James Cook

An New, Genuine and Complete History of the Whole of Capt.

Cook's Voyages

Undertaken and Performed by Royal Authority

James Cook

An New, Genuine and Complete History of the Whole of Capt. Cook's Voyages
Undertaken and Performed by Royal Authority

ISBN/EAN: 9783337192136

Printed in Europe, USA, Canada, Australia, Japan

Cover: Foto ©Raphael Reischuk / pixelio.de

More available books at **www.hansebooks.com**

A New, Genuine, and Complete

HISTORY of

THE WHOLE OF

Capt. Cook's Voyages,

UNDERTAKEN AND PERFORMED

By ROYAL AUTHORITY.

Being the moſt Accurate, Elegant, and Perfect
Edition of the whole WORKS and DISCOVERIES of
that celebrated Circumnavigator, ever publiſhed.

The whole Written in a more pleaſing and elegant
Stile than any other Work of the Kind and Size.

A Full and Satisfactory HISTORY of

Capt. COOK's FIRST VOYAGE round the WORLD,
undertaken and performed by Order of his preſent MAJESTY, in his MAJESTY's Ship, the
ENDEAVOUR, principally for making Diſcoveries in
the SOUTHERN HEMISPHERE, &c. &c.

Begun the latter End of Auguſt 1768, and concluded the 12th of June 1771; containing a Period
of nearly THREE YEARS, in which was compleated
the Circumnavigation of the Globe.

INTRODUCTION.

VOYAGES being conſidered as the grand repoſitory of uſeful and intereſting knowledge,
have juſtly engaged the attention of mankind in all
ages. In this ample field the attention of curioſity

is gratified by a vaft variety of interefting fcenes; and works of this kind are of national confequence, while, at the fame time, they afford a rich fund of pleafure to all thofe who delight to fpend a leifure hour in rational amufement. With refpect to Captain Cook's *firft* * *Voyage* round the world, which was in the ENDEAVOUR, it has fo much attracted the notice of the world, that it cannot be too particularly related, nor too nicely examined; and a principal advantage accruing from the following narrative is, that the fame ftories fet in different lights as they ftrike the obferver, cannot fail of being a fource of frefh intelligence; of fhewing former accounts through a new medium, and of placing them in a more ftriking point of accuracy, by judicious corrections, and additional improvements.

The firft voyage, which is the fubject of our prefent narrative, was undertaken by order of his prefent majefty, for making difcoveries in the fouthern hemifphere, &c. *Captain Cook* was appointed commander of the Endeavour; and with him embarked Mr. (now Sir *Jofeph*) *Banks* and Dr. *Solander*, whofe principal objects in this expedition were, to obferve the tranfit of Venus, and to attempt afterwards farther difcoveries. Mr. Jofeph Banks and Dr. Solander were men of diftinguifhed abilities. The firft of thefe gentlemen was poffeffed of confiderable landed property in Lincolnfhire; and, upon his leaving the Univerfity of Oxford, A. D. 1763, he made a voyage to the

---

* It is unneceffary to point out the obvious imperfections of all publications which include only a *fingle* voyage of the very celebrated Capt. Cook; his *three* different *voyages* are fo immediately connected together, that owing to frequent references from one to another, no perfon can form a fatisfactory idea of his valuable difcoveries, who does not read his *firft, fecond,* and *third voyages* in the *order* in which they were *performed* and *written:* in the prefent very *complete, improved* and *genuine Edition* (for which numerous readers have been waiting with impatience) we therefore confider it as our indifpenfible duty to *begin* with a *full account* of his *Firft Voyage*; after which we fhall record an authentic hiftory of his *Second Voyage*; and then proceed to a *faithful* and *accurate relation* of his much admired *Third* and laft *Voyage* round the world, being that principally undertaken for *new difcoveries* in the *Pacific ocean*, &c. &c. and in the profecution of which he unfortunately *loft* his *life*.

coafts

coasts of Newfoundland and Labradore. Notwithstanding the dangers and difficulties that attended his
first expedition, Mr. Banks returned undiscouraged;
and when the Endeavour was equipping for a voyage
to the South Seas, he determined to embark with the
adventurers, from the laudable motive of enriching
his native country with the knowledge of unknown
productions, and new discoveries.

Dr. Solander, whom Mr. Banks engaged to accompany him, had been appointed to a place in the Bri-
tish Museum, then just established, which he filled
with credit to himself, and in which he gave universal
satisfaction. The Doctor was a native of Sweden, and
a man of great learning, being an adept in natural phi-
losophy, and who had studied under the famous Linnæus. Mr. Banks, besides the important and valuable acquisition of this gentleman, took with him two
draughtsmen, the one being intended to paint sub-
jects of natural history, and the other to delineate
figures and landscapes. He had likewise four servants,
two of whom were negroes, and a secretary in his retinue. Both Capt. Cook and Mr. Banks kept accurate and circumstantial journals of this voyage. The
papers of Capt. Cook contained a minute account
of all nautical incidents, and a very particular description of the figure and extent of the countries he
had visited; and in those of Mr. Banks were found a
great variety of incidents which had not come under
the inspection of Capt. Cook; besides, some officers,
and the more intelligent of the ship's crew, have
communicated to their friends, innumerable natural
and artificial curiosities, with descriptions of the
people, and countries, their productions, manners,
customs, religion, policy, and language. Materials so
interesting and copious, will be thought quite suffi-
cient to furnish the public with the following New
and Complete Edition of the whole of Capt. Cook's
Voyages, &c. in which will be contained all the curious remarks made by several gentlemen engaged in
these celebrated expeditions; and it is our intention

to

to place every important incident in various points of view, that our readers may be complete judges of the valuable nature of the new difcoveries, and of the preference which is due to this elegant, though Cheap Edition.

The preparations for this important work have been fuitable to its ineftimable value, and our earneft concern for its credit; while wealth and fcience have united their powers for the purpofes of public benefit. Many of the firft literary charaĉters of the age have favoured us with their affiftance : not only the great outlines of nature, but the variety of fhades within have been carefully attended to, and not a fingle material fhall be neglected which may embellifh the narratives, and give life and beauty particularly to all the *Three refpective Voyages* of this unparalleled Navigator. We therefore fubmit this undertaking to the judgment of the public, founding our claims to their favour on MERIT ALONE, knowing, it is only on THIS folid foundation we can hope and expect their encouragement and protection.

BOOK

BOOK I.

CHAP. I.

*The departure of the Endeavour from Plymouth—Her
passage io the island of Madeira—A description of its
natural curiosities and trade—A particular account of
Funchiale, the capital of Madeira—The passage from
Madeira to Rio de Janeiro—An account of this capital
of the Portuguese dominions in South America, and of the
circumjacent country—Incidents that happened while the
Endeavour lay in the harbour of Rio de Janeiro.*

THE Endeavour, a bark of three hundred and
twenty tons, which had been originally built
for the Coal-trade, was appointed to the service of
Capt. Cook's first voyage round the world, having
on board ten carriage and twelve swivel guns. On
August the 26th, 1768, we therefore got under sail,
and took our departure from Plymouth. On the 31st,
we saw several of those birds, called by seamen Mother
Carey's Chickens, and which they think prognisticate
a storm. On the 2d of September we saw land between Cape Finisterre, and Cape Ortegal, on the
coast of Gallicia in Spain. In this course some marine
animals were discovered, hitherto unnoticed by na-
turalists. One of these, described as a new species,
is of an angular form, near three inches in length,
and one thick. It has a hollow passage quite through
it, and a brown spot at one end. Four of these animals appeared to adhere together by their sides;
but when put into water, they separated, and swam
about, shining with a brightness resembling the vivid
colour of a gem. We also discovered another animal, exceeding in variety and brightness any thing
we had seen; even in colour and splendor equal to
those of an opal. At the distance of about ten leagues
from Cape Finisterre, we caught among the rigging
of the ship several birds not described by Linnæus.
On

On the 12th we difcovered Puerto Santo and Madeira, and on the day following, moored with the ftream anchor in the road of Funchiale. In heaving up the anchor, Mr. Weir, the mafter's mate, was unfortunately carried overboard and drowned.

Upon approaching the ifland of Madeira from the fea, it appears exceeding beautiful, the fides of the hills being covered with plantations of vines, which are green when all kinds of herbage, except here and there, are burnt up, which was the cafe at this time.

On the 13th in the forenoon the boat came from the officers of health, no one being fuffered to land from on board a fhip without their permiffion. When this was granted, we landed at Funchiale, the chief town in the ifland, and proceeded directly to the houfe of Mr. Cheap, a confiderable merchant, and at that time the Englifh conful there, who received us with a brotherly kindnefs, and treated us with a princely liberality. We continued on the ifland only five days, during which time the feafon was the worft in the year for fearching after natural curiofities; however, the two gentlemen, Dr. Solander and Mr. Banks, pufhed their excurfions about three miles from the town, and collected a few plants in flower, by the obliging attention of Dr. Heberden, the chief phyfician of the ifland, and brother to Dr. Heberden of London. Mr. Banks enquired after and found the tree called Laura Indicus, the wood of which he fuppofes to be what is called the Madeira mahogany, as there is no real mahogany upon the ifland.

The inhabitants of Madeira have no other article of trade than wine, which is made by preffing the juice out in a fquare wooden veffel. The fize of this is proportioned to the quantity of wine; and the fervants, having taken off their ftockings and jackets, get into it, and with their elbows and feet prefs out as much of the juice as they can. In like manner the ftalks, being tied together, are preffed under a fquare piece of wood, by a lever with a ftone faftened to the end of it.

During

During our ſtay upon this iſland we ſaw no wheel-carriages of any ſort, nor have the people any thing that reſembles them, except a hollow board, or ſledge, upon which thoſe wine veſſels are drawn that are too big to be carried by hand. They have alſo horſes and mules very proper for their roads, but their wine is, notwithſtanding, brought to town from the vine-yards where it is made, in veſſels of goat-ſkins, which are carried by men on their heads.

Nature has been very liberal in her gifts to Madeira. The inhabitants are not without ingenuity, but they want induſtry. The ſoil is ſo very rich, and there is ſuch a variety in the climate, that there is ſcarcely any article either of the neceſſaries or luxuries of life, which cannot probably be cultivated here. On the hills, walnuts, cheſnuts, and apples flouriſh, almoſt without culture. Pine-apples, mangoes, guanas, and bananas, grow almoſt ſpontaneouſly in the town. They have corn which is large grained and fine, and it might be produced in plenty; but for want of be-ing attended to, all they conſume is imported from other countries. Beef, mutton, and pork are re-markably good, and the captain took ſome of the former on board for his own uſe.

Funchiale (which took its name from Foncho) ſig-nifying fennel in the Portugueſe language) is ſituate at the bottom of a bay, and though it is extenſive in proportion to the reſt of the iſland, it is but poorly built, and the ſtreets are narrow and badly paved. The churches are full of ornaments, with pictures and images of ſaints; the firſt are, for the moſt part, wretchedly executed, and the latter are dreſſed in laced cloaths. The taſte of the convents, eſpecially of the Franciſcans, is better; neatneſs and ſimplicity being united in moſt of the deſigns of the latter. The infirmary alſo is a piece of good architecture, and one of the moſt conſiderable in this place. In this convent is a ſmall chapel, the whole lining of which, both ſides and ceiling, is compoſed of human ſculls and thigh bones: the thigh bones are laid acroſs

I   each

each other, and a fcull is placed in each of the four angles. When we vifited the good fathers, juft before fupper-time, they received us with great civility. " We will not afk you," faid they, " to fupper with us, becaufe we are not prepared; but if you will come to-morrow, though it is a faft-day, we will have a turkey roafted for you." This polite invitation it was not in our power to accept. There are many high hills in this ifland; Pico Ruivo in particular is near 5100 feet high. To a certain height thefe hills are covered with vines, above which are numbers of chefnuts and pine trees ; and above thefe again whole forefts of various forts of trees. The Mirmulano and Paobranco which are found among them, are unknown in Europe. The latter of thefe is very beautiful, and would be a great ornament to our gardens. The number of inhabitants in Madeira are computed to amount to about eighty thoufand ; and the cuftom-houfe duties produce to the king of Portugal a revenue of 20,000l. a year, clear of all expences. But the balance of trade is againft the people ; for all their money going to Lifbon, the currency of the ifland is in Spanifh. This coin confifteth of piftereens, worth about a fhilling ; bitts about fixpence, and half bitts worth about three-pence.

On the 19th of September the Endeavour failed from Madeira, and on the 21ft we faw the iflands called the Salvages, northward of the Canaries. The principal of thefe was about five leagues to the fouth half weft. On the 23d the Peak of Teneriffe bore weft by fouth half fouth. Its appearance at fun fet was very ftriking ; for when moft part of the ifland appeared of a deep black, the mountain ftill reflected rays, and glowed with a warmth of colour which no painting can exprefs. There is no eruption of vifible fire, but a heat iffues from the chinks near the top, too ftrong to be borne by the hand when held near them. The height of this mountain is 15,396 feet, which is but one hundred and forty-eight yards lefs than three miles,

On

On the 30th we saw Bona Vista, one of the Cape de Verd islands, in latitude 16 deg. north, and longitude 21 deg. 51 min. west. In our course to Teneriffe, we observed numbers of flying fish, which appeared very beautiful, their sides resembling burnished silver.

On the 7th of October Mr. Banks went out in a boat, and caught what our sailors call a Portuguese man of war; together with several shell fishes, or testaceous animals, which are always found floating upon the water; and on the 25th this gentleman shot a black-toed gull, not described by Linnæus, and whose dung is of a red colour. We had now variable winds, with some showers of rain, and the air was so damp as to damage our utensils considerably.

On the 25th we crossed the line with the usual ceremonies; and on the 28th when the ship was in the latitude of Ferdinand Noronha, longitude 32 deg. 5 min. west, we began to look out for the island, and for the shoals which are laid down as lying between it and the main; but neither the island nor shoals could be discovered. On the 29th we perceived that luminous appearance of the sea mentioned by navigators, which emitted rays like those of lightning. As Mr. Banks and Dr. Solander were not thoroughly satisfied with any of the causes hitherto assigned for this phænomenon, and supposing it was occasioned by some luminous animals, they threw out a casting net, in order to try by experiment whether they were right in their conjectures. A species of the Medusa was taken, which bore some resemblance to metalline substance greatly heated, and emitted a whitish light; they caught also some crabs which glittered very much; animals which had not before been taken notice of by the curious researchers into the secrets of nature.

As provisions by this time began to grow short, we resolved to put into the harbour of Rio de Janeiro; and on the 8th of November we saw the coast of

Brafil. Upon fpeaking with the crew of a Portuguefe fifhing boat, we were informed by them, that the
land which we faw was to the fouth of Santo Efpirito.
Mr. Banks, having bought of thefe people fome fifh,
was furprized, that they required Englifh fhillings:
he gave them two which he happened to have about
him; for he imagined Spanifh filver to have been the
only currency, and it was not without fome difpute
that they took the reft of the money in piftereens.
The frefh fifh, which was bought for about nineteen
fhillings, ferved the whole fhip's company. We ftood
off and on along fhore till the 12th, having in view
fucceffively Cape Thomas, and an ifland juft without
Cape Frio, and then made fail for Rio de Janeiro
on the 13th in the morning. Capt. Cook fent his
firft lieutenant in the pinnace before to the city, to
inform the governor, that we had put into that port
in order to procure refrefhments, and a pilot to bring
us into proper anchoring ground. The pinnace returned, but the lieutenant had been detained by the
viceroy, till the captain fhould come on fhore. When
the fhip had come to an anchor, a ten-oared boat filled
with foldiers approached, and rowed round her, but
no converfation took place. Afterwards another boat
appeared, which had feveral of the viceroy's officers
on board. They enquired from whence the Endeavour came? what was her cargo? what number of men
and guns fhe carried? and to what port fhe was
bound? which queftions having been punctually and
truly anfwered, the Portuguefe officers apologized for
having detained the lieutenant, and pleaded the cuftom of the place in excufe for their behaviour.

On the 14th Captain Cook went on fhore, and obtained leave to furnifh the fhip with provifions; but
this permiffion was clogged with the conditions of em-
ploying an inhabitant as a factor, and of fending a
foldier in the Endeavour's boat every time fhe came
from fhore to the veffel. To thefe uncivil terms the
Captain made many objections; but the viceroy was
                                                    determined

determined to infift on them, neither would he permit
Mr. Banks and Dr. Solander to remain on fhore, nor
fuffer the former to go up the country to collect
plants. Captain Cook conceiving from thefe and other
marks of jealoufy, that the viceroy thought they were
come to trade, ufed all his endeavours to convince him
of the contrary ; and acquainted him, that they were
bound to the South Seas, to obferve the tranfit of Venus
over the difk of the fun, an object of great confequence to the improvement of navigation ; but the
viceroy by his anfwer feemed to be entirely ignorant
of this phænomenon. An officer was now appointed
to attend the captain, which order he was defired to
underftand as an intended compliment : however,
when he would have declined fuch a ceremony, the
viceroy very politely forced it upon him.

Dr. Solander and Mr. Banks were not a little chagrined on hearing that they would not be permitted to
refide on fhore, and ftill more fo when they underftood,
that they were not even allowed to quit the fhip; for
the viceroy had ordered, that the captain only, with
fuch failors as were required by their duty, fhould
come on fhore. Whether this arofe from his jealoufy
in regard to trade, or from the apprehenfions he entertained of the extraordinary abilities of the two gentlemen in fearch of new difcoveries, it is certain that
they were highly difagreeable to Mr. Banks and the
Doctor, who were refolved, if poffible, to evade the
order. With this view they attempted to go on
fhore, but were ftopped by the guard-boat ; yet feveral of the crew, without the knowledge of the centinel, let themfelves down by a rope from the cabin
window into the boat about midnight, and drove
away with the tide, till they were out of hearing.
They afterwards landed on an unfrequented part of
the country, and were treated by the inhabitants
with great civility.

Capt. Cook, uneafy under the reftrictions of the
viceroy, remonftrated with him ; but the latter would

return

return no other answer, than that the king his master's orders must be obeyed. The captain, thus repulsed, and much displeased, resolved to go no more on shore, rather than, whenever he did so, to be treated as a prisoner in his own boat; for the officer who was so polite as to accompany him, constantly attended him, both to and from the shore. Two memorials were now drawn up and presented to the viceroy, one written by the captain, and the other by Mr. Banks; but the answers returned were by no means satisfactory. Several papers passed between them and the viceroy to no good purpose, the prohibition still remaining as before; from whence the captain thought it necessary in order to vindicate his own compliance, to urge the viceroy to an act of force in the execution of his orders. For this purpose he sent lieutenant Hicks with a packet, giving him his order not to admit of a guard in his boat. As this gentleman was resolved to obey his captain's commands, the officer of the guard boat did not oppose him by force, but acquainted the viceroy with what had happened, on which the lieutenant was sent away with the packet unopened. When returned, he found a guard of soldiers placed in the boat, and insisted on their quitting it. Whereupon the officer seized the boat's crew, and conducted them under an escort to prison, and the lieutenant was sent back to the ship guarded. When the captain was informed of this transaction, he wrote to the viceroy to demand his boat and her crew, inclosing the memorial which Mr. Hicks his lieutenant had brought back. These papers he sent by a petty officer, to avoid continuing the dispute concerning the guard, which must have been kept up by a commissioned officer. An answer was now promised by the viceroy; but before this could arrive, the long boat, which had four pipes of rum on board, was driven to windward, (the rope breaking that was thrown from the ship,) together with a small skiff that was fastened to the boat. Immediate orders were given for manning the

yawl,

yawl, which being difpatched accordingly with proper directions, returned, and brought the people on board the next morning; from whom Capt. Cook learned, that the long-boat having filled with water, they had brought her to a grapling, and quitted her, and falling in with a reef of rocks on ther return, they were forced to cut the faftening of Mr. Banks's little boat, and fend her adrift. The captain now difpatched another letter to his excellency, wherein he informed him of the accident, defired he would affift him with a boat to recover his own, and, at the fame time, renewed his demand of the delivery of the pinnace and her crew. The viceroy granted the requeft, but in his anfwer to the captain's remonftrance, fuggefted fome doubts that he entertained, whether the Endeavour was really a king's fhip, and alfo accufed the crew of fmuggling. Capt. Cook, in his reply, faid, that he was willing to fhew his commiffion, adding, if any attempt fhould be made to carry on a contraband trade, he requefted his excellency would order the offender to be taken into cuftody. The difpute being thus terminated, Mr. Banks attempted to elude the vigilance of the guard, which he found means to do, and got fafe on fhore on the 26th in the morning. He took care to avoid the town, and paffed the day in the fields, where he could beft gratify his curiofity. Mr. Banks found the country people inclined to treat him with civility, and was invited to their habitations. But it was afterwards heard, that fearch had been making for this gentleman when abfent. He and Dr. Solander therefore refolved to run no more rifques in going on fhore, while they remained at this place.

On the 1ft of December, having taken in water and provifions, we got, with leave from the viceroy, a pilot on board; but the wind prevented us from putting to fea. A Spanifh packet from Buenos Ayres, bound for Spain, arriving the next day, the captain of her with great politenefs offered to take our letters to Europe,

Europe. The favour was accepted, and Captain Cook delivered into his hands a packet for the fecretary of the Admiralty, containing copies of all the papers that had paffed between him and the viceroy, leaving the duplicates with his excellency. On the 5th we weighed anchor, and towed down the bay, but were ftopped at Santa Cruz, the principal fortification, the order from the viceroy, to let us pafs, by an unaccountable negligence, not having been fent; fo that it was not till the 7th that we got under fail. When we had paffed the fort the guard-boat left us, and our pilot was difcharged. It was obferved, during our ftay in this harbour, that the air was filled with butterflies, chiefly of one kind, and the greateft part above our maft-head. Of the town and neighbouring country we fhall give the following defcription.

Rio de Janeiro was probably fo called becaufe difcovered on the feftival of St. Januarius, from whence we may fuppofe the river Januarius took its name, and alfo the town, which is the capital of the Portuguefe in America. This town is fituated on the weft fide of the river, from which it is extended about three quarters of a mile. The ground whereon it ftands is a level plain. It is defended on the north fide by a hill, that extends from the river, having a fmall plain, which contains the fuburbs and king's dock. On the fouth is another hill running towards the mountains which are behind the town. This is neither ill defigned nor ill built ; the houfes in general are of ftone, and two ftories high; every houfe having, after the manner of the Portuguefe, a fmall balcony before its windows, and a lattice of wood before the balcony; its circuit is about three miles; and it appears to be equal in fize to the largeft country towns in England. The ftreets are ftraight, and of a convenient breadth, interfecting each other at right angles; the greater part, however, lie in a line with the citadel, called St. Sebaftian, which ftands on the top of a hill that commands the town. The principal

ftreet

street is near 100 feet in width, and extends from
St. Benedict to the foot of Castle-hill. The other
streets are commonly twenty or thirty feet wide.
The houses adjoining to the principal street are three
stories high, but in other places they are very irregular,
though built after the same manner as at Lisbon. Water is conveyed to a fountain in the great square,
from an aqueduct, raised upon two stories of arches.
The water at this fountain, however, is so bad, that
we could not drink it with pleasure. The churches
are richly ornamented, and there is more religious
parade in this place than in any of the popish countries
in Europe. Not a day passes without a procession of
some parish, with various insignia, splendid and
costly in the highest degree. But the inhabitants may
pay their devotions at the shrine of any saint, without
waiting for a procession; for a small cupboard, having
a glass window, and in which is one of these tutelary
gods, is placed before almost every house, and a lamp
is kept constantly burning, left the old proverb
should be verified, " Out of sight, out of mind."
Before these saints the people pray and sing with such
vehemence, that in the night they were distinctly
heard by our sailors on board the ship.

In this town are four convents, the first is that of
the Benedictines, situated near its northern extremity;
the structure affords an agreeable prospect, and contains an elegant chapel, ornamented with several valuable paintings. The second is that of the Carme-
lites, which forms the centre angle of the royal
square, and fronts the harbour; its church was re-
building in a very elegant manner, with fine free
stone brought thither from Lisbon. The third is that
of St. Anthony, situated on the top of a hill, on the
south side of the town; before this convent stands a
large bason of brown granite, in the form of a pa-
rallelogram, which is employed in washing. The
fourth is situated at the eastern extremity of the
                                                          town,

town, and was formerly the jefuit's convent, but is now converted into a military hofpital.

In the right angle of the royal fquare ftands the viceroy's palace; this with the mint, ftables, gaol, &c. compofe one large building, which has two ftories, and is 90 feet from the water. In paffing through the palace, the firft entrance is to a large hall or guard-room, to which there is an afcent of three or four fteps. In the guard-room are ftationed the viceroy's body-guards, who are relieved every morning between eight and nine; and adjoining to the hall are the ftables, the prifon being in the back part of the building. Within the guard-room is a flight of ftairs for afcending to the upper ftory, which divides at a landing-place about half way, and forms two branches, one leading to the right, and the other to the left. The former leads to a faloon, where there are two officers in conftant attendance ; the viceroy's aid-de-camp at the fame time waiting in the anti-chamber to receive meffages and deliver orders.

The left wing of the royal fquare is an irregular building, which confifts chiefly of fhops occupied by trading people. In the centre of this fquare is the fountain, of which we have made mention, as being fupplied with water from a fpring at the diftance of three miles, from which it is brought by an aqueduct. The place is continually crowded with negroes of both fexes waiting to fill their jars. At the corner of every ftreet is an altar. The market place extends from the north-eaft end of the fquare along the fhore, and this fituation is very convenient for the fifhing boats, and thofe who bring vegetables from the other fide of the river to market. Negroes are almoft the only people who fell the different commodities ex-pofed in the market, and they employ their leifure time in fpinning cotton.

The form of government is in its conftitution mixed, but in fact very defpotic; the viceroy and civil magif-trate of the town frequently committing perfons to
prifon,

prifon, or tranfporting them to Lifbon, at their own pleafure. In order to prevent the people from making excurfions into the country, in fearch after gold and diamonds, certain bounds are prefcribed them, fometimes at a few, and fometimes at many miles diftance from the town; and if a man is taken up by the guard without the bounds, where they conftantly patrole, he is immediately fent to prifon.

The inhabitants of Rio de Janeiro are exceeding numerous, and confift of Portuguefe, Negroes, and Indians, which laft were the original natives of the country. The townfhip of Rio is but a fmall part of the Capitanea, or province; yet it is faid to contain 37,000 white people, and 629,000 blacks, many of whom are free, making together 666,000, in the proportion of 17 to 1.

The military is compofed of twelve regiments of regular troops, fix being Portuguefe, and fix Creoles, and twelve regiments of provincial militia. The inhabitants are fervilely fubmiffive to the regulars, and it has been faid, that if any of them fhould omit the compliment of taking off his hat, when he meets an officer, he would be immediately knocked down. But the fubordination of the officers to the viceroy is equally mortifying, for they are obliged to wait three times every day to know, or receive his commands: the anfwer frequently is, " there is nothing new."

In Rio de Janeiro the gentry keep their chaifes, which are drawn by mules; the ladies however ufe a fedan chair, boarded before and behind, with curtains on each fide, which is carried by two negroes on a pole connected with the top of the chair, by two rods, coming from under its bottom, one on each fide, and refting to the top. The apothecaries fhops commonly ferve the purpofes of coffee-houfes, as the people meet in them to drink capillaire, and play at back-gammon. When the gentry are feen abroad, they are well dreffed, though at home but loofely covered. The fhop-keepers have generally fhort hair, and wear linen jackets with fleeves. The women in general, as in moft of the Portuguefe and Spanifh fettlements in South America, are more ready to grant amorous favours than thofe of any other civilized parts of the world. As foon as the evening began, females appeared at the windows on every fide, who diftinguifhed fuch of the men as beft pleafed their fancies by throwing down nofegays; and Dr. Solander and two other gentlemen received fo many of thefe love-tokens, that they threw them away by hat-fulls.

Without the Jefuits college on the fhore, is a village called Neuftra Seignora del Gloria, which is joined to the town by a very few intervening houfes. Three or four hundred yards, within the Jefuit's-college, ftands a very high caftle, but it is falling to decay. The bifhop's palace is about three hundred yards behind the Benedictine convent, and contiguous to it is a magazine of arms, furrounded by a rampart.

The inhabitants of Rio de Janeiro maintain a whalefifhery, which fupplies them with lamp oil. They import brandy from the Azores, and their flaves and Eaft India goods from their fettlements in Africa, their wine from Madeira, and their European goods from Lifbon. The current coin is Portuguefe, which is ftruck here; the filver pieces are called petacks, of different value; and the copper are five and ten ree pieces. This place is very ufeful for fhips that are in want of refrefhment. They water, as we have before obferved, at the fountain in the great fquare, but the water is not good. We landed our cafks on a fmooth fandy beach, which is not more than a hundred yards diftant from the fountain, and upon application to the viceroy a centinel is appointed to look after them. The harbour is fafe and commodious, and diftinguifhed by a remarkable hill, in the fhape of a cone, at the weft point of the bay. The entrance is not wide, but it is eafy, from the fea breeze which prevails from noon to fun-fet, for

any

any ſhip to enter before the wind. The entrance of
the narrow part is defended by two forts, La Cruz,
and Lozia; they are about three quarters of a mile
from each other. The bottom being rocky, renders
it dangerous to anchor there, but to avoid it ſhips
muſt keep in the mid-channel. The coaſt abounds
with a variety of fiſh, among which are dolphins and
mackarel. Proviſions, except wheaten bread and
flour, are eaſily procured. Yams and caſſada are in
plenty. Beef both freſh and jerked may be bought
at two-pence farthing a pound, but it is very lean.
The people jerk their beef, by taking out the bones,
and cutting it into large but thin ſlices. They then
cure it with ſalt, and dry it in the ſhade. It eats very
well, and, if kept dry, will remain good a long time
at ſea. Mutton is ſcarcely to be procured. Hogs
and poultry are dear. Garden ſtuff and fruit are in
abundance, but the pumkin only can be preſerved at
ſea. Tobacco alſo is cheap, though not good. Rum,
ſugar, and molaſſes are all excellent, and to be had at
reaſonable prices.

The climate of Rio de Janeiro is healthy, and free
from moſt of thoſe inconveniencies incident to tropical
countries. The air is ſeldom immoderately hot, as
the ſea breeze is generally ſucceeded by a land wind.
The ſeaſons are divided into dry and rainy, though
their commencement of late has been irregular and
uncertain, for the latter had failed for near four
years preceding our arrival; but at this time the rain
had juſt began, and fell in heavy ſhowers during our
ſtay: formerly the ſtreets have been overflowed by
the rain, and rendered impaſſable with canoes.

The adjacent country is mountainous, and chiefly
covered with wood, a ſmall part of it only being cultivated. Near the town the ſoil is looſe and ſandy, but
farther from the river it is a fine black mould. It
produces all the tropical fruits in great plenty, and
without much cultivation, a circumſtance exceeding
agreeable to the inhabitants, who are very indolent.

The mines, which lie far up in the country, are very rich. Their fituation is carefully concealed, and no one can view them, except thofe concerned in working and guarding them. About twelve months before our arrival, the government had detected feveral jewellers in carrying on an illicit trade for diamonds, with flaves in the mines; and immediately afterwards a law paffed, making it felony to work at the trade, or to have any tools fit for it in poffeffion, the civil officers having indifcriminately feized on all that could be found. Near 40,000 negroes are annually imported to dig in the mines, fo pernicious to the human frame are thofe works. In 1776, 20,000 more were draughted from the town to fupply the deficiency of the former number.

C .H A P. II.

The departure of the Endeavour from Rio de Janeiro—
Her passage to the entrance of the Streight of Le Maire—
The inhabitants of Terra del Fuego described—Mr. Banks
and Dr. Solander ascend a mountain in search of plants—
An account of what happened to them in this excursion—
The Endeavour passes through the Streight Le Maire—
An account of her passage, and a further description of
the inhabitants of Terra del Fuego, and its productions—
Remarks respecting the south east part of Terra del Fuego,
and the Streight of Le Maire—Directions for the passage
westward round this part of America, into the South
Seas—The passage of the Endeavour from Cape Horn to
the newly discovered islands—An account of their figure
and appearance—The inhabitants described; with a nar-
rative of the various incidents during the course, and on
the Endeavour's arrival among them. .

O N the 8th of December, 1768, having procured
all necessary supplies, we took our departure
from Rio de Janeiro; and on the 9th an amazing
number of atoms were taken out of the sea. These
were of a yellowish colour, and few of them were
more than the 5th part of an inch long; nor could
the best microscope on board the Endeavour discover
whether they belonged to the vegetable or animal
creation. The sea was tinged in such a manner with
these equivocal substances, as to exhibit broad streaks
of a similar colour, for near the space of a mile in
length, and for several hundred yards in breadth.
Whence they came, or for what designed, neither
Mr. Banks nor Dr. Solander could determine. Perhaps they might be the spawn of some marine animal, unknown to either antient or modern philosophers.

On the 11th we hooked a shark. It proved to be a
female. When opened we took six young ones out of

2   it,

it, five of which were alive, and fwam brifkly in a tub of water, but the fixth appeared to have been dead fome time. From this time we met with no material occurrence till the 22d, when we difcovered numerous birds of the profillaria kind, in latitude 39 deg. 37 min. fouth, and longitude 49 deg. 16 min. weft; we alfo difcovered great numbers of porpoifes of a fingular fpecies, of about 15 feet in length, and of an afh colour. On the 23d we obferved an eclipfe of the moon; and about feven o'clock in the morning, a fmall white cloud appeared in the weft, from which a train of fire iffued, extending itfelf wefterly : about two minutes after, we heard two diftinct loud explofions, immediately fucceeding each other, like thofe of cannon, after which the cloud difappeared. On the 24th we caught a large loggerhead tortoife, weighing one hundred and fifty pounds. We likewife fhot feveral birds, one an albetrofs, which meafured between the tips of its wings nine feet and an inch, and from its beak to the tail two feet one inch and an half. On the 30th we ran upwards of fifty leagues, through vaft numbers of land infects; fome in the air, and others upon the water; they appeared to refemble exactly the flies that are feen in England, though they were thirty leagues from land, and fome of thefe infects are known not to quit it beyond three yards. At this time we judged ourfelves to be nearly oppofite to the bay called Sans Fond (without bottom) where it is fuppofed by fome writers, that the continent of America is divided by a paffage; but it was the opinion of our circumnavigators, that there might be a large river, which probably had occafioned an inundation. On the 31ft we had much thunder, lightning and rain. This day and the three following, we faw feveral whales; likewife a number of birds about the fize of a pigeon, with white bellies and grey beaks.

On the 3d of January, 1769, we faw the appearance of land, in latitude 47 deg. 17 min. fouth, and

longitude

longitude 61 deg. 29 min. 45 sec. west, which we mistook for Pepy's island. In appearance it so much resembled land, that we bore away for it; and it was near two hours and an half before we were convinced, that it was one of those deceptions which sailors call a Fog-bank. At this time our seamen beginning to complain of cold, they were furnished with a pair of trowsers, and a Magellanic jacket, made of a thick woollen stuff called Fearnought. On the 11th, after having passed Falkland's Island, we saw the coast of Terra del Fuego, at the distance of about four leagues from the west to south-east by south. As we ranged along the shore to the south-east, smoke was perceived, made, probably, by the natives as a signal, for it was not to be seen after we had passed by.

On the 14th we entered the Streight of Le Maire, but were afterwards driven out again with such violence (the tide being against us) that the ship's bow-sprit was frequently under water. At length, however, we got anchorage in a small cove, on the east of Cape St. Vincent, the entrance to which our captain named St. Vincent's Bay. The weeds which grow here upon rocky ground are very remarkable; they appear above the surface in eight and nine fathoms water. The leaves are four feet in length; and many of the stalks, though not more than an inch and a half in circumference, above one hundred.

Dr. Solander and Mr. Banks went on shore, where, having continued four hours, they returned about nine in the evening, with upwards of an hundred different plants and flowers, of which none of the European botanists had taken any notice near this bay. The country in general was flat, and the bottom, in particular, was a grassy plain. Here was plenty of wood, water, and fowl, and winter bark was found in great plenty. The trees appeared to be a species of the birch, but neither large nor lofty. The wood was white, and they bore a small leaf. White and red cranberries were found in these parts.

On

On the 18th we came to an anchor in twelve fathom water, upon coral rocks, before a small cove, at the distance of about a mile from the shore. At this time two of the natives came down upon the beach, as if they expected that the strangers would land; but as there was no shelter here, the ship was got under sail again, and the Indians retired disappointed. The same afternoon about two o'clock, we came into the bay of Good Succefs, and the veffel coming to an anchor, the captain went on shore, accompanied by Mr. Banks and Dr. Solander, in order to search for a watering place, and difcourfe with the Indians. Thefe gentlemen had not proceeded above one hundred yards before the captain, when two of the Indians that had feated themfelves rofe up, and threw away the fmall fticks which they held in their hands, as a token of amity. They afterwards returned to their companions, who had remained at fome diftance behind them, and made figns to their guefts to advance, whom they received in a friendly, though uncouth manner. In return for their civility, fome ribbands and beads were diftributed among them. Thus a fort of mutual confidence was eftablifhed, and the reft of the Englifh joined the party, the Indians converfing with them in their way, in an amicable manner. Capt. Cook and his friends took three of them to the ship, dreffed them in jackets, and gave them bread and other provifions, part of which they carried on shore with them ; but they refufed to drink rum or brandy, making figns that it burned their throats, as their proper drink was water. One of thefe people made feveral long and loud fpeeches, but no part of them was intelligible to any of us. Another ftole the covering of a globe, which he concealed under his garment that was made of fkin. After having remained on board about two hours, they returned on shore, Mr. Banks accompanying them. He conducted them to their companions, who feemed no way curious to know what their friends had feen, and the latter

were

were as little difpofed to relate, as the former were to enquire. None of thefe people exceeded five feet ten inches in height, but their bodies appeared large and robuft, though their limbs were fmall. They had broad flat faces, high cheeks, nofes inclining to flatnefs, wide noftrils, fmall black eyes, large mouths, fmall, but indifferent teeth, and ftraight black hair, falling down over their ears and foreheads, the latter being generally fmeared with brown and red paints, and like all the original natives of America, they were beardlefs. Their garments were the fkins of feals and guanicoes, which they wrapped round their fhoulders. The men likewife wore on their heads a bunch of yarn, which fell over their foreheads, and was tied behind with the finews or tendons of fome animals. Many of both fexes were painted on different parts of their bodies with red, white, and brown colours, and had alfo three or four perpendicular lines pricked acrofs their cheeks and nofes. The women had a fmall ftring tied round each ancle, and each wore a flap of fkin faftened round the middle. They carried their children upon their backs, and were generally employed in domeftic labour and drudgery.

Mr. Banks and Dr. Solander, attended by their fervants, fet out from the fhip on the 16th, with a defign of going into the country as far as they could that day, and returning in the evening. Having entered a wood, they afcended a hill through a pathlefs wildernefs till the afternoon. After they had reached what they took for a plain, they were greatly difappointed to find it a fwamp, covered with birch, the bufhes interwoven and fo inflexible that they could not be divided: however, as they were not above three feet high, they ftepped over them, but were up to the ancles in boggy ground. The morning had been very fine, but now the weather became cold and difagreeable; the blafts of wind were very piercing, and the fnow fell thick; neverthelefs they purfued their route in hope of finding a better road. Before they had got

No. 1. E over

over this fwamp, an accident happened that greatly difconcerted them: Mr. Buchan, one of the draughtfmen whom Mr. Banks had taken with him, fell into a fit. It was abfolutely neceffary to ftop and kindle a fire, and fuch as were moft fatigued remained to affift him; but Mr. Banks, Dr. Solander, and Mr. Monkhoufe proceeded, and attained the fpot they had in view, where they found a great variety of plants that gratified their curiofity and repaid their toil. On returning to the company amidft the fnow which now fell in great abundance, they found Mr. Buchan much recovered. They had previoufly fent Mr. Monkhoufe and Mr. Green back to him and thofe that remained with him, in order to bring them to a hill which was conjectured to lie in a better track for returning to the wood, and which was accordingly fixed on as a place of rendezvous. They refolved from this hill to pafs through the fwamp, which this way did not appear to be more than half a mile in extent, into the covert of the wood, in which they propofed building a hut, and kindling a fire, to defend themfelves from the feverity of the weather. Accordingly, the whole party met at the place appointed, about eight in the evening, whilft it was ftill day-light, and proceeded towards the next valley.

Dr. Solander having often paffed over mountains in cold countries, was fenfible, that extreme cold, when joined with fatigue, occafions a drowfinefs that is not eafily refifted; he therefore intreated his friends to keep in motion, however difagreeable it might be to them. His words were—Whoever fits down will fleep, and whoever fleeps will wake no more. — Every one feemed accordingly armed with refolution; but, on a fudden, the cold became fo very intenfe as to threaten the moft dreadful effects. It was now very remarkable, that the Doctor himfelf, who had fo forcibly admonifhed and alarmed his party, was the firft that infifted to be fuffered to repofe. In fpite of the moft earneft intreaties of his friends, he lay down amidft the fnow,

and

and it was with difficulty that they kept him awake. One of the black fervants alfo became weak and faint, and was on the point of following this bad example. Mr. Buchan was therefore detached with a party to make a fire at the firft commodious fpot they could find. Mr. Banks and four more remained with the Doctor and Richmond the black, who with the utmoft difficulty were perfuaded to come on ; and when they had traverfed the greateft part of the fwamp, they ex-preffed their inability of going any farther. When the black was told that if he remained there he would foon be frozen to death, his reply was, That he was fo much exhaufted with fatigue, that death would be a relief to him. Doctor Solander faid, he was not un-willing to go, but that he muft firft take fome fleep, ftill perfifting in acting contrary to the opinion which he himfelf had delivered to the company. Thus re-folved, they both fat down, fupported by fome bufhes, and in a fhort time fell afleep. Intelligence now came from the advanced party, that a fire was kindled about a quarter of a mile farther on the way. Mr. Banks then awakened the Doctor, who had already almoft loft the ufe of his limbs, though it was but a few minutes fince he fat down; neverthelefs, he confented to go on, but every meafure taken to relieve the black proved ineffectual. He remained motionlefs, and they were obliged to leave him to the care of a failor, and the other black fervant, who appeared to be the leaft hurt by the cold, and they were to be relieved as foon as two others were fufficiently warmed, to fill their places. The Doctor, with much difficulty, was got to the fire; and as to thofe who were fent to relieve the companions of Richmond, they returned without having been able to find them. What rendered the mortification ftill greater was, that a bottle of rum (the whole ftock of the party) could not be found, and was judged to have been left with one of the three that were miffing.

A fall of fnow continuing for near two hours, there now remained no hopes of feeing the three abfent per-

fons

fons again. At twelve o'clock, however, a great shouting was heard at a distance, which gave inexpressible
satisfaction to every one prefent. Mr. Banks and four
others went forward and met the sailor, who had just
strength enough left to walk. He was immediately sent
to the fire, and they proceeded to feek for the other
two. They found Richmond upon his legs, but incapable of moving them; the other black was lying
fenfeless upon the ground. All endeavours to bring
them to the fire were fruitless; nor was it possible to
kindle one upon the spot, on account of the snow that
had fallen, and was falling; fo that there remained no
alternative, and they were compelled to leave the two
unfortunate negroes to their fate, after they had made
them a bed of the boughs of fome trees, and covered
them over thick with the fame. As all hands had been
employed in endeavouring to move thefe poor blacks
to the fire, and had been expofed to the cold for near
an hour and an half in the attempt, fome of them began
to be afflicted in the fame manner as thofe whom they
were to relieve. Brifcoe, another fervant of Mr. Banks,
in particular, began to lofe his fenfibility. At laft they
reached the fire, and paffed the night in a very difagreeable manner.

The party that fet out from the fhip had confifted of
twelve; two of thefe were already judged to be dead,
it was doubtful whether the third would be able to return on board, and Mr. Buchan, a fourth, feemed to
be threatened with a return of his fits. The fhip they
reckoned to be at the diftance of a long day's journey,
through an unfrequented wood, in which they might
probably be bewildered till night, and having been
equipped only for a journey of a few hours, they had
not a fufficiency of provifions left to afford the company a fingle meal.

At day-break on the 17th, nothing prefented itfelf to
the view all around but fnow, which covered alike the
trees and the ground; and the blafts of wind were fo
frequent and violent, that their journey feemed to be
                                        rendered

London ; Published as the Act directs, by Alex Hogg, at the Kings Arms, No 16 Paternoster Row.

rendered impracticable, and they had reafon to dread perifhing with cold and famine. However, about fix in the morning, they were flattered with a dawn of hope of being delivered, by difcovering the fun through the clouds, which gradually diminifhed. Before their fetting out, meffengers were difpatched to the unhappy negroes; but thefe returned with the melancholy news of their death. Though the fky had flattered the hopes of the furvivors, the fnow continued falling very faft, a circumftance which impeded their journey; but a breeze fpringing up about eight o'clock, added to the influence of the fun, began to clear the air, and the fnow falling in large flakes from the trees, gave tokens of a thaw. Hunger prevailing over every other confideration, induced our travellers to divide the fmall remainder of their provifions, and to fet forward on their journey about ten in the morning. To their great aftonifhment and fatisfaction, in about three hours they found themfelves on the fhore, and much nearer to the fhip than their moft fanguine expectations could have fuggefted. When they looked back upon their former route from the fea, they found, that inftead of afcending the hill in a direct line, they had made a circle almoft round the country. On their return, thefe wanderers received fuch congratulations from thofe on board, as can more eafily be imagined than expreffed.

Mr. Banks and Dr. Solander went on fhore again on the 20th of this month, landing in the bottom of the bay, where they collected a number of fhells and plants, hitherto unknown. After having returned to dinner, they went to vifit an Indian town, about two miles up the country, the accefs to which, on account of the mud, was difficult. When they approached the town, two of the natives came out to meet them, who began to fhout in their ufual manner. They afterwards conducted Mr. Banks and the Doctor to their town. It was fituate on a fmall hill, over-fhaded with wood, and confifted of about a dozen huts, conftructed without art

art or regularity.   They were compofed of a few poles inclining to each other in the fhape of a fugar-loaf, which were covered on the weather fide with grafs and boughs, and on the other fide a fpace was left open, which ferved at once for a fire-place and a door.   They were of the fame nature of the huts that had been feen at St. Vincent's Bay.   A little grafs ferved for beds and chairs, and their utenfils were a bafket for the hand, a fatchel to hang upon the back, and a bladder for water, out of which they drank through a hole near the top.   This town was inhabited by a tribe of about fifty men, women, and children.   Their bows and arrows were conftructed with neatnefs and ingenuity, being made of wood highly polifhed; and the point, which was either glafs or flint, very fkilfully fitted.   Thefe latter fubftances were obferved among them un-wrought, as alfo cloth, rings, buttons, &c. from whence it was concluded that they fometimes tra-velled to the northward, as no fhip, for years paft, had touched at this part of Terra del Fuego.   The natives here did not fhew any furprife at the fight of fire arms, but appeared to be well acquainted with their ufe.   It is likely that the fpot on which the Doctor and Mr. Banks met them, was not a fixed habitation, as their houfes did not feem as if they were erected to ftand for any long time, and they had no boats or canoes among them.   They did not appear to have any form of government, or any ideas of fubordination.   They feemed to be the very out-cafts of men, and a people that paffed their lives in wandering in a forlorn manner over dreary waftes; their dwelling being a thatched hovel, and their cloathing fcarcely fufficient to keep them from pe-rifhing with cold, even in thefe climates.   Their only food was fhell-fifh, which on any one fpot muft foon be exhaufted; nor had they the rudeft imple-ment of art, not even fo much as was neceffary to drefs their food; yet amidft all this, we are told, that they appeared to enjoy that content, which is feldom

found

found in great and populous cities; a species of content, which if they really enjoyed, it must have arisen
from stupidity, a satisfaction the offspring of the
greatest ignorance. Such is the state of uncultivated
nature; such the rude form which uncivilized man
puts on. The wants of these people seemed to be
few; but some wants all mankind must have, and
even the most simple of them, these poor savages appeared scarcely in a condition to gratify. The calls
of hunger and thirst must be obeyed, or man must
perish; yet the people in question seemed to depend
on chance for the means of answering them. Those
who can be happy in such a situation, can only be so,
because they have not a due feeling of their misery.
We know that there have been admirers of simple
nature amongst the philosophers of all ages and nations; and certainly simple nature has her beauties.
In regard to the vegetative and brute creation, she
operates with resistless energy; her power is prevalent,
as her pencil is inimitable; but when we ascend in
the scale of beings, and come to examine the human
race, what shall we find *them*, without cultivation?
It is here that instinct ends, and reason begins; and
without entering into the question, Whether a state
of nature is a state of war? when we observe the innumerable inconveniences to which those are subject
on whom the light of science never dawned, we may
easily determine in the favour of those arts which
have civilized mankind, formed them into societies,
refined their manners, and taught the nations where
they have prevailed, to protect those rights which
the untutored savages have ever been obliged to
yield to the superior abilities of their better instructed
invaders, and have thus fallen a prey to European
tyranny.

We observed in this place seals, sea-lions, and dogs,
and no other quadrupeds; nevertheless it is probable
there are other kinds of animals in the country; for
Mr. Banks remarked, from a hill, an impression of the

foot-fteps of a large animal on the furface of a bog,
but of what kind it was he could not determine. Not
any land-birds were feen larger than an Englifh black-
bird, hawks and vultures excepted. Ducks and other
water fowls we faw in abundance; alfo fhell-fifh, clams,
and limpets. The country, though uncleared, had neither gnat, mufquito, nor any other noxious or troublefome animals. A great variety of plants were found
by the Doctor and Mr. Banks. The wild celery and
fcurvy-grafs are fuppofed to contain antifcorbutic qualities, which will therefore be of fervice to the crews
of fuch fhips as hereafter may touch at this place, after
a long voyage. The latter is found in abundance near
fprings and in damp places, particularly at the watering place in the bay of Good Succefs, and it refembles
the Englifh cuckow flower, or lady's-fmock. The
wild celery is like what grows in our gardens in England, but the leaves are of a deeper green. This plant
may be found in plenty near the beach, and upon the
land above the fpring tides. In tafte it is between that
of celery and parfley. The grateful feaman, long confined to falt provifions, enjoy this healing vegetable
diet, as a fpecial bleffing of an all gracious Providence, particularly vifible in providing in different
climates different food and nourifhment, fuitable to
his nature, wants and neceffities.

On Sunday, Jan. 22, having got in our wood and
water, we failed out of the bay, and continued our
courfe through the Streight; and in paffing this, notwithftanding the defcription which fome voyagers have
given of Terra del Fuego, we did not find that it had,
agreeable to their reprefentations, fuch a forbidding
afpect. On the contrary, we found the fea coafts and
the fides of the hills cloathed with verdure. Indeed
the fummits of the hills were barren, but the valleys
appeared rich, and a brook was generally found at the
foot of almoft every hill; and though the water had a
reddifh tinge, yet it was far from being ill tafted. Upon
the whole it was the beft we took on board during our
voyage.

voyage. Nine miles weftward of cape St. Diego, the below point that forms the north entrance of the Streight of Le Maire, are three hills, called the Three Brothers; and on Terra del Fuego is another hill, in the form of a fugar-loaf, which ftands on the weft fide not far from the fea. We had not that difficulty mentioned in the hiftory of Lord Anfon's voyage, in finding where the ftreight of Le Maire lies. No fhip can well mifs the ftreight that keeps Terra del Fuego in fight, for it will then be eafily difcovered; and Staten ifland which lies on the eaft fide will be ftill more plainly perceived, for there is no land on Terra del Fuego like it. And let it be further particularly obferved, that the entrance of the ftreight fhould be attempted only with a fair wind, when the weather too is moderate, and likewife, upon the beginning of the tide of flood, which here falls out upon the full and change of the moon, about one or two o'clock; let it alfo be remembered, to keep as near the fhore of Terra del Fuego as the winds will permit.

The ftreight of Le Maire is bounded on the weft by Terra del Fuego, and on the eaft by the weft end of Staten ifland, and is nearly five leagues in length, nor lefs in breadth. The bay of Good Succefs is feated about the middle of it, on the fide of Terra del Fuego, which prefents itfelf at the entrance of the ftreight from the northward; and the fouth end of it may be diftinguifhed by a land mark, refembling a road from the fea to the country. It affords good anchorage, and plenty of wood and water. Staten land did not appear to Captain Cook in the fame manner as it did to Commodore Anfon. That horror and wildnefs, mentioned by the Commodore, were not obferved by our gentlemen; on the contrary, the land appeared to be neither deftitute of wood nor verdure, nor was it covered with fnow; and on the north fide we faw the appearances of bays and harbours. It is probable, that the feafon of the year and other circumftances might concur to occafion fuch different reprefentations of a

No. 2. F land,

land, which all our circumnavigators muſt own to be unfriendly and diſagreeably ſituated. On the weſt ſide of the cape of Good Succeſs, whereby is formed the ſouth weſt entrance of the ſtreight, we ſaw the mouth of Valentine's bay; from whence the land lies in a direction weſt ſouth-weſt for more than twenty leagues, appearing high and mountainous, with ſeveral inlets and bays. Fourteen leagues from the bay of Good Succeſs, ſouth-weſt half-weſt, and nearly three leagues from the ſhore, is New Iſland; terminating to the north-eaſt in a remarkable hillock; and ſeven leagues from hence, ſouth-weſt, lies Evout's iſle; a little to the weſt of the ſouth of which are two ſmall low iſlands, near to each other, called Barnevelt's. Theſe are partly ſurrounded with rocks, which riſe to different heights above the water, and are twenty-four leagues from the ſtreight of Le Maire. Three leagues ſouth weſt by ſouth, from Barnevelt's iſlands, is the ſouth-eaſt point of Hermit's iſlands, which lie ſouth-eaſt and north-weſt. They appeared to us in different points of view, ſometimes as one iſland, and at others as part of the main. From the ſouth-eaſt point of theſe iſlands to Cape Horn, the courſe is ſouth-weſt by ſouth, diſtant three leagues. Hermit, who commanded the Dutch ſquadron in 1624, certainly put into ſome of them, and Chapenham, vice admiral of this ſquadron, firſt diſcovered that Cape Horn was formed by a cluſter of iſlands. Between the ſtreight Le Maire and Cape Horn we found, when near the ſhore, the current ſetting generally ſtrong to the north-eaſt; but we loſt it at the diſtance of fifteen or twenty leagues from land.

January the 26th we took our departure from Cape Horn, and the fartheſt ſouthern latitude we made was 60 deg. 10 min. and our longitude was then 74 deg. 30 min. weſt. Cape Horn is ſituated in 55 deg. 53 min. ſouth latitude, and 68 deg. 13 min. weſt longitude. The weather being very calm, Mr. Banks ſailed in a ſmall boat to ſhoot birds, when he killed ſome ſheer-waters, and albatroſſes. The latter were larger

than

View *of* HORN ISLAND.

than thofe which had been taken to the northward of
the ftreight, and proved to be very good food. At
this time we found ourfelves to be 12 deg. to the weftward, and three and a half to the northward of the
ftreight of Magellan, having, from the eaft entrance
of the ftreight, been three and thirty days in failing
round Cape Horn. Notwithftanding the doubling of
Cape Horn is reprefented as a very dangerous courfe,
and that it is generally thought pafling through the
ftreight of Magellan is lefs perilous, yet the Endeavour doubled it with as little danger as fhe would the
north Foreland on the Kentifh coaft; the heavens were
ferenely fair, the wind temperate, the weather pleafant, and, being near fhore, we had a very diftinct
view of the coaft. The Dolphin, in her laft voyage,
which was performed at the fame feafon with ours, was
not lefs than three months in pafling through the
ftreight of Magellan, not including the time that fhe
lay in Port Famine; and it was the opinion of Captain
Cook, that if we had come through the ftreight, we
fhould not at this time have been in thefe feas;
and fhould have fuffered many inconveniences which
we have not experienced. It is a queftion, Whether it is better to go through the ftreight of Le Maire,
or to ftand to the eaftward, and go round Staten land?
This can only be determined according to particular
circumftances, which may make one or the other more
eligible. The ftreight may be pafled with fafety by attending to the directions already given; but if the
land is fallen in with to the eaftward of the ftreight,
and the wind fhould prove tempeftuous, it would be
beft, in our opinion, to go round Staten land. In any
cafe, however, we cannot approve of running into the
latitude of 61 or 62, before any attempt is made to
ftand to the weftward.

March the 1ft we found ourfelves, both by obfervation and the log, in latitude 38 deg. 44 min. fouth,
and 110 deg. 33 min. weft longitude, a concurrence
very fingular in a run of 660 leagues; and which

proved,

proved, that no current had affected the ship in her course; and it was likewise concluded, that we had not come near land of any confiderable extent; for currents are always found at no great diftance from the fhore. Mr. Banks killed above fixty birds in one day; alfo two foreft flies, fuch as had never yet been defcribed; he alfo found a cuttle-fifh of a fpecies different from thofe generally known in Europe. This fifh had a double row of talons, refembling thofe of a cat, which it could put forth or withdraw at pleafure. When dreffed it made excellent foup. On the 24th our latitude was 22 deg. 11 min. fouth, and 127 deg. 55 min. weft longitude. On the 25th a young marine about twenty threw himfelf overboard, on account of a quarrel about a piece of feal fkin, which he took by way of frolic; but being charged with it as a theft, he took the accufation fo much to heart, that in the dufk of the evening he threw himfelf into the fea and was drowned.

On the 4th of April about 10 o'clock, A. M. Peter Brifcoe, fervant to Mr. Banks, difcovered land to the fouth, at the diftance of about three or four leagues. Capt. Cook immediately gave orders to haul for it, when we found an ifland of an oval form, having a lagoon or lake in the center, that extended over the greater part of it. The furrounding border of land was low and narrow in many places, efpecially towards the fouth, where the beach confifted of a reef of rocks. Three places on the north fide had the fame appearance, fo that on the whole the land feemed to refemble feveral woody iflands. To the weft was a large clump of trees, and in the center two cocoa-nut trees. When within a mile of the north fide, though we caft out a line, no bottom could be found at 130 fathom, nor any good anchorage. This ifland was covered with trees, but we could difcern no other fpecies than the palm and the cocoa-nut. Several of the natives were difcovered on fhore; they appeared to be tall, with heads remarkable large, which probably fome bandage might have increafed.

increased. Their complexion was of the copper colour, and their hair was black. Some of these people were seen abreast of the ship, holding poles or pikes of twice their own height. They appeared also naked ; but when they retired, on the ship's passing by the islands, they put on a light-coloured covering. Some clumps of palm-trees served them for habitations, which at a distance appeared like hilly ground, and the view of the groves was a very agreeable one. Our captain called this place Lagoon Island. It lay in 18 degrees south latitude, and 139 west longitude. In the afternoon we again saw land to the north-west; by sun-set we reached it, when it appeared to be a low island of a circular form, and about a mile in circumference. The land was covered with verdure of various kinds, but no inhabitants were visible, nor any cocoa-nut trees. This island is distant from that of Lagoon about seven leagues north, and 62 west, which our gentlemen on board named Thumb Cap.

On the 5th we continued our course with a favourable wind, and about three o'clock discovered land to the westward. It was low, in form resembling a bow, and in circumference seemed to be ten or twelve leagues. Its length is about three or four leagues, and its width about two hundred yards. The beach was flat, and seemed to have no other herbage upon it than sea-weeds. The resemblance of a bow was preserved in the arch and cord forming the land, while the intermediate space was taken up by water. The arch, in general, was covered with trees of various verdure and different heights. This island, from the smoke that was discovered, appeared to be inhabited, and we gave it the name of Bow Island.

On the 6th about noon, we again saw land to the west, and at three o'clock we came up with it. This land seemed to be divided into two parts, or rather a collection of islands (to which we gave the name of the Groups) to the extent of about nine leagues. The two largest were divided from the others by a streight, the

2   breadth

breadth of which was about half a mile. Some of these islands were ten miles or more in length, but appeared like long narrow strings of land, not above a quarter of a mile in breadth; but they produced trees, however, of different kinds, among which was the cocoa-nut tree. Several of the inhabitants came out in their canoes, and two of them shewed an intention of coming on board; but these, like the rest, stopped at the reef. From the observations made, these people appeared to be about our size, and well made. Their complexion was brown, and they were naked. In general, they had two weapons; one was a long pole, spear pointed, and the other resembled a paddle. Several of their canoes were constructed in such a manner, as not to carry more than three persons; others were fitted up for six or seven; and one of these boats hoisted a sail, which was converted into an awning when a shower of rain fell. Capt. Cook would not stay for any of them, neither could we determine, whether the signals made were meant for defiance, or for invitation; one party waving their hats, and another answering by shouting. In this respect it was not judged prudent to try the experiment, in order to be convinced, as the island appeared of no importance, and the crew not being in want of any thing it could produce. This curiosity was therefore laid aside, in expectation of soon discovering the island, where we had been directed to make our astronomical observations, the natives of which, it was reasonable to conjecture, would make no resistance, having already experienced the danger of opposing an European force.

On the 7th we discovered another island, judged to be in compass about five miles, being very low, and having a piece of water in the center. It appeared to abound in wood, and to be covered with verdure, but we saw no inhabitants upon it. It was named Bird Island, from the number of birds that were seen flying about. This lies in latitude 17 deg. 48 min. south, and 143 deg. 35 min. west longitude; distant ten
leagues,

leagues, in the direction weft half north from the weft end of the Groups.

On the 8th in the afternoon we faw land to the north-ward, and came abreaft of it in the evening, at about five miles diftance. This land feemed to be a chain of low iflands, of an oval figure, and confifted of coral and fand, with a few clumps of fmall trees, and in the middle of it was a lagoon. On account of its appearance, it was called Chain Ifland.

On the 10th, after a tempeftuous night, we came in fight of Ofnaburgh ifland, called by the natives Maitea. This ifland is circular, about four miles in circumference, partly rocky, and partly covered with trees.

C H A P.

C H A P. III.

The Endeavour arrives at Otaheite, or George the Third's Island—Rules established by Capt. Cook for conducting a trade with the natives—An account of several incidents during his stay in this island—An observatory and fort erected—Excursions into the woods—Visits from several of the chiefs—The music of the natives, and their manner of burying their dead, described—Other excursions and incidents, both on board and on shore—First interview with Oberea, the supposed Queen of the island—The fort described—The quadrant stolen, and the consequences—A visit to Tootahah, an Indian chief—A wrestling match described—European seeds are sown—The Indians give our people names.

ON the 11th we made Otaheite, or, as captain Wallis had named it, king George the Third's Island. The calms prevented our approaching it till the morning of the 12th, when a breeze sprung up, and several canoes were seen making towards the ship. Few of them, however, would come near, and those who did could not be persuaded to come on board. They had brought with them young plantains and branches of trees, which were handed up the ship's side, and, by their desire, were stuck in conspicuous parts of the rigging as tokens of peace and friendship. We then purchased their commodities, consisting of cocoa-nuts, bananas, bread-fruit, apples and figs, which were very acceptable to the crew. On the evening of the same day we opened the north-west point of the isle, to which the Dolphin's people had given the name of York Island. We lay off and on all night, and in the morning of the 13th we entered Port Royal Harbour in the island of Otaheite, and anchored within half a mile of the shore. Many of the natives came off immediately in their canoes, and brought with them bread-fruit, cocoa-nuts, apples, and some hogs, which

they

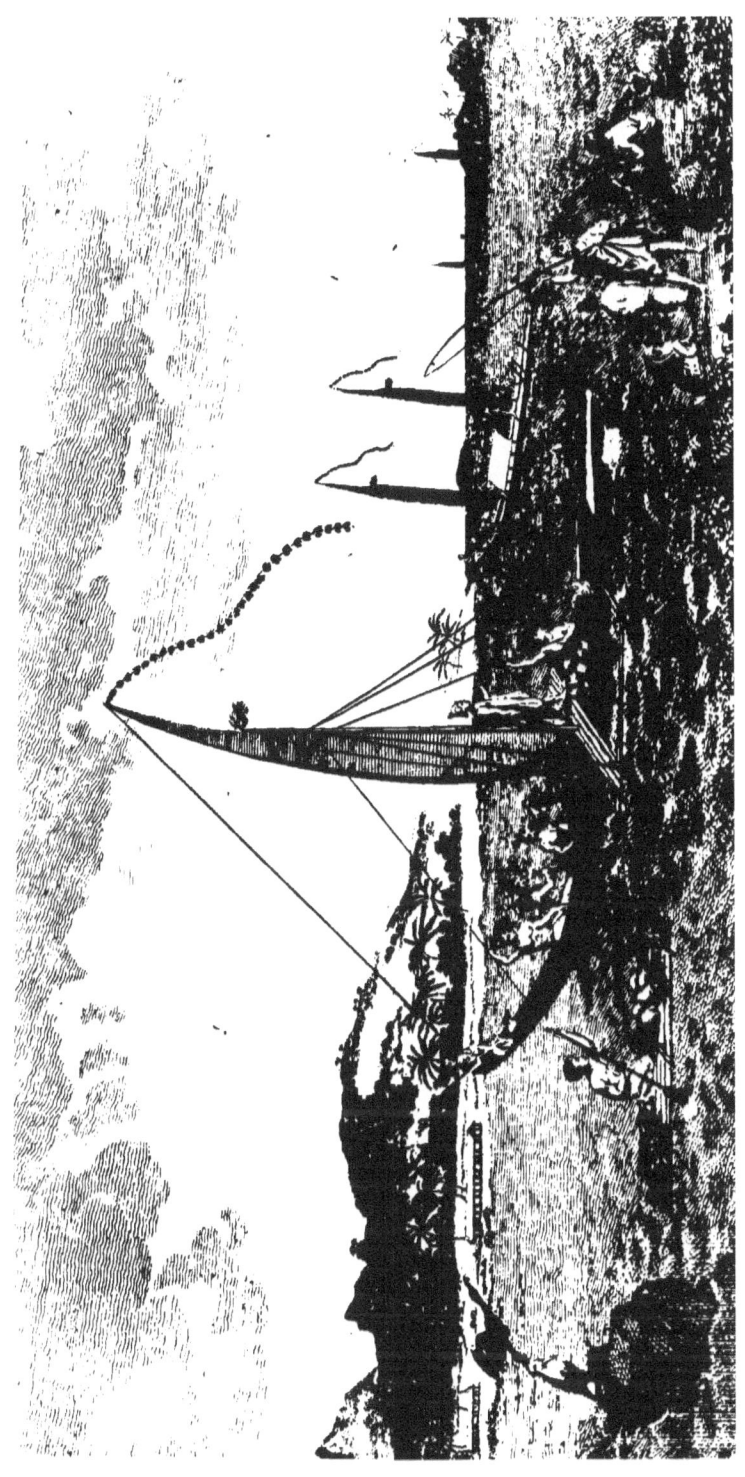

// MILITARY GORGET, *worn* *on the* SOUTH SEA ISLANDS.

Smith sculp.

London; Published as the Act directs, by Alex.ʳ Hogg, at the Kings Arms, Nº.16, Paternoster Row.

they bartered for beads and other trinkets with the
fhip's company. The tree which bears the bread-fruit
is about the fize of a horfe-chefnut: its leaves are near
a foot and a half in length, in fhape oblong, and very
much refemble thofe of the fig-tree. The fruit is not
unlike the cantaloupe melon : it is inclofed in a thin
fkin, and its core is as large as a man's thumb. The
fubftance of this fruit is fomewhat like that of new
bread, and as white as the blanched almond. It muft
be roafted, and when eaten it has the tafte of a flight
fweetnefs.

Among thofe who came on board the Endeavour,
was an elderly man, named Owhaw, known to Mr.
Gore and others who had vifited this ifland with captain Wallis. Owhaw being confidered by our gentlemen as a very ufeful man, they ftudied to pleafe him,
and to gratify all his wifhes. As our continuance in
George's Ifland was not likely to be very fhort, certain
rules were drawn up to be obferved by every perfon on
board his majefty's bark the Endeavour, for the better
eftablifhing a regular trade with the natives. The fubftance of thefe rules were, " That in order to prevent
quarrels and confufion, every one of the fhip's crew
fhould endeavour to treat the inhabitants of Otaheite
with humanity, and by all fair means to cultivate a
friendfhip with them. That no officer, feaman, or
other perfon, belonging to the fhip, excepting fuch
only who were appointed to barter with the natives,
fhould trade, or offer to trade, for any kinds of provifion, fruit, or other produce of the ifland, without having exprefs leave fo to do. That no perfon fhould em-
bezzle, trade, or offer to trade with any part of the
fhip's ftores: and, that no fort of iron, or any thing
made of iron, nor any fort of cloth, or other ufeful articles in the fhip, fhould be given in exchange for any
thing but provifion." Thefe neceffary rules were figned by Capt. Cook, and, being his orders, to the non-
obfervance of them were annexed certain penalties,
befides the punifhment according to the ufual cuftom
of the navy.

No. 2.   G   When

When the bark was properly fecured, Capt. Cook, Mr. Banks, and Dr. Solander, went on fhore, with a party under arms, and their friend the old Indian. They were received by fome hundreds of the natives with awe and reverence, who exchanged the tokens of peace, and offered to conduct them to a fpot of ground, which would be more convenient for them to occupy, than that where they had landed. On their way, the Englifh made the Indians fome prefents, which the latter very thankfully received. They now took a circuit of about four miles through groves of the breadfruit and cocoa-trees. Intermingled with thefe were the dwellings of the natives, which confifted of huts without walls. In the courfe of their journey they found but few fowls or hogs, and underflood, that none of their conductors, nor any of the people they had hitherto feen, were perfons of rank in the ifland. Thofe of our crew, who had before been at Otaheite in the Dolphin, were likewife of opinion, that the queen's refidence had been removed, as no traces of it were now to be difcovered.

Next day, in the morning, before they could leave the fhip, feveral canoes came about her filled with people, whofe drefs denoted them to be of the fuperior clafs. Two of thefe came on board, and each of them fixed upon a friend : one of them chofe Mr. Banks, and the other Captain Cook. The ceremonials confifted of taking off their cloaths in great part, and putting them upon their adopted friends. This compliment was returned by our gentlemen prefenting them with fome trinkets. They then made figns for their new friends to go with them to the place of their abode; and the latter being defirous of being acquainted with the people, and finding out a more convenient harbour, accepted the invitation, and went with them, accompanied by Mr. Banks, Dr. Solander, Captain Cook, and others. We all landed in two boats at the diftance of about three miles, among a great number of the natives, who conducted us to a large habitation, where we were introduced to a middle-aged man, named

Tootahah. When we were feated, he prefented to Mr. Banks a cock, a hen, and a piece of perfumed cloth, which compliment was returned by a prefent from Mr. Banks. We were then conducted to feveral other large dwellings, wherein we walked about with great freedom. The ladies, fo far from fhunning, invited, and even preffed us to be feated. By frequently pointing to the mats upon the ground, and fometimes drawing us down upon them, we had no doubt of their being lefs jealous of obfervation than we were; but the huts that are all open, except a roof, afforded no place of requifite retirement. Walking afterwards along the fhore, we met, accompanied by a great number of natives, another chief, named Tubourai Tamaide, with whom we fettled a treaty of peace, in the manner before defcribed. This chief gave us to underftand, that he had provifions at our fervice, if we chofe to eat, which he produced, and we dined heartily upon bread-fruit, plantains, and fifh. During this vifit, Tomio, the chief's wife, placed herfelf upon the fame mat with Mr. Banks, clofe by him; but as fhe was not young, nor appeared ever to have poffeffed many charms, this gentleman paid little attention to her; and Tomio received an additional mortification, when Mr. Banks beckoned to a pretty girl, who, with fome reluctance, came and placed herfelf by him. The princefs was fomewhat chagrined at this preference given to her rival; neverthelefs fhe continued her affiduities to her gueft. This whimfical fcene was interrupted by an event of a more ferious nature; Dr. Solander having miffed his opera glafs, a complaint was made to the chief, which interrupted the convivial party. The complaint was inforced by Mr. Banks's ftarting up and ftriking the butt-end of his mufquet againft the ground, which ftruck the Indians with fuch a panic, that all of them ran precipitately out of the houfe, except the chief and a few others of the fuperior clafs. That no difadvantageous notions might be entertained of them on account of this circumftance, the chief obferved, with an air of

G 2   great

great probity, That the place which the Doctor had mentioned on this occasion, was not within his diftrict, but that he would fend to the chief of it, and endeavour to recover it, adding, that if this could not be done, he would make the Doctor compenfation, by giving him as much new cloth (of which he produced large quantities) as fhould be thought equal to the value. The cafe however was brought in a little time, and the glafs itfelf foon after, which deprived us of the merit we fhould otherwife have had in refufing the cloth which had been offered us. But it afforded an opportunity of convincing the natives of our generofity, by lavifhing rewards upon them for an action, to which felf-intereft had been the motive, rather than any fentiment of probity; to which, from numerous tranfactions, they appeared to be abfolutely ftrangers. After this adventure was amicably terminated, we returned to the fhip about fix o'clock in the evening. On Saturday the 15th, in the morning, feveral of the chiefs, one of whom was very corpulent, came on board from the other point, bringing with them hogs, bread-fruit, and other refrefhments, in exchange for which they received linen, beads, and other trinkets; but fome of them took the liberty of ftealing the lightening chain. This day the captain, attended by Mr. Banks, and fome of the other gentlemen, went on fhore, to fix on a proper fpot to erect a fort for their defence, during their ftay on the ifland, and the ground was accordingly marked out for that purpofe; a great number of the natives looking on all the while, and behaving in the moft peaceable and friendly manner.

Mr. Banks and his friends having feen few hogs and poultry in their walks, they fufpected that they had been driven up the country; for which reafon they determined to penetrate into the woods, the tent being guarded by a petty officer and a party of marines. On this excurfion feveral of the natives accompanied the Englifh. While the party were on their march, they were alarmed by the difcharge of two pieces fired by the guard of the tent. Owhaw having now called

together

together the captain's party, difperfed all the Indians, except three, who in token of their fidelity broke branches of trees, according to their cuftom, and whom it was thought proper to retain. When they returned to the tent, they found that an Indian having fnatched away one of the centinel's mufquets, a young midfhipman, who commanded the party, was fo imprudent as to give the marines orders to fire, which were obeyed, and many of the natives were wounded; but this did not fatisfy them, as the offender had not fallen, they therefore purfued him and revenged the theft by his death. This action, which was equally inconfiftent with policy and humanity, could not but be very difpleafing to Mr. Banks; but as what had paffed could not be recalled, nothing remained but to endeavour to accommodate matters with the Indians. Accordingly he croffed the river, where he met an old man, through whofe mediation feveral of the natives were prevailed to come over to them, and to give the ufual tokens of friendfhip. The next morning, however, they faw but few of the natives on the banks, and none came on board, from whence it was concluded that the treatment they had received the former day was not yet forgotten, and the Englifh were confirmed in this opinion by Owhaw's having left them. In confequence of thefe circumftances, the captain brought the fhip nearer to the fhore, and moored her in fuch a manner as to make her broad-fide bear on the fpot which they had marked out for erecting their little fortification. But in the evening the captain and fome of the gentlemen going on fhore, the Indians came round them, and trafficked with them as ufual.

Mr. Banks on the 17th, had the misfortune to lofe Mr. Buchan. The fame day they received a vifit from Tubourai Tamaide, and Tootahah. They brought with them fome plantain branches, and till thefe were received, they would not venture on board. They bartered fome bread-fruit and a hog, which was ready dreffed, for nails, with the Englifh.

The fort began to be erected on the 18th. And now
fome

some of the company were employed in throwing up
intrenchments, whilst others were busied in cutting
fascines and pickets, in which work the Indians assisted
them. They fortified three sides of the place, with intrenchments and pallisadoes, and upon the other which
was flanked by a river, where a breast-work was formed
by the water-casks. The natives brought down such
quantities of bread fruit and cocoa-nuts this day, that
it was necessary to refuse them, and to let them know
that none would be wanting for two days. Mr. Banks
slept for the first time on shore this night. None of the
Indians attempted to approach his tent, he had however taken the precaution of placing centinels about it,
for its defence, in case any attack should be meditated.

Tubourai Tamaide visited Mr. Banks at his tent on
Wednesday the 19th, and brought with him his wife
and family with the materials for erecting a house, intending to build it near the fort. He afterwards asked
that gentleman to accompany him to the woods. On
their arrival at a place where he sometimes resided, he
presented his guests with two garments, one of which
was of red cloth, and the other was made of fine matting; having thus clothed Mr. Banks, he conducted
him to the ship, and staid to dinner with his wife and
son. They had a dish served up that day, which was
prepared by the attendants of Tubourai Tamaide, which
seemed like wheat flour, and being mixed with cocoa-
nut liquor, it was stirred about till it became a jelly.
Its flavour was something like blanc mange. A sort of
market was now established without the lines of the fort,
which was tolerably well supplied, and Tubourai Tamaide was a frequent guest to Mr. Banks, and the
other English gentlemen. He was the only native that
attempted to use a knife and fork, being fond of adopt-
ing European manners. Mr. Monkhouse the surgeon
being abroad on his evening walk, reported that he
had seen the body of a man who had been shot from
the tent, of which he gave the following account——
" The corpse was deposited in a shed, close to the
house where the deceased had resided when he was
                                                    alive,

alive, and others were within ten yards of it. It was about fifteen feet in length, and eleven in breadth, and the height was proportionable. The fides and one end were inclofed with a fort of wicker work; the other end was entirely open. The body lay on a bier, the frame of which was of wood, fupported by pofts about five feet high, and was covered with a mat, over which lay a white cloth : by the fide of it lay a wooden mace, and towards the head two cocoa fhells; towards the feet was a bunch of green leaves, and fmall dried boughs tied together, and ftuck in the ground, near which was a ftone about the fize of a cocoa-nut; here were alfo placed a young plantain tree, and a ftone axe. A great many palm nuts were hung in ftrings at the open end of the fhed; and the ftem of a palm-tree was ftuck up on the outfide of it, upon which was placed a cocoa-fhell filled with water. At the fide of one of the pofts there hung a little bag with fome roafted pieces of bread-fruit." The natives were not pleafed at his approaching the body, their jealoufy appearing plainly in their countenances and geftures.

On the 22d we were entertained by fome of the muficians of the country, who performed on an inftrument fomewhat refembling a German flute, but the performer blew through his noftril inftead of his mouth, and others accompanied this inftrument, finging only one tune. Some of the Indians brought their axes to grind and repair, moft of which they had obtained from Captain Wallis and his people in the Dolphin; but a French one occafioned a little fpeculation, and at length upon enquiry, it appeared to have been left here by M. de Bougainville.

On the 24th Mr. Banks and Dr. Solander made an excurfion into the country, and found it level and fertile along the fhore, for about two miles to the eaftward; after which the hills reached quite to the water's edge; and farther on they ran out into the fea. Having paffed thefe hills, which continued about three miles, we came to an extenfive plain, abounding with good habitations, and the people feemed to enjoy a confiderable fhare of property. The place was rendered

dered still more agreeable by a wide river issuing from a valley, and which watered it. We crossed this river, when perceiving the country to be barren, we resolved to return. Just as we were about so to do, we were offered some refreshment by a man, which some writers have expressed to be a mixture of many nations, but different from all, his skin being of a dead white, though some parts of his body were not so white as others; and his hair, eye-brows and beard were as white as his skin. His eyes appeared like those that are blood shot, and he seemed as if he was near-sighted. Upon our return, the excessive joy of Tubourai Tamaide and his women is not to be expressed.

On the 25th, in the evening, several of the gentlemens knives being missing, Mr. Banks, who had lost his among the rest, accused Tubourai Tamaide of having taken it, which as he was innocent, occasioned him a great deal of unmerited anxiety. He made signs, while the tears started from his eyes, that if he had ever been guilty of such a theft as was imputed to him, he would suffer his throat to be cut. But though he was innocent, it was plain from many instances, that the natives of this island were very much addicted to thieving: though Mr. Banks's servant had mislaid the knife in question, yet the rest were produced in a rag, by one of the natives.

When the guns on the 26th, which were six swivels, had been mounted on the fort, the Indians seemed to be in great trouble, and several of the fishermen removed, fearing, notwithstanding all the marks of friendship which had been shewn to them by our people, they should, within a few days, be fired at from the fort: yet the next day, being the 27th, Tubourai Tamaide came with three women, and a friend of his, who was a remarkable glutton, into the fort to dine with us, and after dinner returned to his own house in the wood. In a short time after he came back to complain to Mr. Banks, of a butcher, who had threatened to cut his wife's throat, because she would not barter a stone hatchet for a nail. It appearing clearly that the offender
der

der had infringed one of the rules enjoined by the Captain for trading with the natives, he was flogged on board in their fight. When the firft ftroke had been given they were humane enough to interfere, and intreated earneftly that the culprit might be untied; but when this favour was denied them, they fhewed ftrong figns of concern, and burft into tears.

On the 28th, Terapo, one of Tubourai Tamaide's female attendants, came down to the fort in the greateft affliction, the tears gufhing from her eyes. Mr. Banks feeing her full of lamentation and forrow, infifted upon knowing the caufe, but inftead of anfwering, fhe ftruck herfelf feveral times with a fhark's tooth upon her head, till an effufion of blood followed, while her diftrefs was difregarded by feveral other Indians, who continued laughing and talking with the utmoft un-concern. After this, fhe gathered up fome pieces of cloth, which fhe had thrown down to catch the blood, and threw them into the fea, as if fhe wifhed to pre-vent the leaft trace and mark of her abfurd behaviour. She then bathed in the river, and with remarkable chearfulnefs returned to the tent, as if nothing extraor-dinary had happened. During the forenoon of this day the Indian canoes were continually coming in, and people of both fexes filled the tents of the fort. Mr. Molineux, mafter of the Endeavour, feeing a woman whofe name was Oberea, he declared fhe was the fame perfon, whom he judged to be the queen of the ifland when he was there with Capt. Wallis. The eyes of every one were now fixed on her, of whom fo much had been faid by the crew of the Dolphin, and in the account given of her by the captain. With regard to her perfon, fhe was tall and rather large made; fhe was about forty years of age, her fkin white, and her eyes had great expreffion in them: fhe had been handfome, but her beauty was now upon the decline. It was not long before an offer was made to conduct her on board the fhip, which fhe accepted. Many prefents were made her, particularly a child's doll, which fhe viewed very attentively. Capt. Cook accompanied her on shore, and when we landed, she presented him with a hog and some plantains, in return for his presents, which were carried to the fort in procession, Oberea and the Captain bringing up the rear. In the way they met Tootahah, who, though not king, seemed to be at this time invested with sovereign authority. Envy is found among those who are supposed to be the children of simple nature. Her influence was plainly visible in a matter which to us was rather a subject of laughter than of serious consideration. Tootahah no sooner saw the doll, than he discovered strong symptoms of jealousy, nor could any method be found of conciliating his friendship, but that of complimenting him with a baby also. A doll was now preferable to a hatchet; but a very short time taught the Indians the superior value of iron, which, on account of its usefulness, prevailed over every other consideration. To such of the men who came from time to time on board, the ship's provisions seemed to be very acceptable, but the women did not chuse to taste them; and though they were courted to dine with our gentlemen, yet, for reasons known only to themselves, they preferred the eating of plantains with the servants.

On the 29th, near noon, Mr. Banks paid a visit to Oberea, but was informed that she was asleep under the awning of her canoe; and, going to call her up, was surprized at finding her in bed with a young fellow of about twenty-five years of age, a discovery which caused him to retire rather disconcerted; but he soon understood that a commerce of this kind was by no means considered as scandalous, the ladies frequently courting the men to amorous dalliance, of which they made no secret; and as to young Obadee, found in bed with the queen, he was well known by every one to be the object of her lascivious hours. The queen soon got up, and dressed herself to wait upon Mr. Banks, and, after having, as a token of her particular regard, put on him a suit of fine cloth, they proceeded together to the tents. In the evening Mr. Banks visited Tubourai Tamaide. He was astonished

to

to find this chief and his family in tears, and not being able to difcover the caufe, he foon took leave of them. Upon his return the officers told him, that Owhaw had foretold, that the guns would be fired within four days, and as this was the eve of the third day, they were alarmed at the fituation they judged themfelves to be in. As we were apprehenfive of ill confequences from this prepoffeffion, the centinels were doubled at the fort, and we thought it neceffary to keep under arms; but Mr. Banks walking round the point, at two in the morning, and finding nothing that might tend to encourage his fufpicions, he dropped them, and refted fecure in the fort. This our little fortification was now complete. A bank of earth four feet and an half high on the infide, and a ditch without ten feet broad and fix deep, formed the north and fouth fides. On the weft, oppofite the bay, was another bank (with pallifadoes upon it) four feet high; but a ditch was unneceffary, the works being at high-water mark. Upon the river's bank, on the eaft-fide, was a range of water cafks, filled with water. This being thought the weakeft fide, we planted two four pounders, and mounted fix fwivel guns, which commanded the only two avenues from the woods. We had about forty-five men in this fort, including the officers, and other gentlemen who refided on fhore.

On the 30th Tomio came in great hafte to our tents, and taking Mr. Banks by the arm, told him that Tubourai Tamaide was dying, owing to fomewhat that had been given him by our people, and intreated him inftantly to go to him. Accordingly Mr. Banks went, and found the Indian very fick. He had been vomiting, and had thrown up a leaf which they faid contained fome of the poifon. Mr. Banks having examined the leaf, found it was nothing but tobacco, which the Indian had begged of fome of the fhip's company.

The matter, however, appeared in a very ferious light to Tubourai Tamaide, who really concluded from the violent ficknefs he fuffered, that he had fwallowed

fome

fome deadly drug, the terror of which no doubt contributed to make him yet more fick. While Mr. Banks was examining the leaf, he looked up to him, as if he had been juft on the point of death. But when the nature of this dreadful poifon was found out, he only ordered him to drink of cocoa-nut milk, which foon reftored him to health, and he was as chearful as before the accident happened. Thefe people feemed in particular inftances to be fometimes ftrangely afflicted from flight caufes.

On the 1ft of May, Captain Cook having produced an iron adze, which was made in imitation of the ftone ones ufed by the natives, fhewed it to Tootahah, as a curiofity. The latter fnatched it up and infifted on having it; and though he was offered the choice of any of the articles in the chefts which were opened before him, yet he would not accept of any thing in its ftead. A chief dined with us that day, who had been on board fome time before, accompanied by fome of his women that ufed to feed him. He now came alone; and when all things were fet ready for dinner, the captain helped him to fome victuals, fuppofing that he would have difpenfed with the ceremony of being fed; but he was deceived; for the chief never attempted to eat, and would have gone without his dinner, if one of the fervants had not fed him. The next morning, May 2, we took the aftronomical quadrant and fome of the inftruments on fhore that afternoon; and to our great furprife when we wanted to make ufe of the quadrant, the next day, it was not to be found; a matter which was looked upon as the more extraordinary, as a centinel had been placed for the whole night within a few yards of the place where it was depofited. Our own people, at firft, were fufpected of being concerned in this theft, and, as the inftrument had never been taken out of the cafe, it was fufpected that fome perfon might have carried it off, under the fuppofition that its contents were articles ufed in traffic. A ftrict fearch was made in and about the fort, and a confiderable reward offered in order to

obtain

obtain it again. But all this proving fruitlefs, Mr. Banks, accompanied by Mr. Green and fome other gentlemen, fet out for the woods, where they thought they might probably get fome tidings of what was ftolen. In their way, they met with Tubourai Tamaide and fome of the natives. This chief was made to underftand by figns, that they had loft the quadrant, and that as fome of his countrymen muft have taken it, they infifted upon being fhewn the place where it was concealed. Having proceeded a few miles together, after fome enquiry, Tubourai Tamaide was informed who the thief was, and it was found that he was then at a place about four miles diftant. As they had no arms but a brace of piftols, not caring to truft themfelves fo far from the fort, a meffage was difpatched to Captain Cook, requefting him to fend out a party to fupport them. The captain accordingly fet out with a party properly armed, after having laid an embargo upon all the canoes in the bay.

In the mean time, Mr. Banks and Mr. Green proceeded on their way, and at the place which had been mentioned, were met by one of Tubourai Tamaide's own people, bringing with him part of the quadrant; the cafe and the other parts of the inftrument were recovered foon afterwards, when it was found that it had received no real injury, though it had been taken to pieces.

When they returned in the evening, they were much furprifed to find Tootahah under confinement in the fort, while a croud of the natives furrounded the gate, difcovering marks of the greateft anxiety for the fate of their chief. The occafion of his detention originated from the conduct of the Indians: alarmed at Capt. Cook's having gone up the country with an armed party, moft of the natives left the fort that evening, and one of the canoes attempted to quit the bay. The lieutenant who commanded on board the fhip, having it in charge not to fuffer any canoe to depart, fent a boat to detain her, but fhe no fooner approached, than the Indians jumped into the fea. Tootahah being of the

the number, was taken up, and fent by the lieutenant
to the officer that commanded at the fort, who concluded he fhould do right to detain him prifoner, while the
poor chief thought of nothing but being put to death,
till Capt. Cook caufed him to be returned, to the great
joy of his countrymen. But the natives were ftill inclined to bear this affair in their minds; and as a proof
of it, they neglected to fupply the market with provifions. Mr. Banks walking into the woods, heard
great murmurings concerning the treatment of Tootahah, who, as they faid, had been ill ufed and beaten,
though Mr. Banks declared he was quite ignorant of
his having received fuch treatment.

The chief now fent for fuch hogs to be reftored as
he had left behind him, at firft intending them as a
prefent, which by this time, perhaps, he did not think
the Englifh had merited; but they refufed to fend them
unlefs he would come himfelf, thinking by an interview
to promote a reconciliation; and this they were the
more defious of, as they were told it would be a fortnight before he would pay them a vifit.

On the 3d provifions were extremely fcarce, as the
markets continued to be ill fupplied on the account
already mentioned; and it was not without fome difficulty, that Mr. Banks got a few bafkets of bread-fruit
from Tubourai Tamaide. Tootahah on the 4th fent
for an axe and a fhirt in return for the hogs, which
were accordingly promifed to be brought him the
next day. He fent again early in the morning of the
5th, and Mr. Banks and the Doctor fet out in the pinnace, taking with them one of Tootahah's people, and
foon reached Eparre, where he refided, which was a
few miles to the weftward. When they arrived there,
they found a great number of the natives waiting for
them on the fhore, and were conducted directly to the
chief, the people notwithftanding the offence they had
fo lately taken, fhouting out in their language, " Tootahah is your friend." He was fitting under a tree,
and fome old men were ftanding about him. Having
made figns for them to be feated, he afked for the axe,
which

which was then given him by Capt. Cook, as alfo the
fhirt that he had demanded, and a broad-cloth garment,
which latter he put on, and was well pleafed with the
prefent. They ate a mouthful together in the boat,
and were afterwards conducted to a large court-yard
on one fide of the chief's houfe, where they were to be
entertained with wreftling after the manner of the
country. He himfelf fat at the upper end of the area,
having feveral of his principal men on each fide of him,
who appeared as judges of the fport, which was as
follow:

" Ten or twelve combatants entered the area, and
after many fimple ceremonies of challenging, they
engaged, and each endeavoured to throw his antagonift
by mere ftrength: thus they feized each other by the
hand, or other parts of the body, grappling, without
the leaft art, till one, by having a greater hold, or
ftronger mufcular force, threw his antagonift on his
back. The conqueft was applauded by the old men
with a few words repeated in a kind of tune, and with
three huzzas. After one engagement another fucceeded; but if the combatants could not throw each
other in the fpace of a minute, they parted, either by
confent, or the intervention of their friends. Several
women of rank in the country were prefent, but it was
thought they only attended this amufement in compliment to the Englifh gentlemen. A man with a ftick,
who made way for us when we landed, officiated as
mafter of the ceremonies, keeping order among the
people, and thofe of them who preffed forward he
ftruck with his ftick very fmartly. During thefe athle-
tic fports, another party of men performed a dance,
for the fpace of a minute, but neither of thefe parties
took the leaft notice of each other, their attention
being wholly fixed on their own endeavours to pleafe
and conquer. At the conclufion of this entertainment,
not unlike the wreftling matches of remote antiquity,
we were told, that fome hogs, and a large quantity of
bread fruit were preparing for our dinner, very agreeable intelligence to thofe whofe appetites were fharpened

ed by their journey; but our hoft, inftead of fetting his two hogs before us, ordered one of them to be carried into our boat. Here we thought to have enjoyed our good cheer, and yet we neither dined on fhore, nor in the boat, but at the defire of Tubourai Tamaide, proceeded as far as the fhip: no fmall mortification this, as we had to row four miles, while our dinner was growing cold: however, we were at laft gratified with our promifed repaft, of which our chief and his friends had a liberal fhare. This friendly reconciliation between them and us, operated on the natives like a charm: for it was no fooner known that Tubourai Tamaide was on board, than provifions of all kinds were brought to the fort in great plenty.

On the 8th, early in the morning, Mr. Molineux, the mafter, and Mr. Green fet out in the pinnace to the eaftward, in order to procure fome poultry, or hogs. They faw many of the latter, and one turtle, yet could not purchafe either, becaufe they belonged to Tootahah, and without his permiffion, the people could not be prevailed upon to fell them. Hence we concluded that Tootahah was indeed a prince; and we afterwards learnt, that, in this part of the ifland, he acted as regent for a minor, whom we never faw all the time of our ftay here. However, fome time afterwards, having produced fome nails to barter for provifions, we obtained near twenty cocoa-nuts, and fome bread-fruit, for one of the fmalleft fize, fo that we foon had plenty of thefe articles, though no hogs. In this excurfion Mr. Green imagined he had difcovered a tree fixty yards in circumference; but, on his return, he was informed by our two gentlemen, that it was a fpecies of the fig, whofe branches bending down to the earth take frefh root, and thus form a mafs of trunks, which being all united by a common vegetation, might eafily be miftaken for one trunk or body.

On the 9th in the forenoon, Oberea paid us a vifit, accompanied by her favourite Obadee, prefenting us with a hog and fome bread-fruit. This was the firft vifit we had received from this lady, fince the lofs of

our

our quadrant, and the confinement of Tootahah. By this time our forge was fet up and at work, which afforded a new fubject of admiration to the Indians, and to Capt: Cook an additional opportunity of conferring obligations on them, by permitting the fmith, in his leifure hours, to convert the old iron, which they were fuppofed to have procured from the Dolphin, into different kinds of tools. Oberea produced as much old iron as would have made for her another axe; this fhe requefted to have done; however the lady could not be gratified in this particular, upon which fhe brought a broken axe, defiring it might be mended. The axe was mended, and to all appearance fhe was content. On their return home, the Indians took with them the canoe which had lain fome time at the point.

On the 10th we fowed, in ground properly prepared, feeds of melons, and other plants, but none of them came up, except muftard. Mr. Banks thought the feeds were fpoiled by a total exclufion of frefh air, they having all been put into fmall bottles, and fealed up with rofin. We learnt this day, that the Indians called the ifland Otaheite, the name by which we have diftinguifhed it; but we were not fo fortunate in our endeavours to teach them our names; and, after repeated attempts to pronounce them, which proved fruitlefs, they had recourfe to new ones, the productions of their own invention. Capt. Cook they named Toote; Mr. Hicks, Hete. The mafter they called Boba, from his chriftian name Robert; Mr. Gore, Toarro; Dr. Solander, Torano; Mr. Banks, Tapane; Mr. Green, Eteree; Mr. Parkinfon, Patani; Mr. Sporing, Polini; and fo on for the greateft part of the fhip's crew. Thefe perhaps, were fignificant words in their own language; and we are inclined to this opinion, becaufe Mr. Monkhoufe, who commanded the party, that fhot the man for ftealing a mufket, they named Matte, which was not merely an arbitrary found; but in their language it fignified dead.

CHAP. IV.

An extraordinary visit—Divine service attended by the na-
tives of Otaheite—An uncommon sight—Tubourai Tamaide
found guilty of theft—A visit paid to Tootahah—Various
adventures at that time, and an extraordinary amusement
of the Indians—A relation of what happened at the fort,
while preparations were making to observe the Transit of
Venus—The observations made with great success—A par-
ticular account and description of an Indian funeral—An
unusual character among the Indians—A robbery at the
fort—Specimen of Indian cookery—A narrative of various
incidents—A circumnavigation of the island, and occurrences
during this expedition—A burying-place, and a Morai, or
place of worship described—An inland expedition of Mr.
Banks—Preparations made by the crew of the Endeavour
to leave the island of Otaheite—An account of the departure
of the Endeavour, and the behaviour of the natives, parti-
cularly of Tupid, on this occasion.

ON the 12th of this month (May) an uncommon
ceremony was performed by some of the natives.
As Mr. Banks was fitting in his boat, trading with
them as usual, some ladies, who were strangers, advanced in procession towards him. The rest of the
Indians on each side gave way, and formed a lane for
the visitors to pass, who coming up to Mr. Banks, presented him with some parrots feathers, and various
kinds of plants. Tupid, who stood by Mr. Banks, acted
as his master of the ceremonies, and receiving the
branches, which were brought at six different times,
laid them down in the boat. After this some large
bundles of cloth were brought, consisting of nine
pieces, which being divided into three parcels, one of
the women, called Oorattooa, who appeared to be the
principal, stepping upon one of them, pulled up her
cloaths as high as her waist, and then, with an air of
unaffected simplicity, turned round three times. This
ceremony

ceremony fhe repeated, with fimilar circumftances, on the other two parcels of cloth; and the whole being then prefented to Mr. Banks, the ladies went and faluted him; in return for which extraordinary favours, he made them fuch prefents as he thought would beft pleafe them. In the evening the gentlemen of the fort were vifited by Oberea, and Otheorea, her favourite female attendant, who was a very agreeable girl, and whom we were the more pleafed to fee, becaufe it had been reported that fhe was either fick or dead.

On the 13th Tubourai Tamaide offended Mr. Banks, by fnatching his gun out of his hand, and firing it in the air; an action which alfo much furprized that gentleman, as he imagined him totally ignorant of the ufe of it. And as the ignorance of the people of thofe countries in regard to this particular, muft always caufe them to fear their guefts, Mr. Banks therefore made a ferious matter of what, probably, the other meant only as a joke, and, not without threats, gave him to underftand, that for him but to touch the piece was a high infult. The offender made no reply, but fet out immediately, with his family, for Eparre. Great inconvenience being apprehended from this man, and as in many inftances he had been particularly ufeful, Mr. Banks determined to follow him. He fet out the fame evening from the fort, accompanied by Mr. Molineux, and found him in the middle of a large circle of people, the picture of extreme grief, which was alfo vifible in the countenances of his attendants. One of the women expreffed her trouble in the fame manner as Terapo had done, upon another occafion. Mr. Banks loft no time in endeavouring to put an end to all animofity, The chief was foothed into confidence, and, a double canoe being got ready, they all returned together to the fort before fupper: and as a pledge of fincere reconciliation, both he and his wife paffed the night in the tent of Mr. Banks. That very night, notwithftanding their prefence, one of the natives attempted to fcale the

the barricadoes of the fort; but, being difcovered by one of our centinels, he ran away much fafter than any of our people could follow him. The temptation which caufed him to attempt what might have coft him his life, was, doubtlefs the iron and iron tools which were in ufe at the armourer's forge: incitements to theft which none of the Indians could refift,

On Sunday the 14th, in the morning divine fervice was performed at the fort. We hoped to have had the prefence of fome of the Indians, but before the time fixed on for beginning the fervice, moft of them were gone home. Tubourai Tamaide and his wife were prefent, but though they behaved with much decency, they made no enquiries with refpect to the ceremonies, and their brethren were as little inquifitive upon their return. The day thus begun with acts of devotion, was concluded with thofe of lewdnefs exhibited among the natives by way of entertainment. Among the reft a young fellow lay publickly with a girl about twelve years of age, in the prefence of many of our people, and a great number of the Indians, without the leaft fenfe of impropriety or indecency. Oberea, and fome women of the firft rank in the country were fpectators, who even gave inftructions to the girl how to perform her part, which, young as fhe was, feemed unneceffary.

On Monday the 15th, Tubourai Tamaide was detected in having committed a theft. Mr. Banks had a good opinion of this chief, but, when his honefty was put to the teft, a bafket of nails, left in the corner of the tent proved irrefiftible. He confefed the fact of having ftolen four nails, but when reftitution was demanded, Tamaide faid the nails were at Eparre, High words paffed on the occafion, and, in the end, the Indian produced one of the nails, and was to be forgiven on reftoring the reft; but his virtue was not equal to the tafk, and he withdrew himfelf, as ufual, when he had committed any offence. At this time our long-boat was fo much eaten with worms, that it was found neceffary to give her a new bottom. On examining the

the pinnace, thinking fhe might be in the fame ftate, we had the fatisfaction to perceive, that not a worm had touched her. This difference in the condition of the two boats we attributed to the different ingredients with which their bottoms were paid; the long-boat had been paid with varnifh of pine, and the pinnace painted with white lead and oil; which laft coating we think to be the moft eligible for the bottoms of all boats intended for this part of the world.

On the 24th, Mr. Hicks was fent to Tootahah, who had removed from Eparre to a place called Tettahah. The chief having fent feveral times to requeft a vifit from the captain, promifing, at the fame time, that he would acknowledge the favour by a prefent of fome hogs, the bufinefs of Mr. Hicks was, to obtain, if poffible, the hogs, upon eafier terms than the required vifit. He was received in a friendly manner by Tootahah, who, upon his arrival, produced one hog only, but promifed three more that were at a diftance the next morning. Mr. Hicks waited patiently till the appointed time; but when the morning came, he was obliged to depart with the fingle hog that had been prefented to him.

On the 25th, Mr. Banks feeing Tubourai Tamaide and his wife Tomio at the tent for the firft time fince the former had been detected in ftealing the nails, he endeavoured to perfuade him to reftore them, but in vain. As our gentlemen treated him with a referve and coolnefs which he could not but perceive, his ftay was fhort, and he departed in a very abrupt manner; nor could our furgeon the next morning perfuade to effect a reconciliation by bringing down the nails.

On the 27th, Mr. Banks, Dr. Solander, Captain Cook, and fome others, fet out in the pinnace to vifit Tootahah, who had again removed to a place called Atahourou, fix miles from his laft abode; and not being able to go half way thither in a boat, it was almoft evening before we arrived. We found the chief, as ufual, fitting under a tree with a great crowd about

2   him,

him. Having made our prefents in due form, confifting of a yellow ftuff petticoat, and other trifling articles, we were invited to fupper, and to pafs the night
there. Our party confifted of fix only; but the place
was crowded with a greater number than the houfes and
canoes could contain. Among other guefts were Oberea
with her train of attendants. Mr. Banks having accepted of a lodging in Oberea's canoe, left his companions in order to retire to reft. Oberea had the charge
of his cloaths; but notwithftanding her care, they were
ftolen, as were alfo his piftols, his powder horn, and
feveral other things out of his waiftcoat pockets. An
alarm was given to Tootahah, in the next canoe, who
went with Oberea in fearch of the thief, leaving Mr.
Banks with only his breeches and waiftcoat on, and
his mufket uncharged. They foon returned, but without fuccefs. Mr. Banks thought proper to put up with
the lofs at prefent, and retired a fecond time to reft;
juft as he had compofed himfelf to fleep, he was
rouzed by fome mufic, and obferved lights at a little
diftance from the fhore. He then rofe to go and find
his companions. As foon as he approached the lights,
he found the hut where Captain Cook and three others
of the gentlemen lay, when he began to relate his mif-
adventure to them; they told him in return, that they
had loft their ftockings and jackets. In effect Dr. Solander, who joined them the next morning, was the
only one that efcaped being robbed, and he had flept
at a houfe that was a mile diftant. This accident, however, did not prevent Captain Cook, Mr. Banks, and
the reft that were at the hut, from attending to the
mufic, which was a fort of concert called Heiva, and
confifted of drums, flutes, and feveral voices. They
retired again to their repofe, after this entertainment
was over.

Their cloaths, and the other things which had been
ftolen, were never heard of afterwards, but Mr. Banks
got fome cloaths from Oberea, in which he made a
whimfical appearance.

On

On the 28th, we fet out for the boat, having obtained only one hog, which had been intended for our fupper the preceding night; fo that all things confidered, we had little reafon to be fatisfied with our excurfion. On our return to the boat, we had a fpecimen of the agility of the Indian fwimmers, fome of whom, merely for diverfion, fwam in a furf where no European boat could have lived, and where our beft fwimmers muft have perifhed, had they accidentally fallen in with it.

At this time the preparations were made for viewing the tranfit of Venus, and two parties were fent out to make obfervations from different fpots, that in cafe of failing in one place they might fucceed in another. They employed themfelves for fome time in preparing their inftruments, and inftructing thofe gentlemen who were to go out, in the ufe of them; and on Thurfday the firft of June, they fent the long-boat with Mr. Gore, Mr. Monkhoufe (the two obfervers) and Mr. Sporing, the latter of whom was a friend of Mr. Banks, with proper inftruments to Emayo. Others were fent to find out a fpot that might anfwer the purpofe, at a convenient diftance from their principal ftation.

The party that went towards Emayo, after rowing the greater part of the night, having hailed a canoe, were informed of a place by the Indians on board, which was judged proper for their obfervatory, where they accordingly fixed their tents. It was a rock that rofe out of the water about 140 yards from the fhore.

Saturday the 3d (the day of the tranfit) Mr. Banks, as foon as it was light, left them, in order to go and get frefh provifions on the ifland. This gentleman had the fatisfaction to fee the fun-rife without a cloud. The king, whofe name was Tarrao, came to pay him a vifit, as he was trading with the natives, and brought with him Nuna his fifter. As it was cuftomary for the people in thefe parts to be feated at their conferences,

ences, Mr. Banks spread his turban of Indian cloth, which he wore as a hat, upon the ground, on which they all set down. Then a hog and a dog, some cocoa-nuts, and bread-fruit were brought, being the king's present, and Mr. Banks sent for an adze, a shirt, and some beads, which were presented to his majesty, who received them with apparent satisfaction. Tubourai Tamaide, and Tomio, who had gone with Mr. Banks, came from the observatory, when Tomio, who was said to be related to Tarrao, gave him a long nail, and left a shirt as a present for Nuna. Afterwards the king, his sister, and three beautiful young women their attendants, returned with Mr. Banks to the observatory, where he shewed them the transit of Venus, when that planet was upon the sun, and acquainted them, that to view it in that situation was the cause of his undertaking a voyage to those remoter parts. According to this gentleman's account, the produce of this island is nearly the same with that of Otaheite; the people also resembled those of that island: he had seen many of them upon it who were acquainted with the nature of trading articles. The parties that were sent out to make their observations on the transit, had good success in the undertaking: though they differed rather more than might have been expected in their account of the contact.

Mr. Green's account was as follows:

	Hours.	Min.	Sec.	
The first external contact	9	25	4	Morn.
The first internal contact, or total emersion	9	44	4	
The second internal contact, or beginning of the emersion	3	14	8	Afternoon.
The second external contact, or total emersion	3	32	10	

Latitude

A MAN of OTAHEITE, in A MOURNING D

Latitude of the obfervatory 17 deg. 29 min. 15 fec. fouth ;—longitude, 149 deg. 32 min. 30 fec. weft from Greenwich.

While the gentlemen and officers were bufied in viewing the tranfit, fome of the fhip's company hav‑ ing broke into the ftore-room, took the liberty of fteal‑ ing a quantity of fpike-nails. After a ftrict fearch the thief was found out; he had, however, but few of the nails in his poffeffion; but he was ordered to receive two dozen of lafhes, by way of example.

On the 4th, the two parties fent out to obferve the tranfit were abfent; on which account we deferred keeping his majefty's birth-day to the next day, the 5th, when we celebrated the fame; feveral of the Indian chiefs partook of our entertainment, and in turn drank his majefty's health by the name of Kihiargo, the neareft imitation they could produce of king George. About this time an old female of fome diftinction dy‑ ing, gave the Englifh an opportunity of obferving the ceremonies ufed by thefe iflanders in difpofing of the dead bodies of their people; which, as we have ob‑ ferved, they do not directly bury. The reader has al‑ ready feen the defcription of the bier, the placing the bread-fruit, &c. which, according to Tubourai Ta‑ maide's account, was a kind of offering to their gods. In the front of the fquare fpace, a fort of ftile was placed where the relations of the deceafed ftood to give token of their grief. There were under the awning fome pieces of cloth, whereon were the tears and blood of the mourners, who ufed to wound themfelves with a fhark's tooth upon thefe occafions. Four temporary houfes were erected at a fmall diftance, in one of which remained fome of the relations of the deceafed; the chief mourner refided in another; and was dreffed in a particular manner, in order to perform a certain ceremony. When the corpfe is rotten, the bones are buried near the fpot, and thefe places were found to anfwer the purpofes of religious worfhip, though Cap‑ tain Wallis could not perceive the traces of any fuch worship among them. Concerning the ceremony we are about to speak of, the following is the account we have of it, which may not be unentertaining to the curious reader. It was performed on the 10th, and Mr. Banks was so desirous of being present, that he agreed to take a part in it, when he was informed that he could not be a spectator on any other condition. He went accordingly in the evening, to the place where the body was deposited, where he was met by the relations of the deceased, and was afterwards joined by several other persons. Tubourai Tamaide was the principal mourner, whose dress was whimsical, though not altogether ungraceful. Mr. Banks was obliged to quit his European dress, and had no other covering than a small piece of cloth that was tied round his middle; his body was blacked over with charcoal and water, as were the bodies of several others, and among them some females, who were no more covered than himself. The procession then began, and the chief mourner uttered some words which were judged to be a prayer, when he approached the body, and he repeated these words as he came up to his own house. They afterwards went on, by permission, towards the fort. It is usual for the rest of the Indians to shun these processions as much as possible; they accordingly ran into the woods in great haste, as soon as this came in view. From the fort the mourners proceeded along the shore, crossed the river, then entered the woods, passing several houses, which became immediately uninhabited, and during the rest of the procession, which continued for half an hour, not an Indian was visible. Mr. Banks filled an office that they called Niniveh, and there were two others in the same character. When none of the other natives were to be seen, they approached the chief mourner, saying Imatata; then those who had assisted at the ceremony bathed in the river, and resumed their former dress. Such was this uncommon ceremony, in which Mr. Banks performed a principal part, and received applause from Tubourai Tamaide, the chief mourner. What can have introduced among these Indians

dians fo ftrange a cuftom as that of expofing their dead above ground, till the flefh is confumed by putrefaction, and then burying the bones, it is perhaps impoffible to guefs; nor is it lefs difficult to determine, why the repofitories of their dead fhould be alfo places of worfhip.

On the 12th, the Indians having loft fome of their bows and arrows, and ftrings of plaited hair, a complaint was made to the captain. The affair was enquired into, and the fact being well attefted, the offenders received each two dozen of lafhes. The fame day Tubourai Tamaide brought his bow and arrows, in order to decide a challenge of fhooting between him and Mr. Gore; but it appeared they had miftaken each other, Mr. Gore intending to difcharge his arrow at a mark, while the Indian meant only to try who could fhoot fartheft. The challenge was dropped in confequence of the miftake being difcovered; but Tubourai Tamaide, in order to difplay kis fkill, kneeling down, fhot an arrow, unfeathered (as they all are) near the fixth part of a mile, dropping the bow the inftant the arrow was difcharged. Mr. Banks having this morning met feveral of the natives, and being informed, that a mufical entertainment was expected in the evening, he, and the reft of the Englifh gentlemen refolved to be prefent at the fame. They went accordingly, and heard a performance on drums and flutes by a kind of itinerant muficians. The drummers fung to the mufic, and the Englifh were much furprized when they found that they were the fubject of their lays. The fongs they therefore concluded to be extemporary effufions, the rewards whereof were fuch neceffaries as they required.

On the 14th, in the night, an iron coal rake for the oven, was ftole; and many other things having at different times been conveyed away, Capt. Cook judged it of fome confequence, to put an end, if poffible, to fuch practices, by making it their common intereft to prevent it. He had already given ftrict orders, that the centinels fhould not fire upon the Indians, even if

they

they were detected in the fact; but many repeated depredations determined him to make reprizals. About
twenty-seven of their double canoes with fails were
just arrived, containing cargoes of fish; these the captain seized, and then gave notice, that unless the rake,
and all the other things that had been stolen, were returned, the veffels fhould be burnt. The menace produced no other effect than the reftitution of the rake,
all the other things remaining in their poffeffion.
The captain, however, thought fit to give up the cargoes, as the innocent natives were in great diftrefs for
want of them, and in order to prevent the confufion
arifing from difputes concerning the property of the
different lots of goods which they had on board.
About this time another incident had nearly, notwithftanding all our caution, embroiled us with the Indians. The captain having fent a boat on fhore to get
ballaft, the officer not meeting immediately with what
he wanted, began to pull down one of the fepulchral
manfions of the dead; which facrilegious act of violence was immediately oppofed by the enraged iflanders.
Intelligence of this difpute being received by Mr.
Banks, he went to the place, and a reconciliation was
foon effected, which put an end to the difpute, by
fending the boat's crew to the river's fide, where a fufficient quantity of ftones were to be had without a pof-
fibility of giving offence. This was the only inftance
in which they offered to oppofe us; and (except the
affair of the fort, which has been related) the only infult offered to an individual, was, when Mr. Monkhoufe, the furgeon, took a flower from a tree which
grew in one of their fepulchral inclofures. Upon this
occafion, an Indian came fuddenly behind him and
ftruck him; Mr. Monkhoufe laid hold of the affailant,
but two of his countrymen refcued him, and then they
all ran off as faft as they could.

On the 19th in the evening, while the canoes were
ftill detained, Oberea and feveral of her attendants
paid us a vifit. She came from Tootahah's palace, in
a double canoe, and brought with her a hog, bread-

fruit,

fruit, and other prefents, among which was a dog; but not a fingle article of the things that had been ftolen : thefe fhe faid had been taken away by her favourite Obadee, whom fhe had beaten and difmiffed. She feemed however confcious that her ftory did not deferve credit, and appeared at firft much terrified; though fhe furmounted her fears with great fortitude, and was defirous of fleeping with her attendants in Mr. Banks's tent; but this being refufed, fhe was obliged to pafs the night in her canoe. A whole tribe of Indians would have flept in the ball tent, but were not permitted. The next morning Oberea returned, putting herfelf wholly in our power, when we accepted of her prefents, which fhe doubtlefs thought, and juftly too, the moft effectual means to bring about a reconciliation. Two of her attendants were very affiduous in getting themfelves hufbands, in which they fucceeded, by means of the furgeon and one of the lieutenants: they feemed very agreeable till bed-time, and determined to lie in Mr. Banks's tent, which they accordingly did, till the furgeon having fome words with one of them Mr. Banks thruft her out, and fhe was followed by the reft, except Otea-Tea, who cried fome time, and then he turned her out alfo. This had like to have become a ferious affair, a duel being talked of between Mr. Banks and Mr. Monkhoufe, but it was happily avoided. We had been informed that in this ifland dogs were efteemed more delicate food than pork, as thofe bred by the natives to be eaten, fed entirely upon vegetables. The experiment was tried. Tupia undertook to kill and drefs the dog, which he did, by making a hole in the ground, and baking it. We all agreed it was a very good difh.

On the 21ft we were vifited by many of the natives, who brought with them various prefents. Among the reft was a chief, named Oamo, whom we had not yet feen. He had a boy and a young woman with him. The former was carried on a man's back, which we confidered as a piece of ftate, for he was well able to walk. Oberea and fome of the Indians went from
the

the fort to meet them, being bareheaded, and uncovered as low as the waist; circumstances we
had noticed before, and judged them marks of respect,
which was usually shewn to persons of high rank.
When Oamo entered the tent, the young woman,
though seemingly very curious, could not be prevailed
upon to accompany him. The youth was introduced
by Dr. Solander, but as soon as the Indians within saw
him, they took care to have him very soon sent out.
Our curiosity being raised by these circumstances, we
made enquiry concerning the strangers, and were informed, that Oamo was the husband of Oberea, but
that by mutual consent they had been for a considerable time separated, and the boy and girl were their
children. The former was called Terridiri: he was
heir apparent to the sovereignty of the islands, and
when he had attained the proper age, was to marry
his sister. The present sovereign Outou, was a minor,
and the son of a prince, called Whappai. Whappai,
Oamo, and Tootahah, were all brothers; Whappai was
the eldest, and Oamo the second; wherefore Whappai
having no child but Outou, Terridiri was heir to the
sovereignty. To us it appeared singular, that a boy
should reign during the life of his father; but in the
island of Otaheite, a boy succeeds to his father's authority and title as soon as he is born; but a regent being
necessary, that office, though elective, generally falls
upon the father, who holds the reins of government till
the child is of age. The reason that the election had
fallen upon Tootahah was on account of his warlike
exploits among his brethren. Oamo was very inquisi-
tive, asking a number of questions concerning the English, by which he appeared to be a man of under-
standing and penetration. At this time, a woman
named Teetee, who came from the west of the island,
presented to the captain an elegant garment. The
ground was a bright yellow, it was bordered with red,
and there were several crosses in the middle of it,
which they had probably learned from the French.

On the 23d in the morning, one of our hands being

ing miffing, we enquired for him among the natives, and were told he was at Eparre, Tootahah's refidence in the wood, and one of the Indians offered to fetch him back, which he did that evening. On his return he informed us, that he had been taken from the fort, and carried to the top of the bay by three men, who forced him into a canoe, after having ftripped him, and conducted him to Eparre, where he received fome cloaths from Tootahah, who endeavoured to prevail on him to continue there. We had reafon to conclude this account true, for the natives were no fooner acquainted with his return, than they left the fort with precipitation.

On June the 26th, early in the morning, Capt. Cook fetting out in the pinnace with Mr. Banks, failed to the eaftward with a defign of circum-navigating the ifland. They went on fhore in the forenoon, in a diftrict in the government of Ahio, a young chief, who at the tents had frequently been their vifitant. And here alfo they faw feveral other natives whom they knew. Afterwards they proceeded to the harbour where M. Bougainville's veffel lay, when he came to Otaheite, and were fhewn the watering place, and the fpot where he pitched his tent.

Coming to a large bay, when the Englifh gentlemen mentioned their defign of going to the other fide, their Indian guide, whofe name was Titubaola, faid he would not accompany them, and alfo endeavoured to diffuade the captain and his people from going; obferving, " That country was inhabited by people who were not fubject to Tootahah, and who would deftroy them all." Notwithftanding, they refolved to put their defign in execution, loading their pieces with ball; and at laft Titubaola ventured to go with them. Having rowed till it was dark, they reached a narrow ifthmus which fevered the ifland in two parts, and thefe formed diftinct governments. However, as they had not yet got into the hoftile part of the country, it was thought proper to go on fhore to fpend the night where Ooratova, the lady who had paid her compliments in fo extraordinary a manner at the fort, provided them with a fupper,

per, and they proceeded for the other government in
the morning. They afterwards landed in the diftrict
of a chief called Maraitata, and his father was called
Pahairede. The former of thefe names fignifies the
burying place of men, and the other *the ftealer of boats*.
Thefe people gave the captain a very good reception;
fold them a hog for a hatchet, and furnifhed them with
provifions. A crowd of the natives came round the Englifh gentlemen, amongft whom however they met only
two with whom they were acquainted; but they faw
feveral European commodities, yet they perceived none
that came out of the Endeavour. Here they faw two
twelve pound fhot, one of which had the king's broad
arrow upon it, yet the natives faid they had them from
M. Bougainville. They afterwards advanced till they
reached that diftrict which was under the government
of Waheatua, who had a fon: it was not known in whofe
hands the fovereign power was depofited. There they
found a fpacious plain with a river which they were
obliged to pafs over in a canoe, though the Indians that
followed them fwam over without any difficulty. They
proceeded on their journey for a confiderable way along
the fhore, till at laft they were met by the chief, who
had with him an agreeable woman, of about twenty-two
years of age, who was called Toudidde. Her name was
not unknown to the Englifh, who had often heard of it;
and fhe was fuppofed to bear the fame rank here as
Oberea bore in the other part of the ifland. The parts
through which they now paffed, appeared to be better
cultivated than any of the reft, and the burial places
were more in number. They were neat, and ornamented with carvings; and in one a cock was feen, which
was painted with the various colours of the bird.
Though the country was apparently fertile, very little
bread-fruit was to be found here, a nut called Ahee,
furnifhing the principal fubfiftance of the inhabitants.

Being fatigued with their journey, they went on board
their boat, and landed in the evening on an ifland which
was called Otooareite, to feek for refrefhment. Mr.
Banks

Banks going into the woods for this purpofe, when it was dark could difcover only one houfe, wherein he found fome of the nuts before mentioned, and a little bread-fruit. There was a good harbour in the fouthern part of this ifland, and the furrounding country ap- peared to be extremely fruitful. Landing at about three miles diftance they found fome of the natives whom they well knew, yet it was not without difficulty that they obtained a few cocoa-nuts before they de- parted. When they came a little farther to the eaft- ward, they landed again, and here they were met by Mathiabo, the chief, with whom they were not at all acquainted. He fupplied them with bread-fruit and cocoa-nuts, and they purchafed a hog of him for a glafs bottle, which he chofe in preference to all the other articles prefented before him. A turkey-cock and a goofe were feen here, which were much admired by the natives, and were fuppofed to have been left there by Capt. Wallis's people. They obferved in a houfe near the fame place feveral human jaw-bones, which feem- ed frefh, and had not loft any of the teeth, and were faftened to a board, of a femicircular figure; but they could not get any information of the caufe of this ex- traordinary appearance.

When they left the place, the chief piloted them over the fhoals. In the evening they opened the bay on the north-weft fide of the ifland, which anfwered to that on the fouth-eaft in fuch a manner as to inter- fect it at the ifthmus. Several canoes came off here, and fome beautiful women giving tokens that they fhould be glad to fee them on fhore, they readily ac- cepted the invitation.—They met with a very friendly reception from the chief whofe name was Wiverou, who gave directions to fome of his people to affift them in dreffing their provifions, which were now very plen- tiful, and they fupped at Wiverou's houfe in company with Mathiabo. Part of the houfe was allotted for them to fleep in, and foon after fupper they retired to reft. Mathiabo having borrowed a cloak of Mr. Banks, under the notion of ufing it as a coverlet when he lay down, made off with it without being perceived either by that gentleman or his companions. However, news of the robbery being presently brought them by one of the natives, they set out in pursuit of Mathiabo, but had proceeded only a very little way before they were met by a person bringing back the cloak which this chief had given up rather through fear than from any principle of honesty. On their return they found the house entirely deserted ; and, about four in the morning, the centinel gave the alarm that the boat was missing. Captain Cook and Mr. Banks were greatly astonished at this account, and ran to the water-side ; but though it was a clear star-light morning, no boat was to be seen. Their situation was now extremely disagreeable. The party consisted of no more than four, having with them only one musquet and two pocket pistols, without a spare ball or a charge of powder. After having remained some time in a state of anxiety, arising from these circumstances, of which they feared the Indians might take advantage, the boat which had been driven away by the tide, returned; and Mr. Banks and his companions had no sooner breakfasted than they departed. This place is situated on the north side of Tiarrabou, the south east peninsula of the island, about five miles east from the isthmus, with a harbour equal to any in those parts. It was fertile and populous, and the inhabitants every where behaved with great civility.

The last district in Tiarrabou, in which they landed, was governed by a chief named Omoe. He was then building a house, and was very earnest to purchase a hatchet, but the gentlemen had not one left. He would not trade for nails, and they embarked, the chief, however, following them in his canoe with his wife. They were afterwards taken on board, but when they had sailed about a league, desired to be put on shore. Their request was complied with, when the captain met with some of Omoe's people, who brought with them a very large hog. The chief agreed to exchange the hog for an axe and a nail, and to bring the

beaſt to the fort. As the hog was a very fine one, Mr.
Banks accepted the offer. They faw at this place one
of the Indian Eatuas, a fort of image, made of wicker-
work, which refembled a man in figure; it was near
feven feet in height, and was covered with black and
white feathers; on the head were four protuberances,
called by the natives Tata etc, that is, little men.
Having taken their leave of Omoe, the gentlemen fet
out on their return. They went on fhore again, after
they had rowed a few miles, but faw nothing, except a
fepulchral building, which was ornamented in an extraordinary manner. The pavement, on which was
erected a pyramid, was very neat; at a fmall diſtance
there was a ſtone image, very uncouthly carved, but
which the natives feemed to hold in high eſtimation.
They paſſed through the harbour, which was the only
one fit for fhipping, on the fouth of Opoureonou, fituate
about five miles to the weſtward of the iſthmus, between two fmall iſlands, not far from the ſhore, and
within a mile of each other. They were now near the
diſtrict called Paparra, which was that where Oamo and
Oberea governed, and where the travellers intended to
fpend the night. But when Mr. Banks and his company landed, about an hour before it was dark, it appeared they were both fet out to pay them a viſit at the
fort. However, they flept at Oberea's houfe, which
was neat, though not large, and of which there was no
inhabitant but her father, who fhewed them much
civility.

They took this opportunity of walking out upon a
point upon which they had obferved at a diſtance fome
trees called Etoa, which ufually grow upon the burial
places of thefe iſlanders. They call thofe burying
grounds Morai. And here Mr. Banks faw a vaſt building, which he found to be the Morai of Oamo and
Oberea, which was the moſt confiderable piece of architecture in the iſland. It confiſted of an enormous
pile of ſtone work, raifed in the form of a pyramid,
with a flight of ſteps on each fide. It was near 270
feet long, about one third as wide, and between 40 and

50 feet

50 feet high. The foundation confifted of rock ftones;
the fteps were of coral, and the upper part was of
round pebbles, all of the fame fhape and fize. The
rock and coral-ftones were fquared with the utmoft
neatnefs and regularity, and the whole building appeared as compact and firm as if it had been erected by
the beft workmen in Europe. What rendered this laft
circumftance the more extraordinary was the confideration that when this pile was raifed, the Indians muft
have been totally deftitute of iron tools, either to fhape
their ftones or for any other neceffary purpofe, nor had
they mortar to cement them when made fit for ufe; fo
that a ftructure of fuch height and magnitude muft
have been a work of infinite labour and fatigue. In
the centre of the fummit was the reprefentation of a
bird carved in wood; clofe to this was the figure of a
fifh in ftone. The pyramid conftituted part of one fide
of a court or fquare, the fides of which were nearly
equal; and the whole was walled in, and paved with flat
ftones, notwithftanding which pavement, feveral plantains, and trees which the natives call Etoa, grew within the inclofure. At a fmall diftance to the weftward
of this edifice was another paved fquare that contained
feveral fmall ftages, called Ewattas by the natives;
which appeared to be altars, whereon they placed the
offerings to their gods. Mr. Banks afterwards obferved
whole hogs placed upon thefe ftages or altars.

On Friday the 30th, they arrived at Otahorou, where
they found their old acquaintance Tootahah, who received them with great civility, and provided them a
good fupper, and convenient lodging; and though they
had been fo fhamefully plundered the laft time they
flept with this chief, they fpent the night in the greateft
fecurity, none of their cloaths nor any other article being miffing the next morning. They returned to the
fort at Port Royal Harbour on the firft of July, having
difcovered the ifland, including both peninfulas, to be
about 100 miles in circumference.

After their return from this tour, they were very
much in want of bread-fruit, none of which they had
been

been able to provide themfelves with, as they had feen but little in the courfe of their journey; but their Indian friends coming round them, foon fupplied their want of provifions.

On the 3d, Mr. Banks made an excurfion, in order to trace the river up the valley to its fource, and to remark how far the country was inhabited along the banks of it. He took fome Indian guides with him, and after having feen houfes for about fix miles, they came to one which was faid to be the laft that could be met with. The mafter prefented them with cocoanuts and other fruits, and they proceeded on their walk, after a fhort ftay. They often paffed through vaults formed by rocky fragments in the courfe of their journey, in which, as they were told, benighted travellers fometimes took fhelter. Purfuing the courfe of the river about fix miles farther, they found it banked on both fides by rocks almoft 100 feet in height, and nearly perpendicular; a way, howeyer, might be traced up thefe precipices, along which their Indian guides would have conducted them, but they declined the offer, as there did not appear to be any thing at the fummit which could repay them for the toil and dangers of afcending it. Mr. Banks fought in vain for minerals among the rocks, which were naked almoft on all fides, but no mineral fubftances were found. The ftones every where exhibited figns of having been burnt, which was the cafe of all the ftones that were found while they ftaid at Otaheite, and both there and in the neighbouring iflands the traces of fire were evident in the clay upon the hills. On the 4th, a great quantity of the feeds of water-melons, oranges, limes, and other plants, brought from Rio de Janeiro were planted on each fide of the fort, by Mr. Banks, who alfo plentifully fupplied the Indians with them, and planted many of them in the woods. Some melons, the feeds of which had been fown on the firft arrival of the Englifh at the ifland, grew up and flourifhed before they left it.

By this time they began to think of making preparations

rations to depart; but Oamo, Oberea, and their fon
and daughter vifited them before they were ready to fail.
As to the young woman (whofe name was Toimata)
fhe was curious to fee the fort, but Oamo would not
permit her to enter. The fon of Waheatua, chief of
the fouth-eaft peninfula, was alfo here at the fame time;
and they were favoured with the company of the Indian
who had been fo dextrous as to fteal the quadrant, as
above related. The carpenters being ordered to take
down the gates and palifadoes of the fort, to be converted into fire-wood for the Endeavour, one of the natives ftole the ftaple and hook of the gate; he was purfued in vain, but the property was afterwards recovered, and returned to the owners by Tubourai Tamaide.

Before their departure, two circumftances happened
which gave Capt. Cook fome uneafinefs. The firft
was, that two foreign failors having been abroad, one
of them was robbed of his knife, which as he was endeavouring to recover, he was dangeroufly hurt with
a ftone by the natives, and his companion alfo received a flight wound in the head. The offenders
efcaped, and the captain was not anxious to have them
taken, as he did not want to have any difputes with
the Indians.

Between the 8th and 9th, two young marines one
night withdrew themfelves from the fort, and in the
morning were not to be met with. Notice having been
given the next day that the fhip would fail that or the
enfuing day; as they did not return, Capt. Cook began
to be apprehenfive that they defigned to remain on
fhore; but as he was apprifed in fuch a cafe no
effectual means could be taken to recover them without
running a rifque of deftroying the harmony fubfifting
between the Englifh and the natives, he refolved to wait
a day, in hopes of their returning of their own accord.
But as they were ftill miffing on the tenth in the morning, an enquiry was made after them, when the Indians
declared, that they did not propofe to return, having
taken refuge among the mountains, where it was im-

poffible

poffible for them to be difcovered; and added, that each of them had taken a wife. In confequence of this, it was intimated to feveral of the chiefs that were in the fort with the women, among whom were Tubourai Tamaide, Tomio, and Oberea, that they would not be fuffered to quit it till the deferters were produced. They did not fhew any figns of fear or difcontent, but affured the captain that the marines fhould be fent back. In the mean time Mr. Hicks was difpatched in the pinnace to bring Tootahah on board the fhip, and he executed his commiffion without giving any alarm. Night coming on, Capt. Cook thought it not prudent to let the people, whom he had detained as hoftages, remain at the fort; he therefore gave orders to remove them on board, which greatly alarmed them all, efpecially the females, who teftified the moft gloomy apprehenfions by floods of tears. Capt. Cook efcorted Oberea and others to the fhip; but Mr. Banks remained on fhore with fome Indians, whom he thought it of lefs importance to detain. In the evening one of the marines was brought back by fome of the natives, who reported, that the other and two of our men who went to recover them, would be detained while Tootahah was confined. Upon this Mr. Hicks was immediately fent off in the long boat, with a ftrong body of men to refcue the prifoners; at the fame time the captain told Tootahah, that it was incumbent on him to affift them with fome of his people, and to give orders in his name, that the men fhould be fet at liberty; for that he would be expected to anfwer for the event. Tootahah immediately complied, and this party releafed the men without any oppofition.

On the 11th, about feven in the morning, they returned, but without the arms that had been taken from them when they were made prifoners; thefe, however, being reftored foon after, the chiefs on board were allowed to return, and thofe who had been detained on fhore were alfo fet at liberty. On examining the deferters it appeared, that the Indians had told the truth,

they

they having chofen two girls, with whom they would have remained in the ifland. At this time the power of Oberea was not fo great as it was when the Dolphin firft difcovered the ifland. Tupia, whofe name has been often mentioned in this voyage, had been her prime minifter. He was alfo the chief prieft, confequently, well acquainted with the religion of the country. He had a knowledge of navigation, and was thoroughly acquainted with the number, fituation, and inhabitants of the adjacent iflands. This chief had often expreffed a defire to go with us when we continued our voyage.

On the 12th in the morning he came on board, with a boy about twelve years of age, his fervant, named Taiyota, and requefted the gentlemen on board, to let him go with him. As we thought he might be ufeful to us in many particulars, we unanimoufly agreed to comply with his requeft. Tupia then went on fhore for the laft time to bid farewell to his friends, to whom he gave feveral baubles as parting tokens of remembrance.

Mr. Banks, after dinner, being willing to obtain a drawing of the Morai, which Tootahah had in his poffeffion at Eparre, Capt. Cook accompanied him thither in the pinnace, together with Dr. Solander. They immediately upon landing repaired to Tootahah's houfe, where they were met by Oberea and feveral others. A general good underftanding prevailed. Tupia came back with them, and they promifed to vifit the gentlemen early the next day, as they were told the fhip would then fail.

On the 13th thefe friendly people came very early on board, and the fhip was furrounded with a vaft number of canoes, filled with Indians of the lower fort. Between eleven and twelve we weighed anchor; and notwithftanding all the little mifunderftandings between the Englifh and the natives, the latter, who poffeffed a great fund of good nature and much fenfibility, took their leave, weeping in an affectionate manner. As to Tupia he fupported himfelf through

this

London; Published as the Act directs by Alex.ʳ Hogg, at the Kings Arms, N.º 16, P.

A FLY FLAP *of the* Iſland OHITEROA, *a*

Handles *for the* ſame Inſtrument, *made in* Ot

this fcene with a becoming fortitude. Tears flowed from his eyes, it is true, but the effort that he made to conceal them did him an additional honour. He went with Mr. Banks to the maft head, and waving his hand took a laft farewell of his country. Thus we departed from Otaheite, after a ftay of juft three months.

C H A P. V.*

An hiftorical and defcriptive Account of Otaheite—Of the Ifland and its Productions—Of the Inhabitants—their Drefs—Dwellings—Manner of living—Diverfions—Manufactures—Arts—Sciences—Language—Difeafes—Religious Ceremonies—and Government.

PORT Royal bay, in the ifland of Otaheite, as fettled by captain Wallis, we found to be within half a degree of its real fituation ; and point Venus, the northern extremity of this ifland, and the eaftern part of the bay, lies in 149 deg. 30 min. longitude. A

---

* We here beg leave to remark to our very NUMEROUS SUB-SCRIBERS, that this *much admired Work* is not only *far preferable* to *any other publication* of the kind *whatever*, on account of its *Elegance,* (*heapnefs, Authenticity,* and its including a full account of *all Capt. Cook's Voyages Complete,* written in an admirably pleafing and elegant ftyle; but alfo becaufe every *fingle Sheet* of *our Letter-prefs* comprehends at leaft *double* the *quantity* of *Matter* given in *other Works* of the kind, which, by *fpinning out the fubject* to an *unneceffary length,* is offered to the public at more than *double* the *Price.* Publications of this kind, which contain *only* a *fingle Voyage* of the *celebrated* CAPT. COOK, we find are alfo *univerfally objected to* by the *public :* fo that by the publication of this *cheap* OCTAVO EDITION of ALL Capt. COOK's VOYAGES, &c. COMPLETE, the public at large will be *agreeably accommodated,* not only by being poffeffed *at an eafy Rate* of fuch a *vaft Quantity of Matter* included by our CLOSE *Method of Printing,* but likewife by acquiring at the fame Time all the SPLENDID COPPER-PLATES, *carefully, elegantly* and *accurately taken* from the ORIGINALS, in *Numbers,* price *only Sixpence* each.

No. 3.   M   reef

reef of coral rocks furround the ifland, forming feveral excellent bays, among which, and equal to the
beft of them, is Port Royal. This bay, called by the
natives Matavai, may eafily be difcovered by a remarkable high mountain in the center of the ifland, bearing
due fouth from Point Venus. To fail into it, either
keep the weft point of the reef that lies before Point
Venus, clofe on board, or give it a birth of near half
a mile, in order to avoid a fmall fhoal of coral rocks,
whereon there is but two fathom and a half of water. The moft proper ground for anchoring is on the
eaftern fide of the bay. The fhore is a fine fandy beach,
behind which runs a river of frefh water, very convenient for a fleet of fhips. The only wood for firing
upon the whole ifland is that of fruit trees, which muft
be purchafed of the natives, or it is impoffible to live
on friendly terms with them. The face of the country is very uneven. It rifes in ridges that run up into
the middle of the ifland, where they form mountains
which may be feen at the diftance of fixty miles. Between thefe ridges and the fea is a border of low land
of different breadths in different parts, but not exceeding any where a mile and a half. The foil being watered by a number of excellent rivulets, is extremely
fertile, and covered with various kinds of fruit trees,
which form almoft one continued wood. Even the
tops of the ridges are not without their produce in
fome parts. The only parts of the ifland that are inhabited, are the low lands, lying between the foot of
the ridges and the fea. The houfes do not form villages, but are ranged along the whole border, at about
fifty yards diftant from each other. Before them are
little groups of the plantain trees, which furnifh them
with cloth. According to Tupia's account, this ifland
could furnifh above fix thoufand fighting men. The
produce is bread-fruit, cocoa-nuts, bananas, fweet potatoes, yams, jumbu, a delicious fruit, fugar-cane, the
paper mulberry; feveral forts of figs, with many other
plants and trees, all which the earth produces fponta-
neoufly,

neoufly, or with little culture. But here are no European fruit, garden-ftuff, pulfe, nor grain of any kind. The tame animals are hogs, dogs, and poultry; the wild, ducks, pigeons, parroquets, and a few other birds. The only quadrupeds are rats, and not a ferpent is to be found. In the fea is a great variety of excellent fifh, which conftitutes their chief luxury, and to catch it their chief employment.

The people in general are of a larger make than the Europeans. The males are moftly tall, robuft, and finely fhaped ; the women of the higher clafs above the fize of our Englifh ladies, but thofe of inferior rank are below our ftandard, and fome of them very fhort. Their natural complexion is a fine clear olive, or what we call a brunette, their fkin delicately fmooth, and agreeably foft. Their faces in general are handfome, and their eyes full of fenfibility. Their teeth are remarkably white and regular, their hair for the moft part black, and their breath is entirely free from any difagreeable fmell. The men, unlike the original inhabitants of America, have long beards, which they wear in various fhapes. Circumcifion is generally practifed among them from a motive of cleanlinefs, and they have a term of reproach with which they upbraid thofe who do not adopt this cuftom. Both fexes always eradicate the hair from their arm-pits, and they reproached our gentlemen with want of cleanlinefs : their motions are eafy and graceful, and their behaviour, when unprovoked, affable and courteous. Contrary to the cuftom of moft other nations, the women of this country cut their hair fhort, whereas the men wear it long, fometimes hanging loofe upon their fhoulders, at other times tied in a knot on the crown of the head, in which they ftick the feathers of birds of various colours. A piece of cloth, of the manufacture of the country, is frequently tied round the head of both fexes in the manner of a turban, and the women plait very curioufly human hair into long ftrings, which being folded into branches, are tied on their

M 2 foreheads

foreheads by way of ornament. They have a cuftom practifed in many hot countries, of anointing their hair with cocoa-nut oil, the fmell of which is not very agreeable. Having, among their various inventions no forts of combs, they were infefted with vermin, which they quickly got rid of when furnifhed with thofe convenient inftruments.

They ftain their bodies by indenting or pricking the flefh with a fmall inftrument made of bone, cut into fhort teeth, which indentures they fill with a dark blue or blackifh mixture, prepared from the fmoke of an oily nut (burnt by them inftead of candles) and water. This operation, called by the natives Tattaowing, is exceedingly painful, and leaves an indelible mark on the fkin. It is ufually performed when they are about ten or twelve years of age, and on different parts of the body; but thofe which fuffer moft feverely are the breech and the loins, which are marked with arches, carried one above another a confiderable way up the back. Mr. Banks was prefent at an operation of tattaowing, performed upon the pofteriors of a girl about twelve years old. It was executed with an inftrument that had twenty teeth, and at each ftroke, which was repeated every moment, ferum mixed with blood iffued. She bore the pain with great refolution for feveral minutes; but at length it became fo intolerable, that fhe murmured and burft into moft violent lamentations; but her operator was inexorable, whilft fome females prefent both chid and beat her. Mr. Banks was a fpectator for near an hour, during which time one fide only was tattaowed, the other having undergone the ceremony fome time before, and the arches upon the loins, which are the moft painful, but which they moft value, were yet to be made.

They cloath themfelves in cloth and matting of various kinds: the firft they wear in fine, the latter in wet weather. Thefe are in different forms, no fhape being preferved in the pieces, nor are they fewed together. The women of a fuperior clafs wear three

of

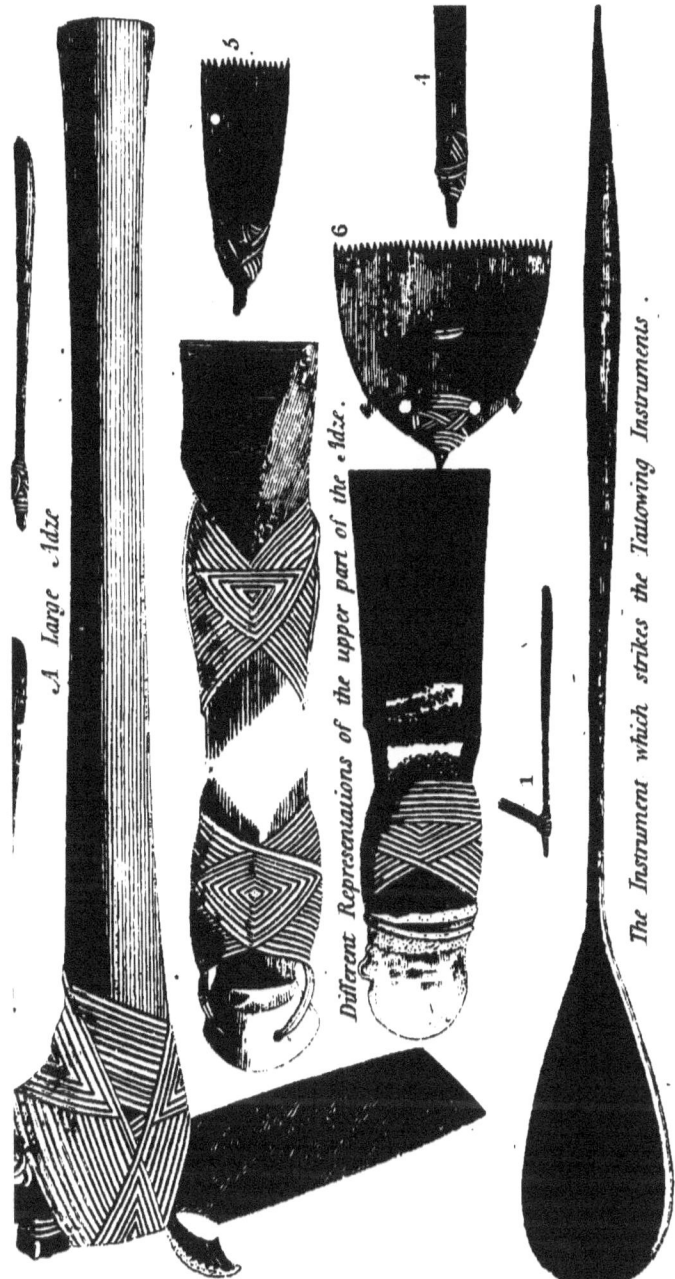

A large Adze.

Different Representations of the upper part of the Adze.

The Instrument which strikes the Tattowing Instruments.

5

4

6

1

or four pieces. One, which is of confiderable length, they wrap feveral times round their waift, and it falls down to the middle of the leg. Two or three other fhort pieces, with a hole cut in the middle of each, are placed on one another, and their heads coming through the holes, the long ends hang before and behind, both fides being open, by which means they have the free ufe of their arms.

The mens drefs is very fimilar, differing only in this inftance, that one part of the garment inftead of falling below the knees is brought between the legs. This drefs is worn by all ranks of people, the only diftinction being quantity in the fuperior clafs. At noon both fexes appear almoft naked, wearing only a piece of cloth that is tied round the waift. Their faces are fhaded from the fun with fmall bonnets, made of cocoa-nut leaves or matting, which are conftructed in a few minutes. The men fometime wear a fort of wig of human or dog's hair, or of cocoa-nut ftrings, woven on a fingle thread, faftened under the hair, and hanging down behind. Both men and women wore ear-rings on one fide, confifting of fhells, ftones, berries, or fmall pearls; but they foon gave the preference to the beads brought by the Endeavour's company. The boys and girls go quite naked; the firft till they are feven or eight years old; the latter till they are about five.

The natives of Otaheite feldom ufe their houfes but to fleep in, or to avoid the rain, as they eat in the open air, under the fhade of a tree. In thofe there are no divifions or apartments. Their cloaths ferve them for covering in the night. The mafter and his wife repofe in the middle; then the married people; next the un-married females; then the unmarried men; and in fair weather the fervants fleep in the open air. The houfes of the chiefs, however, differ in fome particulars. There are thofe that are very fmall, and fo conftructed as to be carried in canoes: all fides of them are inclofed with the leaves of the cocoa-nut; the air neverthelefs penetrates. In thefe the chief and his wife only fleep.

We

We likewife faw houfes that are general receptacles for the inhabitants of a diftrict, many of them being more than 200 feet in length, 40 in breath, and 70 or 80 feet high. They are conftructed at the common expence, and have an area on one fide, furrounded with low palifadoes; but like the others without walls.

Their cookery confifts chiefly in baking, the manner of doing which has been before noticed. When a chief kills a hog, which is but feldom, he divides it equally among his vaffals. Dogs and fowls are more common food. When the bread-fruit is not in feafon, cocoanuts, bananas, plantains, &c. are fubftituted in its ftead. They bake their bread-fruit in a manner which renders it fomewhat like a mealy potatoe. Of this three difhes are made, by beating them up with bananas, plantains, or four pafte, which is called by them Mahie.

Sour pafte is made by taking bread-fruit not thoroughly ripe, and laying it in heaps covered with leaves, by which means it ferments. The core is then taken out, and the fruit put into a hole lined with grafs: it is then again covered with leaves, upon which large ftones are placed; this produces a fecond fermentation; after which it grows four, without any other change for a long time. They take it from this hole as they have occafion for it, and make it into balls. It is then rolled up in plantain leaves and baked. As it will keep for fome weeks, they eat it both hot and cold. Such is the food of this people, their fauce to which is only falt water. As to their drink it is generally confined to water, or the milk of the cocoa-nut, though fome of them would drink fo freely of our Englifh liquors as to become quite intoxicated, fuch inftances, however, were occafioned more by ignorance than defign, as they were never known to practice a debauch of this kind a fecond time. We were told, it is true, that their chiefs fometimes became inebriated by drinking the juice of a plant called Ava, but of this we faw not a fingle inftance during the time we remained on the ifland.

The chief eats generally alone, unlefs when vifited

by

by a ftrañger, who is permitted fometimes to be his
mefs-mate. Net having known the ufe of a table, they
fit on the ground, and leaves of trees fpread before
them ferve as a table-cloth. Their attendants, who are
numerous, having placed a bafket by the chiefs, containing their provifions, and cocoa-nut fhells of frefh
and falt water, fet themfelves down around them.
They then begin their meals with the ceremony of
wafhing their mouths and hands; after which they eat
a handful of bread-fruit and fifh, dipt in falt water
alternately, till the whole is confumed, taking a fip of
falt water between almoft every morfel. The bread-
fruit and fifh is fucceeded by a fecond courfe, confifting
of either plantains or apples, which they never eat
without being pared. During this time a foft fluid
of pafte is prepared from the bread-fruit, which they
drink out of cocoa-nut fhells: this concludes the meal;
and their hands and mouths are again wafhed as at the
beginning. Thefe people eat an aftonifhing quantity
of food at a meal. Mr. Banks and others faw one of
them devour three fifh of the fize of a fmall carp,
four bread-fruits, as large as a common melon, thirteen
or fourteen plantains feven inches long, and above half
as big round; to all which was added a quart of the
pafte by way of drink, to digeft the whole.

The inhabitants of this ifland, though apparently
fond of the pleafures of fociety, have yet an averfion
to holding any intercourfe with each other at their
meals; and they are fo rigid in the obfervation of this
cuftom, that even brothers and fifters have their feparate
bafkets of provifions, and generally fit at the diftance
of fome yards when they eat, with their backs to
each other, and not exchanging a word during the
whole time of their repaft. The middle aged of fuperior rank go ufually to fleep after dinner; but,
which is fomewhat remarkable, older people are not
fo indolent.

Mufic, dancing, wreftling, and fhooting with the
bow, conftitute the greateft part of their diverfions.
Flutes

Flutes and drums are the only mufical inftruments among them. Their drums are formed of a circular piece of wood, hollow at one end only. Thefe are co-vered with the fkin of a fhark, and beaten with the hand inftead of a ftick. Their fongs are extempore, and frequently in rhime, but they confift only of two lines; thefe couplets are often fung by way of evening amufements, between fun-fet and bed-time; during which interval they burn candles made of an oily nut, fixing them one above another upon a fmall ftick that is run through the middle: fome of thefe candles will burn a long time, and afford a pretty good light. Among other amufements, they have a dance called Timorodee, which is generally performed by ten or a dozen young females, who put themfelves into the moft wanton attitudes, keeping time during the per-formance with the greateft nicety and exactnefs. Pregnant women are excluded from thefe dances.

One of the worft cuftoms of the people of Otaheite, is that which feveral of the principal people of the ifland have adopted of uniting in an affociation, wherein no woman confines herfelf to any particular man, by which means they obtain a perpetual fociety. Thefe focieties are called Arreoy. The members have meet-ings where the men amufe themfelves with wreftling, and the women dance the Timorodee in fuch a man-ner as is moft likely to excite the defires of the other fex, and which were frequently gratified in the affem-bly. A much worfe practice is the confequence of this. If any of the women prove with child, the in-fant is deftroyed, unlefs the mother's natural affection fhould prevail with her to preferve its life, which, however, is forfeited unlefs fhe can procure a man to adopt it. And where fhe fuccceds in this, fhe is expelled from the fociety, being called Whan-nownow, which fignifies a bearer of children, by way of reproach.

Perfonal cleanlinefs is much efteemed among thefe Indians. Both fexes are particular in wafhing three

times

times a day, viz. when they rife in the morning, at noon, and before they go to reft. They are alfo very cleanly in their cloaths, fo that no difagreeable effluvia are found to arife in the largeft communities.

Cloth is the chief manufacture of Otaheite, and of this there are three forts, all which are made out of the bark of different trees, namely, the mulberry, the bread-fruit, and a tree which bears fome refemblance to the Weft-Indian wild fig-tree. The firft of thefe produces the fineft cloth, which is feldom worn but by thofe of the firft rank. The next fort is made of the bread-fruit tree, and the laft of that which refembles the wild fig-tree. But this laft fort, though the coarfeft, is fcarcer than the other two, which are manufactured only in fmall quantities, as the fame manner is ufed in manufacturing all thefe cloths. The following defcription will fuffice for the reader's information.

The bark of the tree being ftripped off, is foaked in water for two or three days; they then take it out, and feparate the inner bark from the external coat, by fcraping it with a fhell, after which it is fpread out on plantain leaves, placing two or three layers over one another, care being taken to make it of an equal thicknefs in every part. In this ftate it continues till it is almoft dry, when it adheres fo firmly that it may be taken from the ground without breaking. After this procefs, it is laid on a fmooth board, and beaten with an inftrument made for that purpofe, of the compact heavy wood called Etoa. The inftrument is about fourteen inches long, and about feven in circumference; is of a quadrangular fhape, and each of the four fides is marked with longitudinal grooves or furrows, differing in this inftance, that there is a regular gradation in the width and depth of the grooves on each of the fides; the coarfer fide not containing more than ten of thefe furrows, while the fineft is furnifhed with above fifty. It is with that fide of the mallet where the grooves are deepeft and wideft that they begin to beat their cloth, and proceeding regularly, finifh

No. 3.   N   with

with that which has the greateſt number. By this beating, the cloth is extended in a manner ſimilar to the
gold that is formed into leaves by the hammer; and it
is alſo marked with ſmall channels reſembling thoſe
which are viſible on paper, but rather deeper; it is in
general beat very thin; when they want it thicker than
common, they take two or three pieces and paſte them
together with a kind of glue prepared from a root called
Pea. This cloth becomes exceedingly white by bleach-
ing, and is dyed of a red, yellow, brown, or black colour; the firſt is exceeding beautiful, and equal, if not
ſuperior to any in Europe. They make the red colour
from a mixture of the juices of two vegetables, neither
of which uſed ſeparately has this effect: matting of
various kinds is another conſiderable manufacture, in
which they excel, in many reſpects, the Europeans.
They make uſe of the coarſer ſort to ſleep on, and in
wet weather they wear the finer. They excel in the
baſket and wicker-work; both men and women employ themſelves at it, and can make a great number
of different patterns. They make ropes and lines of
all ſizes of the bark of the Poerou, and their nets for
fiſhing are made of theſe lines; the fibres of the cocoa-
nut they make thread of, ſuch as they uſe to faſten together the ſeveral parts of their canoes; the forms of
which are various, according to the uſe to which they
are applied. Their fiſhing lines are eſteemed the beſt
in the world, made of the bark of the Erowa, a kind of
nettle which grows on the mountains; they are ſtrong
enough to hold the heavieſt and moſt vigorous fiſh,
ſuch as bonettas and albicores; in ſhort, they are extremely ingenious in every expedient for taking all
kinds of fiſh.

The tools which theſe people make uſe of for building houſes, conſtructing canoes, hewing ſtones, and for
felling, cleaving, carving, and poliſhing timber, conſiſts of nothing more than an adze of ſtone, and a chiſ-
ſel of bone, moſt commonly that of a man's arm; and
for a file or poliſher, they make uſe of a raſp of coral
and

and coral fand. The blades of their adzes are extremely tough, but not very hard ; they make them of
various fizes, thofe for felling wood weigh fix or feven
pounds, and others which are ufed for carving, only a
few ounces: they are obliged every minute to fharpen
them on a ftone, which is always kept near them for
that purpofe. The moft difficult tafk they meet with in
the ufe of thefe tools, is the felling of a tree, which em-
ploys a great number of hands for feveral days together.
The tree which is in general ufe is called Aoie, the
ftem of which is ftraight and tall. Some of their
fmaller boats are made of the bread-fruit tree, which
is wrought without much difficulty, being of a light
fpongy nature. Inftead of planes they ufe their adzes
with great dexterity. Their canoes are all fhaped with
the hand, the Indians not being acquainted with the
method of warping a plank.

Of thefe they have two kinds, one they call Ivahahs,
the other Pahies; the former is ufed for fhort voyages
at fea, and the latter for long ones. Thefe boats do
not differ either in fhape or fize, but they are in no
degree proportionate, being from fixty to feventy feet
in length, and not more than the thirtieth part in
breadth. Some are employed in going from one ifland
to another, and others ufed for fifhing. There is alfo
the Ivahah, which ferves for war ; thefe are by far the
longeft, and the head and ftern are confiderably above
the body. Thefe Ivahahs are faftened together, fide
by fide, when they go to fea, at the diftance of a few feet,
by ftrong wooden poles, which are laid acrofs them
and joined to each fide. A ftage or platform is raifed
on the fore part, about ten or twelve feet long, upon
which ftand the fighting men, whofe miffile weapons
are flings and fpears. Beneath thefe ftages the rowers
fit, who fupply the place of thofe who are wounded.
The fifhing Ivahahs are from thirty or forty to ten feet
in length, and thofe for travelling have a fmall houfe
fixed on board, which is faftened upon the fore-part,
for the better accommodation of perfons of rank, who

N 2   occupy

occupy them both day and night. The Pahies differ
also in size, being from sixty to seventy feet long, they
are also very narrow, and are sometimes used for fighting, but chiefly for long voyages. In going from one
island to another, they are out sometimes a month, and
often at sea a fortnight or twenty days, and if they had
convenience to stow more provisions, they could stay
out much longer. These vessels are very useful in landing, and putting off from the shore in a surf, for by
their great length and high stern they landed dry,
when the Endeavour's boats could scarcely land
at all.

They are very curious in the construction of these
boats, the chief parts or pieces whereof are formed se-
parately without either saw, plane, chissel, or any other
iron tool, which renders their fabrication more surpris-
ing and worthy observation. These parts being prepared, the keel is fixed upon blocks, and the planks
are supported with props, till they are sewed or joined
together with strong plaited thongs, which are passed
several times through holes bored with a chissel or bone
such as they commonly make use of, and when finished,
they are sufficiently tight without caulking. They keep
these boats with great care in a kind of shed, built on
purpose to contain them.

Mr. Banks and Dr. Solander were at a loss to find
out their method of dividing time, they always made use
of the term Malama, which signifies the moon; whenever they spoke of time, either past or to come, they
reckon thirteen of these moons, beginning again when
they are expired. This proves that they have some idea
of the solar year; but these gentlemen could not discover how they computed their months, to make thirteen equal to the year, as they said these months consisted of twenty-nine days, one day in which the moon
was invisible being included. They, however, knew
the prevailing weather that was to be expected, as well
as the fruits that would be in season. As to the day,
they divide it into twelve equal parts, six of which be-

long

long to the day, and the other fix to the night. When they enumerate, they reckon from one to ten, making ufe of their fingers, and changing hands, till they come to the number which they intended to exprefs; and joining expreffive figns to their words, in the courfe of their converfation. But they are not fo expert in meafuring diftances, for when they attempt defcribing the fpace between one place and another, they are obliged to exprefs it by the time that would be taken in paffing it.

With regard to their language, it is foft, as it a-bounds with vowels, and eafy to be pronounced; but very few of their nouns or verbs being declineable, it muft confequently be rather imperfect. However, we found means to be mutually underftood without much difficulty. The following fpecimen will poffibly enable the reader to form fome notion of the language of thofe iflanders.

Aheine, *a woman*
Aihoo, *a garment*
Ainao, *take care*
Aree, *a chief*
Aouna, *to-day*
Aoy, *water*
Eahoo, *the nofe*
Eawow, *to fcold*
Eei, *to eat*
Eeyo, *look you*
Emoto, *to box*
Epanoo, *a drum*
Epecnei, *an echo*
Epehe, *a fong*
Erowroo, *the head*
Huaheine, *a wife*
Itopa, *to fall*
Kipoo a meemhee, *a cham-ber-pot*
Mahana, *a day*
Marroowhai, *dry*

Matau, *the eyes*
Matte roah, *to die*
Mayneenee, *to tickle*
Meyoooo, *the nails*
Midee, *a child*
Mutee, *a kifs*
Myty, *good*
Neeheeo, *good night*
Oboboa, *to morrow*
Oowhau, *the thighs*
Ore' dehaiya, *a large nail*
Ore' eeteea, *a fmall nail*
Otaowa, *yefterday*
Pahie, *a fhip*
Parawei, *a fhirt*
Poa, *a night*
Poe, *ear rings*
Tane, *a hufband*
Tatta te hommanne maitai, *a good-natured perfon*
Tea, *white*

Teine,

Teine, *a brother*

Tooaheine, *a sister*

Touanahoe, *you and I*

Toonoah, *a mole in the skin*

Tumatua, *a bonnet*

Wahoa, *fire*

Waow, *I.*

The natives of this country are feldom afflicted with any difeafes, except fometimes an accidental fit of the cholic; but they are fubject to the erifypelas, attended with cutaneous eruptions fomewhat refembling the leprofy; and if they have it to any confiderable degree, they are excluded from fociety and live alone, in a fmall houfe in fome unfrequented part of the ifland. The management of the fick belongs to the priefts, whofe method of cure confifts generally of prayers and ceremonies, which are repeated till they recover or die. If the former happens, it is attributed to their mode of proceeding; if the patient dies, then they urge that the difeafe was incurable.

The religion of thefe iflanders appears to be very myfterious; and as the language adapted to it, was different from that which was fpoken on other occafions, we were not able to gain much knowledge of it. Tupia, who gave us all the information that we got in regard to this particular, informed us, that his countrymen imagined every thing in the creation to proceed from the conjunction of two perfons. One of thefe two firft (being the fupreme deity) they called Taroataihetoomo, and the other Tapapa; and the year which they called Tettowmatatayo, they fuppofe to be the daughter of thefe two. They alfo imagine an inferior fort of deities, known by the name of Eatuas, two of whom, they fay, formerly inhabited the earth, and they fuppofe that the firft man and woman defcended from them. The Supreme Being they ftile " The caufer of earthquakes;" but more frequently addrefs their prayers to Tane, whom they conceive to be a fon of the firft progenitors of nature. They believe in the exiftence of the foul in a feparate ftate, and fuppofe that there are two fituations differing in the degrees of happinefs, which they confider as receptacles for different ranks, but not as places of rewards and punifhments.

Their

Their notion is, that the chiefs and principal people will have the preference to thofe of lower ranks. For as to their actions they cannot conceive them to influence their future ftate, as they believe the deity takes no cognizance of them. The office of the prieft is hereditary; there are feveral of them of all ranks: the chief is refpected next to their kings ; and they are in general fuperior to the natives, not only in point of divine knowledge, but alfo in that of aftronomy and navigation. They are not at all concerned with the ceremony of marriage, which is only a fimple agreement between the man and the woman, and when they chufe to feparate, the matter is accomplifhed with as little ceremony as was thought neceffary to bring them together. Thefe people do not appear to worfhip images of any kind ; but they enter their Morais with great awe and humility, their bodies being uncovered to the waift when they bring their offering to their altar.

As to their form of government, there is a fort of fubordination among them which refembles the early ftate of all the nations of Europe when under the feudal fyftem, which referved authority to a fmall number, putting the reft intirely in their power. The ranks of the people of this ifland were thefe, Earce Rahie, fignifying a king or fupreme governor ; Earee, anfwering to the title of baron ; Mannahoonies, to that of vaffal ; and Toutou, under which name was included the loweft orders of the people, fuch as are called villains according to the old law term. The Earce Rahie, of which there are two here, one belonging to each peninfula, had great refpect fhewn them by all ranks. The Earces are lords of one or more of the diftricts, into which thefe governments are divided ; and they feparate their territories into lots, which are given among the Mannahoonies, who refpectively cultivate the fhare that they hold under the baron. But they are only nominal cultivators ; this, as well as all other laborious work, being done by the Toutou, or lower clafs of the people. The fovereign, or Earce Rahie, and the baron, or Earce, are fucceeded in titles and honours by their

children,

children, as foon as they are born ; but their eftates remain in their poffeffion, and fubject to the management of their parents. Every diftrict under the command of an Earee furnifhes a proportionate number of fighting men, for the defence of the common caufe, in cafe of a general attack ; and they are all fubject to the command of the Earee Rahie. Their weapons confift of flings, in the ufe of which they are very dextrous, and of long clubs remarkably hard, with which they fight obftinately and cruelly, giving no quarter to their enemies in time of battle.

While we ftaid at Otaheite, there was a good underftanding between the Earees of the two peninfulas, though it feems that the Earee of Tearrebau called himfelf king of the whole ifland ; this was a mere nominal claim, and was confidered as fuch by the inhabitants. There is not any thing among them fubftituted for money, or a general medium by which every defirable object may be purchafed or procured ; neither can any permanent good be obtained by force or fraud. The general commerce with women fets afide almoft every excitement to commit adultery. In a word, in a government fo little polifhed, though diftributive juftice cannot be regularly adminiftered ; as, at the fame time, there can be but few crimes whereon to exercife it, the want of this juftice is not fo feverely felt as in more civilized focieties.

Soon after our arrival at this ifland, we were apprifed of the natives having the French difeafe among them. The iflanders called it by a name expreffive of its effects, obferving that the hair and nails of thofe who were firft infected by it, fell off, and the flefh rotted from the bones, while their countrymen, and even neareft relations, who were unaffected, were fo much terrified at its fymptoms, that the unhappy fufferer was often forfaken by them, and left to perifh in the moft horrible conditions.

Thus have we given an accurate, full, and complete defcription of the ifland in its prefent ftate ; we fhall only add a few remarks, which we apprehend may be

of

of ufe to fuch gentlemen in the navy, who may hereafter have it in their orders to touch at the fame. As
this ifland can be ufeful only by fupplying fhips with
refrefhments in their paffage through thefe feas, it
might be made to anfwer fully this important end; European cattle, plants, garden ftuff, and the moft
ufeful vegetables, would doubtlefs flourifh in fo rich
a foil. The climate is remarkably fine, the heat is
not troublefome, nor do the winds blow conftantly from
the eaft. We had frequently a frefh gale from the
S. W. fometimes, though very feldom, from the N. W.
We learnt from Tupia, that fouth wefterly winds prevail in October, November and December, and we have
no doubt but this is true. At the time the winds are
variable, they are always accompanied by a fwell from
the S. W. or W. S. W. The fame fwell happens on a
calm, and when the atmofphere is loaded with clouds,
which fhews that the winds are variable, or wefterly
out at fea, for with a trade wind the weather is clear.
In thefe parts the trade wind does not extend farther to
the fouth than twenty degrees, beyond which we generally found a gale from the weftward. The tides here
are perhaps as inconfiderable as in any part of the world.
A fouth or fouth by weft moon makes high water in the
harbour of Matavai, and its perpendicular height feldom exceeds ten or twelve inches.

C H A P. VI.

*The Endeavour continues her Voyage—Vifits the Iflands in
the Neighbourhood of Otaheite—An Account of feveral
Incidents, and of various Particulars relative to the
Inhabitants—The Paffage of the Endeavour from Ote-
roah to New Zealand—Events on going afhore, and
Incidents while the Ship was in Poverty Bay—This
and the adjacent Country defcribed—Excurfions to Cape
Turnagain, and return to Tolaga—The Inhabitants defcribed, and a Narrative of what happened while we*

No. 4.   O   *were*

*were on that Part of the Coaſt—The Range from Tolaga
to Mercury Bay—Incidents that happend on board the
Endeavour and aſhore—A Deſcription of the Country
and its fortified Villages—She ſails from Mercury Bay
to the Bay of Iſlands—A Deſcription of the Indians on
the Banks of the River Thames—And of the Timber
that grows there—Interviews and Skirmiſhes with the
Natives on an Iſland, and on different Parts of the Coaſt
—Range from the Bay of Iſlands round North Cape.*

ON the 13th of July, 1769, after leaving the iſland of
Otaheite, we continued our courſe, with clear
weather and a gentle breeze; and were informed by
Tupia, that four iſlands which he called Huaheine,
Ulietea, Otaha, and Bolabola, were at the diſtance of
about one or two days ſail; and that hogs, fowls, and
other refreſhments, very ſcarce on board, were to be
got there in great abundance. He alſo mentioned an
iſland to the northward, which he called Tethuroa.
It is ſituated north half weſt eight leagues diſtant from
the northern extremity of Otaheite. It was a ſmall low
iſland, but as Tupia ſaid, without any ſettled inhabitants. On the 15th we made but little way, on account of the calms which ſucceeded the light breezes.
Tupia often prayed to his god Tane for a wind, and
boaſted of his ſucceſs, which indeed he took care to
inſure, by never applying to Tane, till he ſaw a breeze
ſo near, that he knew it muſt reach the ſhip before his
prayer was concluded.

On the 16th we ſounded near the north-weſt part of
the iſland of Huaheine, but found no bottom at 70 fathoms. Several canoes put off; but the Indians ſeemed fearful of coming near the bark till the ſight of Tupia
removed their apprehenſions. They then came along
ſide, and the king of the iſland, with his queen, came on
board. They ſeemed ſurprized at whatever was ſhewn
them, but made no enquiries after any thing but what
was offered to their notice. After ſome time they
became more familiar; and the king, whoſe name
was

was Oree, as a token of amity, propofed exchanging
names with Capt. Cook, which was readily accepted.
We found the people here nearly fimilar to thofe of
Otaheite in almoft every particular ; but if Tupia might
be credited, they are not like them addicted to thieving.
Having anchored in a fmall but convenient harbour,
on the weft fide of the ifland, (called by the natives
Owparre) we went on fhore with Mr. Banks, and fome
other gentlemen, accompanied by the king and Tupia.
The moment we landed Tupia uncovered himfelf as
low as the waift, and defired Mr. Monkhoufe to follow
his example.   Being feated he now began a fpeech, or
prayer, which lafted about twenty minutes ; the king,
who ftood oppofite to him, anfwering in what feemed
fet replies.   During this harangue, Tupia delivered,
at different times, a handkerchief, a black filk neckcloth,
fome plantains, and beads, as prefents to their Eatua,
or deity ; and in return for our Eatua, we received a
hog, fome young plantains, and two bunches of feathers, all which were carried on board.   Thefe ceremonies were confidered as a kind of ratification of a
treaty between us and the king of Huaheine.
   On the 17th we went again on fhore, and made an
excurfion into the country, the productions of which
greatly refembled thofe of Otaheite ; the rocks and
clay feemed, indeed, more burnt : the boat houfes were
curious and remarkable large.   The level part of the
country affords the moft beautiful landfcapes that the
imagination can poffibly form an idea of.   The foil is
exceedingly fertile, and the fhore is lined with fruit trees
of different kinds, particularly the cocoa-nut ; however, in fome places there were falt fwamps and la-
goons which produced neither trees nor plants.
   On the 18th we went again on fhore, and Tupia being engaged with his friends, we took with us Taiyota,
his boy.   Mr. Banks propofed taking a more perfect
view of a kind of cheft, or ark, which he had before obferved.   The lid of this ark was neatly fewed on, and
thatched in a peculiar manner with palm-nut leaves.
      3   It

It was placed on two poles, and supported by small carved arches of wood. These poles served to remove it from one place to another, in the manner of our sedan-chairs. We remarked, that this chest was of a form resembling the ark of the Lord among the Jews; but it is still more remarkable, that enquiring of Tupia's servant what it was called, he told us Ewharre-no-Eatua, the House of God; though he could give no account of its meaning or use. Our trade with the natives went on slowly; we got however eleven pigs, and were not without hopes of obtaining more the next morning.

On the 19th we offered them some hatchets, for which we procured three very large hogs. As we intended to fail in the afternoon, king Oree, and others of the natives came on board to take their leave. Captain Cook presented to Oree a small pewter plate, stamped with this inscription, " His Britannic Majesty's ship Endeavour, Captain Cook, commander, 16 July, 1769." We gave him also some medals, or counters, resembling our English coin, and other trifles, which he promised to keep in order to remember us. The island of Huaheine lies in 16 deg. 43 min. south latitude, and 150 deg. 52 min. west longitude; about 30 leagues distant from Otaheite, and is twenty miles in circumference. Its productions are a month forwarder than those of the last mentioned island, as we found by several of the fruits, &c. Mr. Banks collected only a few new plants, but found a species of the scorpion which he had not before seen. The inhabitants are very lazy, but are stouter and larger made than those of Otaheite; the women very fair, and we thought them handsome. Both sexes seemed to be less timid, and less curious. They made no enquiries when on board the ship, and, when we fired a gun, though apparently frightened, yet they did not fall down, as our friends at Otaheite constantly did when we came among them; but it is to be considered, that the former had never experienced its power of dispensing death. We

now

now made fale for the ifland of Ulietea, diftant feven
or eight leagues from Huaheine.

On the 20th, by the direction of Tupia, we anchored in a bay, formed by a reef, on the north fide of
the ifland. Two canoes foon came off from the fhore,
and the natives brought with them two fmall hogs,
which they exchanged for fome nails and beads. The
captain, Mr. Banks, and other gentlemen now went on
fhore, accompanied by Tupia, who introduced them
with the fame kind of ceremonies that had taken place
on their landing at Huaheine; after which Captain
Cook took poffeffion of this and the three neighbouring iflands, Huaheine, Otaha, and Bolabola, in the
name of his Britannic majefty. We then walked to a
large Morai, called by the natives Tabodeboatea,
which we found different from the fepulchral monuments of Otaheite, being compofed of four walls, a-
bout eight or nine feet high, and built of large coral
ftones, furrounding a court of about 30 feet fquare.
At a fmall diftance we found an altar, or ewhatta,
whereupon lay the laft oblation, or facrifice, a hog
about eighty pounds weight, which had been offered
whole, and vary nicely roafted. We alfo faw four or
five Ewharre-no-eatua, or houfes of God, to which carriage poles were fitted. From hence we proceeded to a
long houfe, where among rolls of cloth, we faw the
model of a canoe, about three feet long, to which were
faftened eight human jaw-bones : we concluded they
were trophies of war : but Tupia affirmed they were
the jaw-bones of the natives of this ifland. Night now
advanced with quick paces, but Mr. Banks and the
Doctor continued their walk along the fhore, and faw
another Ewharre-no-eatua, alfo a tree of the fig
kind, the trunk of which, (the nature whereof has
been already defcribed) was forty-two paces in circumference.

On the 21ft the mafter was fent to infpect the fouthern part of the ifland, and a lieutenant was difpatched
in the yawl to found the harbour where the Endeavour
lay. While the Captain went in the pinnace to take a
view

view of that part of the ifland which lay to the northward.   Mr. Banks and the gentlemen were again on
fhore, trading with the natives, and fearching after the
productions and curiofities of the country.   They difcovered, however, not one particular worthy of notice.

The hazy weather and brifk gales prevented us from
getting under fail, till the 24th, when we put to fea,
and fteered northward within the reef, towards an opening, at the diftance of about five or fix leagues, in effecting which we were in great danger of ftriking on a
rock, the man who founded, crying out on a fudden
"Two fathoms," which could not but alarm us greatly;
but either the mafter was miftaken, or the fhip went
along the edge of a coral rock, many of which in the
neighbourhood of thefe iflands as are fteep as a wall.

The bay where the Endeavour lay at anchor, called
Oopoa, is capacious enough to hold a great number of
fhipping, and fecured from the fea by a reef of rocks.
Its fituation is off the cafternmoft part of the ifland.
The provifions confift of cocoa-nuts, yams, plantains,
and a few hogs and fowls.   The country round about
the place where we landed was not fo plentiful as at
Otaheite or Huaheine.   The fouthermoft opening in
the reef, or channel into the harbour, by which we
entered, is little more than a cable's length wide; it
lies off the eaftermoft point of the ifland, and may be
found by a fmall woody ifland, which lies to the fouth-
eaft of it, called Oatara; north-weft from which are
two other iflots called Opururu and Tamou.   Between
thefe is the channel through which we went out of the
harbour, and it is a full quarter of a mile wide.

On the 25th we were within a league or two of the
ifland of Otoha; but could not get near enough to
land, the wind having proved contrary.   In the morning, Mr. Banks and Dr. Solander went in the long-boat
with the mafter, in order to found a harbour on the
eaft fide of the ifland, which they found fafe and convenient.   We then went on fhore and purchafed a large
quantity of plantains, and fome hogs and fowls.   The
produce

produce of this ifland was much the fame with that of Ulietea, but it feemed to be more barren. We received the fame compliment from the Indians here, as was ufual for them to pay their own kings, which was by uncovering their fhoulders, and wrapping their cloaths round their bodies. We made fail to the northward, and at eight o'clock on the 29th, we were under the high peaks of Bolabola. We found the ifland inacceffible in this part, and likewife that it was impoffible to weather the fouth end of it till late at night. On the 30th, we difcovered an ifland which Tupia called Maurua, but faid it was fmall, furrounded by a reef, and without any commodious harbour, but inhabited, and yielded nearly the fame produce as the adjacent iflands. In the middle is a high round hill which may be feen at eleven or twelve leagues diftance. In the afternoon, finding ourfelves to windward of fome harbour that lay on the we ftfide of Ulietea, we intended to put into one of them, in order to ftop a leak which had fprung in the powder-room, and to take in fome additional ballaft. The wind being right againft us, we plied on and off till the afternoon of the firft of Auguft, when we came to an anchor in the entrance of the channel, which led into one of the harbours.

On Wednefday the 2d, in the morning, when the tide turned, we came into a proper place for mooring in 28 fathom. Many of the natives came off, and brought hogs, fowls, and plantains, which were purchafed upon very moderate terms. Mr. Banks and Dr. Solander went on fhore, and fpent the day very agreeably; the natives fhewing them great refpect: being conducted to the houfes of the chief people, they found thofe who had ran haftily before them, ftanding on each fide of a long mat fpread upon the ground, and the family fitting at the farther end of it. In one houfe they obferved fome very young girls dreffed in the neateft manner, who kept their places waiting for the ftrangers to accoft them; thefe girls were the moft beautiful the gentlemen had ever feen. One of them, about feven or eight years old, was dreffed in a red gown, and her

head

head was decorated with a great quantity of plaited hair;. this ornament is called Tamou, and is held in great eftimation among them.   She was fitting at the upper end of one of their long mats, on which none of the people prefent prefumed to fet a foot; and her head was reclined on the arm of a decent looking woman, who appeared to be her nurfe; when Mr. Banks and Dr. Solander approached her, fhe ftretched out her hand to receive fome beads, which they prefented to her, with an air of fuch dignity and gracefulnefs, as would have done honour to the firft princefs in Europe.

In one of the houfes we were entertained with a dance, different from any we had feen before. The performer put upon his head a large piece of wicker-work, about four feet long, of a cylindrical form, covered with feathers, and edged round with fhark's teeth. With this head-drefs, which is called a Whou, he began to dance with a flow motion; frequently moving his head, fo as to defcribe a circle with the top of his wicker cap, and fometimes throwing it fo near the faces of the by-ftanders as to make them jump back: this they confidered as an excellent piece of humour, and it always produced a hearty laugh, when practifed upon any of the Englifh gentlemen..

On Thurfday the 3d, as Mr. Banks and the doctor were going along the fhore to the noi thward, with a defign to purchafe ftock, they met with a company of dancers, who retarded the progrefs of their excurfion. The company was compofed of fix men and two women dancers, with three drums. They were informed that thefe dancers were fome of the principal people of the ifland, and though they were an itinerant troop, they did not, like the ftrolling parties of Otaheite, receive any gratuity from the by-ftanders. The women wore a confiderable quantity of tamou, or plaited hair, ornamented with flowers of the cape-jeffamine, which were ftuck in with tafte, and made an elegant head-drefs. The womens necks, breafts and arms, were naked; the other parts of their bodies were covered with

with black cloth, which was faftened clofe round them,
and by the fide of each breaft, next the arms, was a
fmall plume of black feathers, worn like a nofegay.
Thus apparelled, they advanced fideways, keeping time
with great exactnefs to the drums, which beat quick
and loud; foon after they began to fhake themfelves
in a very whimfical manner, and put their bodies into
a variety of ftrange poftures, fometimes fitting down,
and at others falling with their faces to the ground, and
refting on their knees and elbows, moving their fingers
at the fame time with a quicknefs fcarcely to be credited. The chief dexterity, however, of the dancers,
as well as the amufement of the fpectators, confifted in
the lafcivioufnefs of their attitudes and geftures. Between the dances of the women a kind of dramatic interlude was performed by the men, confifting of dia-
logue as well as dancing; but for want of a fufficient
knowledge of their language, we could not learn the
fubject of this interlude.

Mr. Banks, Dr. Solander and fome other gentlemen,
were prefent at a more regular dramatic entertainment
the next day. The performers, who were all men,
were divided into two parties, one dreffed in brown,
and the other in white, by way of diftinction. Tupia
being prefent, informed them that the party in brown,
acted the parts of a mafter and his fervants, and the
party in white, a gang of thieves; the mafter having
produced a bafket of meat, which he gave in charge to
his fervants, which party exhibited a variety of expedients, in endeavouring to fteal this bafket, and the
brown as many in preventing the accomplifhment of
their defign. After fome time had been fpent in this
manner, thofe to whom the bafket was intrufted, laying
themfelves down on the ground round it, pretended to
fall afleep; the other party availing themfelves of this
opportunity, ftole gently upon them, and carried off
their booty; the fervants awaking foon after, difcovered their lofs, but they made no fearch after the bafket,
and began to dance with as much alacrity as before.

On Saturday the 5th, fome hogs and fowls, and fe-

veral large pieces of cloth, many of them being fifty
or fixty yards in length, together with a quantity of
plantains and cocoa-nuts, were fent to Captain Cook,
as a prefent from the Earce Rahie of the ifland of Bolabola, accompanied with a meffage, importing that
he was then on the ifland, and intended waiting on the
captain.

On the 6th, the king of Bolabola did not vifit us
agreeable to his promife; his abfence, however, was
not in the leaft regretted, as he fent three young women
to demand fomething in return for his prefent. After
dinner, we fet out to pay the king a vifit on fhore, fince
he did not think proper to come on board. As this
man was the Earee Rahie of the Bolabola man, who had
conquered this, and were the dread of all the neighbouring iflands, we were greatly difappointed inftead
of finding a vigorous enterprifing young chief, to fee a
poor feeble old dotard, half blind, and finking under
the weight of age and infirmities. He received us without either that ftate or ceremony which we had hitherto met with among the other chiefs.

On Wednefday the 9th, having ftopped a leak, and
taken on board a frefh ftock of provifions, we failed
out of the harbour. Though we were feveral leagues
diftant from the ifland of Bolabola, Tupia earneftly
intreated Captain Cook, that a fhot might be fired towards it; which, to gratify him, the captain complied
with. This was fuppofed to have been intended by
Tupia as a mark of his refentment againft the inhabitants of that place, as they had formerly taken from
him large poffeffions which he held in the ifland of
Ulietea, of which ifland Tupia was a native, and a fubordinate chief, but was driven out by thefe warriors.
We had great plenty of provifions, as well of hogs, as
of vegetables, during the time we continued in the
neighbourhood of thefe iflands, fo that we were not
obliged to ufe any confiderable quantity of the fhip's
provifions, and we had flattered ourfelves, that the
fowls and hogs would have fupplied us with frefh provifions during the courfe of our voyage to the fouth-

ward, but in this we were unhappily difappointed, for as the hogs could not be brought to eat any European grain, or any provender whatever, that the fhip afforded, we were reduced to the difagreeable neceffity of killing them immediately on leaving thofe iflands; and the fowls all died of a difeafe in their heads, with which they were feized foon after they had been carried on board. Being detained longer at Ulictea in repairing the fhip than we expected, we did not go on fhore at Bolabola; but after giving the general name of the Society Iflands, to the iflands of Huaheine, Ulietea, Bolabola, Otaha, and Mauruia, which lie between the latitude of 16 deg. 10 min. and 18 deg. 55 min. fouth, we purfued our courfe, ftanding fouthwardly for an ifland, to which we were directed by Tupia, at above 100 leagues diftant. This we difcovered on Sunday the 13th, and were informed by him, that it was called Obiterea.

On the 14th we ftood in for land, and faw feveral of the inhabitants coming along the fhore. One of the lieutenants was difpatched in the pinnace to found for anchorage, and to obtain what intelligence could be got from the natives concerning any land, that might be farther to the fouth. Mr. Banks, Dr. Solander, and Tupia, went with the lieutenant in the boat. When they approached the fhore, they obferved, that the Indians were armed with long lances. A number of them were foon drawn together on the beach, and two jumped into the water, endeavouring to gain the boat; but fhe foon left them and fome others that had made the fame attempt, far enough behind her. Having doubled the point where they intended to land, they opened a large bay, and faw another party of the natives ftanding at the end of it, armed like thofe whom they had feen before. Preparations were then made for landing, on which a canoe full of Indians came off towards them. Obferving this, Tupia received orders to acquaint them that the Englifh did not intend to offer them violence, but meant to traffic with them for nails, which were produced. Thus informed they

came

came along-fide the boat, and took fome nails that
were given them, being feemingly well pleafed with the
prefent. Yet a few minutes after, feveral of thefe people boarded the boat, defigning to drag her on fhore ;
but fome mufquets being difcharged over their heads
they leaped into the fea, and having reached the canoe,
put back with all poffible expedition, joining their
countrymen who ftood ready to receive them.   The
boat immediately purfued the fugitives, but the crew
finding the furf extremely violent, did not venture to
land there, but coafted along fhore to try if they could
not find a more convenient place. Soon after the canoe
got on fhore, a man oppofite the boat flourifhed his
weapon, calling out at the fame time with a fhrill
voice, which was a mark of defiance, as Tupia explained it to the Englifh.—Not being able to find a
proper landing-place, they returned, with an intention
to attempt it where the canoe went on fhore; whereupon another warrior repeated the defiance : his appearance was more formidable than that of the other;
he had a high cap on made of the tail feathers of a
bird, and his body was painted with various colours.
When he thought fit to retire, a grave man came forward, who afked Tupia feveral queftions, relating to
the place from whence the veffel came, as, Who were
the perfons on board? Whither they were bound? &c.
After this it was propofed that the people in the boat
fhould go on fhore and trade with them if they would
lay afide their weapons; but the latter would not agree
to this, unlefs the Englifh would do the like. As this
propofal was by no means an equal one, when it was
confidered that the hazard muft for many reafons be
greater to the boat's crew than the Indians, and as per-
fidy was dreaded, it was not complied with. Befides,
fince neither the bay which the Endeavour entered, nor
any other part of the ifland furnifhed good harbour or
anchorage, it was refolved not to attempt landing any
more, but to fail from hence to the fouthward.

The natives are very tall, well proportioned, and
have long hair, which, like the inhabitants of the other

iflands,

iflands, they tie in a bunch on the top of their heads, they are likewife tataowed in different parts of their bodies, but not on their pofteriors. The ifle does not fhoot up into high peaks like the others that they vifited, but is more level and uniform, and divided into fmall hillocks, fome of which are covered with groves of trees. However, none of thofe bearing the bread fruit were feen, and not many cocoa-trees, but a great number of thofe called Etoa, were feen on the fea coaft of this ifland. Both the nature of their cloth, and their manner of wearing it, differed in many refpects from what had been obferved in the progrefs of our voyage. All the garments that thefe people wore, were dyed yellow, and painted with a variety of colours on the outfide. One piece formed their whole habit, having a hole in it through which they put their heads. This reached as far as their knees, and was tied clofe round their bodies with a kind of yellowifh fafh. Some of them alfo wore caps of the fame kind, as we have already mentioned, and others bound round their heads a piece of cloth which refembled a turban.

On the 15th we failed from this ifland with a fine breeze; but on the 16th it was hazy, and we bore away for what refembled feveral high peaks of land. The weather clearing up, we were convinced of our miftake, and refumed our courfe accordingly. We faw a comet on the 30th, about four o'clock, which was then about 60 deg. above the horizon. Land was difcovered at weft by north on Thurfday the 7th of October, and in the morning of the 8th, we came to an anchor oppofite the mouth of a fmall river, not above half a league from the coaft.

Captain Cook, Mr. Banks, Dr. Solander, and fome other gentlemen, having left the pinnace at the mouth of the river, proceeded a little farther up, when we landed, leaving the yawl to the care of fome of our boys, and went up to a few fmall houfes in the neighbourhood. Some of the natives that had concealed themfelves in the neighbourhood took advantage of our abfence from the boat, and rufhed out, advancing and

brand-

brandifhing their long wooden lances. On this our boys dropped down the ftream. The cockfwain of the pinnace then fired a mufquetoon over their heads, but it did not prevent them from following the boat, in confequence of which he levelled his piece, and fhot one of them dead on the fpot. Struck with aftonifh-ment at the death of their companion, the others re-mained motionlefs for fome time, but as foon as they recovered their fright, retreated to the woods with the utmoft precipitation. The report of the gun brought the advanced party back to the boats, and both the pinnace and yawl returned immediately to the fhip.

On the 9th, a great number of the natives were feen near the place where the gentlemen in the yawl had landed the preceding evening, and the greateft part of them appeared to be unarmed. The long-boat, pin-nace, and yawl, being manned with marines and failors, Capt. Cook, with the reft of the gentlemen, and Tupia, went on fhore, and landed on the oppofite fide of the river, over againft a fpot where feveral Indians were fit-ting on the ground. Thefe immediately ftarted up, and began to handle their weapons, each producing either a long pike, or a kind of truncheon made of ftone with a ftring through the handle of it, which they twifted round their wrifts. Tupia was directed to fpeak to them in his language; and we were agreeably furprized to find that he was well underftood, the natives fpeak-ing in his language, though in a different dialect. Their intentions at firft appeared to be very hoftile, brandifhing their weapons in the ufual threatening man-ner; upon which a mufquet was fired at fome diftance from them : the ball happened to fall into the water, at which they appeared rather terrified, and defifted from their menaces. Having now drawn up the marines, we advanced nearer to the fide of the river. Tupia, again fpeaking, informed them of our defire to traffic with them for provifions: to this they confented, pro-vided we would go over to them to the other fide of the river. The propofal was agreed to, upon condition that the natives would quit their weapons; but the

moft

moft folemn affurances of friendfhip could not prevail with them to make fuch a conceffion. Not thinking it prudent therefore to crofs the river, we, in our turn, intreated the Indians to come over to us, and after fome time prevailed on one of them fo to do. He was prefently followed by feveral others. They did not appear to value the beads and iron which we offered in the way of barter, but propofed to exchange their weapons for ours; which being objected to, they endeavoured feveral times to fnatch our arms from us, but being on our guard, from the information given us by Tupia that they were ftill our enemies, their attempts were repeatedly fruftrated; and Tupia, by our direction gave them to underftand, that any further offers of violence would be punifhed with inftant death. One of them, neverthelefs, had the audacity to fnatch Mr. Green's dagger when his back was turned to them, and retiring a few paces, flourifhed it over his head; but his temerity coft him his life; for Mr. Monkhoufe fired a mufquet loaded with ball, and he inftantly dropped. Soon after, though not before we had difcharged our pieces loaded with fmall fhot only, they retreated flowly up the country, and we returned to our boats.

The behaviour of the Indians, added to our want of frefh water, induced Capt. Cook to continue his voyage round the bay, with a hope of getting fome of the natives aboard, that by civil ufage he might convey through them a favourable idea of us to their countrymen, and thereby fettle a good correfpondence with them. An event occurred which, though attended with difagreeable circumftances, promifed to facilitate this defign. Two canoes appeared, making towards land, and Capt. Cook propofed intercepting them with our boats. One of them got clear off, but the Indians in the other, finding it impoffible to efcape, began to attack our people in the boats with their paddles. This compelled the Endeavour's people to fire upon them, when four of the Indians were killed, and the other three, who were young men, jumped into the water, and

and endeavoured to fwim to fhore; they were, however, taken up, and conveyed on board. At firft they di-covered all the figns of fear and terror, thinking they fhould be killed; but Tupia, by repeated affurances of friendfhip, removed their apprehenfions, and they afterwards eat heartily of the fhip's provifions. Hav-ing retired to reft in the evening, they flept very quietly for fome hours, but about midnight, their fears returning, they appeared in great agitation, frequently making loud and difmal groans. Again the kind ca-reffes and friendly promifes of Tupia operated fo ef-fectually, that they became calm, and fung a fong, which at the dead of night had a pleafing effect. The next morning, after they were dreffed according to the mode of their own country, and were ornamented with necklaces and bracelets, preparations were made for fending them to their countrymen, at which they ex-preffed great fatisfaction; but finding the boat ap-proaching Capt. Cook's firft landing place, they inti-mated that the inhabitants were foes, and that after killing their enemies, they always eat them. The cap-tain, neverthelefs, judged it expedient to land near the fame fpot, which he accordingly did with Mr. Banks, Doctor Solander, and Tupia, refolving at the fame time to protect the youths from any injury that might be of-fered them. Thefe had fcarcely departed on their re-turn to their friends, when two large parties of Indians advanced haftily towards them, upon which they again flew to us for protection. When the Indians drew near, one of the boys difcovered his uncle among them, and a converfation enfued acrofs the river, in which the boy gave a juft account of our hofpitality, and took great pains to difplay his finery. A fhort time after this converfation the uncle fwam acrofs the river, bring-ing with him a green bough, a token of friendfhip, which we received as fuch, and feveral prefents were made him. Notwithftanding the prefence of this re-lation, all three of the boys, by their own defire, re-turned to the fhip, but as the captain intended to fail the next morning, he fent them afhore in the evening,

though

though much againſt their inclination. The names of
theſe boys were Toahowrange, Koikerange, and Ma-
ragovete. They informed us of a particular kind of
deer upon the iſland, and that there were likewiſe tars,
capers, romara, yams; a kind of long pepper, bald
coote, and black birds.

On the 11th at ſix o'clock in the morning, we weighed, and ſet ſail, in hopes of finding a better anchoring
place, Capt. Cook having given the bay (called by the
natives Toaneora) the name of Poverty Bay; and the
ſouth-weſt point he called young Nick's Head, on account of its firſt having been perceived by a lad on
board, named Nicholas Young. In the afternoon we
were becalmed; and ſeveral canoes full of Indians came
off from the ſhore, who received many preſents, and
afterwards bartered even their cloaths, and ſome of
their paddles, ſo eager were they to be poſſeſſed of European commodities. A ſingle tree formed the bottom
of their canoes, and the upper part conſiſted of two
planks ſewed together; theſe were painted red, re-
preſenting many uncommon figures, and very curi-
ouſly wrought. The Indians were armed with blud-
geons, made of wood, and of the bone of a large animal: they called them Patoo-Patoo; and they were
well contrived for cloſe fighting.

Having finiſhed their traffic, they ſet off in ſuch a
hurry, that they forgot three of their companions, who
remained on board all night. Theſe teſtified their fears
and apprehenſions, notwithſtanding Tupia took great
pains to convince them they were in no danger; and
about ſeven o'clock the next morning a canoe came off,
with four Indians on board. It was at firſt with difficulty the Indians in the ſhip could prevail on thoſe in
the canoe to come near them, and not till after the
former had aſſured them, that the Engliſh did not eat
men. The chief came on board, whoſe face was tataowed, with a remarkable patoo in his hand, and in
this canoe the three Indians left the ſhip. Capt. Cook
gave the name of Cape Table to a point of land about
ſeven leagues to the ſouth of Poverty Bay: its figure

greatly refembling a table, and the ifland, called by the natives Teahowry, he named Portland Ifland, it being very fimilar to that of the fame name in the Britifh Channel. It is joined to the main by a chain of rocks near a mile in length, partly above water. There are feveral fhoals, called fhambles, about three miles to the north-eaft of Portland, one of which the Endeavour narrowly efcaped ; there is, however, a paffage between them with twenty fathom water. Some parts of Portland Ifland, as well as the main, were cultivated ; and pumice ftone in great quantities lying along the fhore, within the bay, indicated that there was a volcano in the ifland. High palings upon the ridges of hills were alfo vifible in two places, which were judged to be defigned for religious purpofes.

On the 12th feveral Indians came off in a canoe; they were disfigured in a ftrange manner, danced and fang, and at times appeared to be peaceably inclined, but at others to menace hoftilities. Notwithftanding Tupia ftrongly invited them to come on board, none of them would quit the canoe. Whilft the Endeavour was getting clear of the fhambles, five canoes full of Indians came off, and feemed to threaten the people on board, by brandifhing their lances, and other hoftile geftures. A four-pounder, loaded with grape-fhot, was therefore ordered to be fired, but not pointed at them. This had the defired effect, and made them drop a-ftern. Two more canoes came off whilft the Endeavour lay at anchor, but the Indians on board behaved very peaceably and quiet, and received feveral prefents, but would not come on board.

On Friday the 13th in the morning, we made for an inlet, but finding it not fheltered, ftood out again ; and were chafed by a canoe filled with Indians, but the Endeavour out-failed them. She purfued her courfe round the bay, but did not find an opening. The next morning we had a view of the inland country. It was mountainous, and covered with fnow in the interior parts, but the land towards the fea was flat and uncultivated, and in many places there were groves of high trees.

trees. Nine canoes full of Indians came from the ſhore, and five of them, after having confulted together, purſued the Endeavour, apparently with a hoſtile de-ſign. Tupia was defired to acquaint them that im-mediate deſtruction would enſue if they perſevered in their attempts; but words had no influence, and a four-pounder, with grape-ſhot was fired, to give them ſome notion of the arms of their opponents. They were terrified at this kind of reaſoning, and paddled away faſter than they came. Tupia then hailed the fugitives and acquainted them that if they came in a peaceable manner, and left their arms behind, no annoyance would be offered them; one of the canoes ſubmitting to the terms, came along-ſide the ſhip, and received many preſents; but the other canoes returning, and perſiſting in the ſame menacing behaviour, interrupted this friendly intercourſe.

On the 15th we were viſited by ſome fiſhing-boats, the people in which, conducted themſelves in an amica-ble manner. Though the fiſh which they had on board had been caught ſo long that they were not eatable, Capt. Cook purchaſed them merely for the ſake of promoting a trade with the natives. In the afternoon a canoe with a number of armed Indians came up, and one of them, who was remarkably cloathed, with a black ſkin, found means to defraud the captain of a piece of red baize, under pretence of bartering the ſkin he had on for it. As ſoon as he had got the baize into his poſ-ſeſſion, inſtead of giving the ſkin in return, agreeable to his bargain, he rolled them up together, and order-ed the canoe to put off from the ſhip, turning a deaf ear to the repeated remonſtrance of the captain againſt his unjuſt behaviour. After a ſhort time this canoe, together with the fiſhing boats which had put off at the ſame time, came back to the ſhip, and trade was again begun. During this ſecond traffic with the Indians, one of them unexpectedly ſeized Tupia's little boy Taiyota, and pulling him into his canoe, inſtantly put off, and paddled away with the utmoſt ſpeed; ſeveral muſquets were immediately diſcharged at the people in

the

the canoe, and one of them receiving a wound, they all let go the boy, who before was held down in the bottom of the canoe. Taiyota taking the advantage of their consternation, immediately jumped into the sea, and swam back towards the Endeavour ; he was taken on board without receiving any harm; but his strength was so much exhausted with the weight of his cloaths, that it was with great difficulty he reached the ship. In consequence of this attempt to carry off Taiyota, Capt. Cook called the cape off which it happened, Cape Kidnappers, lying in latitude 39 deg. 43 min. south, and longitude 182 deg. 24 min. west, and is very distinguishable by the high cliffs and white rocks that surrounded it. The distance of this cape from Portland Island is about 13 leagues, and it forms the south point of a bay which was denominated Hawke's Bay, in honour of Admiral Hawke.

Taiyota, having recovered from his fright, produced a fish and informed Tupia that he intended to offer it to his Eatua or God, in gratitude for his happy escape ; this being approved of by the other Indian, the fish was cast into the sea. Capt. Cook now passed by a small island which was supposed to be inhabited only by fishermen, as it seemed to be barren, and Bare Island was the name given to it, and to a head-land in latitude 40 deg. 34 min. south, and longitude 182 deg. 55 min. west, because the Endeavour turned, he gave the name of Cape Turnagain. It was never certainly known whether New Zealand was an island before this vessel touched there : on this account, the lords of the admiralty had instructed Capt. Cook to sail along the coasts as far as 40 degrees south, and if the land extended farther, to return to the northward again. It was for this reason that the captain altered his course, when he arrived at the cape above-mentioned : the wind having likewise veered about to the south, he returned, sailing along the coast nearly in his former track. Between this and Cape Kidnappers Bay, the land is unequal, and somewhat resembles our downs and small villages, and many inhabitants were observed. The ship came abreast

abreaſt of a peninſula, in Portland Iſland, named Tera-
kako, on Wedneſday the 19th. At this time a canoe
with five Indians came up to the veſſel. There were
two chiefs among them, who came on board, and ſtaid
all night. One of theſe was a very comely perſon, and
had an open and agreeable countenance. They were
extremely grateful for the preſents which they received,
and diſplayed no ſmall degree of curioſity. They would
not eat or drink, but the ſervants devoured the victuals
ſet before them with a moſt voracious appetite.

We gave the name of Gable End Foreland to a remarkable head-land, which we paſſed on the 19th.
Three canoes appeared here, and one Indian came on
board to whom we gave ſmall preſents before he withdrew.

Many of theſe Indians wore pieces of green-ſtone
round their necks which were tranſparent, and reſembled an emerald. Theſe being examined, appeared to
be a ſpecies of the nephritic ſtone. Several pieces of it
were procured by Mr. Banks, and it appeared that this
furniſhed the iſlanders with their principal ornaments.
The form of ſome of their faces was agreeable; their
noſes were rather prominent than flat. Their dialect
was not ſo guttural as that of others, and their language
nearly reſembled that of Otaheite.

On Friday the 20th we anchored in a bay two leagues
to the north of the Foreland. To this bay we were invited by the natives in canoes, who behaved very amicably, and pointed to a place where they ſaid we ſhould
find plenty of freſh water. We determined here to get
ſome knowledge of the country, though the harbour was
not ſo good a ſhelter from the weather as we expected.
Two chiefs, whom we ſaw in the canoes, came on board,
they were dreſſed in jackets, the one ornamented with
tufts of red feathers, the other with dogs-ſkin. We
preſented to them linen and ſome ſpike nails, but they
did not value the laſt ſo much as the inhabitants of the
other iſlands. The reſt of the Indians traded with us
without the leaſt impoſition, and we directed Tupia to
acquaint them of our views in coming thither; and
promiſe,

promife, that they fhould receive no injury, if they offered none to us. In the afternoon the chief return-ed ; and towards the evening we went on fhore, accom-panied by the Captain, Dr. Solander, and Mr. Banks. We were courteoufly received by the inhabitants, who did not appear in numerous bodies, and in other in-ftances were fcrupuloufly attentive not to give offence. We made them feveral fmall prefents, and in this agreeable tour round the bay, we had the pleafure of finding two ftreams of frefh water. We remained on fhore all night, and the next day Mr. Banks and Dr. Solander difcovered feveral birds, among which were quails and large pigeons. Many ftages for drying fifh were obferved near where we landed, and fome houfes with fences. We faw dogs with pointed ears, and very ugly. Sweet potatoes, like thofe which grow in Ame-rica were found. The cloth plant grew fpontaneous. In the neighbouring valleys the lands were laid out in regular plantations ; and in the bay we caught plenty of crabs, cray-fifh, and horfe-mackarel, larger than thofe upon the Englifh coafts. The low lands were planted with cacoes; the hollows with gourds ; but as to the woods they were almoft impaffable, on account of the number of fupple-jacks which grew there. We went into feveral of the houfes belonging to the natives, and met with a very civil reception ; and, without the leaft referve, they fhewed us whatever we defired to fee. At times we found them at their meals, which our prefence never interrupted. At this feafon fifh conftituted their chief food ; with which they eat, in-ftead of bread, roots of a kind of fern ; thefe when roafted upon a fire are fweet and clammy : in tafte not difagreeable, though rather unpleafant from the num-ber of their fibres. They have doubtlefs in other fea-fons of the year an abundance of excellent vege-tables.

The women of this place paint their faces with a mix-ture of red ocre and oil, which, as they are very plain, renders them in appearance more homely. This kind of daubing being generally wet upon their cheeks and foreheads,

2

forehcads, was eafily transferred to thofe who faluted them, as was frequently vifible upon the nofes of our people. The young ones, who were complete coquets, wore a petticoat, under which was a girdle, made of the blades of grafs ftrongly perfumed, to which was pendant a fmall bunch of the leaves of fome fragrant plant. The faces of the men were not in general painted; but they were daubed with dry red ocre from head to foot, their apparel not excepted. Though in perfonal cleanlinefs they were not equal to our friends at Otaheite, yet in fome particulars they furpaffed them; for their dwellings were furnifhed with privies, and they had dunghills upon which their offals and filth were depofited. Among the females chaftity was light-ly efteemed. They reforted frequently to the watering place, where they freely beftowed every favour that was requefted. An officer meeting with an elderly woman, he accompanied her to her houfe, and having prefented her with fome cloth and beads, a young girl was fingled out, with whom he was given to underftand he might retire. Soon after an elderly man, with two women came in as vifitors, who with much formality faluted the whole company, after the cuftom of the place, which is by gently joining the tips of their nofes together. On his return, which was on Saturday the 21ft, he was furnifhed with a guide, who whenever they came to a brook or rivulet took him on his back to prevent his being wet. Many of the natives were cu-rioufly tataowed, an old man in particular, was marked on the breaft with curious figures. One of them had an axe made of the green ftone, which we could not purchafe, though fundry things were offered in exchange. Thefe Indians at night dance in a very uncouth manner, with antic geftures, lolling out their tongues and making ftrange grimaces. In their dances old men as well as the young ones are capital performers.

In the evening, Mr. Banks, being apprehenfive that we might be left on fhore after it was dark, applied to the Indians for one of their canoes to convey us on board the fhip. This they granted with an obliging manner.

manner. We were eight in number, and not being
ufed to a veffel that required a nice balance, we overfet
her in the furf. No one however was drowned, but it
was concluded, to prevent a fimilar accident, that half
our number fhould go at one time. Mr. Banks, Dr.
Solander, Tupia, and Taiyota, were the firft party who
embarked again, and arrived fafe at the fhip, as did
the remainder of our company, all not a little pleafed
with the good nature of our Indian friends, who chearfully contributed their affiftance, upon our fecond trip.
During our ftay on fhore, feveral of them went out in
their canoes and trafficked with the fhip's company.
At firft they preferred the cloth of Otaheite to that of
Europe, but in the courfe of a day it decreafed in its
value five hundred per cent. Thefe people expreffed
ftrong marks of aftonifhment when fhewn the bark and
her apparatus. This bay, which we now determined
to quit, the natives call Tegadoo, and it is fituated in
38 deg. 10 min. fouth latitude.

On the 22d in the evening, being Sunday, we weighed
anchor and put to fea, but the wind being contrary
we ftood for another bay a little to the fouth, called
by the natives Tolaga, in order to complete our wood
and water, and to extend our correfpondence with the
natives. In this bay we came to an anchor, in about
eleven fathom water, with a good fandy bottom, the
north point of the bay bearing north by eaft, and the
fouth point fouth eaft. We found a watering-place in
a fmall cove a little within the fouth-point of the bay,
which bore fouth by eaft, diftant about a mile. Several canoes with Indians on board, trafficked with us
very fairly for glafs bottles.

On Monday the 23d in the afternoon, we went on
fhore accompanied by Mr. Banks, Dr. Solander, and
the captain. We examined and found the water extremely good; alfo plenty of wood; and the natives
fhewed us as much civility as thofe from whom we had
lately departed. At this watering-place we fet up an
aftronomical quadrant, and took feveral folar and lu-
nary obfervations. In the morning of the 24th, Mr.
Gore

London Published by Alexᵈ Hogg at the Kings Arms, Nᵒ 16 Paternoster Row.

A Curiously ARCHED ROCK on the Coast of NEW ZEALAND.

South sculp.

Gore and the marines were fent on fhore to guard the people employed in cutting wood and filling the cafks with water. Capt. Cook, Mr. Banks, and the doctor alfo went on fhore: the latter were employed in collecting plants. In our walks through the vales we faw many houfes uninhabited, the natives refiding chiefly in fheds, on the ridges of the hills, which are very fteep. In a valley between two very high hills, we faw a curious rock that formed a large arch, oppofite the fea. This cavern was in length about feventy feet, in breadth thirty, and near fifty in height, commanding a view of the bay and hills on the other fide, which had a very pleafing effect. Indeed the whole country about the bay is agreeable beyond defcription, and, if properly cultivated, would be a moft fertile fpot. The hills are cloathed with beautiful flowering fhrubs, intermixed with a number of tall, ftately palms, which perfume the air, making it perfectly odoriferous. Mr. Banks and the doctor, among other trees that yielded a fine tranfparent gum, difcovered the cabbage-tree, the produce whereof when boiled, was very good. We met with various kinds of edible herbage in great abundance, and many trees that produced fruit fit to eat. The plant from which the cloth is made, is a kind of Hemerocallis; its leaves afford a ftrong gloffy flax, equally adapted to cloathing, and making of ropes. Sweet potatoes and plantains are cultivated near the houfes.

On our return we met an old man who entertained us with the military exercifes of the natives, which are performed with the Patoo-Patoo and the lance. The former has been already mentioned, and is ufed as a battle-axe: the latter is eighteen or twenty feet in length, made of extreme hard wood, and fharpened at each end. A ftake was fubftituted for a fuppofed enemy. The old warrior firft attacked him with his lance, advancing with a moft furious afpect. Having pierced him, the patoo-patoo was ufed to demolifh his head, at which he ftruck with a force which would at one blow have fplit any man's fkull; from whence we concluded no quarter was given by thefe people to their foes in time of action.

The natives in this part are not very numerous. They are tolerably well fhaped, but lean and tall. Their faces refemble thofe of the Europeans. Their nofes are aquiline, their eyes dark coloured, their hair black, which is tied upon the top of their heads, and the mens beards are of a moderate length. Their tataowing is done very curioufly, in various figures, which makes their fkin refemble carving; it is confined to the principal men, the females and fervants ufing only red paint, with which they daub their faces, that otherwife would not be difagreeable. Their cloth is white, glofly, and very even; it is worn principally by the men, though it is wrought by the women, who, indeed, are condemned to all drudgery and labour.

On the 25th we fet up the armourers forge on fhore for neceffary ufes, and got our wood and water without the leaft moleftation from the natives, with whom we exchanged glafs bottles and beads for different forts of fifh. Mr. Banks and Dr. Solander went again in fearch of plants. Tupia, who was with them, engaged in a converfation with one of the priefts, and they feemed to agree in their opinions upon the fubject of religion. Tupia, in the courfe of this conference, enquired whether the report of their eating men was founded in truth, to which the prieft anfwered, it was, but that they eat none but declared foes, after they were killed in war. This idea fo favage and barbarous, proved, however, that they carried their refentment even beyond death.

On the 17th, Capt. Cook and Dr. Solander went to infpect the bay, when the doctor was not a little furprifed to find the natives in the poffeffion of a boy's top, which they knew how to fpin by whipping it, and he purchafed it out of curiofity. Mr. Banks was during this time employed in attaining the fummit of a fteep hill, that had previoufly engaged their attention, and near it he found many inhabited houfes. There were two rows of poles about fourteen or fifteen feet high,

high, covered over with sticks, which made an avenue of about five feet in width, extending near a hundred yards down the hill, in an irregular line: the intent of this erection was not discovered. When the gentlemen met at the watering place, the Indians sang their war song, which was a strange medley of shouting, sighing, and grimace, at which the women assisted. The next day Capt. Cook and other gentlemen went upon the island at the entrance of the bay, and met with a canoe that was 67 feet in length, six in breadth, and four in height; her bottom, which was sharp, consisted of three trunks of trees, and the sides and head were curiously carved.

We also came to a large unfinished house. The posts which supported it were ornamented with carvings, that did not appear to be done upon the spot, and as the inhabitants seemed to set great value upon works of this kind, future navigators might find their advantage in carrying such articles to trade with. Though the posts of this house were judged to be brought here, the people seemed to have a taste for carving; as their boats, paddles, and tops of walking sticks evince. Their favourite figure is a volute or spiral, which is sometimes single, double, and triple, and is done with great exactness, though the only instruments we saw were an axe made of stone, and a chissel. Their taste, however, is extremely whimsical and extravagant, scarcely ever imitating nature. Their huts are built under trees, their form is an oblong square: the door low on the side, and the windows are at the ends; reeds covered with thatch compose the walls; the beams of the eaves, which come to the ground, are covered with thatch; most of the houses had been deserted, through fear of the English, upon their landing. There are many beautiful parrots, and great numbers of birds of different kinds, particularly one whose note resembles the European black-bird; but here is no ground fowl or poultry, nor any quadrupedes, excepts rats and dogs, and these were not numerous. The dogs are considered as delicate food, and their skins serve for

ornaments

ornaments to their apparel. There is a great variety of fish in the bay, shell and cray fish are very plentiful, some of the latter weigh near 12 pounds.

Sunday, October the 29th, we set sail from this bay. It is situate in latitude 38 deg. 22 min. south, four leagues to the north of Gable End Foreland; there are two high rocks at the entrance of the bay, which form a cove very good for procuring wood and water. There is a high rocky island off the north point of the bay, which affords good anchorage, having a fine sandy bottom, and from seven to thirteen fathom water, and is likewise sheltered from all but the north-east wind. We obtained nothing here in trade but some sweet potatoes, and a little fish. This is a very hilly country, though it presents the eye with an agreeable verdure, various woods and many small plantations. Mr. Banks found a great number of trees in the woods, quite unknown to Europeans, the fire wood resembled the maple-tree, and produced a gum of whitish colour; other trees yielded a gum of a deep yellow green. The only roots were yams and sweet potatoes, though the soil appears very proper for producing every species of vegetables.

On Monday the 30th, sailing to the northward, we fell in with a small island about a mile distant from the north-east point of the main, and this being the most eastern part of it, the captain named it East Cape, and the island East Island; it was but small, and appeared barren. The cape is in latitude 37 deg. 42 min. 30 sec. south. There are many small bays from Tolaga Bay to East Cape. Having doubled the cape, many villages presented themselves to view, and the adjacent land appeared cultivated. In the evening of the 30th, Lieutenant Hicks discovered a bay to which his name was given. Next morning, about nine, several canoes came off from shore with a number of armed men, who appeared to have hostile intentions. Before these had reached the ship, another canoe, larger than any that had yet been seen, full of armed Indians, came off, and made towards the Endeavour with great expedition.

pedition. The captain now judging it expedient to prevent, if poffible, their attacking him, ordered a gun to be fired over their heads. This not producing the defired effect, another gun was fired with ball, which threw them into fuch confternation that they immediately returned much fafter than they came. This precipitate retreat, induced the captain to give the cape, off which it happened, the name of Cape Runaway; it lies in latitude 37 deg. 32 min. fouth, and longitude 181 deg. 48 min. weft.

On the 31ft, we found that the land, which during this day's run appeared like an ifland, was one, and we named the fame White Ifland.

On the 1ft of November, at day-break, not lefs than between 40 and 50 canoes were feen, feveral of which came off as before, threatening to attack the Englifh. One of their chiefs flourifhed his pike, and made feveral harangues, feeming to bid defiance to thofe on board the veffel. At laft, after repeated invitations, they came clofe along-fide; but inftead of fhewing a difpofition to trade, the haranguing chief uttered a fentence, and took up a ftone which he threw againft the fhip, and immediately after they feized their arms. They were informed by Tupia, of the dreadful confequences of commencing hoftilities; but this admonition they feemed little to regard. A piece of cloth, however, happening to attract their eyes, they began to be more mild and reafonable. A quantity of cray fifh, mufcles, and conger eels was now purchafed. No fraud was attempted by this company of Indians, but fome others that came after them, took goods from the veffel without making proper returns. As one of them that had rendered himfelf remarkable for thefe practices, and feemed proud of his fkill in them, was putting off with his canoe, a mufquet was fired over his head, which circumftance produced good order for the prefent. Yet when thefe favages began to traffic with the failors, they renewed their frauds; and one of them was bold enough to feize fome linen that was hung to dry, and run away with it. In order to induce him to

return,

return, a mufquet was firft fired over his head, but this not anfwering the end, he was fhot in the back with fmall fhot, yet he ftill perfevered in his defign. This being perceived by his countrymen, they dropped a-ftern, and fet up the fong of defiance. In confequence of their behaviour, though they made no preparations to attack the veffel, the captain gave orders to fire a four pounder, which paffed over them; but its effect on the water terrified them fo much, that they retreated with precipitation to the fhore.

In the afternoon, about two o'clock, we difcovered a pretty high ifland to the weftward. Some time after perceiving other rocks and iflands in the fame quarter, but not being able to weather them before night came on, we bore up between them and the main land. In the evening a double canoe, built after the fame fafhion as thofe of Otaheite, came up, when Tupia entered into a friendly converfation with the Indians, and was told that the ifland, clofe to which we lay, was called Mowtohora. It was but a few miles from the main land, pretty high, but of no great extent. We imagined the difpofition of the Indians, from their talk with Tupia, to be in our favour, but, when it was dark they began their ufual falute, by pouring a volley of ftones into the fhip and then retreated. South-weft by weft of this ifland, upon the main land, and in the center of a large plain, is a high circular mountain, to which we gave the name of Mount Edgecombe. It is very confpicuous, and is feated in latitude 37 deg. 59 min. longitude 193 deg. 7 min.

The next morning, being the 2nd, a number of canoes appeared, and one, which proved to be the fame that had pelted us the night before, came up. After converfing with Tupia, and behaving peaceably about an hour, they complimented us with another volley of ftones. We returned the falute by firing a mufket, which made them inftantly take to their paddles. Between ten and eleven we failed between a low flat ifland and the main land. The laft appeared to be of a moderate height, but level, full of plantations and villages.

lages. The villages were upon the high land next
the fea, more extenfive than any we had feen, and furrounded by a ditch, and a bank with rails on the top
of it. There were fome inclofures that refembled forts,
and the whole had the appearance of places calculated
for defence.

On the 3d, we paffed the night near a fmall ifland,
which Capt. Cook named the Mayor; and at feven in
the morning, diftant from hence about fix leagues, we
difcovered a clufter of fmall iflands, which we called
the Court of Aldermen. Thefe were twelve miles from
the main, between which were other fmall iflands,
moftly barren, but very high. The afpect of the main
land was now much changed, the foil appearing to be
barren, and the country very thinly inhabited. The
chief who governed the diftrict from Cape Turnagain
to this coaft was named Teratu. In the afternoon
three canoes, built differently from thofe already mentioned, came along-fide the Endeavour. They were
formed of the trunks of whole trees, rendered hollow
by burning; but they were not carved, nor in any manner ornamented. We now failed towards an inlet that
had been difcovered, and having anchored in feven fathom water, the fhip was foon furrounded by a number of canoes, and the people on board them did not
feem difpofed for fome time to commit any acts of hof-
tility. A bird being fhot by one of our crew, fome Indians, without fhewing any furprife brought it on
board; and for their civility the captain gave them a
piece of cloth. But this favour operated upon them
in a different manner than was expected; for when it
was dark, they begun a fong of defiance, and endeavoured to carry off the buoy of the anchor; and notwithftanding fome mufquets were fired at them, they
feemed rather to be irritated than frightened. They
even threatened to return the next morning; but on
Sunday night eleven of them were to be feen, and thefe
retired when they found the fhip's crew were upon
their guard.

On the 4th at day break no lefs than twelve canoes

made

made their appearance, containing near two hundred men, armed with spears, lances, and stones, who seemed determined to attack the ship, and would have boarded her, had they known on what quarter they could best have made their attack. While they were paddling round her, which kept the crew upon the watch in the rain, Tupia, at the request of the captain, used a number of dissuasive arguments, to prevent their carrying their apparent designs into execution; but we could not pacify them by the fire of our musquets: they then laid aside their hostile intentions, and began to trade; yet they could not refrain from their fraudulent practices; for after they had fairly bartered two of their weapons, they would not deliver up a third, for which they had received cloth, and only laughed at those who demanded an equivalent. The offender was wounded with small shot; but his countrymen took not the least notice of him, and continued to trade without any discompofure. When another canoe was struck for their mal-practices, the natives behaved in the same manner; but if a round was fired over or near them, they all paddled away. Thus we found, that theft and chicane, were as prevalent among the inhabitants of New Zealand, as those of Otaheite. In searching for an anchoring place, the captain saw a fortified village upon a high point, and having fixed upon a proper spot, he returned; upon which we weighed, run in nearer to the shore, and cast anchor upon a sandy bottom, in four fathom and a half water. The south point of the bay bore due east, distant one mile, and a river which the boats can enter at low water south south-east, distant a mile and an half.

On the 5th, in the morning, the Indians came off to the ship again, who behaved much better than they had done the preceding day. An old man in particular named Tojava, testified his prudence and honesty, to whom, and a friend with him, the captain presented some nails, and two pieces of English cloth. Tojava informed us, that they were often visited by free-booters from the north, who stripped them of all they could lay

their

their hands on, and at times made captives of their wives and children ; and that being ignorant who the Englifh were upon their firft arrival, the natives had been much alarmed, but were now fatisfied of their good intentions. He added, that for their fecurity againft thofe plunderers, their houfes were built conti-guous to the tops of. the rocks, where they could bet-ter defend themfelves. Probably their poverty and mi-fery may be afcribed to the ravages of thofe who fre-quently ftript them of every neceffary of life. Having difpatched the long-boat and pinnace into the bay to haul and dredge for fifh, but with little fuccefs, the In-dians on the banks teftified their friendfhip by every poffible means. They brought us great quantities of fifh dreffed and dried, which though indifferent, we purchafed, that trade might not be difcouraged. They alfo fupplied us with wood and good water. While we were out with our guns, the people who ftaid by the boats faw two of the natives fight. The battle was begun with their lances; but fome old men taking thefe away, they were obliged to decide the quarrel, like Englifhmen, with their fifts. For fome time they boxed with great vigour and perfeverance, but at length they all retired behind a little hill, fo that our people were prevented from feeing the iffue of the combat. At this time the Endeavour being very foul, fhe was heeled, and her bottom fcrubbed in the bay.

On the 8th, we were vifited by feveral canoes, in one of which was Tojava, who, defcrying two canoes, haftened back again to the fhore, apprehending they were freebooters ; but finding his miftake, he foon re-turned ; and the Indians fupplied us with as much ex-cellent fifh as ferved the whole fhip's company. This day a variety of plants were collected by Mr. Banks and Doctor Solander, who had never obferved any of the kind before. They ftaid on fhore till near dark, when they obferved how the natives difpofed of themfelves during the night. They had no fhelter but a few fhrubs. The men lay neareft the fea in a femicircular form ; and the women and children moft diftant from it. They had no king whofe fovereignty they acknow-

No. 5. S ledged,

ledged, a circumstance not to be paralleled on any other parts of the coast.

Early in the morning of the 9th the Indians brought in their canoes a prodigious quantity of mackarel, of which one sort were exactly the same with those caught in England. They sold them at a low rate, and they were not less welcome to us on that account. These canoes were succeeded by others equally loaded with the same sort of fish; and the cargoes purchased were so great, that every one of the ship's company who could get salt, cured as many as would serve him for a month's provision. The Indians frequently resort to the bay in parties to gather shell-fish, of which it affords an incredible plenty. Indeed wherever we went, whether on the hills, or through the vales, in the woods or on the plains, we saw many waggon loads of shells in heaps, some of which appeared fresh, others very old.

This being a very clear day, Mr. Green, the astronomer, landed with other gentlemen to observe the transit of Mercury. The observation of the ingress was made by Mr. Green alone, and Capt. Cook took the sun's altitude to ascertain the time. While the observation was making, a canoe, with various commodities on board, came along-side the ship; and Mr. Gore, the officer who had then the command, being desirous of encouraging them to traffic, produced a piece of Otaheitean cloth, of more value than any they had yet seen, which was immediately seized by one of the Indians, who obstinately refused either to return it, or give any thing in exchange: he paid dearly however for his temerity, being shot dead upon the spot. The death of this young Indian alarmed all the rest; they fled with great precipitancy, and, for the present, could not be induced to renew their traffic with the English. But when the Indians on shore had heard the particulars related by Tojava, who greatly condemned the conduct of the deceased, they seemed to think that he had merited his fate. His name was Otirreeonooe. This transaction happened, as has been mentioned, whilst the observation was making of the transit of Mercury, when

the

the weather was fo favourable, that the whole tranfit was viewed, without a cloud intervening. The tranfit commenced feven hours, 20 min. 58 fec. By Mr. Green's obfervation the internal contact was at 12 hours, eight min. 57 fec. the external at 12 hours nine min. 55 fec. the latitude 30 deg. 48 min. five fec. In confequence of this obfervation having been made here, this bay was called Mercury Bay.

On the 10th, Mr. Banks, Dr. Solander, and the captain went in boats to infpect a large river that runs into the bay. They found it broader fome miles within than at the mouth, and interfected into a number of ftreams, by feveral fmall iflands, which were covered with trees. On the caft fide of the river, the gentlemen fhot fome fhags, which proved very good eating. The fhore abounded with fifh of various kinds, fuch as cockles, clams, and oyfters; and here were alfo ducks, fhags, and curlieus, with other wild fowl in great plenty. At the mouth of the river there was good anchorage in five fathom water. The gentlemen were received with great hofpitality by the inhabitants of a little village on the eaft fide of the river. There are there the remains of a fort called Eppah, on a peninfula that projects into the river, and it was calculated for defending a fmall number againft a greater force. From the remains, it neverthelefs feemed to have been taken and partly deftroyed. The Indians fup before fun-fet, when they eat fifh and birds baked or roafted; they roaft them upon a ftick, ftuck in the ground near the fire, and bake them in the manner the dog was baked, which the gentlemen eat at George's Ifland. A female mourner was prefent at one of their fuppers; fhe was feated upon the ground, and wept inceffantly, at the fame time repeating fome fentences in a doleful manner, but which Tupia could not explain; at the termination of each period fhe cut herfelf with a fhell upon her breaft, her hands, or her face; notwithftanding this bloody fpectacle greatly affected the gentlemen prefent, yet all the Indians who fat by her, except one, were quite unmoved. The gentlemen faw fome, who from the depth of their fcars

S 2   muft,

muft, upon thefe occafions, have wounded themfelves more violently.

Great plenty of oyfters were procured from a bed which had been difcovered, and they proved exceedingly good. Next day the fhip was vifited by two canoes, with unknown Indians; after fome invitation they came on board, and they all trafficked without any fraud. Two fortified villages being deferted, the Captain, with Mr. Bank, and Dr. Solander, went to examine them. The fmalleft was romantically fituated upon a rock, which was arched; this village did not confift of above five or fix houfes, fenced round. There was but one path, which was very narrow, that conducted to it. The gentlemen were invited by the inhabitants to pay them a vifit, but not having time to fpare, took another route, after having made prefents to the females. A body of men, women, and children now approached the gentlemen; thefe proved to be the inhabitants of another town, which they propofed vifiting. They gave many teftimonies of their friendly difpofitions; among others they uttered the word Heromai, which according to Tupia's interpretation, implied peace, and appeared much fatisfied, when informed the gentlemen intended vifiting their habitations. Their town was named Wharretouwa. It is feated on a point of land over the fea, on the north fide of the bay, and was pailed round, and defended by a double ditch. Within the ditch a ftage is erected for defending the place in cafe of an attack; near this ftage, quantities of darts and ftones are depofited that they may always be in readinefs to repel the affailants. There is another ftage to command the path that leads to the town; and there were fome out-works. The place feemed calculated to hold out a confiderable time againft an enemy armed with no other weapons than thofe of the Indians. It appeared however deficient in water for holding out a fiege. Inftead of bread, they had fern root, which was here in great plenty, with dried fifh. Very little of the land was cultivated, and fweet potatoes and yams were the only vegetables to be found. There are two rocks near the fort of this

fortification,

fortification, both feparated from the main land; they are very fmall, neverthelefs they are not without dwelling-houfes and little fortifications. In their engagements, thefe Indians throw ftones with their hands, being deftitute of a fling, and thofe and lances are their only miffible weapons; they have, befides the patoo-patoo, already defcribed, a ftaff about five feet in length and another fhorter. We failed from this bay, after having taken poffeffion of it in the name of the king of Great Britain, on the 15th of November. Tojava, who vifited us in his canoe juft before our departure, faid, he fhould prepare to retire to his fort as foon as the Englifh were gone, as the relations of Otirreonooe had threatened to take his life, as a forfeit for that of the deceafed, Tojava being judged partial in this affair to the Englifh.

Towards the north-weft, a number of iflands of different fizes appeared, which were named Mercury Iflands; Mercury Bay lies in latitude 36 deg. 47 min. fouth; longitude 184 deg. 4 min. weft, and has a fmall entrance at its mouth. On account of the number of oyfters found in the river, the captain gave it the name of Oyfter River: Mangrove River (which the captain fo called from the great number of thofe trees that grew near it) is the moft fecure place for fhipping, being at the head of the bay. The north-weft fide of this bay and river appeared much more fertile than the eaft fide. The inhabitants, though numerous, have no plantations. Their canoes are very indifferently conftructed, and are not ornamented at all. They lie under continual apprehenfions of Terratu, being confidered by him as rebels. Shore iron fand is to be found in plenty on this coaft, which proves that there are mines of metal up the country, it being brought down from thence by a rivulet.

On the 18th in the morning, we fteered between the main, and an ifland which feemed very fertile, and as extenfive as Ulietea. Several canors filled with Indians, came along-fide here, and the Indians fang their war fong, but the Endeavour's people paying them no attention, they threw a volley of ftones, and then paddled

dled away; however they prefently returned their infults.
Tupia fpoke to them, making ufe of his old arguments,
that inevitable deftruction would enfue if they perfifted;
they anfwered by brandifhing their weapons, intimating, that if the Englifh durft come on fhore, they
would deftroy them all. Tupia ftill continued in ex-
poftulating with them, but to no purpofe : and they
foon gave another volley of ftones ; but upon a mufquet being fired at one of their boats, they made a precipitate retreat. We caft anchor in 23 fathom water
in the evening, and early the next morning failed up an
inlet. Soon after two canoes came off, and fome of the
Indians came on board: they knew Tojava very well,
and called Tupia by his name. Having received from
us fome prefents, they retired peaceably, and apparently
highly gratified.

On Monday the 20th, after having run five leagues
from the place where we had anchored the night before, we came to an anchor in a bay called by the
natives Ooahaouragee. Capt. Cook, Mr. Banks, Dr.
Solander, and others fet off in the pinnace to examine
the bottom of the bay, and found the inlet end of a
river, about nine miles above the fhip. We entered
into the fame with the firft of the flood, and before we
had proceeded three miles, the water was perfectly frefh.
Here we faw an Indian town, built upon a fmall dry
fand-bank, and entirely furrounded by a deep mud ;
the inhabitants of which with much cordiality invited
us to land, and gave us a moft friendly reception. We
were now fourteen miles up the river, and finding little
alteration in the face of the country, we landed on the
weft fide to examine the lofty trees which adorned its
banks, and were of a kind that we had not feen before.
At the entrance of a wood we met with one ninety-
eight feet high from the ground, quite ftrait, and nineteen feet in circumference ; and as we advanced we
found others ftill larger. The wood of thefe trees is
very heavy, not fit for mafts but would make exceeding
fine planks. Our carpenter, who was with us, obferved, that the timber refembled that of the pitch pine
which is lightened by tapping. There were alfo trees
of

of other kinds, all unknown to us, fpecimens of which
we brought away. We reimbarked about three o'clock
with the firft of the ebb, and Capt. Cook gave to the
river the name of the Thames, it having a refemblance
to the river of that name in England. It is not fo deep,
but it is as broad as the Thames is at Greenwich, and
the tide of flood is as ftrong. On the evening of the
21ft we reached the fhip, all extremely tired, but happy
at being on board.

On the 22d, early in the morning, we made fail,
and kept plying till the flood obliged us once more to
come to an anchor. The captain and Dr. Solander
went on fhore to the weft, but made no obfervations
worth relating. After thefe gentlemen departed, the
fhip was furrounded with canoes, which kept Mr.
Banks on board, that he might trade with the Indians,
who bartered their arms and cloaths for paper, taking
no unfair advantages. But though they were in general honeft in their dealings, one of them took a
fancy to a half minute glafs, and being detected in fe-
creting the fame, it was refolved to give him a fmatch
of the cat-o'-nine-tails. The Indians interfered to ftop
the current of juftice; but being oppofed they got
their arms from their canoes, and fome of the people
in them attempted to get on board. Mr. Banks and
Tupia now coming upon deck, the Indians applied to
Tupia, who informed them of the nature of the offender's intended punifhment, and that he had no influence over Mr. Hicks, the commanding officer. They
appeared pacified, and the criminal received not only
a dozen, but afterwards a good drubbing from an old
man, who was thought to be his father. The canoes
immediately went off, the Indians faying, they fhould
be afraid to return again on board. Tupia, however,
brought them back, but they feemed to have loft that
confidence which they before repofed in us. Their
ftay was fhort, and after their departure we faw them
not again, though they had promifed to return with
fome fifh.

On the 23d, the weather ftill continuing unfavourable, and the wind contrary, we kept plying down the
river,

river, anchoring between the tides; and at the north weft extremity of the Thames, we paſſed a point of land which the captain called Point Rodney; and another, at the north eaſt extremity, when we entered the bay, he named Cape Colville, in honour of Lord Colville. Not being able to approach land, we had but a diſtant view of the main for a courſe of near thirty miles. Under the name of the river Thames, the captain comprehended the whole bay. Cape Colville is to be diſtinguiſhed by a high rock, and lies in 36 deg. 26 min. of ſouth latitude, and 194 deg. 27 min. weft longitude. The Thames runs ſouth by eaſt from the ſouthern point of the cape. In ſome parts it is three leagues over, for about fourteen leagues, after which it becomes narrow. In ſome parts of the bay the water is 26 fathoms deep; the depth diminiſhes gradually, and in general the anchorage is good. To ſome iſlands that ſhelter it from the ſea Captain Cook gave the name of Barrier Iſlands; they ſtretch north-weft and ſouth-eaſt ten leagues. The country ſeemed to be thinly inhabited; the natives are well made, ſtrong, and active; their bodies are painted with red ocre, and their canoes, which are well conſtructed, were ornamented with carved work.

On the 24th, we continued ſteering along the ſhore between the iſlands and the main; and in the evening anchored in an open bay, in about fourteen fathom water. Here we caught a large number of fiſh of the ſcienne, or bream kind, enough to ſupply the whole ſhip's company with proviſion for two days. From our ſucceſs Capt. Cook named this place Bream Bay, and the extreme points at the north end of the bay he called Bream Head. Several pointed rocks ſtand in a range upon the top of it, and ſome ſmall iſlands which lie before it were called the Hen and Chickens. It is ſituated in latitude 35 deg. 46 min. ſeventeen leagues north-weft of Cape Colville. There is an extent of land, of about thirty miles, between Point Rodney and Bream Head, woody and low. No inhabitants were viſible; but from the fires perceived at night, we concluded it was inhabited.

I   On

On the 25th, early in the morning, we left the bay, and continued our courfe flowly to the northward; at noon our latitude was 36 deg. 36 min. fouth, and we faw fome iflands which we named the Poor Knights, at north-eaft by north, diftant three leagues; the norther-moft land in fight bore N. N. W. we were now at the diftance of two miles from the fhore, and had twenty-fix fathom water. Upon the iflands were a few towns that appeared fortified, and the land round them feemed well inhabited.

On the 26th, towards night, feven large canoes came off to us, with about two hundred men. Some of the Indians came on board, and let us know, that they had an account of our arrival. Thefe were followed by two larger canoes, adorned with carving. The In-dians, after having held a conference, came a-long fide of the veffel. They were armed with various weapons, and feemed to be of the higher order. Their patoo-pa-toos were made of ftone and whale-bone, ornamented with dog's hair, and were held in high eftimation. Their complexion was darker than that of thofe to the fouth, and their faces were ftained with amoco. They were given to .pilfering, of which one of them gave an inftance pretending to barter a piece of talc, wrought into the fhape of an axe, for a piece of cloth ; nor was he difpofed to fulfil his agreement, till we compelled him to do it, by firing a mufquet over his head, which brought him back to the fhip, and he returned the cloth. At three in the afternoon we paffed a remark-able high point of land, bearing weft, and it was called Cape Brett, in honour of Sir Piercy Brett. At the point of this cape is a round high hillock, and north-eaft by north, diftant about a mile, is a curious arched rock, like that which has been already defcribed. This cape, or at leaft part of it, is called by the natives Mo-tugogo, and lies in 35 deg. 10 min. 30 fec. fouth lati-tude, and in 185 deg. 23 min. weft longitude. To the fouth-weft by weft is a bay, in which is many fmall iflands, and the point at the north-weft entrance the captain named Point Pococke. There are many villages on the main as well as on the iflands, which appeared well inhabited, and feveral canoes filled with Indians made to the fhip, and in the courfe of bartering fhewed the fame inclination to defraud as their neighbours. Thefe Indians were ftrong and well proportioned; their hair black, and tied up in a bunch ftuck with feathers: their chiefs had garments made of fine cloth, decorated with dog's fkin; and they were tataowed like thofe who had laft appeared.

On the 27th, at eight in the morning, we found ourfelves within a mile of many fmall iflands, laying clofe under the main, at the diftance of twenty-two miles from Cape Brett. Here we lay about two hours, during which time feveral canoes came off from the iflands, which we called Cavalles, the name of fome fifh which we purchafed of the Indians. Thefe people were very infolent, ufing many frantic geftures, and pelting us with ftones. Nor did they give over their infults, till fome fmall fhot hit one who had a ftone in his hand. A general terror was now fpread among them, and they all made a very precipitate retreat. For feveral days the wind was fo very unfavourable, that the veffel rather loft than gained ground.

On the 29th, having weathered Cape Brett, we bore away to leeward, and got into a large bay, where we anchored on the fouth-weft fide of feveral iflands, and fuddenly came into four fathoms and a half water. Upon founding, we found we had got upon a bank, and accordingly weighed and dropped over it, and anchored again in ten fathoms and a half, after which we were furrounded by thirty-three large canoes, containing near three hundred Indians all armed. Some of them were admitted on board, and Captain Cook gave a piece of broad cloth to one of the chiefs, and fome fmall prefents to the other. They traded peaceably for fome time, being terrified at the fire-arms, with the effects of which they were not unacquainted; but whilft the captain was at dinner, on a fignal given by one of the chiefs, all the Indians quitted the fhip, and attempted to tow away the buoy; a mufquet was now fired over them, but it produced no effect; fmall fhot was then fired at them, but it did not reach them. A

mufquet

mufquet loaded with ball, was therefore ordered to be fired, and Otegoowgoow (fon of one of the chiefs) was wounded in the thigh by it, which induced them immediately to throw the buoy overboard. To complete their confufion, a round fhot was fired, which reached the fhore, and as foon as they landed, they ran in fearch of it. If thefe Indians had been under any kind of military difcipline, they might have proved a much more formidable enemy; but acting thus, without any plan or regulation, they only expofed themfelves to the annoyance of the fire-arms, whilft they could not poffibly fucceed in any of their defigns. The Captain, Mr. Banks, and Dr. Solander, landed upon the ifland, and the Indians in the canoes foon after came on fhore. The gentlemen were in a fmall cove, and were prefently furrounded by near 400 armed Indians; but the captain not fufpecting any hoftile defign on the part of the natives, remained peaceably difpofed. The gentlemen, marching towards them, drew a line, intimating that they were not to pafs it: they did not infringe upon this boundary for fome time; but at length, they fang the fong of defiance, and began to dance, whilft a party attempted to draw the Endeavour's boat on fhore; thefe fignals for an attack being immediately followed by the Indians breaking in upon the line, the gentlemen judged it time to defend themfelves, and accordingly the captain fired his mufquet, loaded with fmall fhot, which was feconded by Mr. Banks's difcharging his piece, and two of the men followed his example. This threw the Indians into confufion, and they retreated, but were rallied again by one of the chiefs, who fhouted and waved his patoo-patoo. The Doctor now pointed his mufquet at this hero, and hit him: this ftopped his career, and he took to flight with the other Indians. They retired to an eminence in a collected body, and feemed dubious whether they fhould return to the charge. They were now at too great a diftance for a ball to reach them, but thefe operations being obferved from the fhip, fhe brought her broadfide to bear, and by firing over them, foon difperfed them. The Indians had in their fkirmifh two of their

T 2   people

people wounded, but none killed : peace being thus re-
stored, the gentlemen began to gather celery and other
herbs, but suspecting that some of the natives were
lurking about with evil designs, they repaired to a cave,
which was at a small distance.   Here they found the
chief, who had that day received a present from the
captain ; he came forth with his wife and brother, and
solicited their clemency.   It appeared, that one of the
wounded Indians was a brother of this chief, who was
under great anxiety lest the wound should prove mortal,
but his grief was in a great degree alleviated, when he
was made acquainted with the different effects of small
shot and ball ; he was at the same time assured, that
upon any farther hostilities being committed, ball would
be used.   This interview terminated very cordially, after some trifling presents were made to the chief and
his companions.   The prudence of the gentlemen cannot be much commended : for had these 400 Indians
bodly rushed in upon them at once with their weapons,
the musquetry could have done very little execution ;
but supposing twenty or thirty of the Indians had been
wounded, as it does not appear their pieces were loaded
with ball, but only small shot, there would have remained a sufficent number to have massacred them, as
it appears they do not give any quarter, and none could
have been expected upon this occasion. It is true, when
the ship brought her broadside to bear, she might have
made great havock amongst the Indians ; but this
would have been too late to save the party on shore.—
Being in their boats, the English rowed to another part
of the same island, when landing and gaining an eminence, they had a very agreeable and romantic view of
a great number of small islands, well inhabited and cultivated.   The inhabitants of an adjacent town approached unarmed, and testified great humility and
submission.   Some of the party on shore who had been
very violent for having the Indians punished for their
fraudulent conduct, were now guilty of trespasses equally
reprehensible, having forced into some of the plantations, and dug up potatoes.   The captain, upon this
occasion shewed strict justice in punishing each of the

offenders

offenders with twelve lafhes: one of them being very refractory upon this occafion, and complaining of the hardfhip, thinking an Englifhman had a right to plunder an Indian with impunity, received fix additional lafhes for his reward.

On the 30th, it being a dead calm, two boats were fent to found the harbour ; when many canoes came up and traded with great probity; the gentlemen wen* again on fhore and met with a very civil reception from the natives ; and this friendly intercourfe continued all the time they remained in the bay, which was feveral days. Being upon a vifit to the old chief, he fhewed them the inftruments ufed in tataowing, which were very like thofe employed at Otaheite upon the like occafion. They faw the man who had been wounded by the ball, when the attempt was made to carry off the fhip's buoy ; and though it had gone through the flefhy part of his arm, it did not feem to give him the leaft pain or uneafinefs.

On Tuefday the 5th of December in the morning, we weighed anchor, but were foon becalmed, and a ftrong current fetting towards the fhore, we were driven in with fuch rapidity, that we expected every moment to be run upon the breakers, which appeared above water not more than a cable's length diftance, and we were fo near the land, that Tupia, who was totally ignorant of the danger, held a converfation with the Indians, who were ftanding on the beach. We were happily relieved however from this alarming fitua·tion by a frefh breeze fuddingly fpringing up from the fhore. The bay which we had left was called the Bay of Iflands, on account of the numerous iflands it contains ; we caught but few fifh while we lay there, but procured great plenty from the natives, who were extremely expert in fifhing, and difplayed great ingenuity in the form of their nets, which were made of a kind of grafs ; they were two or three hundred fathoms in length, and remarkably ftrong, and they have them in fuch plenty that it is fcarcely poffible to go a hundred yards without meeting with numbers lying in heaps. Thefe people did not appear to be under the government

ment of any particular chief or sovereign, and they seemed to live in a perfect state of friendship, notwithstanding their villages were fortified. According to their observations upon the tides, the flood comes from the south, and there is a current from the west.

On the 7th of December, being Thursday, several observations of the sun and moon were made, whereby we found our latitude to be 185 deg. 36 min. west. In the afternoon we were close under the Cavalles. Several canoes put off and followed the Endeavour, but a light breeze springing up, we did not wait for them. The next morning, being the 8th, at ten o'clock we tacked and stood in for the shore, from which we were distant nearly six leagues. By day-light on the 9th we were in with the land, about seven leagues to the westward of the Cavalles; and soon after came to a deep bay, which was named Doubtless Bay. The entrance thereto is formed by two points, distant from each other five miles, and which lie west north-west and east south-east. The wind preventing us putting in here, we steered for the westermost land in sight, and before we got the length of it, we were becalmed. During the calm we were visited by several canoes; but the Indians having heard of our guns, were afraid to come on board; however we bought some of their fish, and learned from them, by the assistance of Tupia, that we were about two days sail from a place called Moore Whennua, where the land changed its shape, and turning to the south extended no more westward. This place was concluded to be the land discovered by Tasman, which he called Cape Maria Van Diemen. They also informed us, that to the north-north-west there was an extensive country discovered by their ancestors, which they named Ulimaroa, where the inhabitants lived upon hogs, called in their language Booah, the very name given them, by those who inhabited the South-sea Islands.

On Sunday the 10th, a breeze springing up, we stood off to the north, and found by observation our latitude to be 34 deg. 44 min. south. On the 11th, early in the morning the land, with which we stood in, appeared
low

low and barren, but not deftitute of inhabitants. It
forms a peninfula, which the captain called Knuckle
Point, and the bay that lies contiguous thereto he
named Sandy Bay. In the middle of this is a high
mountain, which we called Mount Camel, on account
of its refemblance to that animal. We faw one village
on the weft fide of this mount, and another on the eaft
fide. Several canoes put off but could not reach the
fhip, which tacked, and ftood to the northward, till the
afternoon of the 12th, when fhe ftood to the north-eaft.
Towards night we were brought under double reefed
topfails ; and in the morning it was fo tempeftuous as
to fplit the main topfail and the fore mizen-top fails.
Early in the morning of the 14th we faw land to the
fouthward, at the diftance of eight or nine leagues ; and
on the 15th we tacked and ftood to the weftward.
On the 16th we difcovered land from the maft head,
bearing fouth-fouth-weft. On Sunday the 17th we
tacked in thirty five fathom, and found we had not
gained one inch to windward the laft twenty-four
hours. We faw a point of land, the northern extremity
of New Zealand, which Capt. Cook named North
Cape. It lies in latitude 34 deg. 22 min. fouth, and
in 185 deg. 55 min. weft longitude ; we continued
ftanding off and on till the 23d, when about feven
o'clock we difcovered land bearing fouth half eaft.
   On the 24th we faw the fame land fouth-eaft by fouth
four leagues diftant, which we judged to be the Iflands
of the Three Kings. The chief of thefe is in latitude
34 deg. 12 min. fouth, and 187 deg. 48 min. weft
longitude, and diftant about 14 or 15 leagues from
North Cape. Mr. Banks went out in the long-boat
and fhot fome birds that nearly refembled geefe, and
they were very good eating. On Chriftmas-day, December the 25th, we tacked, and ftood to the fouthward.
On the 26th we had no land in fight, and were twenty
leagues to the weftward of North Cape. At mid-night
we tacked and ftood to the northward. On the 27th
it blew a ftorm from the eaft, accompanied with heavy
fhowers of rain, which compelled us to bring the fhip
to, under her mainfail. The gale continued till Thurf-

I   day

day the 28th, when it fell about two o'clock in the morning; but at eight encreafed to a hurricane, with a prodigious fea. At noon the gale fomewhat abated, but we had ftill heavy fqualls. On the 29th in the evening, we wore and ftood to the north-weft. On Saturday the 30th, we faw land bearing north-eaft, which we concluded to be Maria van Diemen; and it corresponded with the account we had received of it from the Indians. We wore at mid-night, and ftood to the fouth-eaft. On the 31ft we tacked at feven in the evening, and ftood to the weftward. We were now diftant from the neareft land about three leagues, and had fomewhat more than forty fathom water.

C H A P. VII.

The Endeavour continues her Voyage, January the 1ft 1770, round North Cape to Queen Charlotte's Sound—That part of the Coaft defcribed—Tranfactions in the Sound—She fails between two Iflands, and returns to Cape Turnagain—A fhocking Cuftom of the Inhabitants—A Vifit to a Hippah, and other remarkable Particulars—The Circum-navigation of this Country completed—The Coaft and Admiralty Bay defcribed—The Departure of the Endeavour from New Zealand, and other remarkable Particulars—A defcriptive Account of New Zealand—Its firft Difcovery by Tafman—Situation and Productions—An Account of the Inhabitants—Their Drefs, Ornaments, and Manner of Life—Their canoes, Navigation, Tillage, Weapons, Mufic, Government, Religion, and Language—The Arguments in Favour of a Southern Continent controverted.

A. D. 1770. JAnuary the 1ft, on Monday at fix in the morning, being New Year's Day, we tacked, and ftood to the eaftward. At noon we ftood to the weftward; found our latitude to be 34 deg. 37 min. fouth; our diftance from the Three Kings ten or eleven leagues; and from Cape Maria van Diemen
about

about four leagues and an half, in fifty-four fathom water. On the third we saw land; it was high and flat, trending away to the south-east, beyond the reach of the naked eye. It is remarkable, that at midsummer we met with a violent gale of wind, in latitude 35, south; and that we were three weeks in getting ten leagues to the westward, and five weeks in getting fifty leagues, for at this time it was so long since we passed Cape Brett.

On the morning of the 4th we stood along shore. The coast appeared sandy, barren, dreary, and inhospitable. Steering northward on the 6th we saw land again, which we supposed to be Cape Maria. On the 7th we had light breezes, and were at times becalmed, when we saw a sun-fish, short and thick, with two large fins, but scarcely any tail, resembling a shark in colour and size. We continued steering east till the 9th, when we were off a point of land, which Capt. Cook named Woody Head. From the south-west we also saw a small island, and called it Gannet Island. Another point, remarkably high to the east-north-east, the captain named Albetrofs Point; on the north side whereof a bay is formed, promising good anchorage. At about two or three leagues distance from Albetrofs Point, to the north-east we discovered a remarkable high mountain, the peak of which is equal in height to that of Teneriffe. Its summit was covered with snow, and we gave it the name of mount Egmont, in honour of the earl of that name. It lies is in latitude 39 deg. 16 min. south, and 185 deg. 15 min. west longitude. The country round it is exceeding pleasant, having an agreeable verdure interfected with woods, and the coast forms an extensive cape which Capt. Cook named Cape Egmont. To the north of this are two small islands, in the form of a sugar-loaf. This day being the 13th we had heavy showers of rain, accompanied with thunder and lightening. We continued to steer along the shore at the distance of between two and three leagues, and between seven and eight had a transient view of Mount Edgcombe, which bore north-west distant about ten leagues.

No. 5.   U   On

On the 14th when failing fouth-eaft by fouth, the coaft ran more foutherly, and foon after five in the morning we faw land, for which we hauled up. At noon the north-weft extremity bore fouth 63 weft; and fome high land, in appearance an ifland, bore fouth-fouth-eaft, diftant five leagues. We were now in a bay, and by obfervation in latitude 40 deg. 27 min. fouth, longitude 184 deg. 39 min. weft. In the evening at eight o'clock, the land that bore fouth 63 weft, now bore north 59 weft, diftant feven leagues, and appeared like an ifland. Between this land and Cape Egmont lies the bay, on the weft-fide of which we were at this time. The land here is high and beautifully variegated with hills and vales. At this place Capt. Cook propofed to careen the fhip, and to take in a frefh fupply of wood and water. Accordingly,

On the 15th at day-break, we fteered for an inlet, when, it being almoft a calm, the fhip was carried by a current, or the tide, within a cable's length of the fhore; but by the affiftance of the boats fhe got clear. While effecting this, we faw a fea-lion, anfwering the defcription given of a male one in Commodore Anfon's voyages. About one o'clock in the afternoon we hauled round the fouth-weft point of the ifland, and the inhabitants of a village were immediately upon feeing us up in arms. At two we anchored in a very fafe cove on the north-weft fide of the bay, and moored in eleven fathom water, with a foft ground. In paffing the point of the bay we had obferved an armed centinel on duty, who was twice relieved; and now four canoes came off, for purpofe, as we imagined, of reconnoitring; for none of the Indians would venture on board, except an old man who feemed of elevated rank. His countrymen expoftulated with him, laid hold of him, and took great pains to prevent his coming aboard, but they could not divert him from his purpofe. We received him with the utmoft civility and hofpitality. Tupia and the old man joined nofes, according to the cuftom of the country, and having received feveral prefents, he retired to his affociates, who began to dance and laugh, and then retired to their fortified village. Whether their expreffions

fions of joy were tokens of enmity or friendſhip we could not determine, having ſeen them dance when inclined both to war and peace. Capt. Cook and other gentlemen now went on ſhore, at the bottom of the cove, where they met with plenty of wood, and a fine ſtream of excellent water, and on hauling the ſeine were very ſuccefsful, having caught three hundred weight of fiſh in a ſhort time, which was equally diſtributed among the ſhip's company.

On the 16th, at day-break, we were employed in careening the bark, when three canoes came off with a great number of Indians, who brought ſeveral of their women with them, which circumſtance was thought to be a favourable preſage of their peaceable diſpoſition ; but they ſoon convinced us of our miſtake, by attempting to ſtop the long boat ; upon which Captain Cook had recourſe to the old expedient of firing ſhot over their heads, which intimidated them for the preſent ; they ſoon gave freſh proofs of treacherous defigns ; for one of them ſnatched at ſome paper from our market-man, and miſſing it, put himſelf in a threatening attitude ; whereupon ſome ſhot was fired, which wounded him in the knee ; but Tupia ſtill continued converſing with his companions, making enquiries concerning their traditions reſpecting the antiquities of their country. He alſo aſked them, if they had ever before ſeen a ſhip as large as the Endeavour ? to which they replied, that they had not, nor ever heard, that ſuch a veſſel had been on their coaſt, though Taſman certainly touched here, it being only four miles ſouth of Murderer's Bay. In all the coves of this bay we found plenty of cuttle fiſh, breams, barracootas, gurnard, mackarel, dog-fiſh, ſoles, dabs, mullets, drums, ſcorpenas, or rock-fiſh, cole-fiſh, ſhags, chimeras, &c. The inhabitants catch their fiſh in the following manner. Their net is cylindrical, extended by ſeveral hoops at the bottom, and contracted at the top. The fiſh going in to feed upon the bait are caught in great abundance. In this iſland are birds of various kinds, and in great numbers, particularly parrots, wood-pigeons, water hens, hawks, and many different ſinging

U 2 birds.

birds. An herb, a fpecies of Philadelphus, was ufed here inftead of tea, and a plant called Teegoomme, refembling rug-cloaks, ferved the natives for garments. The environs of the cove where the Endeavour lay is covered entirely with wood, and the fupple jacks are fo numerous, that it is with difficulty that paffengers can purfue their way; here is a numerous fand-fly, that is very difagreeable. The tops of many hills were covered with fern. The air of the country is very moift, and has fome qualities that promote putrefaction, as birds that had been fhot but a few hours were found with maggots in them. The women who accompanied the men in their canoes, wore a head-drefs, which we had no where met with before; it was compofed of black feathers, tied in a bunch on the top of the head, which greatly increafed its height. The manner of their difpofing of their dead is very different to what is practifed in their fouthern iflands, they tie a large ftone to the body, and throw it into the fea. We faw the body of a woman who had been difpofed of this way, but which, by fome accident had difengaged itfelf from the ftone, and was floating upon the water. The captain, Mr. Banks, and the doctor vifited another cove, about two miles from the fhip. There was a family of Indians who were greatly alarmed at the approach of thefe gentlemen, all running away except one; but upon Tupia's converfing with him, the others returned. They found, by the provifions of this family, that they were cannibals, here being feveral human bones that had been lately dreffed and picked, and it appeared that a fhort time before, fix of their enemies having fallen into their hands, they had killed four and eaten them, and that the other two were drowned in endeavouring to make their efcape. They made no fecret of this abominable cuftom, but anfwered Tupia, who was defired to afcertain the fact, with great compofure, that his conjectures were juft, that they were the bones of a man, and teftified by figns, that they thought human flefh delicious food. Upon being afked, Why they had not eaten the body of the woman that had been floating upon the water? they anfwered,

She

She died of a diforder, and that moreover fhe was related to them, and they never ate any but their enemies,
Upon Mr. Banks ftill teftifying fome doubts concerning
the fact, one of the Indians drew the bone of a man's
arm through his mouth, and this gentleman had the
curiofity to bring it away with him. There was a woman in this family whofe arms and legs were cut in a
fhocking manner, and it appeared fhe had thus wounded herfelf becaufe her hufband had lately been killed
and eaten by the enemy. Some of the Indians brought
four fkulls one day to fell, which they rated at a very
high price. The brains had been taken out, and probably eaten, but the fkull and hair remained. They
feemed to have been dried by fire, in order to preferve
them from prutrefaction. The gentlemen likewife faw
the bail of a canoe, which was made of a human fkull.
On the whole their ideas were fo horrid and brutifh,
that they feemed to pride themfelves upon their cruelty
and barbarity, and took a particular pleafure in fhewing the manner in which they killed their enemies, it
being confidered as very meritorious to be expert at this
deftruction. The method ufed was to knock them
down with their patoo-patoos, and then rip up their
bellies.

Great numbers of birds ufually begun their melody
about two o'clock in the morning, and ferenaded us till
the time of their rifing. This harmony was very a-
greeable, as the fhip lay at a convenient diftance from
the fhore to hear it. Thefe feathered chorifters, like
the Englifh nightingales, never fing in the day-time.

On the 17th, the fhip was vifited by a canoe from the
hippah, or village; it contained, among others, the
aged Indian, of fuperior diftinction, who had firft vifited the Englifh upon their arrival. In a conference
which Tupia had with him, he teftified his apprehenfions, that their enemies would very foon vifit them,
and repay the compliment, for killing and eating the
four men. On the 18th we received no vifit from the
Indians; but going out in the pinnace to infpect the
bay, we faw a fingle man in a canoe fifhing, in the
manner already defcribed. It was remarkable, that
this

this man did not pay the leaft attention to the people in the pinnace, but continued to purfue his employ-ment even when we came along-fide of him, without once looking at us. Some of the Endeavour's people being on fhore, found three human hip bones, clofe to an oven; thefe were brought on board, as well as the hair of a man's head, which was found in a tree. The next day a forge was fet up to repair the iron-work; and fome Indians vifited the fhip with plenty of fifh which they bartered very fairly for nails.

On the 20th, in the morning, Mr. Banks purchafed of the old Indian a man's head, which he feemed very unwilling to part with; the fkull had been fractured by a blow, and the brains were extracted, and like the others, it was preferved from putrefaction. From the care with which they kept thefe fkulls, and the reluct-ance with which they bartered any, it was imagined they were confidered as trophies of war, and teftimo-nials of their valour. In this day's excurfion, we did not meet with a fingle native; the ground on every fide was quite uncultivated; but we difcovered a very good harbour. The fucceeding day the fhip's company were allowed to go on fhore for their amufement, and the gentlemen employed themfelves in fifhing, in which they were very fuccefsful Some of the company in their excurfion met with fortifications that had not the advantage of an elevated fituation, but were furround-ed by two or three wide ditches, with a draw-bridge, fuch as, though fimple in its ftructure, was capable of anfwering every purpofe againft the arms of the na-tives. Within thefe ditches is a fence, made with ftakes, fixed in the earth. A decifive conqueft or vic-tory over the befieged, occafions an entire depopula-tion of that diftrict, as the vanquifhed, not only thofe who are killed, but the prifoners likewife are devoured by the victors.

The 22d was employed by Mr. Banks and Dr. So-lander, in collecting of plants, whilft Capt. Cook made fome obfervations on the main land on the fouth-eaft fide of the inlet, which confifted of a chain of high hills, and formed part of the fouth-weft fide of the

the ftreight; the oppofite fide extended far to the eaft: He alfo difcovered a village, and many houfes that had been deferted, and another village that appeared to be inhabited. There were many fmall iflands round the coaft, that feemed intirely barren, and what few inha-bitants were upon them lived principally upon fifh. On the 24th, we vifited a hippah, which was fituated on a very high rock, hollow underneath, forming a fine natural arch, one fide of which joined to the land, and the other rofe out of the fea. The inhabitants re-ceived us with great civility, and very readily fhewed us every thing that was curious. This hippah was partly furrounded with palifadoes, and it had a fighting ftage, like that already defcribed. Here we met with a crofs refembling a crucifix, which was erected as a monu-ment for a deceafed perfon; but could not learn how his body was difpofed of. From a converfation that Tupia had with thefe people, a difcovery was made that an officer being in a boat near this village, and fome canoes coming off, made him imagine they had hoftile defigns, and he fired upon them with ball, which made them retire with much precipitation, but they could not effect their retreat, before one of them was wounded. What made this rafh action the more to be lamented was, that the Indians gave afterwards every poffible affurance that their intentions upon this occafion were entirely friendly.

On the 25th, the Captain, Mr. Banks, and Dr. So-lander, went on fhore to fhoot, when they met with a numerous family, who were among the creeks catching fifh: they behaved very civil, and received fome tri-fling prefents from the gentlemen, who were loaded by way of return with the kiffes and embraces of both fexes, young and old. The next day, being the 26th, they made another excurfion in the boat, in order to take a view of the ftreight, that paffes between the eaftern and weftern feas. To this end they attained the fummit of a hill, but it being hazy in the horifon, they could fee but to a fmall diftance to the eaft; how-ever, it was refolved to explore the paffage in the fhip when they fhould put to fea. Before their departure
from

from this hill, they erected a pyramid with stones, and
left some musket balls, small shot and beads, that were
likely to stand the test of time, and would be memorials, that this place had been visited by Europeans.
On our return, having descended the hill, we made a
hearty meal of the shaggs and fish, procured by our
guns and lines ; and which were dressed by the boat's
crew in the place we had appointed. Here we were re-
spectfully received by another Indian family, who
added to their civilities strong expressions of kindness
and pleasure. They shewed us where to get water,
with every other office as was in their power. From
hence we visited another hippah, seated on a rock almost inacceffible: it consisted of about one hundred
houses and a fighting stage. We made the friendly inhabitants some small presents of paper, beads, and
nails, and they in return furnished us with dried fish.
On the 27th and 28th our company were engaged in
making necessary repairs, catching fish, and getting the
Endeavour ready to continue her voyage.

On Monday the 29th, we were visited by our old
friend Topoa in company with other Indians, from
whom we heard, that the man who had received a
wound near the hippah, was dead ; but this report
proved afterwards groundless ; and we found that Topoa's discourses were not always to be taken literally.
During the time the bark was preparing for sea, Mr.
Banks and Dr. Solander often went on shore ; but their
walks were circumscribed by the luxuriant climbers'
which filled up the space between the trees, and rendered the woods impassable. Capt. Cook also made
several observations on the coast to the north-west, and
perceived many islands, forming bays, in which there
appeared to be good anchorage for shipping. He also
erected another pyramid of stones, in which he put
some bullets, &c. as before, with the addition of a
piece of our silver coin, and placed part of an old
pendant on the top, to distinguish it. Returning to
the ship he met with many of the natives, of whom he
purchased a small quantity of fish.

On Tuesday, the 30th, some of our people, who

were fent out early in the morning to gather celery, met with about twenty Indians, among whom were five or fix women, whofe hufbands had lately been made captives. They fat down upon the ground together, and cut many parts of their bodies in a moft fhocking manner, with fhells, and fharp pieces of talc or jafper, in teftimony of their exceffive grief. But what made the horrid fpectacle more terrible, was, that the male Indians who were with them, paid not the leaft attention to it, but with the greateft unconcern imaginable, employed themfelves in repairing their huts. This day the carpenter having prepared two pofts, they were fet up as memorials, being infcribed with the date of the year, the month, and the fhip's name. One of them we erected at the watering place, with the union-flag hoifted upon the top; and the other in the ifland that lies neareft the fea, called by the natives Motuara; and the inhabitants being informed, that thofe pofts were fet up to acquaint other adventurers that the Endeavour had touched at this place, they promifed never to deftroy them. Capt. Cook then gave fomething to every one prefent, and to Topoa our old friend, he prefented a filver three-pence, dated 1736, and fome fpike nails which had the king's broad arrow cut deep upon them. After which he honoured this inlet with the name of Queen Charlotte's Sound; and at the fame time took poffeffion of it in the name and for the ufe of his prefent majefty. The whole of this day's bufinefs concluded with drinking a bottle of wine to the queen's health. The bottle was given to the old man, who received the prefent with ftrong figns of joy. We muft not omit here to obferve, that Topoa being queftioned concerning a paffage into the eaftern-fea, anfwered, that there was certainly fuch a paffage. He alfo faid, that the land to the fouth-weft of the ftreight, where we then were, confifted of two whennuas or iflands, named Tovy Poenamoo, which fignifies " the water of green talc;" which might probably be the name of a place where the Indians got their green talc, or ftone, of which they make their ornaments and cutting tools. He alfo told us, there was

No. 5.   X   a third

a third whennua, eaftward of the ftreight, called Ea-
heinomauwee, of confiderable extent; the circumnavigation of which would take up many moons: he added,
that the land on the borders of the ftreight, contiguous
to this inlet, was called Tiera Witte. Having procured
this intelligence, and concluded the ceremonies at fixing
up the monumental memorial, we returned to the fhip.
The old man attended us in his canoe, and returned
home after dinner.

Wednefday the 31ft, having taken in our wood and
water, we difpatched one party to make brooms, and
another to catch fifh. Toward the clofe of the evening
we had a ftrong gale from the north-weft, with fuch
heavy fhowers, that our fweet little warblers on fhore
fufpended their wild notes, with which till now they
had conftantly ferenaded us during the night, affording
us a pleafure not to be expreffed, and the lofs of which
we could not at this time refrain from regretting.

On the 1ft of February the gale increafed to a ftorm,
with heavy gufts from the main land, which obliged us
to let go another anchor. Towards night they became
more moderate, but the rain poured down with impetuofity, that the brook at our watering place overflowed its banks, and carried away to our lofs ten cafks
full of water.

On Saturday the 3d, we went over to the hippah
on the eaft-fide of Charlotte's Sound, and procured
a confiderable quantity of fifh. The people here confirmed all that Topoa had told us refpecting the ftreight,
and the unknown country. At noon when we took
leave of them, fome fhewed figns of forrow, others of
joy that we were going. When returning to the fhip
fome of our company made an excurfion along the
fhore northward, to traffic for a further fupply of fifh,
but without fuccefs. Sunday the 4th, Mr. Banks and
Dr. Solander were engaged in collecting fhells, and different kinds of feeds.

On the 5th we got under fail, but the wind foon falling, we came again to anchor a little above Motuara.
Topoa here paid us a vifit to bid us farewell. Being
queftioned whether he had ever heard, that fuch a vef-

fel

fel as ours had ever vifited the country, he replied in the negative ; but faid, there was a tradition of a fmall veffel having come from Ulimora, a diftant country in the north, in which were only four men, who on their landing, were all put to death. The people of the Bay of Iflands and Tupia had fome confufed traditionary notions about Ulimora, but from their accounts we could draw no certain conciufion. This day Mr. Banks and Dr. Solander went again on fhore in fearch of natural curiofities, and by accident met with a very amiable Indian family, among whom was a widow, and a pretty youth about ten years of age. The woman mourned for her hufband, according to the cuftom of the country, with tears of blood; and the child, by the death of his father, was the proprietor of the land where we had cut our wood. The mother and fon were fitting upon matts, the reft of the family of both fexes, about feventeen in number, fat round them. They behaved with the utmoft hofpitality and courtefy, and endeavoured to prevail with us to ftay all night ; but expecting the fhip to fail, we could not accept of their prefling invitation. This family feemed the moft intelligent of any Indians we had hitherto coverfed with, which made us regret our late acquaintance with them ; for had we fallen into their company before, we fhould probably have gained more information from them in one day, than we had been able to acquire during our whole ftay upon the coaft.

Monday the 6th, in the morning the Endeavour failed out of the bay, which, from the favage cuftom of eating human flefh, we called Cannibal Bay. We bent our courfe to an opening in the eaft ; and when in the mouth of the ftreight were becalmed in latitude 41° fouth, and 184 deg. 45 min. weft longitude. The two points that form the entrance we called Cape Koamaro, and Point Jackfon. The land forming the harbour or cove in which we lay is called by the Indians Totarranue; the harbour itfelf, named by the captain Ship Cove, is very convenient and fafe. It is fituated on the weft-fide of the cove, and is the fouthermoft of the three coves within the ifland of Motuara, between which

and

and the iſland of Hamote, or between Motuara or weſtern-ſhore is the entrance. In the laſt of theſe inlets are two ledges of rocks, three fathom under water, which may eaſily be known by the ſea-weed that grows upon them. Attention muſt alſo be paid to the tides, which, when there is little wind, flow about nine or ten o'clock at the full and change of the moon, and riſe and fall about ſeven feet and a half, paſſing through the ſtreight from the ſouth-eaſt. The land about this ſound, which we ſaw at the diſtance of twenty leagues, conſiſts entirely of high hills, and deep valleys, well ſtored with a variety of excellent timber, fit for all purpoſes except maſts, for which it is two hard and heavy. On the ſhore we found plenty of ſhags, and a few other ſpecies of wild fowl, that are very acceptable food to thoſe who have lived long upon ſalt proviſions. The number of inhabitants is not greater than four hundred, who are ſcattered along the coaſt, and upon any appearance of danger retire to their Hippahs or forts, in which ſituation we found them. They are poor, and their canoes without ornaments. The traffic we had with them was wholly for fiſh; but they had ſome knowledge of iron, which the natives of other parts had not. On our arrival they were much pleaſed with our paper; but when they knew it would be ſpoiled by the wet, they would not have it. Engliſh broad-cloth, and red Kerſey they highly eſteemed.

Leaving the ſound we ſtood over to the eaſtward, and were carried by the rapidity of the current very cloſe to one of the two iſlands that lie off Cape Koamaroo, at the entrance of Queen Charlotte's Sound. At this time we were every moment in danger of being daſhed to pieces againſt the rocks, but after having veered out 150 fathoms of cable, the ſhip was brought up, when the rocks were not more than two cables length from us. Thus we remained, being obliged to wait for the tide's ebbing, which did not take place till after midnight.

On the 7th, at eight o'clock in the morning we weighed anchor, and a freſh breeze with a tide of ebb hurried us through the ſtreight with great ſwiftneſs.

The

The narroweft part of this ftraight lies between Cape Tierrawitte and Cape Koamaroo, the diftance between which we judged to be five leagues. The length of the ftraight we could not determine. In pafling it, we think it fafeft to keep to the north-eaft fhore, for on this fide we faw nothing to fear. Cape Tierrawitte lies in 41 deg. 44 min. of fouth latitude, and 183 deg. 45 min. of weft longitude. And Cape Koamaroo is 41 deg. 34 min. fouth, and in 113 deg. 30 min. weft longitude. About nine leagues from the former cape, and under the fame fhore north, is a high ifland, which the captain called Entry Ifle. We were now facing a deep bay which we called Cloudy Bay. Some of our gentlemen doubting whether Eahienomauwee was an ifland, we fteered fouth-eaft, in order to clear up this doubt; but the wind fhifting we ftood caftward, and fteered north-eaft by eaft all night. The next morning they were off Cape Pallifer, and found that the land ftretched away to the north-eaftward of Cape Turnagain. In the afternoon, three canoes came off, having feveral Indians on board. Thefe made a good appearance, and were ornamented like thofe on the northern coaft. There was no difficulty in perfuading them to come on board, where they demeaned themfelves very civilly; and a mutual exchange of prefents took place. As they afked for nails it was concluded that they heard of the Englifh, by means of the inhabitants of fome of the other places at which we had touched. Their drefs refembled that of the natives of Hudfon's Bay. One old man was tataowed in a very particular manner, he had likewife a red ftreak acrofs his nofe; and his hair and beard were remarkable for their whitenefs. The upper garment that he wore was made of flax, and had a wrought border: under this was a fort of petticoat of a cloth called Aooree Waow. Teeth aud green ftones decorated his ears: he fpoke in a foft and low key, and it was concluded, from his deportment, that he was a perfon of diftinguifhed rank among his countrymen, and thefe people withdrew greatly fatisfied with the prefents that they had received.

On the 9th, in the morning, we difcovered that Eahienomauwee

Eahienomauwee was really an island. About sixty
Indians in four double canoes came within a stone's
throw of the ship, on the 14th of February. As they
surveyed her with surprize, Tupia endeavoured to per-
suade them to come nearer, but this they could not be
prevailed on to do. On this account the island was denominated the Island of Lookers-on. Five leagues
distant from the coast of Tovy Poenamoo, we saw an
island which was called after Mr. Banks's name; a
few Indians appeared on it, and in one place they difcovered a smoke, so that it was plain the place was inhabited. Mr. Banks going out in his boat for the purpose of shooting, killed some of the Port Egmont hens,
which were like thofe found on the isle of Fare, and
the first that they had seen upon this coast. A point
of land was observed on Sunday the 25th, in latitude
45 deg. 35 min. south, to which Capt. Cook gave the
name of Cape Saunders, in honour of Admiral Saunders. We kept off from the shore, which appeared to
be interspersed with trees, and covered with green hills,
but no inhabitants were difcovered.

On the 4th of March, several whales and seals were
seen; and on the 9th we saw a ledge of rocks, and soon
after another ledge at three leagues diftance from the
shore, which we passed in the night to the northward,
and at day-break observed the others under our bows,
which was a fortunate escape; and in consideration of
their having been so nearly caught among these, they
were denominated the Traps. We called the southern-
most point of land, the South Cape, and found it to
be the southern extremity of the whole coast. Proceeding northward, the next day we fell in with a barren rock about fifteen miles from the main land,
which was very high, and appeared to be about a mile
in circumference; and this was named Solander's
Island.

On the 13th, we difcovered a bay containing several
islands, where we concluded if there was depth of water,
shipping might find shelter from all winds. Dusky
Bay was the appellation given to it by the captain, and
five high peaked rocks, for which it was remarkable,
caused

caufed the point to be called Five Fingers. The wef-
termoft point of land upon the whole coaft, to the
fouthward of Dufky Bay, we called Weft Cape. The
next day we paffed a fmall narrow opening, where
there feemed to be a good harbour formed by an ifland,
the land behind which exhibited a profpect of mountains covered with fnow.

On the 16th, we paffed a point which confifted of
high red cliffs, and received the name of Cafcade Point,
on account of feveral fmall ftreams which fell down it.
In the morning of the 18th the valleys were obferved
covered with fnow as well as the mountains, which
feemed to have fallen the night before, when we had
rain at fea. Thus we paffed the whole north-weft coaft
of Tovy Poenamoo, which had nothing worth our obfervation but a ridge of naked and barren rocks covered
with fnow, fome of which we conjectured might probably have remained there ever fince the creation. As
far as the eye could reach, the profpects were in general
wild, craggy, and defolate; fcarcely any thing but rocks
to be feen, the moft of which Dr. Hawkefworth def-
cribes as having nothing but a kind of hollows, and
dreadful fiffures inftead of valleys between them. From
this uncomfortable country we determined to depart,
having failed round the whole country by the 27th of
this month. Capt. Cook therefore went on fhore in
the long-boat, and having found a place proper for
mooring the fhip, and a good watering place, the crew
began to fill their cafks, while the carpenter was employed in cutting wood. The captain, Mr. Banks, and
Dr. Solander, went in the pinnace to examine the bay,
and the neighbouring country. Landing there they
found feveral plants of a fpecies which was before unknown to them ; no inhabitants appeared ; but they
faw feveral huts which feemed to have been deferted a
long time before: all the wood and water being taken
on board, the veffel was ready to fail by the time that
they returned in the evening, and it was now refolved
at a council of war to fteer for the coaft of New Holland, in the courfe of their return by the way of the
Eaft-Indies.

I On

On the 31ft, we took our departure from an eaftern point of land, to which we gave the name of Cape Farewel, calling the bay out of which we failed, Admiralty Bay; and two capes, Cape Stephens, and Cape Jackfon, (the names of the two fecretaries of the Admiralty board.) We called a bay between the ifland and Cape Farewell, Blind Bay, which was fuppofed to have been the fame that was called Murderers Bay, by Tafman, the firft difcoverer of New Zealand, but though he named it Staten Ifland, wifhing to take poffeffion of it for the States General, yet being attacked here by the Indians he never went on fhore to effect his purpofe. This coaft, now more accurately examined, is difcovered to confift of two iflands, which were before thought to be a part of the fouthern continent fo much fought after.

They are fituated between the 34th and 48th deg. of fouth latitude, and between 181 deg. and 194 deg. weft longitude. The northern ifland is called Eahienomauwee, and the fouthern is named Tovy Poenamoo by the natives. The former, though mountainous in fome places, is ftored with wood, and in every valley there is a rivulet. The foil in thofe valleys is light, but fertile and well adapted for the plentiful production of all the fruits, plants and corn of Europe. The fummer, though not hotter, is in general of a more equal temperature than in England; and from the vegetables that were found here it was concluded, that the winters were not fo fevere. The only quadrupeds that were difcovered were dogs and rats, and of the latter very few, but the former the inhabitants (like thofe of Otaheite) breed for food. There are feals and whales on the coafts, and we once faw a fea-lion. The birds are hawks, owls, quails, and fome melodious fong birds. There are ducks, and fhags of feveral forts, like thofe of Europe, and the gannet, which is of the fame fort. Albetroffes, fheerwaters, penguins, and pintados, alfo vifit the coaft. The infects found here are, butterflies, flefh-flies, beetles, fand flies, and mufquitos.

Tovy Poenamoo is barren and mountainous, and appeared to be almoft deftitute of inhabitants.

The fea that wafhes thefe iflands abounds with delicate and wholefome fifh. Whenever the veffel came to an anchor, enough were caught with hook and line only, to fupply the whole fhip's company; and when we fifhed with nets, every mefs in the fhip, where the people were induftrious, falted as much as fupplied them for feveral weeks. There were many forts of fifh here which we had never before feen, and which the failors named according to their fancies. They were fold on moderate terms to the crew: among the reft, fifh like the fkate, eels, congers, oyfters, flat-fifh refembling foles and flounders, cockles and various forts of mackarel were found in abundance upon the coaft.

Here are forefts abounding with trees, producing large, ftrait and clean timber. One tree about the fize of our oak, was diftinguifhed by a fcarlet flower, compofed of feveral fibres, and another which grows in fwampy ground, very ftrait and tall, bearing fmall bunches of berries, and a leaf refembling that of the yew-tree. About 400 fpecies of plants were found, all of which are unknown in England, except garden night-fhade, fow thiftle, two or three kinds of fern, and one or two forts of grafs. We found wild celery, and a kind of creffes, in great abundance, on the fea-fhore; and of eatable plants raifed by cultivation, only cocoas, yams, and fweet potatoes. There are plantations of many acres of thefe yams and potatoes. The inhabitants likewife cultivate the gourd; and the Chinefe paper mulberry-tree is to be found, but in no abundance.

In New Zealand is only one fhrub or tree, which produces fruit, which is a kind of berry almoft taftelefs; but they have a plant which anfwers all the ufes of hemp and flax. There are two kinds of this plant, the leaves of one of which are yellow, and the other a deep red, and both of them refemble the leaves of flags. Of thefe leaves they make lines and cordage, and much ftronger than any thing of the kind in Europe. Thefe leaves they likewife fplit into breadths, and tying the flips together, form their fifhing nets. Their common apparel, by a fimple procefs, is made from the leaves, and their finer, by another preparation, is made from

No. 6.   Y   the

the fibres. This plant is found both in high and low ground, in dry mould and in deep bogs; but as it grows largeft in the latter, that feems to be its proper foil,

The natives are as large as the largeft Europeans. Their complexion is brown, but little more fo than that of a Spaniard. They are full of flefh, but not lazy and luxurious; and are ftout and well fhaped. The women poffefs not that delicacy, which diftinguifhes the European ladies; but their voice chiefly diftinguifhes them from the men. The men are active in a high degree; their hair is black, and their teeth are white and even. The features of both fexes are regular; they enjoy perfect health, and live to an advanced age. They appeared to be of a gentle difpofition, and treat each other with the utmoft kindnefs; but they are per- petually at war, every little diftrict being at enmity with all the reft. This is owing, moft probably, to the want of food in fufficient quantities at certain times. As they have neither black cattle, fheep, hogs, nor goats; fo their chief food was fifh, which being not always to be had, they are in danger of dying through hunger. They have a few dogs; and when no fifh is to be gotten, they have only vegetables, fuch as yams and potatoes, to feed on: and if by any accident thefe fail them, their fituation muft be deplorable. Not- withftanding the cuftom of eating their enemies, the circumftances and temper of thefe people is in fa- vour of thofe who might fettle among them as a co- lony.

The inhabitants of New Zealand are as modeft and referved in their behaviour and converfation as the moft polite nations of Europe. The women, indeed, were not dead to the fofter impreffions; but their mode of confent was in their idea as harmlefs as the confent to marriage with us, and equally binding for the ftipu- lated time. If any of the Englifh addreffed one of their women, he was informed, that the confent of her friends muft be obtained, which ufually followed, on his ma- king a prefent. This done he was obliged to treat his temporary wife as delicately as we do in England. A gentleman

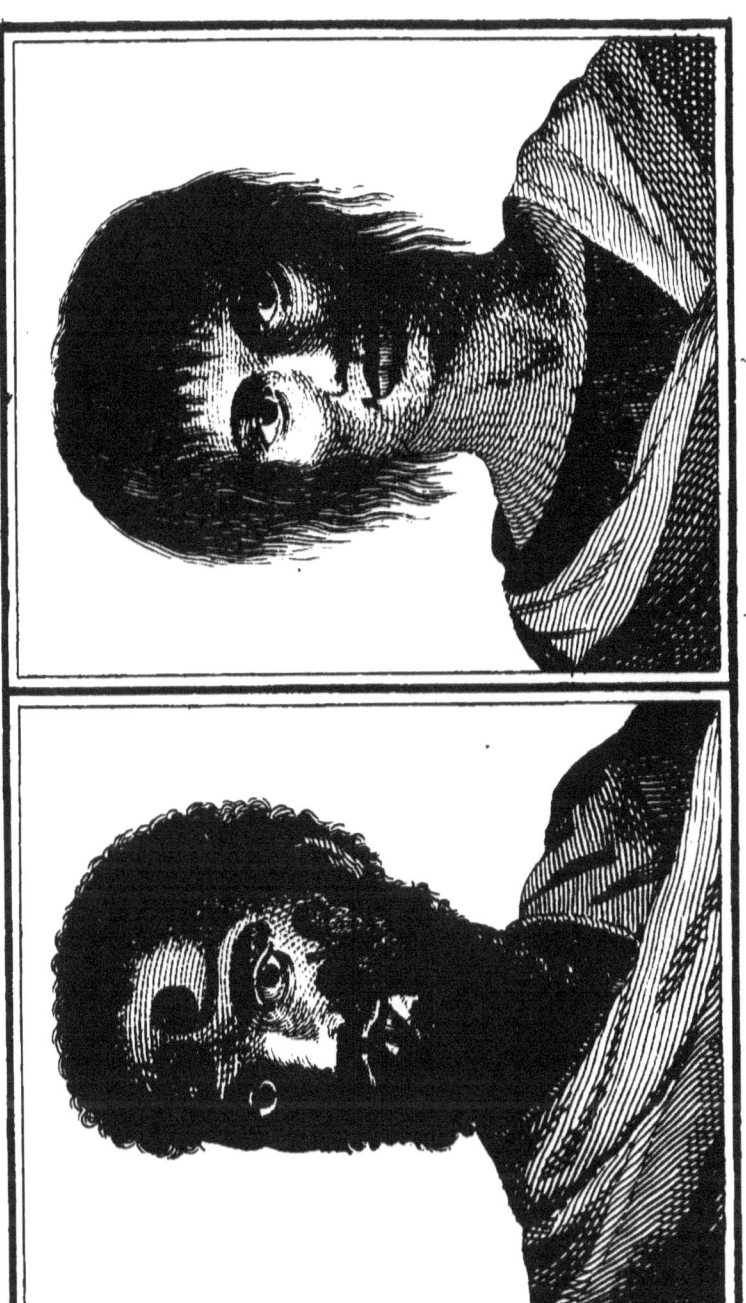

A MAN of NEW-ZEALAND. A WOMAN of NEW-ZEALAND.

gentleman who failed in the Endeavour, having addressed a family of some rank, received an answer, of which the following is an exact translation. " Any of " these young ladies will think themselves honoured by " your addresses, but you must first make me a present, " and you must then come and sleep with us on shore, " for day-light must by no means be a witness of what " passes between you."

These Indians anoint their hair with oil melted from the fat of fish or birds. The poor people use that which is rancid, so that they smell very disagreeable; but those of superior rank make use of that which is fresh. They wear combs both of bone and wood, which is considered as an ornament when stuck upright in the hair. The men tie their hair in a bunch on the crown of the head, and adorn it with feathers of birds, which they likewise sometimes place on each side of the temples. They commonly wear short beards. The hair of the women sometimes flows over their shoulders, and sometimes is cut short. Both sexes, but the men more than the women, mark their bodies with black stains, called amoco. In general the women stain only the lips, but sometimes mark other parts with black patches: the men on the contrary put on additional marks from year to year, so that those who are very ancient are almost covered. Exclusive of the amoco, they mark themselves with furrows. Those furrows made a hideous appearance, the edges being indented, and the whole quite black. The ornaments of the face are drawn in the spiral form with equal elegance and correctness, both cheeks being marked exactly alike; while paintings on their bodies resemble fillagree work, and the foliage in old chafed ornaments; but no two faces or bodies are painted exactly after the same model. The people of New Zealand, frequently left the breech free from these marks, which the inhabitants of Otaheite adorned beyond any other. These Indians likewise paint their bodies by rubbing them with red ocre, either dry or mixed with oil.

Their dress is formed of the leaves of the flag split into slips, which are interwoven and made into a kind

of

of matting, the ends, which are feven or eight inches in length, hanging out on the upper fide. One piece of this matting being tied over the fhoulders, reaches to the knees : the other piece being wrapped round the waift falls almoft to the ground. Thefe two pieces are faftened to a ftring, which by means of a bodkin of bone is paffed through, and tacks them together. The men wear the lower garment only at particular times.

They have two kinds of cloth befides the coarfe matting or fhag above-mentioned ; one of which is as coarfe, but beyond all proportion ftronger than the Englifh canvas ; the other which is formed of the fibres of a plant, drawn into threads which crofs and bind each other, refembles the matting on which we place our difhes at table.

They make boarders of different colours to both thefe forts of cloth, refembling girls famplers, and finifhed with great neatnefs and elegance. What they confider as the moft ornamental part of their drefs is the fur of dogs, which they cut into ftripes, and few on different parts of their apparel. As dogs are not plenty, they difpofe their ftripes with œconomy. They have a few dreffes-ornamented with feathers; and one man was feen covered wholly with thofe of the red parrot.

The women never tie their hair on the top of their head, nor adorn it with feathers ; and are lefs anxious about drefs than the men. Their lower garment is bound tight round them, except when they go out fifhing, and then they are careful that the men fhall not fee them. It once happened that fome of the fhip's crew furprifed them in this fituation, when fome of them hid themfelves among the rocks, and the reft kept their bodies under water till they had formed a girdle and apron of weeds; and their whole behaviour manifefted the moft refined ideas of female modefty.

The ears of both fexes were bored, and the holes ftretched fo as to admit a man's finger. The ornaments of their ears are feathers, cloth, bones, and fome-times bits of wood ; a great many of them made ufe of the nails which were given them by the Englifh, for this purpofe, and the women fometimes adorned
their

their ears with white down of the albetrofs, which they fpread before and behind the whole in a large bunch. They likewife hung to their ears by ftrings, chiffels, bodkins, the teeth of dogs, and the teeth and nails of their deceafed friends. The arms and ancles of the women are adorned with fhells and bones, or any thing elfe through which they can pafs a ftring. The men wear a piece of green talc or whalebone, with the refemblance of a man carved on it, hanging to a ftring round the neck. We faw one man who had the griftle of his nofe perforated, and a feather paffed through it, projecting over each cheek.

Thefe people fhew lefs ingenuity in the ftructure of their houfes, than in any thing elfe belonging to them ; they are from fixteen to twenty-four feet long, ten or twelve wide, and fix or eight in height. The frame is of flight fticks of wood, and the walls and roof are made of dry grafs pretty firmly compacted. Some of them are lined with bark of trees, and the ridge of the houfe is formed by a pole which runs from one end to the other. The door is only high enough to admit a perfon crawling on hands and knees, and the roof is floping. There is a fquare hole near the door, ferving both for window and chimney, near which is the fire place. A plank is placed over the door, adorned with a fort of carving, and this they confider as an ornamental piece of furniture. The fide-walls and roof projecting two or three feet beyond the walls at each end form a fort of portico where benches are placed to fit on. The fire is made in the middle of a hollow fquare in the floor, which is inclofed with wood or ftone. They fleep near the walls, where the ground is covered with ftraw for their beds. Some who can afford it, whofe families are large, have three or four houfes, inclofed in their court-yard. Their clothes, arms, feathers, fome ill made tools, and a cheft, in which all thefe are depofited, form all the furniture of the infide of the houfe Their hammers to beat fern-root, gourds to hold water, and bafkets to contain provifions, are placed without the houfe. One houfe was found near 40 feet long, 20 wide, and 14 high. Its fides were

adorned

adorned with carved planks of workmanſhip ſuperior to the reſt; but the building appeared to have been left unfiniſhed. Though the people ſleep warm enough at home, they ſeem to deſpiſe the inclemency of the weather, when they go in ſearch of fiſh or fern roots. Sometimes, indeed, they place a ſmall defence to windward, but frequently ſleep undreſſed with their arms placed round them, without the leaſt ſhelter whatever.

Beſides the fern-root, which ſerves them for bread, they feed on albetroſſes, penguins, and ſome other birds. Whatever they eat is either roaſted or baked, as they have no veſſel in which water can be boiled. We ſaw no plantations of cocoas, potatoes, and yams, to the ſouthward, though there were many in the northern parts. The natives drink no other liquor than water, and enjoy perfect and uninterrupted health. When wounded in battle, the wound heals in a very ſhort time without the application of medicine; and the very old people carry no other marks of decay about them than the loſs of their hair, and teeth, and a failure of their muſcular ſtrength: but enjoy an equal ſhare of health and chearfulneſs with the youngeſt.

The canoes of this country are not unlike the whale-boats of New England, being long and narrow. The larger ſort ſeem to be built for war, and will hold from 30 to 100 men. One of theſe at Tolaga meaſured near 70 feet in length, ſix in width, and four in depth. It was ſharp at the bottom, and conſiſted of three lengths, about two or three inches thick, and tied firmly together with ſtrong plaiting; each ſide was found of one entire plank, about twelve inches broad, and about an inch and a half thick, which was fitted to the bottom part with equal ſtrength and ingenuity. Several thwarts were laid from one ſide to the other, to which they were ſecurely faſtened, in order to ſtrengthen the canoes. Some few of their canoes at Mercury Bay and Opooragc, are all made entirely of one trunk of wood, which is made hollow by fire; but by far the greater part are built after the plan above deſcribed. The ſmaller boats which are uſed chiefly in fiſhing, are adorned at head and ſtern with the figure of a man, the

3   eyes

eyes of which are compofed of white fhells: a tongue of enormous fize is thruft out of the mouth, and the whole face a picture of the moft abfolute deformity. The grander canoes, which are intended for war, are ornamented with open work, and covered with fringes of black feathers, which gives the whole an air of per-fect elegance; the fide-boards which are carved in a rude manner, are embellifhed with tufts of white fea-thers. Thefe veffels are rowed with a kind of paddles, between five and fix feet in length, the blade of which is a long oval, gradually decreafing till it reaches the handle; and the velocity with which they row with thefe paddles is very furprifing. Their fails are com-pofed of a kind of mat or netting, which is extended between two upright poles, one of which is fixed on each fide. Two ropes, faftened to the top of each pole, ferve inftead of fheets. The veffels are fteered by two men having fuch a paddle, and fitting in the ftern; but they can only fail before the wind, in which direction they move with confiderable fwiftnefs.

The Indians ufe axes, adzes, and chiffels, with which laft they likewife bore holes. The chiffels are made of jafper, or of the bone of a man's arm; their axes and adzes of a hard black ftone. They ufe their fmall jafper tools till they are blunted, and then throw them away, having no inftrument to fharpen them with. The Indians at Tolaga having been prefented with a piece of glafs, drilled a hole through it, and hung it round the neck. A fmall bit of jafper was thought to have been the tool they ufed in drilling it.

Their tillage is excellent, owing to the neceffity they are under of cultivating or running the rifque of ftarv-ing. At Tegadoo their crops were juft put into the ground, and the furface of the field was as fmooth as a garden, the roots were ranged in regular lines, and to every root there remained a hillock. A long narrow ftake, fharpened to an edge at bottom, with a piece fixed acrofs a little above it, for the convenience of driving it into the ground with the foot, fupplies the place both of plough and fpade. The foil being light, their work is not very laborious, and with this inftru-ment

ment alone they will turn up ground of fix or feven
acres in extent.

The feine, the large net which has been already noticed, is produced by the united labour, and is probably the joint property of a whole town.   Their fifh-
hooks are of fhell or bone ; and they have bafkets of
wicker-work to hold the fifh.   Their warlike weapons
are fpears, darts, battle-axes, and the patoo-patoo.
The fpear, which is pointed at each end, is about fixteen feet in length, and they hold it in the middle, fo ·
that it is difficult to parry a pufh from it.   Whether
they fight in boats or on fhore the battle is hand to hand,
fo that they muft make bloody work of it.   They
truft chiefly in the patoo-patoo, which is faftened to
their wrifts, by means of a ftrong ftrap, that it may
not be wrefted out of their hands.   Thefe are worn in
the girdles of people of a fuperior rank, as a military
ornament.   They have a kind of ftaff of diftinction,
which is carried by the principal warriors.   It is formed
of a whale's rib, is quite white, and adorned with
carving, feathers, and the hair of their dogs.   Sometimes they had a ftick fix feet long, inlaid with fhells,
and otherwife ornamented like a military ftaff.   This
honourable mark of diftinction was commonly in the
hands of the aged, who were alfo more daubed with
the amoco.

When they came to attack us, one or more of thefe
old men thus diftinguifhed, were ufually in each canoe.
It is their cuftom to ftop about 50 or 60 yards from a
fhip, when the chiefs rifing from their feat, put on a
dog's fkin garment, and, holding out their decorated
ftaff, direct them how to proceed.   When they were
too far from the fhip to reach it with their miffile weapons, then the defiance was given, and the words
ufually were Karomai haromai, harre uta a patoo-patoo, " Come on fhore, come on fhore, and we will
kill you all with our patoo-patoos."   While they thus
threatened us, they approached gradually the bark, till
clofe along-fide ; yet talking at intervals in a peaceable·
manner, and anfwering whatever queftions we afked
them.   Then again their menaces were renewed, till
                                                   encouraged

encouraged by our fuppofed timidity, they began the war-fong and dance, the fure prelude of an attack, which always followed, and fometimes continued until the firing of fmall fhot repulfed them ; but at others, they vented their paffion, by throwing a few ftones at the fhip, in the way of infulting us.

The contortions of thefe favage Indians are nume-rous; their limbs are diftorted, and their faces are agitated with ftrange convulfive motions. Their tongue hangs out of their mouths to an amazing length, and their eye-lids are drawn fo as to form a circle round the eye. At the fame time they fhake their darts, brandifh their fpears, and wave their patoo-patoos to and fro in the air. There is an admirable vigour and activity in their dancing; and in their fong they keep time with fuch exactnefs, that 60 or 100 paddles when ftruck againft the fides of their boats at once, make only a fingle report. In times of peace they fometimes fing in a manner refembling the war-fong, but the dance is omitted. The women, whofe voices are exceeding melodious and foft, fing likewife in a mufical, but mournful manner. One of their in-ftruments of mufic is a fhell, from which they produce a found not unlike that made with a common horn ; the other is a fmall wooden pipe, refembling a child's nine-pin, not fuperior in found to a child's whiftle. We never heard them attempt to fing to them, or to produce any meafured notes like what we call a tune.

As to the horrid cuftom of eating human flefh, pre-valent among them, to what has been already faid on this head, we fhall only add, that in moft of the coves, upon landing, we found near the places where fires had been made, flefh bones of men ; and among the heads that were brought on board, fome of them had a kind of falfe eyes, and ornaments in their cars, as if alive. The head purchafed by Mr. Banks, and fold with great reluctance, was that of a young perfon, and, by the contufions on one fide, appeared to have received many violent blows. There had been lately a fkirmifh, and we fuppofed the young man had been killed with the reft.

No. 6.　　　　　　Z　　　　　　The

The hippahs or villages of thefe people, of which there are feveral between the bay of Plenty and Queen Charlotte's found, are all fortified. In thefe they conftantly refide; but near Tolaga, Hawk's Bay, and Poverty Bay, only fingle houfes are to be feen, at a confiderable diftance from each other. On the fides of the hills were erected long ftages, fupplied with darts and ftones, thought by us to be retreats in time of action; as it appeared that from fuch places they could combat with their enemies to great advantage. A magazine of provifions, confifting of dried fifh, and fern roots, was alfo difcovered in thefe fortifications.

The inhabitants of this part of the country were all fubjects of Teratu, who refided near the Bay of Plenty; and to their being thus united under one chief, they owed a fecurity unknown to thofe of other parts. Several inferior governors are in the dominions of Teratu, to whom the moft implicit obedience is paid. One of the inhabitants having robbed a failor belonging to the Endeavour, complaint was made to a chief, who chaftized the thief by kicking and ftriking him, which correction he bore with unrefifting humility. The inhabitants of the fouthern parts formed little focieties, who had all things in common, particularly fifhing nets and fine apparel. The latter, probably obtained in war, were kept in a little hut, deftined for that ufe, in the center of the town, and the feveral parts of the nets, being made by different families, were afterwards joined together for public ufe. Lefs account, in the opinion of Tupia, is made of the women here than in the South Sea iflands. Both fexes eat together; but how they divide their labour, we cannot determine with certainty, though we are inclined to believe that the men cultivate the ground, make nets, catch birds, and go out in their canoes to fifh; while the women are employed in weaving cloth, collecting fhell-fifh, and in dreffing food.

As to the religion of thefe people, they acknowledge one Supreme Being, and feveral fubordinate deities. Their mode of worfhip we could not learn, nor was any place proper for that purpofe feen. There was indeed

deed a fmall fquare area, encompaffed with ftones, in the middle of which hung a bafket of fern-roots on one of their fpades. This they faid was an offering to their gods, to obtain from them a plentiful crop of provifions. They gave the fame account of the origin of the world, and the production of mankind, as our friends in Otaheite. Tupia, however, feemed to have much more deep and extenfive knowledge of thefe fubjects than any of the people of this ifland, and when he fometimes delivered a long difcourfe, he was fure of a numerous audience, who heard with remarkable reverence and attention.

With regard to the manner of difpofing of their dead, we could form no certain opinion. The fouthern diftrict faid, they difpofed of their dead by throwing them into the fea; but thofe of the north buried them in the ground. We faw, however, not the leaft fign of any grave or monument; but the body of many among the living, bore the marks of wounds, in token of grief for the lofs of their friends and relations. Some of their fcars were newly made, a proof that their friends had died while we were there; yet no one faw any thing like a funeral ceremony or proceffion, the reafon is, becaufe they affected to conceal every thing refpecting the dead with the utmoft fecrecy.

We obferved a great fimilitude between the drefs, furniture, boats, and nets of the New Zealanders, and the natives of the South Sea iflands, which evidently demonftrates that the common anceftors of both were *ab origine* natives of the fame country. Indeed the inhabitants of thefe different places have a tradition, that their anceftors fprang from another country many years fince, and they both agree that this country was called Heawige. This is alfo certain, that Tupia when he accofted the people here in the language of his own country, was perfectly underftood; but perhaps a yet ftronger proof that their origin was the fame, will arife from a fpecimen of their language, which we fhall evince by a lift of words in both languages, according to the dialect of the northern and fouthern iflands of which New Zealand confifts; whence it will appear,

that

that the language of Otaheite does not differ more
from that of New Zealand, than the language of the
two iflands from each other.

The LANGUAGE of

NEW ZEALAND.		OTAHEITE.	ENGLISH.
Northern.	*Southern.*		
Eareete	Eareete	Earee	*A chief.*
Taata	Taata	Taata	*A man.*
Whahine	Whahine	Ivahine	*A woman.*
Eupo	Heaowpoho	Eupo	*The head.*
Macauwe	Heoo-oo	Roourou	*The hair.*
Terringa	Hetaheyei	Terrea	*The ear.*
Erai	Hcai	Erai	*The forehead.*
Mata	Hemata	Mata	*The eyes.*
Paparinga	Hepapaeh	Paparea	*The cheeks.*
Ahewh	Heeih	Ahew	*The nofe.*
Hangoutou	Hegaowai	Outou	*The mouth.*
Ecouwai	Hakaoewai	——	*The chin.*
Haringaringu	——	Rema	*The arm.*
Maticara	Hermaigawh	Maneow	*The finger.*
Ateraboo	——	Oboo	*The belly.*
Apeto	Heeapeto	Peto	*The navel.*
Haromai	Heromai	Harromai	*Come hither.*
Heica	Heica	Eyea	*Fiſh.*
Kooura	Kooura	Tooura	*A lobſter.*
Taro	Taro	Taro	*Cocoas.*
Cumala	Cumala	Cumala	*Potatoes.*
Tuphwhe	Tuphwhe	Tuphwhe	*Yams.*
Mannu	Mannu	Mannu	*Birds.*
Kaoura	Kaoura	Oure	*No.*
Tahai	——	Tahai	*One.*
Rua	——	Rua	*Two.*
Torou	——	Torou	*Three.*
Ha	——	Hea	*Four.*
Rema	——	Rema	*Five.*
Ono	——	Ono	*Six.*
Etu	——	Hetu	*Seven.*
Warou	——	Warou	*Eight.*
Iva	——	Heva	*Nine.*
		Angahourou	

NEW ZEALAND.		OTAHEITE.	ENGLISH.
Northern.	Southern.		
Angahourou	——	Ahourou	*Ten.*
Hennihew	Hencaho	Nihio	*The teeth.* .
Mehow	——	Mattai	*The wind.*
Amootoo	—·——	Teto	*A thief.*
Mataketake	——	Mataitai	*To examine.*
Eheara	——	Heiva	*To sing.*
Keno	Keno	Eno	*Bad.*
Eratou	Eratou	Eraou	*Trees.*
Toubouna	Toubouna	Toubouna	*Grandfather.*
Owy Terra	———	Owy Terra	{ *What do you call this or that.*

Hence it appears evidently that the language of New Zealand and Otaheite, is radically one and the fame. The dialect indeed is different as in England, where the word is pronounced *gate* in Middlefex, and *geate* in Yorkfhire ; and as the northern and fouthern words were taken down by two different perfons, one might poffibly ufe more words than the other to exprefs the fame found. Befides, in the fouthern parts they put the articles *ke* or *ko* before a noun, as we do thofe of *the* or *a :* it is alfo common to add the word *oeia* after another word, as we fay *certainly,* or *yes indeed* ; and by not attending fufficiently to this, our gentlemen fometimes, judging by the ear only, formed words of an enormous length : for example, one of them afking a native the name of the ifland, called Matuaro, he replied, with the particle *ke* prefixed *Ke-matuaro* ; and upon the queftion being repeated, the Indian added *oeia,* which made the word *Ke-matuaro-oeia ;* and upon infpecting the log-book, Capt. Cook found Matuaro transformed into *Cumettiwarroweia.* Now a fimilar orthographical difference might happen, or a like miftake might be made by a foreigner in writing an Englifh word. Suppofe a New Zealander to enquire, when near to afk, *What village is this?* The anfwer might be, *It is Hackney indeed.* The Indian then for the information of his countrymen, had he the ufe of letters, might record,

record, that he had paffed through, or been at a place called by the Englifh *Itifhackneyindeed*. We were ourfelves at firft led into many ridiculous miftakes, from not knowing that the article ufed in the South-Sea Iflands, is *to* or *ta*, inftead of *ke* or *ko*.

We have fuppofed, that the original inhabitants of thefe iflands, and thofe in the South-Seas, came from the fame country; but what country that is, or where fituated, remains ftill a fubject of enquiry. In this we all agreed, that the original natives were not of America, which lies to the eaftward; and unlefs there fhould be a continent to the fouthward, in a temperate latitude, we cannot but conclude that they emigrated from the weftward.

Before we clofe this account of New Zealand, we beg leave farther to obferve, that hitherto our navigation has been very unfavourable to the fuppofition of a Southern Continent. The navigators who have fupported the pofitions upon which this is founded, are Tafman, Juan Fernandes, Hermite, Quiros, and Roggewein; but the track of the Endeavour has totally fubverted all their theoretical arguments. Upon a view of the chart it will appear, that a large fpace extends quite to the tropics, which has not been explored by us nor any other navigators; yet we believe there is no cape of any Southern Continent, and no Southern Continent to the northward of 40 deg. fouth. Of what may lie farther to the fouthward of 40 deg. we can give no opinion; yet are far from difcouraging any future attempts after new difcoveries: for a voyage like this may be of public utility. Should no continent be found, new iflands within the tropics may be difcovered. Tupia in a rough chart of his own drawing laid down no lefs than feventy-four; and he gave us an account of above one hundred and thirty, which no European veffel has ever yet vifited.

C H A P. VIII.

*Paffage from New Zealand to Botany Bay, in New Hol-
land—Various Incidents related—A Defcription of the
Country and its Inhabitants—The Endeavour fails from
Botany Bay to Trinity Bay—With a further Account of
the Country—Her dangerous Situation in her Paffage
from Trinity Bay to Endeavour River.*

ON Saturday the 31ft of March, 1770, we failed
from Cape Farewell, having fine weather and a
fair wind. This cape lies in latitude 40 deg. 33 min.
S. and in 186 deg. W. longitude. The fame day we
fteered weftward, with a frefh gale till the 2nd of
April, when by obfervation we found our latitude to be
40 deg. and our longitude from Cape Farewell, 2 deg.
31 min. Weft. On the ninth in the morning, when in
latitude 38 deg. 29 min. S. we faw a tropic bird, a fight
very unufual in fo high a latitude. On the 15th we faw
an egg bird, and a gannet. As thefe birds never go
far from land we founded all night, but had no ground
at 130 fathom water. The day following a fmall land
bird perched on the rigging, but we had no ground at
120 fathom. Tuefday the 17th, we had frefh gales
with fqualls and dark weather in the morning; and in
the afternoon a hard gale and a great fea from the
fouthward, which obliged us to run under our fore-fail
and mizen all night. On the 18th in the morning,
we were vifited by a pintado bird, and fome Port-
Egmont hens, an infallible fign that land was near,
which we difcovered at fix o'clock in the morning of the
19th, four or five leagues diftant. To the fouthermoft
point in fight, we gave the name of Point Hicks, the
name of our firft lieutenant who difcovered it. At
noon, in latitude 37 deg. 5 min. and 210 deg. 29 min.
W. longitude, another remarkable point of the fame
land bore N. 20 E. diftant about four leagues. This
point rifing in a round hillock, extremely like the Ram

4   Head

Head at the entrance of Plymouth Sound, Capt. Cook
therefore gave it the same name. What we had yet
seen of the land was low and level; the shore white and
sandy; and the inland parts covered with wood and
verdure. At this time we saw three water-spouts at
once; two between us and the shore, and the third at
some distance upon our larboard quarter. In the
evening, at six o'clock, the northermost point of land
was distant about two leagues, which we named Cape
Howe. On the following day we had a distant view of
the country, which was in general covered with wood,
and interspersed with several small lawns. It appeared
to be inhabited, as smoke was seen in several places.
At four o'clock the next morning, we saw a high mountain, which from its shape, was called Mount Dromedary, under which there is a point which received the
name of Point Dromedary. In the evening we were
opposite a point of land which rose perpendicular, and
was called Point Upright. On Sunday the 22d, we
were so near the shore, as to see several of the inhabitants on the coast, who were of a very dark complexion,
if not perfect negroes. At noon we saw a remarkable
pecked hill, to which the captain gave the name of the
Pigeon House, from its resemblance of such a building.
The trees on this island were both tall and large,
but we saw no place fit to give shelter even to a boat.

The captain gave the name of Cape George to a
point of land discovered on St. George's-day, two
leagues to the north of which the sea formed a bay,
which, from its shape, was called Long Nose; eight
leagues from which lies Red Point, so called from the
colour of the soil in its neighbourhood. On the 27th,
we saw several inhabitants walking along the shore,
four of them carrying a canoe on their shoulders, but
as they did not attempt to come off to the ship, the
captain took Messrs. Banks and Solander, and Tupia in
the yawl, and employed four men to row them to that
part of the shore where they saw the natives, near which
four small canoes lay close in land. The Indians sat
on the rocks till the yawl was a quarter of a mile from
the shore, and then they ran away into the woods. The
surf

furf beating violently on the beech, prevented the boat
from landing; the gentlemen were therefore obliged to
make what obfervations they could at a diftance. The
canoes refembled generally the fmaller fort of thofe of
New Zealand. They faw a great number of cabbage
trees on fhore; the other trees were of the palm kind,
and there was no underwood among them. At five in
the evening they returned to the fhip, and a light breeze
fpringing up, we failed to the northward, where we difcovered feveral people on fhore, who, on our approach,
retired to an eminence, foon after which two canoes arrived on the fhore, and four men, who came in them,
joined the others. The pinnace having been fent a-
head to found, arrived near the fpot where the Indians
had ftationed themfelves, on which one of them hid
himfelf among the rocks near the landing place, and
the others retreated farther up the hill. The pinnace
keeping along fhore, the Indians walked near in a line
with her; they were armed with long pikes, and a
weapon refembling a fcymitar, and, by various figns
and words, invited the boat's crew to land; thofe who
did not follow the boat, having obferved the approach
of the fhip, brandifhed their weapons, and threw themfelves into threatening attitudes. The bodies, thighs,
and legs of two of thefe, were painted with white
ftreaks, and their faces were almoft covered with a
white powder. They talked together with great emo-
tion, and each of them held one of the above mentioned weapons. The fhip having come to an anchor, we
obferved a few huts, in which were fome of the natives;
and faw fome canoes, in each of which was a man employed in ftriking fifh with a kind of fpear. We had
anchored oppofite a village of about eight houfes, and
obferved an old woman and three children come out of
a wood, laden with fuel for a fire; they were met by
three fmaller children, all of whom, as well as the woman, were quite naked. The old woman frequently
looked at the fhip with the utmoft indifference, and, as
foon as fhe had made a fire, the fifhermen brought
their canoes on fhore, and they fet about dreffing their
dinner with as much compofure, as if a fhip had been

No. 6.   A a   no

no extraordinary fight. Having formed a defign of landing, we manned the boats, and took Tupia with us, and we had no fooner come near the fhore, than two men advanced, as if to difpute our fetting foot on land. They were each of them armed with different kinds of weapons. They called out aloud in a harfh tone, warra warra wai! the meaning of which Tupia did not underftand. The captain threw them beads, nails, and other trifles, which they took up, and feemed very well pleafed with. He then made fignals that he wanted water, and ufed every poffible means to convince them that no injury was intended. They made figns to the boat's crew to land, on which we put the boat in, but we had no fooner done fo, than the two Indians came again to oppofe us. A mufquet was now fired between them, on the report of which, one of them dropped a bundle of lances, which he immediately fnatched up again in great hafte. One of them then threw a ftone at the boat, on which the captain ordered a mufquet loaded with fmall fhot to be fired, which wounding the eldeft of them on the legs, he retired haftily to one of the houfes that ftood at fome little diftance. The people in the boats now landed, imagining that the wound which this man had received would put an end to the conteft. In this, however, we were miftaken, for he immediately returned with a kind of fhield, of an oval figure, painted white in the middle, with two holes in it to fee through. They now advanced with great intrepidity, and both difcharged their lances at the boat's crew, but did not wound any of them. Another mufquet was fired at them, on which they threw another lance, and then took to their heels. We now went up to the huts, in one of which we found the children, who had fecreted themfelves behind fome bark. We looked at them, but left them without its being known we had feen them, and having thrown feveral pieces of cloth, ribbands, beads, and other things into the hut, we took feveral of their lances, and then reimbarked in the boat. The canoes on this coaft were about 13 feet in length, each made of the bark of a fingle tree, tied up at the ends, and kept open in the middle by the means of

 fticks

ſticks placed acroſs them; their paddles were very ſmall, and two were uſed at a time.

We now ſailed to the north point of the bay, and found plenty of freſh water. On taking a view of the hut where we had ſeen the children, we had the mortification to find that every Indian was fled, and that they had left all the preſents behind them. The captain now went in the pinnace to inſpect the bay, and ſaw ſeveral of the natives, who all fled as he approached them. Some of the men having been ſent to get wood and water, they no ſooner went on board to dinner, than the natives came down to the place, and examined the caſks with great attention, but did not offer to remove them. When the people were on ſhore in the afternoon, about twenty of the natives, all armed, advanced within a trifling diſtance of them, and then ſtopped, while two of their number approached ſtill nearer. Mr. Hicks, the commanding officer on ſhore, went towards them, with preſents in his hands, and endeavoured, by every poſſible means, to aſſure them of his friendly intentions, but to no purpoſe, for they retired before he came up to them. In the evening, Meſſrs. Banks and Solander, went with the captain to a cove north of the bay, where they caught between three and four hundred weight of fiſh, at four hauls.

On Monday the 30th, the natives came down to the huts before it was light, and were repeatedly heard to ſhout very loud, and ſoon after day-break they were ſeen on the beach, but quickly retired about a mile, and kindled ſeveral fires in the woods. This day ſome of the ſhip's crew being employed in cutting graſs at a diſtance from the main body, while the natives purſued them, but ſtopping within fifty or ſixty yards of them, they ſhouted ſeveral times, and retreated to the woods. In the evening they behaved exactly in the ſame manner, when the captain followed them alone and unarmed for ſome time, but they ſtill retired as he approached.

On Tueſday, May the firſt, the ſouth point of the bay was named Sutherland Point, one of the ſeamen of the name of Sutherland, having died that day, was

buried

buried on fhore; and more prefents were left in the huts, fuch as looking-glaffes, combs, &c. but the former ones had not been taken away. Making an excurfion about the country, we found it agreeably variegated with wood and lawn, the trees being ftrait and tall, and without underwood. The country might be cultivated without cutting down one of them. The grafs grows in large tufts, almoft clofe to each other, and there is a great plenty of it. In this excurfion, we met with many places where the inhabitants had flept without fhelter, and one man, who ran away the moment he beheld us. More prefents were left in their huts, and at their fleeping-places, in hopes of producing a friendly intercourfe. We faw the dung of an animal which fed on grafs, and traced the foot-fteps of another, which had claws like a dog, and was about the fize of a wolf: alfo the track of a fmall animal, whofe foot was like that of a pole-cat; and faw one animal alive, about the fize of a rabbit. We found fome wood that had been felled, and the bark ftript off by the natives, and feveral growing trees, in which fteps had been cut, for the convenience of afcending them. The woods abound with a vaft variety of beautiful birds, among which were cockatooes, and parroquets, which flew in large flocks. The fecond lieutenant, Mr. Gore, having been with a boat in order to drudge for oyfters, faw fome Indians, who made figns for him to come on fhore, which he declined: having finifhed his bufinefs, he fent the boat away, and went by land with a midfhipman, to join the party that was getting water. In their way they met with more than 20 of the natives, who followed them fo clofe as to come within a few yards of them; Mr. Gore ftopped and faced them, on which the Indians ftopped alfo, and when he proceeded again, they followed him; but they did not attack him though they had each man a lance. The Indians coming in fight of the water-cafks, ftood at the diftance of a quarter of a mile, while Mr. Gore and his companion reached their fhip-mates in fafety. Two or three of the waterers now advanced towards the Indians, but obferving they did not retire, they very

                                                imprudently

imprudently turned about, and retreated haftily: this apparent fign of cowardice infpired the favages, who difcharged four of their lances at the fugitives, which flying beyond them, they efcaped unhurt. They now ftopped to pick up the lances.; on which the Indians retired in their turn. At this inftant the captain came up with Meffrs. Banks and Solander, and Tupia advancing made figns of friendfhip;. but the poor natives would not ftay their coming up to them. On the following day they went again on fhore, where many plants were collected by Dr. Solander, and Mr. Banks. They faw feveral parties of the Indians, who all ran away on their approach. Tupia having learnt to fhoot, frequently ftayed alone to fhoot parrots, and the Indians conftantly fled away from .him with as much precipitation as from the Englifh. On the 3d of May, fourteen or fifteen Indians, in the fame number of canoes, were engaged in ftriking fifh within half a mile of the watering-place. At this time a party of the fhip's crew were fhooting near the fifhermen, one of whom Mr. Banks obferved to haul up his canoe on the beach, and approach the people who were fhooting. He watched their motions unobferved by them, for more than a quarter of an hour, then put off his boat and returned to his fifhing. At this time the captain, with Dr. Solander and another gentleman, went to the head of the bay to try to form fome connection with the Indians. On their firft landing they found feveral of the Indians on fhore, who immediately retreated to their canoes, and rowed off. They went up the country, where they found the foil to be a deep black mould, which appeared to be calculated for the production of any kind of grain. They faw fome of the fineft meadows that were ever beheld, and met with a few rocky places, the ftone of which is fandy, and feemed to be admirably adapted for building. In the woods they found a tree bearing cherries, if fhape and colour may intitle them to that name, the juice of which was agreeably tart. They now returned to their boat, and feeing a fire at a diftance, rowed towards it ; but the Indians fled at their coming near them. Near the

I   beach

beach they found feven canoes, and as many fires, from which they judged that each fifherman had dreffed his own dinner. There were oyfters lying on the fpot, and fome mufcles roafting on the fire. They ate of thefe fifh, and left them fome beads and other trifles in return. They now returned to the fhip, and in the evening Mr. Banks went out with his gun, and faw a great number of quails, fome of which he fhot, and they proved to be the fame kind as thofe of England. On the following day a midfhipman having ftayed from his companions, came fuddenly to an old man and woman, and fome children, who were fitting naked under a tree together: they feemed afraid of him, but did not run away. The man wore a long beard, and both he and the woman were grey-headed; but the woman's hair was cut fhort. This day likewife, two of another party met with fix Indians on the border of a wood, one of whom calling out very loud, a lance was thrown from a wood, which narrowly miffed them. The Indians now ran off, and, in looking round they faw a youth defcend from a tree, who had doubtlefs been placed there for the purpofe of throwing the lance at them. This day the captain went up the country on the north fide of the bay, which he found to refemble the moory grounds of England; but the land was thinly covered with plants about 16 inches high. The hills rife gradually behind each other, for a confiderable diftance, and between them is marfhy ground. Thofe who had been fent out to fifh this day, met with great fuccefs, and the fecond lieutenant ftruck a fifh called the Stingray, which weighed near two hundred and fifty pounds. The next morning a fifh of the fame kind was taken, which weighed three hundred and fifty pounds. The name of Botany Bay was given to this place from the large number of plants collected by Meffrs. Banks and Solander. This country produces two kinds of wood which may be deemed timber, one of which is tall and ftrait like the pine, and the other is hard, heavy, and dark-coloured, like lignum vitæ; it yields a red gum, like dragon's blood; and bears fome refemblance of the Englifh oak. There are

are mangroves in abundance, feveral kinds of palm, and a few fhrubs. Among other kinds of birds, crows were found here, exactly like thofe of England. There is great plenty of water-fowls, among the flats of fand and mud; one of which is fhaped like a pelican, is larger than a fwan, and has black and white feathers. Thefe banks of mud abound with cockles, mufcles, oyfters, and other fhell-fifh, which greatly contribute towards the fupport of the natives, who fometimes drefs them on fhore, and at other times in their canoes. They likewife caught many other kinds of fifh with hooks and line.

While the captain remained in the harbour, the Englifh colours were difplayed on fhore, daily, and the name of the fhip, with the date of the year, was carved on a tree near the place where we took in our water.

On Sunday the 6th of May, we failed from Botany Bay, and at noon were off a harbour, which was called Port Jackfon, and in the evening, near a bay, to which we gave the name of Broken Bay. The next day at noon, the northermoft land in fight projected fo as to juftify the calling it Cape Three Points. On Wednefday the 9th, we faw two exceeding beautiful rainbows, the colours of which were ftrong and lively, and thofe of the inner one fo bright, as to reflect its fhadow on the water. They formed a complete femicircle, and the fpace between them was much darker than the reft of the fky. On Thurfday we paffed a rocky point, which was named Point Stephens. Next day faw fmoke in feveral places on fhore, and in the evening difcovered three remarkable high hills near each other, which the captain named the Three Brothers. They lie in latitude 31 deg. 40 min. and may be feen thirteen or fourteen leagues from the fhore.

Sunday, the 13th, we faw the fmoke of fires, on a point of land, which was therefore called Cape Smokey. As we proceeded from Botany Bay, northward, the land appeared high and well covered with wood. In the afternoon, we difcovered fome rocky

iflands

iflands between us and the land, the fouthermoft of which is in latitude 30 deg. 10 min. and the northermoft in 29 deg. 58 min. On Tuefday morning, by the affiftance of our glaffes, we difcerned about a fcore of Indians, each loaded with a bundle, which we imagined to be palm leaves for covering their houfes. We traced them for more than an hour, during which time they took not the leaft notice of the fhip; at length they left the beach, and were loft behind a hill, which they gained by a gentle afcent. At noon, in latitude 28 deg. 37 min. 30 fec. fouth, and in 206 deg. 30 min. weft longitude, the captain difcovered a high point of land, and named it Cape Byron. We continued to fteer along the fhore with a frefh gale, and in the evening we difcovered breakers at a confiderable diftance from the fhore, fo that we were obliged to tack, and get into deeper water; which having done, we lay with the head of the veffel to the land till the next morning, when we were furprized to find ourfelves farther to the fouthward than we had been the preceding evening, notwithftanding we had a foutherly wind all night. The breakers lie in latitude 28 deg. 22 min. fouth. In the morning we paffed the breakers, near a peaked mountain, which we named Mount Warning, fituated in 28 deg. 22 min. fouth latitude. The point off which thefe fhoals lie, Capt. Cook named Point Danger. We purfued our courfe, and the next day fay more breakers, near a point, which we diftinguifhed by the name of Point Look-out; to the north of which the fhore forms a wide open bay, which we called Moreton's Bay, and the north point thereof Cape Moreton. Near this are three hills, which we called the Glafs Houfes, from the very ftrong refemblance they bore to fuch buildings.

On Friday, the 18th, at two in the morning, we defcried a point fo unequal, that it looks like two fmall iflands under the land, and it was therefore called Double Ifland Point. At noon, by the help of glaffes, we difcovered fome fands, which lay in patches of feveral acres. We obferved they were moveable, and that they had not been long in their prefent fituation;

for

for we faw trees half buried, and the tops of others ftill green. At this time two beautiful water-fnakes fwam by the fhip, in every refpect refembling land fnakes, except that their tails were flat and broad, probably to ferve them inftead of fins in fwimming.

Saturday, the 19th at noon, we failed about four leagues from the land, and at one o'clock faw a point, whereon a number of Indians were affembled, from whence it was called Indian Head. Soon afterwards we faw many more of the natives; alfo fmoke in the day time, and fires by night. The next day we faw a point, which was named Sandy Point, from two large tracts of white fand that were on it. Soon after we paffed a fhoal, which we called Break Sea Spit, be-caufe we had now fmooth water, after having long en-countered a high fea. For fome days paft we had feen the fea birds, called boobies, none of which we had met with before; and which, from half an hour after, were continually paffing the fhip in large flights: from which it was conjectured, that there was an inlet or river of fhallow water to the fouthward, where they went to feed in the day time, returning in the evening to fome iflands to the northward. In honour of Capt. Hervey we named this bay, Hervey's Bay.

On Tuefday, the 22nd, at fix in the morning, by the help of our glaffes, when a-breaft of the fouth point of a large bay, in which the captain intended to an-chor, we difcovered, that the land was covered with palm-nut-trees, none of which we had feen fince we had quitted the iflands within the tropic. On the 23d, early in the morning, Capt. Cook attended by feveral gentlemen, and Tupia, went on fhore to exa-mine the country. The wind blew fo frefh, and we found it fo cold, that being at fome diftance from the fhore, we took with us our cloaks. We landed a lit-tle within the point of a bay, which led into a large lagoon, by the fides of which grows the true mangrove, fuch as is found in the Weft-Indies, as it does alfo on fome bogs, and fwamps of falt water which we difco-vered. In thefe mangroves were many nefts of ants of a fingular kind, being as green as grafs. When the

No 6.   B b   branches

branches were moved, they came forth in great numbers, and bit the difturber moft feverely. Thefe trees
likewife afforded fhelter for immenfe numbers of green
caterpillars, whofe bodies were covered with hairs,
which, on the touch, occafioned a pain fimilar to the
fting of a nettle, but much more acute. Thefe infects
were ranged fide by fide on the leaves, thirty or forty
together, in a regular manner. Among the fand-banks
we faw birds larger than fwans, which we imagined
were pelicans; and fhot a kind of buftard, which
weighed feventeen pounds. This bird proved very delicate food, on which account we named this bay, Buftard Bay. We likewife fhot a duck of a moft beautiful
plumage, with a white beak. We found an abundance
of oyfters, of various forts, and among the reft fome hammer oyfters of a curious kind. The country here is
much worfe than that about Botany Bay, the foil being
dry and fandy, but the fides of the hills are covered with
trees, which grow feparately without underwood. We
faw the tree that yields a gum like the *fanguis draconis*,
but the leaves are longer than the fame kind of trees in
other parts, and hang down like thofe of a weeping
willow. While we were in the woods, feveral of the
natives took a furvey of the fhip and then departed.
We faw on fhore fires in many places, and repairing to
one of them, found a dozen burning near them. The
people were gone, but had left fome fhells and bones of
fifh they had juft eaten. We perceived likewife feveral pieces of foft bark about the length and breadth of
a man, which we judged had been ufed as beds. The
whole was in a thicket of clofe trees, which afforded
good fhelter from the wind. This kind of encamp-
ment was in a thicket well defended from the wind.
The place feemed to be much trodden, and as there
was no appearance of a houfe, it was imagined that
they fpent their nights, as well as their days, in the
open air: even Tupia fhook his head and exclaimed,
Taata Enos! " Poor Wretches!"

On Thurfday, the 24th, we made fail out of the bay,
and on the day following were a-breaft of a point,
which being immediately under the tropic, the captain
named

named Cape Capricorn, on the weft fide whereof we faw an amazing number of large birds refembling the pelican, fome of which were near five feet high. We now anchored in twelve fathom water, having the main land and barren iflands in a manner all round us.

Sunday, the 27th, we ftood between the range of almoft barren iflands, and the main land, which appeared mountainous. We had here very fhallow water, and anchored in fixteen feet, which was not more than the fhip drew. Mr. Banks tried to fifh from the cabin windows, but the water was too fhallow. The ground indeed was covered with crabs, which greedily feized the bait, and held it till they were above water. Thefe crabs were of two kinds, one of a very fine blue, with a white belly; and the other marked with blue on the joints, and having three brown fpots on the back.

On Monday, the 28th, in the morning, we failed to the northward, and to the northermoft point of land we gave the name of Cape Manifold, from the number of high hills appearing above it. Between this cape and the fhore is a bay which we called Keppel's, and to feveral iflands, we gave the name of the fame admiral. This day being determined to keep the main land clofe aboard, which continued to trend away to the weft, we got among another clufter of iflands. Here we were greatly alarmed, having on a fudden but three fathom water, in a ripling tide; we immediately put the fhip about, and hoifted out the boat in fearch of deeper water; after which we ftood to the weft with an eafy fail, and in the evening came to the entrance of a bay. In the afternoon, having founded round the fhip, and found that there was water fufficient to carry her over the fhoal, we weighed, and ftood to the weftward, having fent a boat a-head to found, and at fix in the evening we anchored in ten fathom, with a fandy bottom, at about two miles diftant from the main.

On Tuefday, the 29th, we had thoughts of laying the fhip afhore, and cleaning her bottom, and therefore landed with the mafter in fearch of a convenient place for that purpofe. In this excurfion Dr. Solander and Mr. Banks accompanied us; we found walking ex-

tremely incommodious, the ground being covered
with grafs, the feeds of which were fharp and bearded,
fo that they were continually fticking in our cloaths,
whence they worked forwards to the flefh by means of
the beard.   We were alfo perpetually tormented with
the ftings of mufquetos.   Several places were found
convenient to lay down the fhip afhore, but to our
great difappointment, we could meet with no frefh
water.   We proceeded, however, up the country, and
in the interior part, we found gum trees, on the
branches whereof were white ants nefts formed of clay,
as big as a bufhel.   On another tree we faw black ants,
which perforated all the twigs, and after they had
eaten out the pith, formed their lodging in the hollows which contained it; yet the trees were in a flou-
rifhing condition.   We alfo faw in the air many thoufands of butterflies, which ever way we looked ; and
every bough was covered with incredible numbers.
On the dry ground we difcovered, fuppofed to have
been left by the tide, a fifh about the fize of a min-
now, having two ftrong breaft fins, with which it leaped
away as nimbly as a frog : it did not appear to be
weakened by being out of the water, nor even to prefer that element to the land, for when feen in the water
it leaped on fhore, and purfued its way.   It was likewife remarked, that where there were fmall ftones projecting above the water, it chofe rather to leap from
one ftone to another, than to pafs through the water.

On Wednefday, the 30th, Capt. Cook, and other gentlemen, went afhore, and having gained the fummit of
a hill, took a furvey of the coaft, and the adjacent
iflands, which being done, the captain proceeded with
Dr. Solander up an inlet, that had been difcovered
the preceding day ; but the weather proving unfavourable, and from a fear of being bewildered among
the fhoals in the night, they returned to the fhip, having feen the whole day, only two Indians, who followed
the boat a confiderable way along fhore ; but the tide
running ftrong, the captain thought it not prudent to
wait for them.   While thefe gentlemen were tracing
the inlet, Mr. Banks, with a party, endeavoured to

penetrate

penetrate into the country, and having met with a piece of fwampy ground, we refolved to pafs it; but before we got half way, we found the mud almoft knee deep. The bottom was covered with branches of trees, interwoven on the furface of the fwamp, on which we fometimes kept our footing; fometimes our feet flipt through; and fometimes we were fo entangled among them, as not to be able to free ourfelves but by groping in the mud and flime with our hands. However, we croffed it in about an hour, and judged it might be about a quarter of a mile over. Having performed this difagreeable tafk, we came to a fpot, where had been four fmall fires, near which were fome bones of fifh that had been roafted; alfo grafs laid in heaps, whereon four or five perfons probably had flept. Our fecond lieutenant, Mr. Gore, at another place, faw the track of a large animal, near a gully of water; he alfo heard the founds of human voices, but did not fee the people. At this place two turtles, fome water fowl, and a few fmall birds, were feen. As no water was to be found in our different excurfions, for feveral of our crew were alfo rambling about, the captain called the inlet where the fhip lay, Thirfty Sound. It lies in latitude 22 deg. 10 min. fouth, and in 210 deg. 18 min. weft longitude, and may be known by a group of iflands that lie right before it, between three and four leagues out at fea. We had not a fingle inducement to ftay longer in a place, where we could not be fupplied with frefh water, nor with provifion of any kind. We caught neither fifh nor wild fowl; nor could we get a fhot at the fame kind of water-fowl, which we had feen in Botany Bay. Therefore on the 31ft at fix o'clock, A. M. we weighed anchor, and put to fea. We kept without the iflands that lie in fhore, and to the N. W. of Thirfty Sound, as there appeared to be no fafe paffage between them and the main, at the fame time we had a number of iflands without us, extending as far as we could fee. Pier Head, the N. W. point of Thirfty Sound, bore S. E. diftant fix leagues, being half way between the iflands which are off the caft point of the weftern inlet, and three fmall iflands that lie directly without them.

them. Having failed round thefe laft, we came to an anchor in fifteen fathom water, and the weather being dark, hazy, and rainy, we remained under the lee of them till feven o'clock of the next morning.

On the 1ft of June, we got under fail, and our latitude by obfervation was 21 deg. 29 min. fouth. We had now quite open the weftern inlet, which we have diftinguiſhed by the name of Bread Sound. A point of land which forms its N. W. entrance, we named Cape Palmerſton, lying in 21 deg. 30 min. S. latitude, and in 210 deg. 54 min. W. longitude. Between this cape and Cape Townſhend is the bay, which we have called the Bay of Inlets. At eight in the evening, we anchored in eleven fathom, with a fandy bottom, about two leagues from the main land.

Saturday the 2nd, we got under fail, and at noon, in latitude 20 deg. 56 min. we faw a high promontory, which we named Cape Hilſborough. It bore W. half N. diſtant feven miles. The land appeared to abound in wood and herbage, and is diverſified with hills, plains, and valleys. A chain of iſlands large and fmall are fituated at a diſtance from the coaſt and under the land, from fome of which we faw fmoke afcending in different places.

On Sunday, the 3d, we difcovered a point of land, which we called Cape Conway, and between that and Cape Hilſborough, a bay to which we gave the name of Repulfe Bay. The land about Cape Conway forms a moſt beautiful landfcape, being diverſified with hills, dales, woods, and verdant lawns. By the help of our glaſſes we difcovered two men and a woman on one of the iſlands, and a canoe with an outrigger like thofe of Otaheite. This day we named the iſlands Cumberland Iſlands, in honour of the duke; and a paſſage which we had difcovered, was called Whitfunday paſſage, from the day on which it was feen. At day-break, on Monday the 4th, we were abreaſt of a point, which we called Cape Glouceſter. Names were alfo given this day to three other places, namely, Holborne Iſle, Edgcumbe Bay, and Cape Upſtart, which laſt was fo called becaufe it rifes abruptly from the low lands that fur-

round

round it. Inland are some hills or mountains, which, like the cape, afford but a barren profpect.

On Tuefday the 5th, we were about four leagues from land, and our latitude by obfervation was 19 deg. 12 min. S. We faw very large columns of fmoke ri-fing from the low lands. We continued to fteer W. N. W. as the land lay, till noon on the 6th, when our latitude by obfervation was 19 deg. 1 min. S. at which time we had the mouth of a bay all open, diftant two leagues. This we named Cleveland Bay; and the eaft point Cape Cleveland. The weft, which had the ap-pearance of an ifland, we called Magnetical ifland, be-caufe the compafs did not traverfe well when we were near it: they are both high, as is the main land be-tween them, the whole forming a furface the moft rugged, rocky, and barren of any we had feen upon the coaft: yet it was not without inhabitants, for we faw fmoke in feveral parts of the bottom of the bay.

Thurfday the 7th, at day-break we were a-breaft of the eaftern part of this land, and in the afternoon faw feveral large columns of fmoke upon the main; alfo canoes, and fome trees, which we thought were thofe of the cocoa-nut; in fearch of which, as they would have been at this time very acceptable, Mr. Banks and Dr. Solander went afhore with lieutenant Hicks; but in the evening they returned with only a few plants, ga-thered from the cabbage-palm, and which had been miftaken for the cocoa-tree.

On Friday, the 8th, we ftood away for the norther-moft point in fight, to which we gave the name of Point Hillock. Between this and Magnetical Ifle the fhore forms Halifax Bay, which affords fhelter from all winds. At fix in the evening we were a-breaft of a point of land, which we named Cape Sandwich. From hence the land trends W. and afterwards N. forming a fine large bay, which was named Rockingham Bay. We now ranged northward along the fhore, towards a clufter of iflands, on one of which about forty or fifty men, women, and children were ftanding together, all ftark naked, and looking at the fhip with a curiofity never obferved among thefe people before. At noon
our

our latitude, by obfervation, was 17 deg. 59 min. and we were a-breaft of the north point of Rockingham Bay, which bore from us W. diftant about two miles. This boundary of the bay is formed by an ifland of con-fiderable height, which we diftinguifhed by the name of Dunk Ifle.

On Saturday, the 9th, in the morning, we were a-breaft of fome fmall iflands, which were named Frankland's Ifles. At noon we were in the middle of the channel, and by obfervation in latitude 16 deg. 57 min. S. and in longitude 214 deg. 6 min. W. with twenty fathom water. The point on the main of which we were now abreaft Capt. Cook named Cape Grafton. Having hauled round this, we found a bay three miles to the weftward, in which we anchored; and called the ifland Green Ifland. Here Mr. Banks and Dr. Solan-der went afhore with the captain, with a view of pro-curing water, which not being to be had eafily, they foon returned aboard, and the next day we arrived near Trinity Bay, fo called becaufe difcovered on Trinity Sunday.

Sunday, the 10th, was remarkable for the dangerous fituation of the Endeavour, as was Tuefday the 12th ; for her prefervation and deliverance, as chriftians, or only moral philofophers, we ought to add, agreeable to the will of an over-ruling providence, who fhut up the fea with doors, who appointed for it a decreed place, and faid, Thus far thou fhalt come, and here fhall thy proud waves be ftayed. As no accident remarkably unfortunate had befallen us, during a navigation of more than thirteen hundred miles, upon a coaft every where abounding with the moft dangerous rocks and fhoals, no name of diftrefs had hitherto been given to any cape or point of land which we had feen. But we now gave the name of Cape Tribulation, to a point we had juft feen fartheft to the northward, be-caufe here we became acquainted with misfortune. The cape lies in latitude 16 deg. 6 min. S. and 214 deg. 39 min. W. longitude.

This day, Sunday the 10th, at fix in the evening we fhortened fail, and hauled off fhore clofe upon a wind, to avoid the danger of some rocks, which were seen a-head, and to observe whether any islands lay in the offing, as we were near the latitude of those islands, said to have been discovered by Quiros. We kept standing off from six o'clock till near nine, with a fine breeze and bright moon. We had got into twenty-one fathom water, when suddenly we fell into twelve, ten, and eight fathom, in a few minutes. Every man was instantly ordered to his station, and we were on the point of anchoring, when, on a sudden, we had again deep water, so that we thought all danger at an end, concluding we had sailed over the tail of some shoals, which we had seen in the evening. We had twenty fathoms and up-wards before ten o'clock, and this depth continuing some time, the gentlemen, who had hitherto been upon duty, retired to rest; but in less than an hour the water shallowed at once from twenty to seventeen fathoms, and before soundings could be taken the ship struck upon a rock, and remained immoveable. Every one was in-stantly on deck, with countenances fully expressive of the horrors of our situation. Knowing we were not near the shore, we concluded that we were upon a rock of coral, the points of which are sharp, and the surface so rough, as to grind away whatever it rubbed against, even with the gentlest motion. All the sails being im-mediately taken in, and our boats hoisted out, we found, that the ship had been lifted over a ledge of the rock, and lay in a hollow within it. Finding the water was deepest a-stern, we carried out the anchor from the starboard quarter, and applied our whole force to the capstan, in hopes to get the vessel off, but in vain. She now beat so violently against the rock, that the crew could scarcely keep on their legs. The moon shone bright, by the light of which we could see the sheath-ing-boards float from the bottom of the vessel, till at length the false keel followed, so that we expected in-stant destruction. Our best chance of escaping seemed now to be by lightening her; but having struck at high water, we should have been in our present situation after the vessel should draw as much less water as the water had sunk; our anxiety abated a little, on finding that

No. 7.   C c   the

the ship settled on the rocks as the tide ebbed, and we flattered ourselves, that, if the ship should keep together till next tide, we might have some chance of floating her. We therefore instantly started the water in the hold, and pumped it up. The decayed stores, oil-jars, casks, ballast, six guns, and other things, were thrown overboard, in order to get at the heavier articles; and in this business we were employed till day-break, during all which time not an oath was sworn, so much were the minds of the sailors impressed with a sense of their danger.

On Monday the 11th, at day-light, we saw land at eight leagues distance, but not a single island between us and the main, on which part of the crew might have been landed, while the boat went on shore with the rest: so that the destruction of the greater part of us would have been inevitable had the ship gone to pieces. It happened that the wind died away to a dead calm before noon. As we expected high-water about eleven o'clock, every thing was prepared to make another effort to free the ship, but the tide fell so much short of that in the night, that she did not float by 18 inches, though we had thrown over-board near fifty tons weight: we therefore renewed our toil, and threw over-board every thing that could possibly be spared; as the tide fell, the water poured in so rapidly, that we could scarce keep her free by the constant working of two pumps. Our only hope now depended on the midnight tide, and preparations were accordingly made for another effort to get the ship off. The tide began to rise at five o'clock, when the leak likewise increased to such a degree, that two pumps more were manned, but only one of them would work; three, therefore, were kept going till nine o'clock, at which time the ship righted; but so much water had been admitted by the leak, that we expected she would sink as soon as the water should bear her off the rock. Our situation was now deplorable, beyond description, almost all hope being at an end. We knew that when the fatal moment should arrive, all authority would be at an end. The boats were incapable of conveying all on shore, and we

I

dreaded a conteft for the preference, as more fhocking than the fhipwreck itfelf: yet it was confidered, that thofe who might be left on board, would eventually meet with a milder fate than thofe who, by gaining the fhore, would have no chance but to linger out the remains of life among the rudeft favages in the univerfe, and in a country, where fire-arms would barely enable them to fupport themfelves in a moft wretched fituation. At twenty minutes after ten the fhip floated, and was heaved into deep water, when we were happy to find that fhe did not admit more water than fhe had done before: yet as the leak had for a confiderable time gained on the pumps, there was now three feet nine inches water in the hold. By this time the men were fo worn by fatigue of mind and body, that none of them could pump more than five or fix minutes at a time, and then threw themfelves, quite fpent, on the deck, amidft a ftream of water which came from the pumps. The fucceeding man being fatigued in his turn, threw himfelf down in the fame manner, while the former jumped up and renewed his labour, thus mutually ftruggling for life, till the following accident had like to have given them up a prey to abfolute defpair, and thereby infured our deftruction. Between the infide lining of the fhip's bottom, which is called the cieling, and the outfide planking, there is a fpace of about feventeen or eighteen inches. The man who had hitherto taken the depth of water at the well, had taken it no farther than the cieling, but being now relieved by another perfon, who took the depth of the outfide plank, it appeared by this miftake, that the leak had fuddenly gained upon the pumps, the whole difference between the two planks. This circumftance deprived us of all hopes, and fcarce any one thought it worth while to labour, for the longer prefervation of a life which muft fo foon have a period: but the miftake was foon difcovered; and the joy arifing from fuch unexpected good news infpired the men with fo much vigour, that before eight o'clock in the morning, they had pumped out confiderably more water than they had fhipped. We now talked of nothing but getting the

fhip

ship into fome harbour, and fet heartily to work to get in the anchors; one of which, and the cable of another, we loft; but thefe were now confidered as trifles. Having a good breeze from fea, we got under fail at eleven o'clock, and fteered for land. As we could not difcover the exact fituation of the leak, we had no profpect of ftopping it within fide of the veffel, but on Tuefday the 12th, the following expedient, which one of the midfhipmen had formerly feen tried with fuccefs, was adopted. We took an old ftudding fail, and having mixed a large quantity of oakham and wool, chopped fmall, it was ftitched down in handfuls on the fail, as lightly as poffible, the dung of fheep and other filth being fpread over it. Thus prepared, the fail was hauled under the fhip, by ropes, which kept it extended till it came under the leak, when the fuction carried in the oakham and wool from the furface of the fail. This experiment fucceeded fo well, that inftead of three pumps, the water was eafily kept under with one.

We had hitherto no farther view than to run the fhip into fome harbour, and build a veffel from her materials, in which we might reach the Eaft-Indies; but we now began to think of finding a proper place to repair her damage, and then to purfue her voyage on its original plan. At fix in the evening we anchored feven leagues from the fhore; and found that the fhip made 15 inches water an hour during the night; but as the pumps could clear this quantity, we were not uneafy. At nine in the morning we paffed two iflands, which were called Hope Iflands, becaufe the reaching of them had been the object of our wifhes, at the time of the fhipwreck. In the afternoon, the mafter was fent out with two boats to found and fearch for a harbour where the fhip might be repaired, and we anchored at fun-fet, in four fathoms water, two miles from the fhore. One of the mates being fent out in the pinnace, returned at nine o'clock, reporting, that he had found fuch a harbour as was wanted, at the diftance of two leagues.

Wednefday the 13th, at fix o'clock we failed, having previoufly fent two boats a-head, to point out the fhoals that we faw in our way. We foon anchored about a
mile

mile from the shore, when the captain went out, and found the channel very narrow, but the harbour was better adapted to our present purpose, than any place we had seen in the whole course of the voyage. As it blew very fresh this day and the following night, we could not venture to run into the harbour, but remained at anchor during the two succeeding days, in the course of which we observed four Indians on the hills, who stopped and made two fires.

Our men, by this time, began to be afflicted with the scurvey; and our Indian friend Tupia was so ill with it, that he had livid spots on both his legs. Mr. Green the astronomer was likewise ill of the same disorder; so that our being detained from landing was every way disagreeable. The wind continued fresh till the 17th, and then we resolved to push in for the harbour, and twice ran the ship a-ground; the second time she stuck fast, on which we took down the booms, fore-yard, and fore-top masts, and made a raft on the side of the ship; and, as the tide happened to be rising, she floated at one o'clock. We soon got her into the harbour, where she was moored along the side of a beach, and the anchors, cables, &c. immediately taken out of her.

C H A P. IX.

The Ship is refitted in Endeavour River—Transactions during that Time—The Country, its Inhabitants and Productions described—A Description of the Harbour, the adjacent Country, and several Islands near the Coast—The Range from Endeavour River to the northern Extremity of the Country—And the Dangers of that Navigation—The Endeavour departs from South Wales—That Country, its Product and People described, with a Specimen of the Language.

ON Monday, the 18th, in the morning, we erected a tent for the sick, who were brought on shore as soon as it was ready for their reception. We likewise
built

built a stage from the ship to the shore, and set up a
tent to hold the provisions and stores, that were landed
the same day. The boat was now dispatched in search
of fish for the refreshment of the sick, but she returned
without getting any; but Tupia employed himself
in angling, and living entirely upon what he caught,
recovered his health very fast. In an excursion Mr.
Banks made up the country, he saw the frames of several huts, and Cap'. Cook having ascended one of the
highest hills, observed the land to be stoney and
barren, and the low land near the river over-run with
mangroves, among which the salt-water flowed every
tide.

Tuesday, the 19th, the smith's forge was set up, and
the armourer prepared the necessary iron-work for the
repair of the vessel. The officers stores, ballast, water,
&c. were likewise ordered out, in order to lighten the
ship. This day Mr. Banks crossed the river to view
the country, which he observed to be little else than
sand hills. He saw vast flocks of pigeons, most
beautiful birds, of which he shot several. On Wednesday the 20th, as we were removing the coals, the
water rushed in, near the foremast, about three feet from
the keel; so that it was resolved to clear the hold
entirely; which being done on Friday the 22nd,
we warped the ship higher up the harbour, to a station more proper for laying her ashore, in order to stop
the leak. Early in the morning, the tide having left
her, we proceeded to examine the leak, when it appeared that the rocks had cut through four planks into the
timbers, and that three other planks were damaged.
In these breaches not a splinter was to be seen, the
whole being smooth as if cut away by an instrument :
but it was the will of an omnipotent being, that the
vessel should be preserved by a very singular circumstance : for though one of the holes was large enough
to have sunk her, even with eight pumps constantly at
work, yet this inlet to our destruction was partly stopped
up, by a fragment of the rock being left sticking
therein. We likewise found some pieces of the oakham, wool, &c. which had got between the timbers,
and

Thornton sculp

An Animal *found on the* Coast *of* NEW HOLLAN
called KANGUROO.

and ſtopped thoſe parts of the leak that the ſtone had left open. Excluſive of the leak, great damage was done to various parts of the ſhip's bottom. While the ſmiths were employed in making nails and bolts, the car‑ penters began to work on the veſſel; and ſome of the people were ſent on the other ſide of the river to ſhoot pigeons for the ſick. They found a ſtream of freſh water, ſeveral inhabitants of the Indians, and ſaw a mouſe-coloured animal, exceeding ſwift, and about the ſize of a greyhound.

On Saturday the 23d, a boat was diſpatched to haul the ſeine, and returned at noon with only three fiſh, and yet we ſaw them in plenty leaping about the harbour. This day many of the crew ſaw the animal above- mentioned; and one of the ſeamen declared he had ſeen the devil, which John thus deſcribed, " He was, ſays he, as large as a one gallon keg, and very like it: he had horns and wings, yet he crept ſo ſlowly through the graſs, that if I had not been afeard, I might have touched him." This formidable apparition we after- wards diſcovered to have been a batt, which we muſt acknowledge has a frightful appearance, it being black, and full as large as a partridge; but the man's own ap- prehenſions had furniſhed his devil with horns.

Sunday, Mr. Gore and a party of men ſent out with him, procured a bunch or two of wild plantains, and a few palm cabbages, for the refreſhment of the ſick : and this day the Captain and Mr. Banks ſaw the animal already mentioned. It had a long-tail that it carried like a greyhound, leaped like a deer, and the point of its foot reſembled that of a goat. The repairs of the ſhip on the ſtarboard ſide having been finiſhed the pre- ceding day, the carpenters now began to work under her larboard bow; and being examined abaft it appear- ed ſhe had received very little injury in that quarter. Mr. Banks having removed his whole collection of plants into the bread room, they were this day under water, by which ſome of them were totally deſtroyed; however by great care moſt of them were reſtored to a ſtate of preſervation. A plant was found this day, the 25th, the leaves of which were almoſt as good as

ſpinnage;

ſpinnage; alſo a fruit of a deep purple colour, and the
ſize of a golden pippin, which after having been kept
a few days taſted like a damſon. On Tueſday, the
26th, the carpenter was engaged in caulking the ſhip,
and the men in other neceſſary buſineſs; and on the
27th the armourer continued to work at the forge, and
the carpenter on the ſhip; while the captain made ſeveral hauls with the large net, but caught only between
twenty and thirty fiſh, which were diſtributed among
the ſick, and thoſe who were not yet quite recovered.
We began this day to move ſome of the weight from
the after-part of the ſhip forward, to eaſe her. On the
28th, Mr. Banks with ſome ſeamen went up into the
country, to whom he ſhewed a plant which ſerved them
for greens, and which the inhabitants of the Weſt-In-
dies call Indian Kale. Here we ſaw a tree notched for
climbing; alſo neſts of white ants from a few inches to
five feet in height; prints of mens feet, and the tracks
of three or four animals were likewiſe diſcovered.

On Friday the 29th, at two o'clock in the morning,
Capt. Cook with Mr. Green, obſerved an emerſion of
Jupiter's firſt ſatellite: the time here was 2 hours 18
min. 53 ſec. which makes the longitude of this place
214 deg. 42 min. 30 ſec. W. and the latitude 15 deg.
26 min. S. At dawn of day the boat was ſent out to
haul for fiſh, and took what made an allowance of one
pound and a half to each man. One of our midſhip-
men, this day abroad with his gun, reported, that he
had ſeen a wolf, reſembling exactly the ſame ſpecies in
America, at which he ſhot, but could not kill it. The
next morning, being the 30th, the captain aſcended a
hill to take a view of the ſea, when he obſerved innumerable ſand banks and ſhoals, in every direction; but
to the northward there was an appearance of a paſſage,
which ſeemed the only way to ſteer clear of the ſur-
rounding dangers, eſpecially as the wind blows con-
ſtantly from the S. E. Mr. Gore ſaw this day two ſtraw
coloured animals of the ſize of a hare, but ſhaped
like a dog. In the afternoon the people returned with
ſuch a quantity of fiſh, that two pounds and a half
were diſtributed to each man; and plenty of greens
had

had been gathered, which when boiled with peas made an excellent mefs, and we all thought this day's fare an unfpeakable refrefhment.

On Sunday, the 1ft of July, all the crew had permiffion to go on fhore, except one from each mefs, part of whom were again fent out with the feine, and were again equally fuccefsful. Some of our people who went up in the country, gave an account of their having feen feveral animals, and a fire about a mile up the river. On Tuefday the 3d, the mafter, who had been fent in the pinnace, returned, and reported, that he had found a paffage out to fea, between fhoals which confifted of coral rocks, many whereof were dry at low water. He found fome cockles fo large, that one of them was more than fufficient for two men; likewife plenty of other fhell-fifh, of which he brought a fupply to the fhip, in his return to which he had landed in a bay where fome Indians were at fupper; but they inftantly retired, leaving fome fea eggs by a fire for dreffing them. This day we made another attempt to float the fhip, and happily fucceeded at high water; when we found, that by the pofition fhe had lain in, one of her planks was fprung, fo that it was again neceffary to lay her afhore. An alligator fwam by her feveral times at high water.

Wednefday the 4th was employed in trimming her upon an even keel, warping her over, and laying her down on a fand-bank, on the fouth fide of the river; and on the next day, the 5th, fhe was again floated, and moored off the beach, in order to receive the ftores on board. This day we croffed the harbour, and found on a fandy beach a great number of fruits, not difcovered before; among others a cocoa-nut, which Tupia faid had been opened by a crab, and was judged to be what the Dutch call Beurs Krabbe. The vegetable fubftances which Mr. Banks picked up were encrufted with marine productions, and covered with barnacles, a proof of their having been tranfplanted, probably from Terra del Efperito Santo. This gentleman with a party having failed up the river on the 6th, to make an excurfion up the country, returned on the

No. 7.   D d   8th.

8th. Having followed the courfe of the river, they found it at length contracted into a narrow channel, bounded by fteep banks, adorned with trees of a moft beautiful appearance, among which was the bark tree. The land was low and covered with grafs, and feemed capable of being cultivated to great advantage. The night, though we had made a fire on the banks of the river, was rendered extremely difagreeable by the ftings of the mufquitos, that caufe an almoft intolerable torment. Going in purfuit of game, we faw four animals, two of which were chafed by Mr. Banks's greyhound, but they greatly outftripped him in fpeed, by leaping over the long thick grafs, which incommoded the dog in running. It was obferved of the animals, that they bounded forward on two legs inftead of running on four. Having returned to the boat we proceeded up the river, till it contracted to a brook of frefh water, but in which the tide rofe confiderably. Having ftopped to pafs the night, with hope of fome reft, we faw a fmoke at a diftance, on which three of us approached it, but the Indians were gone. We faw the impreffions of feet on the fand, below high-water mark, and found a fire ftill burning in the hollow of an old tree. At a fmall diftance were feveral huts, and we obferved ovens dug in the ground : the remains of a recent meal were likewife apparent. We now retired to our refting-place, and flept on plantain leaves, with a bunch of grafs for our pillows, on the fide of a fandbank, under the fhelter of a bufh. The tide favouring our return in the morning, we loft no time in getting back to the fhip. The mafter, who had been feven leagues at fea, returned foon after Mr. Banks, bringing with him three turtles, which he took with a boathook, and which together weighed near eight hundred pounds. He was fent out next morning, and Mr. Banks accompanied him with proper inftruments for catching turtle : but not being fuccefsful, he would not go back that night, fo that Mr. Banks, after collecting fome fhells and marine productions, returned in his own fmall boat. In the morning the fecond lieutenant was fent to bring the mafter back, foon after which four Indians,

dians, in a fmall canoe, were within fight. The captain now determined to take no notice of thefe people, as the moft likely way to be noticed by them. This project anfwered; two of them came within mufquet fhot of the veffel, where they converfed very loud; in return, the people on board fhouted, and made figns of invitation. The Indians gradually approached, with their lances held up; not in a menacing manner, but as if they meant to intimate that they were capable of defending themfelves. They came almoft along-fide, when the captain threw them cloth, nails, paper, &c. which did not feem to attract their notice, at length one of the failors threw a fmall fifh, which fo pleafed them, that they hinted their defigns of bringing their companions, and immediately rowed for the fhore. In the interim, Tupia and fome of the crew landed on the oppofite fhore. The four Indians now came quite along-fide the fhip, and having received farther prefents, landed where Tupia and the failors had gone. They had each two lances, and a ftick with which they threw them. Advancing towards the Englifh, Tupia perfuaded them to lay down their arms, and fit by him, which they readily did. Others of the crew now going on fhore, the Indians feemed jealous, left they fhould get between them and their arms, but care was taken to convince them that no fuch thing was intended, and more trifles were prefented to them. The crew ftaid with them till dinner-time, and then made figns of invitation for them to go to the fhip and eat; but this they declined, and retired in their canoe. Thefe men were of the common ftature, with very fmall limbs; their complexion was of a deep chocolate; their hair black, either lank or curled, but not of the woolly kind; the breafts and upper lip of one of them were painted with ftreaks of white, which he called carbanda, and fome part of their bodies had been painted red. Their teeth were white and even, their eyes bright, and their features rather pleafing; their voices mufical, and they repeated feveral Englifh words with great readinefs.

The next morning, the vifit of three of thefe Indians was renewed, and they brought with them a,

fourth,

fourth, whom they called Yaparico, who appeared to
be a perfon of fome confequence. The b ne of a bird,
about fix inches long, was thruft through the griftle of
his nofe; and indeed all the inhabitants of this place
had their nofes bored, for the reception of fuch an ornament. Thefe people being all naked, the captain
gave one of them an old fhirt, which he bound round
his head like a turban, inftead of ufing it to cover any
part of his body. They brought a fifh to the fhip,
which was fuppofed to be in payment for that given
them the day before: after ftaying fome time with apparent fatisfaction, they fuddenly leaped into their canoe, and rowed off, from a jealoufy of fome of the
gentlemen who were examining it.

On the 12th of July, three Indians vifited Tupia's
tent, and after remaining fome time, went for two
others, whom they introduced by name. Some fifh
was offered them, but they feemed not much to regard
it; after eating a little, they gave the remainder to
Mr. Banks's dog. Some ribbands which had been
given them, to which medals were fufpended round
their necks, were fo changed by fmoke, that it was
difficult to judge what colour they had been, and the
fmoke had made their fkins look darker than their natural colour, from whence it was thought that they had
flept clofe to their fires, as a preventative againft the
fting of the mufquitos. Both the ftrangers had bones
through their nofes, and a piece of bark tied over their
foreheads; and one of them had an ornament of ftrings
round his arm; and an elegant necklace made of fhells.
Their canoe was about ten feet long, and calculated to
hold four perfons, and when it was in fhallow water
they moved it by the help of poles. Their lances had
only a 'fingle point, and fome of them were barbed
with fifh-bones. On the 14th Mr. Gore fhot one of the
moufe-coloured animals above-mentioned. It chanced
to be a young one, weighing more than 38 pounds;
but when they are full grown, they are as large as a
fheep. The fkin of this beaft which is called Kanga-
roo, is covered with fhort fur, and is of a dark moufe
colour; the head and ears are fomewhat like thofe of a
hare;

hare; this animal was dreffed for dinner, and proved
fine eating. The fhip's crew fed on turtle almoft every
day, which were finer than thofe eaten in England,
owing to their being killed before their natural fat was
wafted, and their juices changed.

On the 17th, Mr. Banks and Dr. Solander went with
the captain into the woods, and faw four Indians in a
canoe, who went on fhore, and walked up without figu
of fear. They accepted fome beads, and departed,
intimating that they did not chufe to be followed.
The natives being now become familiar with the fhip's
crew, one of them was defired to throw his lance, which
he did with fuch dexterity and force, that though it was
not above four feet from the ground at the higheft, it
penetrated deeply into a tree at the diftance of fifty
yards. The natives now came on board the fhip, and
were well pleafed with their entertainment.

On the 19th, we faw feveral of the women, who, as
well as the men, were quite naked. We were this day
vifited by ten Indians, who feemed refolved to have
one of the turtles that was on board, which they repeatedly made figns for, and being as repeatedly refufed, they expreffed the utmoft rage and refentment,
one of them in particular, having received a denial
from Mr. Banks, he ftamped, and pufhed him away in
a moft violent manner. At length they laid hands on
two of the turtles, and drew them to the fide of the
fhip where the canoe lay, but the failors took them
away. They made feveral fimilar attempts, but being
equally unfuccefsful, they leaped fuddenly into their
canoe, and rowed off. At this inftant the captain,
with Mr Banks, and five or fix of the feamen, went
on fhore, where they arrived before the Indians, and
where many of the crew were already employed. As
foon as the Indians landed, one of them fnatched a
fire'brand from under a pitch-kettle, and running to
the windward of what effects were left on fhore, fet fire
to the dry grafs, which burned rapidly, fcorched a pig
to death, burned part of the fmith's forge, and would
have deftroyed a tent of Mr. Banks, but that fome people came from the fhip juft in time to get it out of the
way

way of the flames. In the mean while the Indians went to a place where the fishing-nets lay, and a quantity of linen was laid out to dry, and there again set fire to the grafs, in spite of all persuasion, and even of threats. A musquet loaded with small shot was fired, and one of them being wounded, they ran away, and this second fire was extinguished : but the other burned far into the woods.

The Indians still continued in sight, a musquet charged with ball was fired, the report only of which sent them out of sight ; but their voices being heard in the woods, the captain with a few people went to meet them. Both parties stopped when in sight of each other; at which time an old Indian advanced before the rest a little way, but soon halted, and after having spoke some words, which we could not understand, he retreated to his companions, and they all retired slowly in a body. Having found means to seize some of their darts, we continued following them about a mile, and then sat down upon some rocks, the Indians sitting down also about an hundred yards from us. The old man again came forward, having a lance without a point in his hand ; he stopped several times at different distances, and spoke, whereupon the captain made signs of friendship, which they answered. The old man now returned, and spoke aloud to his companions, who placed their lances against a tree, and came forward in a friendly manner. When they came up to us, we returned the darts we had taken, and we perceived with great satisfaction, that this rendered the reconciliation complete. In this party were four persons whom we had not seen before, who, as usual, were introduced to us by name, but the man who had been wounded in the attempt to burn our nets, was not among them. Having received from us some trinkets, they walked amicably towards the coast, intimating by signs, that they would not fire the grafs again. When we came opposite the ship they sat down, but we could not prevail with them to go on board. They accepted a few musquet balls, the use and effect of which the captain endeavoured to explain. We then left them,

3   and

and when arrived at the ship, we saw the woods burning at the distance of two miles. We had no conception of the fury with which grafs would burn in this hot climate, nor of the difficulty of extinguishing it; but we determined, that if it should ever again be neceffary for us to pitch our tents in fuch a fituation, our firft work should be to clear the ground round us.

Friday the 20th, our ship being ready for fea, the mafter was fent in fearch of a paffage to the northward, but could not find any; while the captain founded and buoyed the bar. This day we faw not any Indians; but the hills for many miles were on fire, which at night made an appearance truly fublime. On the 22nd, we killed a turtle, through both shoulders of which ftuck a wooden harpoon, near fifteen inches long, bearded at the end, and about the thicknefs of a man's finger, refembling fuch as we had feen among the natives. The turtle appeared to have been ftruck a confiderable time, for the wound was perfectly healed. On the 24th, one of the failors, who with others had been fent to gather kale, having ftrayed from the reft, fell in with four Indians at dinner. He was at firft much alarmed, but had prudence enough to conceal his apprehenfions; and fitting down by them gave them his knife, which having examined, they returned. He would then have left them; but they feemed difpofed to detain him, till, by feeling his hands and face, they were convinced he was made of flesh and blood like themfelves. They treated him with great civility, and having kept him about half an hour, they made figns that he might depart. When he left them, not taking the direct way to the ship, they came from the fire and shewed him the neareft way; from whence we concluded, that they well knew from whence he came. We may here obferve, that the language of thefe people feemed to us more harsh than that of the iflanders in the South-Sea. They were continually repeating the word chercau, a term as we imagined of admiration. They alfo cried out, when they faw any thing new, cher, tut, tut, tut, tut! which probably was a fimilar expreffion. Mr. Banks having gone on shore in fearch of plants,
found

found the cloth which had been diftributed among the natives, lying in a heap, as ufelefs lumber. Indeed they feemed to fet very little value upon any thing we had except our turtle, a commodity we were leaft inclined and able to fpare.

Tuefday the 24th, Mr. Banks and Dr. Solander returning from the woods, through a deep valley, found lying on the ground feveral marking nuts, the Anacardium orientale: but they fought in vain for the tree that bore them. On the 26th, as Mr. Banks was again fearching the country to enrich his natural hiftory, he took an animal of the opoffum kind, with two young ones. On the 27th, Mr. Gore fhot a Kanguroo, which weighed eighty-four pounds, though not at its full growth. When dreffed on the 28th, we found it had a much worfe flavour than that we had eaten before.

Sunday the 29th, we got the anchor up, and made all ready to put to fea. A boat was fent out to afcertain what water was upon the bar; when returned, the officer reported, that there was only thirteen feet, which was fix inches lefs than the fhip drew. We therefore this day gave up all hopes of failing. Monday the 30th, we had frefh gales with hazy weather and rain, till Tuefday the 31ft, at two in the morning, when the weather became more moderate. During all this time the pinnace and yawl continued to ply the net and hook with tolerable good fuccefs, bringing in at different times a turtle, and from two to three hundred weight of fifh.

On Wednefday the 1ft of Auguft, the pumps were examined by the carpenter, who found them all in a ftate of decay, and fome quite rotten, owing, as he faid, to the fap having been left in the wood: but as the fhip admitted only an inch of water in an hour, we hoped fhe was ftout enough, and trufted to her foundnefs.

On Saturday the 4th, at feven o'clock in the morning, we once more got under fail, and put to fea. We ftood off E. by N. with the pinnace a-head to keep founding. About noon we came to an anchor, when the harbour from whence we had failed bore S. 70 W. diftant about five leagues. The captain here named the northermoft

point

point of land in fight Cape Bedford, and the harbour we had quitted Endeavour River. Our latitude by obfervation was now 15 deg. 32 min. S. Endeavour River is only a fmall bar harbour, or creek, which runs in a winding channel three or four leagues inland. The depth of water for fhipping is not more than a mile within the bar, and only on the north-fide. At the new and full of the moon, it is high-water between nine and ten o'clock. It muft alfo be remembered, that this part of the coaft is fo barricaded with fhoals, as to make the harbour very difficult of accefs : the fafeft approach is fiom the fouthward, keeping the main land clofe ·upon the board all the way. Over the fouth point is fome high land, but the north point is formed by a low fandy beach. The provifions we procured in this harbour confifted of turtle, oyfters of different forts, cavalhe or fcomber, flat fifh, fkate or ray fifh, purflain, wild beans, and cabbage-palms. Of quadrupedes, there are goats, wolves, pole-cats, a fpotted animal of the viverra kind, and feveral kinds of ferpents, fome of which only are venomous. Dogs are the only tame animals. The land fowls are kites, crows, hawks, loriquets, cockatoos, parrots, pigeons, and fmall birds of various forts, the names of which we could not learn. The water fowls are wild geefe, curlieus, hens, whiftling ducks that perch on trees, and fome few others. The foil of the hills, though ftoney, produces coarfe grafs befides wood, that of the valleys is in general well cloathed, and has the appearance of fertility. The trees here are of various forts, of which the gum trees are the moft common. On each fide of the river are mangroves, which in fome parts extend a mile within the coaft. The country is well watered, and ant-hills are every where in great numbers.

On Saturday the 4th, Capt. Cook went up to the maft-head to look at fome dangerous fhoals, feveral of which he faw above the water. This day fuch a quantity of fifh was caught, as allowed a dividend of two pounds to each man. During the fix following days we attempted to fail between the fhoals and breakers, by which we were every way furrounded. On the 10th we were between a head land and three iflands, which had been difcovered the preceding day. We now entertained hopes of being out of danger; but this not proving to be the cafe, we called the head land Cape Flattery. Some land was now difcovered, and was generally taken for the main; but in the captain's opinion a clufter of iflands. Upon this diverfity of fentiments it was refolved to bring the fhip to an anchor. This done, the captain landed, and from a high point took a furvey of the fea-coaft, by which he was confirmed in his conjecture. On the point where he ftood were feen the prints of human feet, in white fand of an exquifite finenefs; and the place was named Point Lookout. To the northward of this the coaft appeared to be fhoal and flat, for a confiderable diftance, which did not encourage our hope, that the channel we had hitherto found in with the land would continue.

On Saturday the 11th, early in the morning, Mr. Banks and Capt. Cook went to vifit the largeft of the three iflands, and having gained the fummit of the higheft hill, they beheld a reef of rocks, whereon the fea broke in a frightful manner; but the hazy weather preventing a perfect view, they lodged under a bufh during the night, and next day feeing what had the appearance of a channel between the reefs, one of the mates on the 12th, was fent out in the pinnace to examine it; and at noon returned, having found between fifteen and twenty-eight fathom of water; but it blew fo hard, that the mate did not dare to venture into one of the channels, which he faid appeared to be very narrow; but the captain judged he had feen them to a difadvantage. While bufy in his furvey, Mr. Banks was attentive to his favourite purfuit, and collected many plants he had not before feen. This ifland, vifible at twelve leagues diftance, and in general barren, we found to be about eight leagues in circumference. There are fome fandy bays and low-land on the N. W. fide, which is covered with long grafs, and trees of the fame kind with thofe on the main; lizards of a very large fize alfo abounded, fome of which we took. We found alfo frefh water in two places; one running ftream, clofe to the

the fea, was a little brackifh; the other was a ftanding pool perfectly fweet. We were furprized to fee, that, notwithftanding the diftance of this ifland from the main, it was fometimes vifited by the Indians from thence; as was plain from feven or eight frames of their huts which we found. All thefe were built on eminences, and from their fituation, we judged, that the weather here, at certain feafons, is invariably calm and mild. On our return to the fhip, the captain named this place the Lizard Ifland, on account of our having feen no other animals but lizards. When returning, we landed on a low fandy ifland, upon which were birds of various kinds. We took a neft of young eagles, and therefore called the place Eagle Ifland. We found alfo a neft of fome other bird, of a moft enormous fize: it was made with fticks upon the ground, and was not lefs than fix and twenty feet in circumference, and two feet eight inches high. We perceived that this place alfo had been vifited by the Indians. During our abfence from the fhip, the mafter had landed on feveral low iflands, where he had feen great heaps of turtle fhells, and found the fins of them, which the Indians had left hanging on the trees, fo frefh, that they were dreffed and eaten by the boat's crew.

On Sunday the 12th, the officers held a confultation, and we were unanimous in opinion, that it would be beft to quit the coaft altogether, till we could approach it with lefs danger; in confequence of which concurrent opinion, we failed on Monday the 13th, and got through one of the channels in the reef, happy at finding ourfelves once more in the open fea, after having been furrounded by dreadful fhoals and rocks for near three months. We had now failed above 1000 miles, during which run we had been obliged to keep founding, without the intermiffion of a fingle minute; a circumftance which, it is fuppofed, never happened to any fhip but the Endeavour. The paffage through which we paffed into the open fea beyond the reef, is in latitude 14 deg. 32 min. S. and may always be known by the three high iflands within it, which Capt. Cook called the Iflands of Direction, becaufe by thefe

a ftranger

a ſtranger may find a ſafe channel through the reef quite
to the main. The channel lies from Lizard Iſland
N. E. half N. diſtant three leagues, and is about one
third of a mile broad, and much the ſame in length.
The iſlands abound in turtle and other fiſh, and on the
beach we found bamboos, cocoa-nuts, pumice-ſtone, and
the ſeeds of plants, ſuppoſed to be wafted thither by the
trade winds, as the plants themſelves are not natives of
the country.

On Tueſday the 14th, we anchored, and by obſerva-
tion, our latitude was 13 deg. 46 min. S. and at this
time we had no land in ſight. On the 15th we ſteered
a weſterly courſe, in order to get ſight of land, that we
might not overſhoot the paſſage, if a paſſage there was
between this land and New Guinea. Early in the afternoon we had ſight of land, which had the appearance
of hilly iſlands, but it was judged to be part of the main,
and we ſaw breakers between the veſſel and the land,
in which there was an opening; to get clear, we ſet all
our ſails, and ſtood to the northward till midnight, and
then went on a ſouthward tack for about two miles,
when the breeze died away to a dead calm. When
day-light came on we ſaw a dreadful ſurf break at a vaſt
height, within a mile of the ſhip, towards which the
rolling waves carried her with great rapidity. Thus
diſtreſſed, the boats were ſent a-head to tow, and the
head of the veſſel was brought about, but not till ſhe
was within a hundred yards of the rock, between which
and her there was nothing left but the chaſm, and which
had riſen and broke to a wonderful height on the rock;
but in the moment we expected inſtant deſtruction, a
breeze, hardly diſcernable, aided the boats in getting
the veſſel in an oblique direction from the rock. The
hopes, however, afforded by this providential circumſtance, were deſtroyed by a perfect calm, which ſucceeded in a few minutes; yet the breeze once more returned, before we had loſt the little ground which had been
gained. At this time a ſmall opening was ſeen in the
reef, and a young officer being ſent to examine it,
found that its breadth did not much exceed the length
of the ſhip, but that there was ſmooth water on the
other

other side of the rocks. Animated by the defire of preferving life, we now attempted to pafs the opening; but this was impoffible; for it having become high-water in the interim, the ebb tide rufhed through it with amazing impetuofity, carrying the fhip about a quarter of a mile from the reef, and fhe foon reached the diftance of near two miles, by the help of the boats. When the ebb tide was fpent, the tide of flood again drove the veffel very near the rocks, fo that our profpect of deftruction was renewed, when we difcovered another opening, and a light breeze fpringing up, we entered it, and were driven through it, with a rapidity that pre-vented the fhip from ftriking againft either fide of the channel. The fhip now came to an anchor, and our crew were grateful for having regained a ftation, which they had been very lately moft anxious to quit. The name of Providence Channel was given to the opening through which the fhip had thus efcaped the moft im-minent dangers. A high promontory on the main land in fight, was denominated Cape Weymouth, and a bay near it Weymouth Bay. This day the boats went out to fifh, and met with great fuccefs, particularly in catching cockles, fome of which were of fuch an ama-zing fize, as to require the ftrength of two men to move them. Mr. Banks likewife fucceeded in his fearch for rare fhells, and different kinds of coral.

On the 18th, we difcovered feveral fmall iflands, which were called Forbes's Iflands, and had a fight of a high point of land on the main, which was named the Bolt Head. On the 19th, we difcovered feveral other fmall iflands, the land of which was low, barren, and fandy. A point was feen, and called Cape Grenville, and a bay which took the name of Temple Bay. In the afternoon many other iflands were feen, which were denominated Bird Ifles, from their being frequented by numerous flocks of birds. On the 20th, many more fmall iflands were feen, on one of which were a few trees, and feveral Indian huts, fuppofed to have been erected by the natives of the main land, as temporary habitations during their vifit to thefe iflands. On the 21ft we failed through a channel, in which was a number of fhoals;

and

and gave the name of York Cape to a point of the
main land which forms the fide of the channel. A large
bay is formed to the fouth of the cape, which was
called Newcaftle Bay, and in which are feveral little
iflands; on the north-fide of the cape the land is rather
mountainous, but the low parts of the country abound
with trees; the iflands difcovered in the morning of this
day, were called York Ifles. In the afternoon we anchored between fome iflands, and obferved, that the
channel now began to grow wider; we perceived two
diftant points, between which no land could be feen, fo
that the hope of having at length explored a paffage
into the Indian Sea, began to animate every breaft; but,
to bring the matter to a certainty, the captain took a
party, and being accompanied by Meffrs. Solander and
Banks, they landed on an ifland, on which they had
feen a number of Indians, ten of whom were on a hill,
one of them carrying a bow and a bundle of arrows,
the reft armed with lances; and round the necks of two
of them hung ftrings of mother of pearl. Three of
thefe Indians ftood on fhore, as if to oppofe the landing
of the boat, but they retired before it reached the beach.
The captain and his company now afcended a hill, from
whence they had a view of near forty miles, in which
fpace there was nothing that threatened to oppofe their
paffage, fo that the certainty of a channel feemed to be
almoft indubitable. Previous to their leaving the ifland,
Capt. Cook difplayed the Englifh colours, and took poffeffion of all the eaftern coaft of the country, from the
38th deg. of S. latitude to the prefent fpot, by the name
of New South Wales, for his fovereign the King of
Great Britain: and three volleys of fmall arms being
fired, and anfwered by an equal number from the Endeavour, the place received the name of Poffeffion
Ifland. The next morning we faw three naked women
collecting fhell-fifh on the beach; and weighing anchor,
gave the name of Cape Cornwall to the extreme point
of the largeft ifland on the north-weft fide of the paffage: fome low iflands near the middle of the channel
receiving the name of Wallis's Ifle; foon after which
the fhip came to an anchor, and the long-boat was fent
out

out to found. Towards evening we failed again, and the captain landed with Mr. Banks, on a fmall ifland which was frequented by immenfe numbers of birds, the majority of which being boobies, the place received the name of Booby Ifland. We were now advanced to the northern extremity of New Holland, and had the fatisfaction of viewing the open fea to the weftward. The N. E. entrance of the paffage is formed by the main land of New Holland, and by a number of iflands, which took the name of the Prince of Wales's Iflands, and which Capt. Cook imagines may reach to New Guinea ; thefe iflands abound with trees and grafs, and were known to be inhabited, from the fmoke that was feen afcending in many places.

To the paffage we had failed through, Capt. Cook gave the name of Endeavour Streights. New South Wales is a much larger country than any hitherto known, and not deemed a continent, being larger than all Europe, which is proved by the Endeavour's having coafted more than 2000 miles, even if her tract were reduced to a ftrait-line. Northward of the latitude of 33 deg. the country is hilly, yet not mountainous ; but to the fouthward of that latitude, it is moftly low and even ground. The hills in general are diverfified by lawns and woods, and many of the valleys abound with herbage, though, on the whole, it cannot be deemed a fertile country. To the northward the grafs is not fo rich, nor the trees fo high as in the fouthern parts, and almoft every where, even the largeft trees grow at a diftance of not lefs than thirteen yards afunder. In all thefe places where the land forms a bay, the fhore is covered with mangroves, that grow about a mile in land, in a fwampy ground, which the fpring tides always overflow ; in fome parts there are bogs, covered with thick grafs, and plenty of under-wood in the valleys ; the foil in general feems unfit for cultivation, though there are many fpots where the arts of tillage might be attended with fuccefs. There are feveral falt creeks, running in many directions through the country, where there are alfo brooks of frefh water, but there are no rivers of any confiderable extent ; yet it feemed to be well watered,

watered, as the time when the fhip was on the coaft was reckoned the drieft feafon of the year. The gum-tree yields a refin like the dragons blood. Here are three kinds of palm-trees, two of which are found only in the northern diftrict. Nuts fomewhat refembling chefnuts are produced by one of thefe, which were fuppofed to be eatable, yet fome of the feamen having made free with them were taken very ill; two of whom died within a week, and it was not without difficulty that the third was recovered. The fecond fort of palm is much like the Weft Indian cabbage-tree, which yields a cabbage of an agreeable tafte. The third fort abounds in the fouthern part, and produces a fmall cabbage of a very agreeable flavour, with many nuts, which furnifh food for hogs. There is likewife a tree on which grows a purple apple that taftes like a damofcene, as we have before obferved. Befides thefe there is a fig-tree, producing figs, but not of the fineft fort, and they have another which bears a fort of plumb that is flat on the fides like a cheefe. A plant was found here, the leaves of which were like thofe of the bulrufh; it yields a bright yellow refin, that refembles gumbouge, but does not ftain—it had a very agreeable fmell. We found two forts of yams, the one round and covered with ftringy fibres, the other in fhape like a radifh; both of which are of a pleafant tafte. A fruit of a difagreeable flavour was found, in fhape refembling a pine-apple; and another that was much like a cherry, but had a foft kernel. The country produces purflain and wild parfly. We faw here, befides the beaft already mentioned, one that was called a quall, the belly of this animal was quite white, its back was brown with white fpots; and it was like a pole-cat. Vaft numbers of beautiful pigeons were obferved, and the feamen fhot many of them, alfo eagles, hawks, cranes, herons, buftards, crows, parrots, parroquets, cockatoos, and fome other birds of fine plumage, befides quails and doves.

In this country there are but few infects, and the ants and mufquitos are the chief among them. There are four kinds of the former which deferve particular notice. The firft of thefe are entirely green, and live on trees,

where

where they build their nefts in a very curious manner, bending down the leaves, and gluing them together with an animal juice, fuppofed to proceed from their own bodies. While feveral of thefe animals were bufied in this employ, thoufands were joined to keep the leaf in its proper fituation, which, when they were difturbed in their work, flew back with a force that any one would have imagined to be fuperior to their united ftrength; at the fame time they avenged themfelves by feverely ftinging their difturbers. The fecond fpecies of ants here are black, and live in the infide of the branches, after they have worked out the pith. The third fort lodged themfelves in the root of a plant that twines round the trunks of other trees. This they made hollow, and cut into a great number of paffages that ran acrofs each other, yet there was no appearance of the plants having been injured. They are not above half the fize of the red ants of this country. As to the fourth fort they are like the Eaft-Indian white ants, and had one fort of nefts as big as a half-peck loaf which hung from the boughs of trees, and were compofed of feveral minute parts of vegetables, which appeared to be ftuck together by the glutinous juice before mentioned. There was a communication between the cells, and paffages to other nefts upon the fame tree; they had alfo a hollow covered paffage to another neft on the ground, at the root of a different tree. The height of the ground-neft was found to be about fix feet, and the breadth nearly the fame: and the outfide was plaiftered with clay almoft two inches thick. Thefe had a fubterraneous paffage leading to the roots of the trees near which they were conftructed, from whence thefe creatures afcended the trunk and branches by covered ways, calculated for the purpofe. It was concluded, that the ants reforted to thefe ground-nefts during the wet feafon, as they were water proof.

Variety of fifh is fupplied by the feas in thefe parts, among which are mullets, cray-fifh and crabs. Upon the fhoals are found the rock, pearl, and other oyfters, as well as the moft delicate green turtle, befides thofe enormous cockles which have been already mentioned.

No. 7.   F f   Alligators

Alligators are found in the rivers and falt creeks. The country does not appear to be inhabited by numbers any way proportioned to its great extent; not above thirty being ever feen together but once, which was when thofe of both fexes, and all ages got together on a rock off Botany Bay, to view the fhip. None of their villages confifted of more huts than would afford fhelter for fourteen or fifteen men, and thefe were the largeft numbers that were affembled with a view to attack us. No part of the country appeared to be cultivated, whence there muft neceffarily be fewer inhabitants on the inland parts than on the fea-coaft. The men are well made, of the middle fize, and active, in a high degree; but their voices are foft, even to effeminacy. Their colour is chocolate; but they were fo covered with dirt, as to look almoft as black as negroes. Their hair is naturally long and black, but they commonly cropped it fhort; in fome few inftances it is flightly curled, but in common quite ftrait; it is always matted with dirt, yet wholly free from lice; their beards are thick and bufhy, but kept fhort by fingeing. The women were feen only at a diftance, as the men conftantly left them behind when they croffed the river. The chief ornament of thefe people is the bone that is thruft through the nofe, which the failors whimfically called their fprit-fail yard; but befides this they wore necklaces formed of fhells, a fmall cord tied twice or thrice round the arm between the elbow and fhoulder, and a ftring of plaited human hair round the waift. Some few of them had an ornament of fhells hanging acrofs the breaft. Befides thefe ornaments they painted their bodies and limbs white and red, in ftripes of different dimenfions; and they had a circle of white round each eye, and fpots of it on the face. Their ears were bored, but they did not wear ear-rings. They accepted whatever was given them, but feemed to have no idea of making an adequate return; and they would not part with their ornaments for any thing that was offered in exchange. Their bodies were marked with fcars, which they fignified were in remembrance of the deceafed. Their huts were built with fmall rods,

the

the two ends of which were fixed into the ground, fo as
to form the figure of an oven ; they are covered with
pieces of bark and palm-leaves. The door of this
building, which is only high enough to fit upright in,
is oppofite to the fire-places. They fleep with their
heels turned up toward their heads ; and even in this
pofture the hut will not hold more than four people.
In the northern parts, where the weather was warmer,
one fide of the houfes was left open, and the other oppofed to whatever wind might blow at the time there ;
huts were only built for temporary ufe, and left behind
when they removed to other parts of the country ; but
if their ftay was only for a night or two, they had no
other protection from the weather than what the grafs
and bufhes afforded. While the huts on the main land
were turned from the wind, thofe on the iflands were
towards it : a kind of proof that they vifit the iflands
in fine weather, and enjoy the refrefhing breeze while
they flept. Thefe huts are furnifhed with a kind of
bucket for fetching water, made of an oblong piece of
bark tied up at each end with the twig of a tree ; and
this is the only furniture of the houfe. On their backs
they have a kind of bag, of the fize and form of a
cabbage-net, in which they carry their fifh-hooks and
lines, of the fhells of which they make thefe hooks ;
the ornaments which they wear confift of fome points
of darts, and two or three bits of paint ; and in this
narrow compafs lie all their riches. They feed on the
kanguroo, and feveral kinds of birds when they can
catch them ; they likewife eat yams, and various kinds
of fruit ; but the principal article of their exiftence is
fifh. They were frequently obferved with the leaves
of a tree in their mouths, but whether it had the qualities of either tobacco or beetle could not be known ;
but it was obferved not to difcolour the teeth or lips.

From the notches that were feen in a great number
of trees, for the purpofe of climbing them, it was
imagined that their method of taking the kanguroo,
was by ftriking it with their lances as it paffed under the
tree. In thefe likewife, it is probable, that they took
birds, while they were roofting, as they feemed too
fhy

shy to be otherwise catched. Their method of producing fire, and extending the flames of it, is very singular: having wrought one end of a stick into an obtuse point, they place this point upon a piece of dry wood, and turning the upright stick very fast backward and forward between their hands, fire is soon produced, nor is it increased with less celerity. One of the natives was frequently observed to run along the sea coast, leaving fire in various places. The method taken to do this was as follows: before he set off, he wrapped up a little spark of fire in dry grass, and the quickness of his motion soon fanning it into a flame, he then placed it on the ground, and putting a spark of it in another bit of grass ran on again, and increased the number of his fires at pleasure. These fires were supposed to be intended for the taking of the kanguroo, as that animal was so very shy of fire, that when pursued by the dogs, it would not cross places which had been newly burnt, even when the fire was extinguished.

The natives of New South Wales make use of spears or lances, but these are very differently constructed: those that were seen in the southern parts of the country had four prongs, pointed with bone, and barbed, and the points were rubbed with a kind of wax, the smoothness of which made an easier passage into what was struck by them. On the contrary, the lances in the northern parts have only one point; the shafts of them are of different lengths, from eight to fourteen feet, are made of the stalk of a plant not unlike a bulrush, and consists of several joints let into each other, and tied together. The points of these lances are sometimes made of fish-bone, and sometimes of a hard heavy wood; they are barbed with other pieces of wood or stone, so that when they have entered any depth in the body, they cannot be drawn out without tearing the flesh in a shocking manner, or leaving splinters behind them. When the natives intend to wound at a considerable distance, they discharge this instrument with a throwing stick, but if the object be near them, it is thrown from the hand only. The throwing-stick is a

piece

piece of smooth, hard, red wood, half an inch thick, two inches broad, and about three feet in length, having a crofs piece near four inches long at one end, and a small knob at the other. A small hollow is made in the shaft of the lance, near the point, and in this hollow the knob is received, but, on being forced forward, it will easily slip from it. The lance being placed on this throwing-stick, the Indian holds it over his shoulder, shakes it, and then throws both lance and stick with his utmost power, but as the crofs-piece strikes the shoulder the sudden jerk stops the stick, while the lance is driven forward with amazing rapidity, and is generally so well aimed, that a mark at the distance of fifty yards is more certainly struck with it than by a bullet from a gun. These people make use of shields made of the bark of trees, of about eighteen inches broad, and three feet long. Many trees were seen from whence the bark had been taken, and others on which the shields were cut out but not taken away. In the northern parts of this country, the canoes are formed by hollowing the trunk of a tree, and it was conjectured, that this operation must have been performed by fire, as the natives did not appear to have any instruments proper for that purpose. The canoes are in length about fourteen feet, and so narrow, that they would be frequently overset, but that they are provided with an out-rigger. The natives row them with paddles, using both hands in that employment. The canoes in the southern parts are formed only of a piece of bark four yards long, fastened together at each end, and the middle kept open by pieces of wood, passing from side to side. In deep water these are rowed by paddles, of about a foot and a half in length, the rower having one in each hand, but in shallow water they are pushed forward by means of a long stick. As these vessels are extremely light, and draw very little water, the Indians run them on the mud banks in search of shell-fish, some of which, it is probable, they broil and eat as foon as they are taken, as it was remarked that in the centre of these vessels there was usually a fire burning on a quantity of fea-weed. The natives

have

have no tools but a wooden mallet, a kind of wedge, and an adze, made of stone, with some pieces of coral and shells, which may possibly be applied to the purposes of cutting. They polish the points of their lances, and their throwing-sticks, with the leaves of a tree that appears to be the wild fig, which bites with a sharpness, almost equal to that of a rasp. Four people are the greatest number that a canoe will contain: and when more than this number were to pass a river, three were landed out of the first freight, and one man went back for the rest.

The following may serve as a specimen of their language,

NEW HOLLAND.	ENGLISH.
Aco,	The arms.
Aibudje,	To yawn.
Bamma,	A man.
Bonjoo,	The nose.
Boota,	To eat.
Chucula,	To drink.
Cotta,	A dog.
Coyor,	The breast.
Doomboo,	The neck.
Dunjo,	A father.
Eboorbalga,	The thumbs.
Edamal,	The feet.
Eiyamoae,	The crown of the head.
Eya & ba,	That or this.
Galan,	The sun.
Garbar,	The eye-brows.
Gippa,	The belly.
Kere,	The sky.
Kolke,	The nails.
Mailelel,	To swim.
Maianang,	Fire.
Marra,	To go.
Mangal,	The hands.
Meul,	The eyes.
Melea,	The ears.
Mingoore,	To dance.

Mocoo,

NEW HOLLAND.	ENGLISH.
Mocoo,	*The back.*
Morcol,	*The throat.*
Moree,	*The hear of the head.*
Mootjel,	*A woman.*
Mulere,	*The teeth.*
Nakil,	*The little finger.*
Peegoorga,	*The legs.*
Peete,	*The forehead.*
Poapoa,	*Earth.*
Pongo,	*The knees.*
Poona,	*To sleep.*
Poorai,	*Water.*
Poteea,	*Fish.*
Putai	*A turtle.*
Tabugga,	*A fly.*
Tacal,	*The chin.*
Te,	*A, or the.*
Tennapuke,	*The hole made in the nostrils for the bone ornament.*
Tocaya,	*Sit down.*
Tumurre,	*A sun.*
Unjar,	*The tongue.*
Wageegee,	*The head.*
Walloo,	*The temples.*
Waller,	*The beard.*
Walboolbool,	*A butterfly.*
Wonananio,	*Asleep.*
Wulgar,	*The clouds.*
Yembe,	*The lips.*
Zoocoo,	*Wood.*

Though it appeared evident, that the natives of these islands waged war with each other, by the weapons they possessed, yet not a wound received from their enemies appeared on any part of their bodies.

C H A P.

CHAP. X.

*The Endeavour continues her Voyage from South Wales to
New Guinea—An Account of Incidents upon landing
there—She proceeds from New Guinea to the Island of
Savu—Transactions at this Isle—Its Produce and Inhabitants, with a Specimen of their Language—Run from
Savu to Batavia—Transactions while the Endeavour
was refitting at this Place.*

ON the 23d of August, 1770, in the afternoon, after
leaving Booby Island, we had light airs till five
o'clock, when it fell calm, and we came to an anchor
in eight fathom water, with a soft sandy bottom. On
Friday, the 24th, soon after the anchor was weighed,
we got under sail, steering N. W. and in a few hours
one of the boats a-head made the signal for shoal-wa-
ter. We instantly brought the ship to, with all her
sails standing, and a survey being taken of the sea
around her, it was found that she had met with another narrow escape, as she was almost encompassed with
shoals, and was likewise so situated between them, that
she must have struck before the boat's crew had made
the signal, if she had been half the length of a cable
on either side. In the afternoon we made sail with the
ebb tide, and got out of danger before sun-set, when
we brought to for the night.

On Sunday, the 26th, it was the Captain's intention to steer N. W. but having met with those shoals,
we altered our course, and soon got into deep water.
On the 27th we pursued our voyage, shortening sail at
night, and tacking till day-break of the 28th, when
we steered due N. in search of New Guinea. At this
time our latitude by observation was 8 deg. 52 min.
S. We here observed many parts of the sea covered with a kind of brown scum, to which our sailors gave the name of spawn. It is formed of an incredible number of minute particles, each of which,
when seen through the microscope, was found to con-
sist of a considerable number of tubes, and these tubes

were

were fubdivided into little cells. The fcum being burnt, and yielding no fmell like what is produced by animal fubftances, we concluded it was of the vegetable kind. This has often been feen on the coaft of Brazil, and generally makes its appearance near the land. A bird called the Noddy was found this evening among the rigging of the fhip. Land having been this day difcovered from the maft head, we ftood off and on all night, and at day-break we failed towards it with a brifk gale. Between fix and feven in the morning we had fight of a fmall low ifland, at about a league from the main, in latitude 80 deg. 13 min. S. and in longitude 221 deg. 25 min. W. and it has already been diftinguifhed by the names of Bartholomew and Whermoyfen. It appeared a very level ifland, clothed with trees, among which is the cocoa-nut; and we judged it to be inhabited by the fmoke of the fires which were feen in different parts of it. The boats were now fent out to found, as the water was fhallow; but as the fhip, in failing two leagues, had found no increafe in its depth, fignals were made for the boats to return on board. We then ftood out to fea till midnight, tacked, and ftood in for land till the morning.

On Thurfday, the 30th, when about four leagues diftant, we had fight of it, and its appearance was ftill flat and woody. Abundance of the brown fcum was ftill feen on the furface of the fea, and the failors, convinced that it was not fpawn, gave it the whimfical name of fea-faw-duft. We now held a northward courfe, fcarcely within fight of land, and as the water was but juft deep enough to navigate the veffel, many unfuccefsful attempts were made to bring her near enough to get on fhore: it was therefore determined to land in one of the boats, while the fhip kept plying off and on. In confequence of this refolution,

On Monday, Sept. the 3d, Capt. Cook, Mr. Banks, and Dr. Solander, attended by the boat's crew, and Mr. Banks's fervant, fet off from the fhip in the pinnace, being in all twelve perfons well armed. We rowed directly to the fhore, but when come within two hundred yards of it, we found the water fo fhallow, that we

were obliged to leave the boat, in the care of two of the
failors, and wade to land. We had no fooner reached
the fhore, than we faw feveral prints of human feet
on the fand, below high-water mark, from whence it
was evident, that the natives had been there. We
concluded they could be at no great diftance, and as a
thick wood came down within a hundred yards of the
water, we proceeded with caution, that our retreat to
the boat might not be cut off. We walked by the fide
of the wood, and came to a grove of cocoa-nut trees,
not far from which was a fhed, or hut, which had
been covered with leaves, and near it lay a number of
frefh fhells of the fruit. At a fmall diftance of from this
place we found plantains ; and having now advanced
about a quarter of a mile from the boat, three Indians
rufhed out of the wood with a hideous fhout, at about
the diftance of a hundred yards ; and as they ran towards us, the foremoft threw fomething out of his
hand, which flew on one fide of him, and burnt exactly like gun-powder, but made no report ; and the
other two threw their lances at us. No time was to be
loft ; we difcharged our pieces, loaded with fmall fhot
only ; which we imagine they did not feel ; for, without retreating, they caft a third dart : we therefore now
loaded with ball, and fired a fecond time. It is probable fome of them were wounded, as they all took to
their heels with great agility. We improved this interval, in which the deftruction of the natives was no
longer neceffary to our own defence, and with all expedition returned to our boat. In the way we perceived fignals on board, that more Indians were coming
down in a body ; and before we got into the water, we
perceived feveral of them coming round a point at the
diftance of about five hundred yards. When they faw us
they halted, and feemed to wait till their main body
fhould join them. They continued in this ftation, without giving us any interruption, while we entered the water, and waded toward the boat. We now took a view
of them at our leifure. They made much the fame appearance as the New-Hollanders, being nearly of the
fame ftature, and having their hair fhort cropped.

They

They were alfo like them ftark naked. During this time they were fhouting at a diftance, and letting off their fires, which feemed to be difcharged by a fhort piece of ftick, probably a hollow cane, this being fwung fideways, produced fire and fmoke like that occafioned by a mufquet. The crew on board the fhip faw this ftrange appearance, and thought the natives had fire arms. Thofe who went out in the boat, and had rowed a-breaft of them, fired fome mufquets above their heads, the balls of which being heard by the natives rattling among the trees, they retired very deliberately, and our people in the boat returned to the fhip. Upon examining the lances that had been thrown at us, we found they were made of a reed, or bamboo cane, the points of which were of hard wood, and barbed in many places. They were light, ill made, and about four feet long. Such was the force with which they were difcharged, that they went beyond us, though we were at fixty yards diftance, but in what manner they were difcharged we could not determine; probably they might be thrown with a ftick, in the manner practiced by the New Hollanders. This place is in latitude 6 deg. 15 min. S. The whole coaft of this country is low land, but covered with a luxuriance of wood and herbage beyond defcription beautiful. The cocoa-nut, bread-fruit, and plantain tree, all flourifhed here in the higheft perfection, befides moft of the trees, fhrubs, and plants, that are common to the South Sea iflands. This day, Monday, Sept. the 3d, we made fail to the weftward; being refolved to fpend no more time upon this coaft; but before we got under fail, fome of the officers ftrongly urged the Captain to fent a party of men on fhore, to cut down the cocoa-nut trees, for the fake of the fruit. This Capt. Cook, with equal wifdom and humanity, peremptorily refufed, as unjuft and cruel; fenfible that the poor Indians, who could not brook even the landing of a fmall party on their coaft, would have made a vigorous effort to defend their property had it been invaded; confequently many muft have fallen a facrifice on their fide, and perhaps fome of our own people. " I fhould, (fays Capt. Cook)

G g 2

have

have regretted the neceffity of fuch a meafure, if I
had been in want of the neceffaries of life; and certainly it would have been highly criminal when nothing
was to be obtained but two or three hundred green
cocoa-nuts; which would at moft have procured us a
mere tranfient gratification. I might indeed have proceeded farther along the coaft to the northward, or
weftward, in fearch of a place where the fhip might
have lain fo near the fhore, as to cover the people with
her guns when they landed; but this would have ob-
viated only part of the mifchief, and though it might
have fecured us, it would probably in the very act have
been fatal to the natives. Befides, we had reafon to
think that before fuch a place could have been found,
we fhould have been carried fo far to the weftward as
to have been obliged to go to Batavia, on the north
fide of Java, through the ftreights of Sunday: the
fhip alfo was fo very leaky that I doubted whether it
would not be neceffary to heave her down at Batavia,
which was another reafon for making the beft of our
way to that place, efpecially as no difcoveries could be
expected in feas which had already been navigated, and
where every coaft had been laid down by the Dutch
geographers."

On Saturday the 8th, we paffed two fmall iflands, on
one of which Capt. Cook would have landed, but having only ten fathom water, the ground being alfo rocky,
and the wind blowing frefh, we might have endangered
the fafety of the fhip. We now failed at a moderate
rate till next morning at three o'clock; after which we
had no ground with 120 fathoms. Before noon we
had fight of land, which was conjectured to be either
the Arrou Iflands, or Timor Laoct. We were now in
latitude 9 deg. 37 min. S. and in longitude 233 deg.
54 min. W. We ftood off and on during the night,
and on Wednefday the 12th, we faw a number of fires
and fmoke in feveral places, from whence it was conjectured that the place was well peopled. The land
near the fhore was covered with high trees, not unlike
pines; farther back were cocoa-trees and mangroves;
there were many falt-water creeks, and feveral fpots of
ground

ground which appeared to have been cleared by art; and the whole country rofe, by gradual flopes, into hills of a very confiderable height. The land and fea breezes being now very flight, we continued in fight of the ifland for two days, when it was obferved that the hills reached in many places quite to the fea-coaft, and where that was not the cafe, there were large and noble groves of the cocoa-nut tree, which ran about a mile up the county, at which diftance great numbers of houfes and plantations were feen; the plantations were furrounded with fences, and extended nearly to the fummits of the moft lofty hills, yet neither the natives nor cattle were feen on any of them, which was thought a very extraordinary circumftance. Fine groves of the fan palm fhaded the houfes from the rays of the fun.

On the 16th, we had fight of the little ifland called Rotte; and the fame day faw the ifland Semau, at a diftance to tne fouthward of Timor. The ifland of Rotte is chiefly covered with bufhy wood without leaves; but there are a number of fan palm trees on it, growing near the fandy beaches; and the whole confifts of alternate hills and valleys. The ifland of Semau is not fo hilly as Timor, but refembles it greatly in other refpects. At ten o'clock this night a dull reddifh light was feen in the air, many parts of which emitted rays of a brighter colour, which foon vanifhed, and were fucceeded by others of the fame kind. This phœnomenon, which reached about ten degrees above the horizon, bore a confiderable refemblance to the Aurora Borealis, only that the rays of light which it emitted had no tremulous motion: it was furveyed for two hours, during which time its brightnefs continued undiminifhed. As the fhip was now clear of all the iflands which had been laid down in fuch maps as were on board, we made fail during the night, and were furprifed the next morning at the fight of an ifland to the W. S. W. which we flattered ourfelves was a new difcovery. Before noon we had fight of houfes, groves of cocoa-nut trees, and large flocks of fheep. This was a welcome fight to people whofe

health

health was declining for want of refreshment, and it was instantly resolved to attempt the purchase of what we stood so much in need of. The second lieutenant was immediately dispatched in the pinnace, in search of a landing-place; and he took with him such things as it was thought might be acceptable to the natives.— During Mr. Gore's absence, the people on board saw two men on horseback upon the hills, who frequently stopped to take a view of the vessel. The lieutenant soon returned with an account that he had entered a little cove, near which stood a few houses ; that several men advanced and invited him to land ; and that they conversed together so well as they could by signs. He reported that these people were very like the Malays, both in person and dress; and said they had no other arms but a knife which each of them wore in his girdle.

The lieutenant not being able to find any place in which the ship might come to anchor, he was dispatched again with money and goods to buy such necessaries as were immediately wanted for the sick. Dr. Solander attended the lieutenant, and during their absence, the ship stood on and off the shore. Soon after the boat had put off, two other horsemen were seen from the ship, one of whom had a laced hat on, and was dressed in a coat and waistcoat, of the fashion of Europe. These men rode about on shore taking little notice of the boat, but regarding the ship with the utmost attention. As soon as the boat reached the shore, some other persons on horseback, and many on foot hastened to the spot, and it was observed that some cocoa-nuts were put into the boat, from whence it was concluded, that a traffick had commenced with the natives. A signal being made from the boat that the ship might anchor in a bay at some distance, she immediately bore away for it. When the lieutenant came on board, he reported, that he could not purchase any cocoa-nuts, as the owner of them was absent, and that what he had brought were given him, in return for which he had pressed the natives with some linen. The method by which he learned that there was a harbour in the neighbourhood, was by the natives drawing a kind

kind of rude map on the fand, in which the harbour,
and a town near it, was reprefented ; it was likewife
hinted to him, that fruit, fowls, hogs, and fheep might
be there obtained in great abundance. He faw feveral
of the principal inhabitants of the ifland, who had
chains of gold about their necks, and wore fine linen.
The word Portuguefe being frequently repeated by the
Indians, it was conjectured that fome natives of Portugal were in the ifland, and one of the boat's crew being
of that kingdom, he fpoke to the iflanders in his own
language, but foon found that they had only learned a
few words, of which they did not know the meaning.
While the natives were endeavouring to reprefent the
fituation of the town near the harbour, one of them, in
order to be more particular in directions, informed the
Englifh that they would fee fomething which he endeavoured to defcribe by placing his fingers acrofs each
other ; and the Portuguefe failor took it for granted,
that he could mean nothing but a crofs. When the
boat's crew were on the point of returning to the fhip,
the gentleman who had been feen on horfeback in the
drefs of Europe, came down to the beach ; but the
lieutenant did not think it proper to hold a conference
with him, becaufe he had left his commiffion on board
the fhip.

When the fhip had entered the bay, in the evening,
according to the directions received, an Indian town
was feen at a diftance ; upon which a jack was hoifted
on the fore-top-maft head, prefently afterwards three
guns were fired, and Dutch colours were hoifted in
the town ; the fhip, however, held on her way, and
came to an anchor at feven in the evening. The colours being feen hoifted on the beach the next morning,
the captain concluded, that the Dutch had a fettlement
on the ifland, he therefore difpatched the fecond lieutenant to acquaint the governor, or other principal refident, who they were, and that the fhip had put in for
neceffary refrefhments. The lieutenant having landed,
he was received by a kind of guard of fomething more
than twenty Indians, armed with mufquets, who after
they had taken down their colours from the beach, pro-

ceeded

ceeded without the leaft military order; and thus efcorted him to the town, where the colours had been
hoifted the preceding evening. The lieutenant was
now conducted to the Raja, or king of the ifland, to
whom, by means of a Portuguefe interpreter, he made
known his bufinefs. The Raja faid, he was ready to
fupply the fhip with the neceffary refrefhments, but that
he could not trade with any other people than the
Dutch, with whom he was in alliance, without having
firft obtained their confent; he added, however, that
he would make application to the Dutch agent, who
was the only white man among them. To this agent,
whofe name was Lange, and who proved to be the perfon that was feen from the fhip in the European drefs,
a letter was difpatched, and in a few hours he came to
the town, behaved politely to the lieutenant, and told
him he might buy what he thought proper of the inhabitants of the ifland. This offer being freely made, and
readily accepted, the Raja and Mr. Lange intimated
their wifhes to go on board the fhip, and that two
of the boat's crew might be left as hoftages for their
fafe return. The lieutenant gratified them in both
thefe requefts, and took them on board juft before dinner was ferved. It was thought that they would have
fat down without ceremony; but now the Raja intimated his doubts, whether being a black, they would
permit him to fit down with them. The politenefs of
the officers foon removed his fcruples, and the greateft
good humour and feftivity prevailed among them. As
Dr. Solander and another gentleman on board, were tolerable proficients in Dutch, they acted as interpreters
between Mr. Lange and the officers, while fome of the
failors, who underftood Portuguefe, converfed with
fuch of the Raja's attendants as fpoke that language.
Our dinner confifted chiefly of mutton, which when the
Raja had tafted, he requefted of us an Englifh fheep,
and the only one we had left was prefented to him.
Our complaifance in this particular, encouraged the
king to afk for an Englifh dog, and Mr. Banks politely
gave him his greyhound. A fpying-glafs was alfo put
into his hand, Mr. Johan Chriftopher Lange having intimated,

timated, that fuch a prefent would be very acceptable. Our vifitors now informed us, that the ifland abounded with buffaloes, fheep, hogs, and fowls, plenty of which fhould be driven down to the fhore the next day. This put us all in high fpirits, and the liquor circulated rather fafter than either the Indians or the Saxon could bear; but they had, however, the refolution to exprefs a defire to depart, before they were quite intoxicated. When they came upon deck, they were received in the fame manner as when they came aboard, by the marines under arms; and the Raja exprefling a defire to fee them exercife, his curiofity was gratified. They fired three rounds. The king obferved them with great attention, and appeared much furprized at the regularity and expedition of their manœuvres. When they cocked their firelocks, he ftruck the fide of the fhip with his ftick, exclaiming at the fame time violently, " That all the locks made but one click." They were difmiffed with many prefents, and on their departure were faluted with nine guns. Mr. Banks with Dr. Solander accompanied them, and when they put off returned our compliments with three cheers. Our gentlemen on their arrival at the town, tafted their palm-wine, which was the frefh juice of the trees, unfermented. It had a fweet, but not difagreeable tafte, and hopes were entertained, that it might contribute to recover our fick from the fcurvy. The houfes of the natives confifted of only a thatched roof, fupported over a boarded floor, by pillars about four feet high.

Wednefday the 19th, in the morning, Capt. Cook, attended by feveral gentlemen, went on fhore to return the Raja's vifit; but their principal intention was to purchafe the cattle and fowls, which they had been affured the preceding day fhould be driven down to the beach. We were greatly chagrined at finding no fteps had been taken to fulfil this promife: however, we proceeded to the houfe of affembly, which, with a few other houfes, built by the Dutch Eaft-India Company, are diftinguifhed from the reft, by having two pieces of wood, refembling a pair of cows horns, fixed at each end of the roof; and thefe we concluded to be what the

No. 8. Hh Portuguefe

Portuguefe failor conftrued into croffes, from the Indian
having croffed his fingers when he was defcribing the
town. At the houfe of affembly we faw Mr. Lange
and the Raja, whofe name was A Madocho Lomi Djara,
furrounded by many of the principal people; Capt. Cook
having informed them, that he had loaded his boat with
goods, which he wifhed to exchange for neceffary refrefhments, permiffion was given him to land them.
We now endeavoured to make an agreement for the
hogs, fheep, and buffaloes, which were to be paid for
in cafh; but this bufinefs was no fooner hinted than
Mr. Lange took his leave, having firft told the captain,
that he had received a letter from the governor of Concordia, in Timor, the contents of which fhould be dif-
clofed at his return. As the morning was now far advanced, and we had no frefh provifions on board, we
requefted the Raja's permiffion to buy a fmall hog and
fome rice, and to order his people to drefs the dinner
for us. He very obligingly replied, that if we could eat
victuals dreffed by his fubjects, which he could fcarcely
fuppofe, he would do himfelf the honour of entertaining us. A dinner being thus procured, the captain fent
off his boat to bring liquors from the fhip. It was
ready about five o'clock, and after we were feated on
mats, which were fpread on the floor, it was ferved in
fix and thirty bafkets. We were then conducted by
turns to a hole in the floor, near which flood a man
with water in a veffel, made of the leaves of the fan-
palm, who affifted us in wafhing our hands. This done
we returned to our places and expected the king.
Having waited fome time, we enquired the reafon of his
abfence, and were informed that the perfon who gave
the entertainment never partook of it with his guefts;
but that the Raja was ready to come and tafte of what
was provided, if we entertained a thought that the victuals were poifoned. We declared that we did not
harbour any fuch fufpicion, and defired that the cuftom
of the country might not be violated on our account.
When dinner was ended, the wine paffed brifkly, and
we invited the Raja to drink with us, thinking if he
would not eat with us, he might at leaft fhare in the
jollity

jollity of the bottle; but he again excufed himfelf, faying, the man who entertained his guefts fhould never
get drunk with them, and that the fureft way to avoid
this was to refrain from tafting the liquor. The prime
minifter and Mr. Lange were of our party, and we
made a moft luxurious meal. The pork and rice were
excellent, and the broth not to be defpifed; but the
fpoons, made of leaves, were fo fmall, that few of us had
patience to ufe them. We did not drink our wine at
the place where we had dined; and the remains of the
dinner we left to the feamen and fervants, who immediately took our places. They could not difpatch
all we had left; but the Raja's female fervants, who
came to take away the utenfils, obliged them to carry
away what they had not eaten. When we thought the
wine had fo far operated as to open the heart, we took
an opportunity to enquire after the buffaloes and fheep,
of which we had not in all this time heard a fyllable,
though they were to have been at the beach early in the
morning. Mr. Lange, the Saxon Dutchman, now began to communicate to us the contents of the letter,
which he pretended to have received from the governor of Concordia, and wherein he faid, inftructions were
given, that if the fhip fhould touch at this ifland, and
be in want of provifions, fhe fhould be fupplied; but he
was not to permit her to remain longer than was neceffary; nor were any large prefents to be made to the natives of low rank, nor to be even left with their fuperi-
ors to be divided among them after the fhip had failed;
but he added, any trifling civilities received from the Indians might be acknowledged by a prefent of beads,
or other articles of very fmall value. It is probable
that the whole of this ftory was a fiction; and that
by precluding our liberality to the natives, the Saxon
Dutchman hoped more eafily to draw all the prefents
of any value into his own pocket. In the evening we
were informed, that only a few fheep had been brought
to the beach, which had been driven away before our
people could procure money from the fhip to pay for
them. Some fowls however were bought, and a large
quantity of a kind of fyrup made of the juice of the

palm-tree. This, though infinitely fuperior to molaffes or treacle, fold at a very low price. Vexed at being thus difappointed in purchafing the chief articles moft wanted, we remonftrated with Mr. Lange, who now found another fubterfuge. He faid, had we gone down to the beach ourfelves, we might have purchafed what we pleafed; but that the natives were afraid of being impofed on by our feamen with counterfeit money. We could not but feel fome indignation againft a man who had concealed this, being true; or alledged it, being falfe; and Capt. Cook repaired immediately to the beach, but no cattle were to be feen, nor were any at hand to be bought. During his abfence, Lange told Mr. Banks, that the Indians were offended at our not having offered them gold for what we had to fell, and without which nothing could be bought. Mr. Banks did not think it worth his while to hold farther conver-fation with a man who had been guilty of fuch repeat-ed falfities; but rofe up fuddenly, and we all returned on board much diffatisfied with our fruitlefs negotia-tions. The Raja had indeed given a more plaufible reafon for our difappointment: he faid, the buffaloes being far up in the country, there had not been time to bring them down to the beach.

On Thurfday the 20th, Dr. Solander went again afhore with Capt. Cook, and while the former went up to the town to fpeak to Lange, the captain remained on the beach with a view of purchafing provifions. Here he met with the old Indian, who, as he appeared to have fome authority, we had among ourfelves diftin-guifhed by the name of the Prime Minifter. In order to engage this man in our intereft, the captain prefented him with a fpying-glafs; but only a fmall buffalo was offered to be fold. The price was five guineas, nearly twice its real value. Three, however, were offered, which the dealer thought a good price; but faid, he muft acquaint the king with what had been bid before he could ftrike the bargain. A meffenger was immediate-ly difpatched to the Raja, and on his return brought word, that not lefs than five guineas would be taken for the buffalo. The captain abfolutely refufed to give the

fum

fum demanded, which occafioned the fending away a fecond meffenger, and during his abfence, Dr. Solander was feen coming from the town, followed by above a hundred men, fome of whom were armed with muf-quets, and others with lances. Upon enquiring into the meaning of this hoftile appearance, the doctor in-formed us, the purport of a meffage from the king was, according to Mr. Lange's interpretation, that the peo-ple would not trade with us becaufe we had refufed to give them more than half the value for their commo-dities ; and that we were not to expect permiffion to trade upon any terms longer than this day.

A native of Timor, whofe parents were Portuguefe, came down with this party, and delivered to the cap-tain what was pretended to be the order of the Raja, and which was in fubftance the fame that Lange had told Dr. Solander; but it was afterwards difcovered that this man was a confident of Lange's in the fcheme of extortion. The Englifh gentlemen had at the fame time no doubt, but that the fuppofed order of the Raja was a contrivance of thefe men, and while they were debating how to act in this critical conjuncture, anxious to bring the affair to a fpeedy iffue, the Portuguefe be-gan to drive away fuch of the natives as had brought palm-fyrup and fowls to fell, and others who were now bringing fheep and buffaloes to the market. At this juncture Capt. Cook happening to look at the old man who had been diftinguifhed by the name of prime mi-nifter, imagined that he faw in his features a difappro-bation of the prefent proceedings ; and, willing to im-prove the advantage, he grafped the Indian's hand, and gave him an old broad-fword. This well-timed prefent produced all the good effects that could be wifhed ; the prime minifter was enraptured at fo honourable a mark of diftinction, and brandifhing his fword over the head of the impertinent Portuguefe, he made both him and a man who commanded the party, fit down behind him on the ground. The whole bufinefs was now accom-plifhed ; the natives, eager to fupply whatever was wanted, brought their cattle in for fale, and the market was foon ftocked. For the firft two buffaloes, Capt.

Cook

Cook gave ten guineas : but he afterwards purchafed them by way of exchange, giving a mufquet for each, and at this rate he might have bought any number he thought proper. There remained no doubt but that Lange had a profit out of the two that were fold ; and that his reafon for having faid the natives would take nothing but gold for their cattle, was, that he might the more eafily fhare in the produce. Capt. Cook purchafed of the natives of this ifland fome hundred gallons of palm-fyrup, a fmall quantity of garlick, a large number of eggs, fome limes and cocoa-nuts, thirty dozen of fowls, three hogs, fix fheep, and nine buffaloes. We having obtained thefe neceffary articles, now prepared for failing from this place.

The ifland of Savu is fituated in 10 deg. 35 min. S. latitude, and 237 deg. 30 min. W. longitude. Its length is between twenty and thirty miles. But its breadth Capt. Cook could not afcertain, as he only faw the north fide of it. The harbour in which the fhip lay, was called Seba, from a diftrict of the country fo denominated : and there are two other bays on different parts of the ifland. At the time the Endeavour lay there it was near the end of the dry feafon, when it had not rained for almoft feven months, nor was there a running ftream of frefh water to be feen, and the natives were fupplied only by fmall fprings, fituated at a diftance up the country, yet even in this dry feafon the appearance of the ifland was beautiful. Near the coaft the land lies level, and well cloathed with palm, called arecao, and cocoa-nut trees. Farther off, the ground rifes in the moft gradual afcent, and is covered with fair palm-trees even to the tops of the hills, fo as to prefent a regular grove to the view. The rains in this country ceafe in March or April, and fall again in October or November, and thefe rains produce abundance of indico, millett, and maize, which grow beneath the fineft trees in the country. Befides thefe articles, the ifland produces tobacco, cotton, betel, tamarinds, limes, oranges, mangoes, guinea corn, rice, callevances, and water-melons. A fmall quantity of cinnamon was feen, and fome European herbs, fuch as garlick, fennel, celery,

and

and marjoram, befides which, there are fruits of various
kinds, and particularly the blimbi, which has a fharp
tafte, and is a fine pickle, but it is not eaten raw; its
length is from 3 to 4 inches; it is nearly as thick as a
man's thumb, of an oval form, covered with a very thin
fkin, of a very light green, and contains a number of
feeds ranged in the fhape of a ftar. Several buffaloes
were feen on this ifland which were almoft as large as
an ox; and from a pair of enormous horns of this animal, which Mr. Banks faw, it was fuppofed that fome
of them were much larger; yet they did not weigh more
than half as much as an ox of the fame fize; having
loft the greater part of their flefh through the late
dry weather: the meat however was juicy, and of a
delicate flavour. The horns of thefe animals bend
backwards; they had no dew-laps, and fcarce any hair
on their fkins, and their ears were remarkably large.
The other tame animals on the ifland are dogs, cats,
pigeons, fowls, hogs, goats, fheep, affes, and horfes.
Few of the horfes are above twelve hands high, yet they
are full of mettle, and pace naturally in an expeditious manner: the natives ride them with a halter only.
The hogs of this country are fed on the hufks of rice
and palm-fyrup mixed with water, and are remarkably
fine and fat. The fheep is not unlike a goat, and are
therefore called cabaritos; their ears, which are long,
hang down under their horns; their nofes are arched,
and their bodies covered with hair. The fowls are of
the game kind, and though they are rather large, the
hen lays a very fmall egg. The fea-coaft furnifhes
the inhabitants with turtle, but not in any great
abundance.

The people of this ifland are rather below the middle ftature; their hair is black and ftrait, and perfons
of all ranks, as well thofe that are expofed to the weather, as thofe that are not, have one general complexion,
which is the dark brown. The men are well formed
and fprightly, and their features differ much from each
other; the women, on the contrary, have all one fet of
features, are very fhort, and broad built. The men
have filver pincers hanging by ftrings round their
necks,

necks, with which they pluck out the hair of their
beards; and both men and women root out the hair
that grows under their arms; the hair of the womens
heads is tied in a club behind, while the men wear a
kind of turban on their heads, formed of muflin, cotton,
or even with filk handkerchiefs, but the heads of the women have no covering. The drefs of the men confifts of
two pieces of cotton cloth, one of which is bound round
the middle, and the lower edge of it being drawn pretty
tight between the legs, the upper edge is left loofe, fo
as to form a kind of pocket, in which they carry knives
and other things: the other piece being paft under the
former on the back of the wearer, the ends of it are
carried over the fhoulders, and tucked into the pocket
before. The women drew the upper edge of the piece
round the waift tight, while the lower edge dropping to
the knees, make a kind of petticoat: the other piece of
cloth is faftened acrofs the breaft, and under the arms.
This cloth, which is manufactured by the natives, is
dyed blue while in the yarn; and as it is of various
fhades, its look, when it comes to be worn, is very
beautiful.

Their ornaments are very numerous, and confift of
rings, beads worn round the neck and on the wrifts,
and chains of plaited gold wire, are likewife worn by
both fexes; but the women had likewife girdles of
beads round their waifts, which ferved to keep up their
petticoats. Both fexes had their ears bored without a
fingle exception, that we faw, but we never obferved
an ornament in any of them. Nor did we perceive
either man or woman in any thing but what appeared
to be their ordinary drefs, except the king and his minifter, who in general wore a kind of night-gown of
coarfe chintz, and the latter once received us in a black
robe, which appeared to be made of prince's ftuff.
One perfon, in the way of finery, had a filver-headed
cane, marked with a kind of cypher, confifting of the
Roman letters V. O. C. which might have been a prefent
from the Dutch Eaft-India Company, whofe mark it is.
We alfo faw boys about twelve or fourteen years old,
having fpiral circles of thick brafs wire paffed three or
four

four times round their arms, above the elbow; and upon the fame part of the arm, fome of the men had rings of ivory, two inches broad, and about one in thicknefs; thefe we were informed were the fons of the Raja's or chiefs, whofe high births were diftinguifhed by thefe cumbrous ornaments. Moft of the men had their names marked on their arms, and the women had a fquare ornament of flourifhed lines imprinted juft under the bend of the elbow. On enquiry it was found that this practice had been common among the Indians long before they were vifited by any Europeans; and in the neighbouring iflands, it was faid, the inhabitants were marked with circles upon their necks and breafts. We were ftruck with the fimilitude between thefe marks, and thofe made by tattaowing in the South Sea iflands; and M. Boffu's account of fome Indians who dwell on the banks of Akanza, a river in North America, which falls into the Miffiffippi, will afford a probable conjecture how the operation is performed. "The Alkanzas, fays he, have adopted me, and as a mark of my privilege, have imprinted the figure of a roe-buck upon my thigh, which was done in this manner: an Indian having burnt fome ftraw, diluted the afhes with water, and with this mixture, drew the figure upon my fkin; he then retraced it, by pricking the lines with needles, fo as at every puncture juft to draw the blood, and the blood mixing with the afhes of the ftraw, forms a figure which can never be effaced."

The houfes of Savu are all built upon the fame plan, but differ in fize, according to the rank and wealth of the proprietors, being from twenty feet to four hundred, and they are fixed on pofts of about four or five feet from the ground. One end of thefe is driven into the ground, and upon the other is laid a floor of wood, which makes a vacant fpace of four feet between the floor of the houfe and the ground. On this floor are raifed other pillars that fupport a roof of floping fides, which meet in a ridge at the top, like thofe of our barns; the caves of this roof, which is thatched with palm-leaves, reach within two feet of the floor, and over-hang it as much. The fpace within is gene-

No. 8.   I i   rally

rally divided lengthwife into three equal parts; the middle part, or center, is inclofed by a partition of four fides, reaching about fix feet above the floor, and one or two fmall rooms are alfo fometimes taken off from the fides; the reft of the fpace under the roof is open, fo as freely to admit the air and the light. The particular ufes of thefe apartments we could not, during our fhort ftay, learn, except that the clofe room in the cencer was appropriated to the women.

As to the food of thefe people, they eat all the tame animals to be found in the ifland; but they prefer the hog to all others; next to this they admire horfe-flefh; to which fucceeds the buffalo, then poultry; and they prefer cats and dogs to goats and fheep. Fifh, we believe, is not eaten but by the poor, nor by them, except when their duty or bufinefs requires them to be upon the beach, and then each man has a light cafting net, which is girt round his body, and with this he takes any fmall fifh which may come in his way.

The moft remarkable and ufeful tree that grows on the ifland is the fan palm. Its ufes are fo various, that it requires particular notice. At certain times it is a fuccedaneum for all other food both to man and beaft. A kind of wine, called toddy, is extracted from this tree, by cutting the buds, and tying under them fmall bafkets, made of the leaves. The juice which trickles into thefe veffels is collected morning and evening, and is the common drink of all the inhabitants. The natives call this liquor dua or duac, and both the fyrup and fugar, gula. The fyrup is not unlike treacle, but is fomewhat thicker, and has a more agreeable tafte. The fugar is of a redifh brown, probably the fame with the Jugata fugar upon the continent of India, and to our tafte it was more agreeable than any cane fugar, unrefined. We at firft apprehended that the fyrup, of which fome of our people eat great quantities, would have occafioned fluxes, but what effect it produced was rather falutary than hurtful. This fyrup is ufed to fatten hogs, dogs, and fowls; and the inhabitants themfelves have fubfifted upon this alone for feveral months, when other crops have failed, and animal

mal

mal food has been fcarce. With the leaves of this tree the natives thatch their houfes, and make bafkets, cups, umbrellas and tobacco-pipes. They make leaft account of the fruit, and as the buds are wounded for the tuac or toddy, there is very little produced. It is nearly of the fize of a full grown turnip; and the kernels muft be eaten before it is ripe, otherwife they are fo hard, that the teeth will not penetrate them.

As fire-wood is very fcarce, the natives, by the following method, make a very little anfwer the ends of cookery and diftillation. A hollow is dug under ground, like a rabbit burrow, in a horizontal direction, about two yards long, with a hole at each end, one of which is large, and the other fmall. The fire is put in at the large hole, and the fmall one ferves for a draught. Circular holes are made through the earth which covers this cavity, on which are fet earthen pots, large in the middle, and fmaller towards the bottom, fo that the fire acts upon a large part of the furface. They contain generally about eight or ten gallons each, and it is furprifing to fee with what a fmall quantity of fuel they are kept boiling. In this manner they boil all their victuals, and make all their fyrup and fugar. The Peruvian Indians have a contrivance of the fame kind; and perhaps by the poor in other countries it might be adopted with advantage.

In this ifland both fexes are enflaved by the pernicious cuftom of chewing beetle and areca, contracted even while they are children. With thefe they mix a fort of white lime, compofed of coral ftones and fhells, to which is added frequently a fmall quantity of tobacco, whereby their mouths are rendered difguftful both to the fight and the fmell; for the tobacco infects their breath, and the beetle and lime make the teeth both black and rotten. We faw many of both fexes whofe fore teeth were confumed, irregularly, almoft down to the gums, and corroded like iron by ruft. This lofs of teeth has generally been attributed to the tough ftringy coat of the areca nut; but our gentlemen imputed it wholly to the lime; for the teeth are not loofened or broken, as might be the cafe by chewing of

hard

hard and rough fubftances, but they are gradually
wafted, as even metals are by powerful acids ; and they
may not be miftaken who fuppofe that fugar has a bad
effect upon the teeth of Europeans, feeing refined fugar contains a confiderable quantity of lime, and it is
well known, that lime will deftroy bone of any kind.
When the natives are at any time not chewing beetle
and areca, they then are fmoking. The manner of
doing this is by rolling up a fmall quantity of tobacco,
and putting it into one end of a tube, about fix inches
long, as thick as a goofe quill, and made of a palm-
leaf. The women in particular were obferved to fwal-
low the fmoke.

The ifland is divided into five diftricts or nigrees,
each of which is governed by a Raja. Thefe are called
Laai, Seba, Regeeua, Timo, and Maffara. We went
afhore at Seba, and found a Raja that governed with
abfolute authority. He was about five and thirty, and
the moft corpulent man we had feen upon the whole
ifland. But though he governed with an unlimited
authority, he took very little regal pomp upon him,
He was directed almoft implicitly by Mannu Djarme,
the old man, his prime minifter, already mentioned ; yet notwithftanding the power with which he
was invefted, he was univerfally beloved, a fure proof
that he did not abufe it. Mr. Lange informed Capt.
Cook, that the chiefs who had fucceffively prefided over
the five principalities of this ifland, had lived for time
immemorial in the moft cordial friendfhip with each
other ; yet, he faid, the people were of a warlike difpofition, and had always courageoufly defended themfelves againft foreign invaders. We were told alfo, that
the inhabitants of the ifland could raife, on a fhort notice, 7,300 fighting men armed with mufquets; of
which number Laai was faid to furnifh 2,600, Seba
2000, Regeeua 1,500, Timo 800, and Maffara 400.
Befides the arms already mentioned, each man is furnifhed with a large maffy pole-ax, which, in the hands
of people who have courage, muft be a formidable
weapon. In the ufe of their lances thefe people are
faid to be fo expert, that they can pierce a man through
the

the heart at fixty or feventy yards diftance : yet the Raja had always lived at peace with his neighbours. This account of the martial prowefs of the inhabitants of Savu may be true ; but during our ftay we faw no appearance of it. Before the town houfe indeed, we faw about one hundred fpears and targets, which ferved to arm thofe who were fent down to intimidate us at the trading place, but they feemed to be the refufe of old armories, no two being of the fame make or length, for fome were fix, others fixteen feet long. Not one lance was among them, and though the mufquets were clean on the outfide, within they were eaten by the ruft into holes; and the people themfelves appeared to be fo little acquainted with military difcipline, that they came down like a diforderly rabble, every one having a cock, fome tobacco, or other merchandife, and few or none of their cartouch boxes were furnifhed with either powder or ball, but a piece of paper was thruft into the holes to fave appearances. We likewife faw before the houfe of affembly a great gun, fome fwivels, and patararoes : but the great gun lay with the touchhole to the ground, and the fwivels and patararoes were not in their carriages.

The inhabitants of Savu are divided into five ranks, namely, the Rajas, the land owners, the manufacturers, the fervants, and the flaves. The Rajas are chief; the land owners are refpected in proportion to their eftates, and the number of their flaves, which laft are bought and fold with their eftates ; but a fat hog is the price of one if purchafed feparately. Notwithftanding a man may thus fell his flave, or convey him with his lands, yet his power does not extend farther, as he may not even ftrike him without the Raja's permiffion. The eftates of thefe land-holders are of very different extent: fome of them not poffeffing above five flaves, whilft others have 500. When a man of rank goes abroad, one of his flaves follows him with a filver-hilted fword or hanger, ornamented with horfe hair taffels, and another carries a little bag containing tobacco, beetle, areca, and lime. This is all the ftate that even the Rajas themfelves take upon them.

Thefe

These people have a great veneration for antiquity. Their principal boast is of a long line of venerable ancestors. Those houses that have been well tenanted for succeſſive generations, are held in the higheſt eſteem ; even the ſtones which are worn ſmooth by having been ſat upon for ages, derive a certain value from that circumſtance. He whoſe progenitors have bequeathed him any of theſe ſtones, or whoſe wealth has enabled him to purchaſe them, cauſes them to be ranged round his habitation, for his ſervants and ſlaves to ſit upon. The Raja cauſes a large ſtone to be ſet up in the chief town of each diſtrict as a monument of his reign. In the province of Seba, thirteen ſuch ſtones were ſeen as well as the remains of ſeveral others which were much worn. Theſe ſtones were all placed on the top of a hill, and ſome of them were of ſuch an enormous ſize that it was amazing by what means they could have been brought thither ; nor could any information on this head be obtained from the natives : theſe monuments however, indicated that for a ſeries of generations, the iſland had been regularly governed.— When a Raja dies, proclamation is made that all thoſe who have been his ſubjects ſhall hold a ſolemn feſtival. On this they proceed to the hill where theſe ſtones are erected, and feaſt for ſeveral weeks, killing all the animals that ſuit their purpoſe, wherever they can be found, in order to furniſh the treat, which is daily ſerved up on the monumental ſtones. When they have thus exhauſted their whole ſtock, they are compelled to keep a faſt ; and when the feaſt happens to end in the dry ſeaſon, when they cannot get vegetables to eat, they have no other ſubſiſtance than the palm ſyrup and water, till the few animals which have eſcaped the general maſſacre have bred a ſufficient number for a freſh ſupply, except the adjacent diſtrict happens to be in a condition to relieve them.

The natives of Savu have an inſtrument with which they clear the cotton of its ſeeds; it is about ſeven inches in height and fourteen in length. They have alſo a machine with which they ſpin by hand, as was the cuſtom before the invention of ſpinning wheels in Europe.

The

The inhabitants of this ifland were in general robuft and healthy, and had every mark of longevity. The fmall pox, however, is a diftemper with which they are acquainted, and which they dread as much as a peftilence. When any perfon is attacked by it, he is carried to a fpot at a diftance from the houfes, where his food is conveyed to him by means of a long ftick, as no one dares to venture near him. Abandoned by all his friends, he is there left to live or die as it may happen, without being admitted to any comforts of the community.

The Portuguefe very early vifited this ifland, on which they eftablifhed a fettlement, but foon after they were fucceeded by the Dutch, who without formally taking poffeflion of the place, fent a number of trading veffels in order to eftablifh a commerce with the natives. Moft of the Dutch purchafes, it is fuppofed, are confined to a fupply of provifions for the Spice-Iflands, the inhabitants of which breed but a fmall number of cattle. The Dutch Eaft India Company made an agreement with the feveral Rajas of the iflands, that a quantity of rice, maize, and callavances fhould be annually furnifhed to their people, who, in return, were to fupply the Rajas with filk, linen, cutlery wares, and arrack. Certain fmall veffels, each having on board ten Indians, are fent from Timor to bring away the maize and callavances, and a fhip that brings the articles furnifhed by the Dutch, receives the rice on board once a year; and as there are three bays on this coaft, this veffel anchors in each of them in turn. The Dutch articles of commerce are accepted by the Rajas as a prefent; and they and their chief attendants drink of the arrack without intermiflion till it is exhaufted.

It was in tne agreement above-mentioned that the Rajas ftipulated, that a Dutch refident fhould be conftantly on the ifland. Accordingly this Lange, whom we have mentioned, was fent thither in that capacity, and a fort of affiftant with him, whofe father was a Portuguefe, and his mother a native of Timor, with one Frederic Craig, whofe father was a Dutchman, and

2   his

his mother an Indian. Mr. Lange vifits the Raja in ftate, attended by fifty flaves on horfe-back, and if the crops are ripe, orders veffels to convey them immediately to Timor, fo that they are not even houfed upon the ifland. It is likewife part of his bufinefs to perfuade the landholders to plant, if he perceives that they are backward in that particular. This refident had been ten years on the ifland, when the Endeavour touched there, during all which time he had not feen any white perfons, except thofe who came annually in the Dutch veffel, to carry off the rice, as above-mentioned. He was married to a native of Timor, and lived in the fame manner as the natives of Savu, whofe language he fpoke better than any other. He fat on the ground like the Indians, and chewed beetle, and feemed in every thing to refemble them, except in his complexion and the drefs of his conntry. As to Mr. Craig, his affiftant, he was employed in teaching the natives to write and read, and inftructing them in the principles of Chriftianity. Though there was neither clergyman nor church to be feen upon the ifland, yet this Mr. Craig averred, that in the townfhip of Seba only, there were 600 Chriftians: as to the religion of thofe who have not embraced Chriftianity, it is a peculiar fpecies of Paganifm, every one having a god of his own, fomewhat after the manner of the Cemies heretofore mentioned. Their morality, however, is much purer than could be expected from fuch a people. Robberies are fcarcely ever committed. Murder is unknown among them; and though no man is allowed more than one wife, they are ftrangers to adultery, and almoft fo to the crime of fimple fornication. When any difputes arife between the natives, the determination of the Raja is decifive and fatisfactory. Some obfervations were made upon the language of the natives, by the gentlemen, weile the veffel lay here; and a kind of vocabulary formed, a fketch of which we have here inferted:

Momonne,	-	*A man.*
Mobunne,	-	*A woman.*
Catoo,	-	*The head.*

Row

Row catoo,	-	*The hair.*
Matta,	- -	*The eyes.*
Rowna matta,	-	*The eye-lashes.*
Swanga,	-	*The nose.*
Cavaranga,	-	*The cheeks.*
Wodcele,	- -	*The ears.*
Vaio,	- -	*The tongue.*
Lacoco,	- -	*The neck.*
Soofoo,	- -	*The breasts.*
Caboo foofoo	-	*The nipples.*
Dulloo,	- -	*The belly.*
Affoo,	- -	*The navel.*
Tooga,	- -	*The thighs.*
Rootoo,	-	*The knees.*
Baibo,	- -	*The legs.*
Dunceala,	-	*The feet.*
Kiffovei yilla,	-	*The toes.*
Camacoo,	-	*The arms.*
Wulaba,	-	*The hand.*
Cabaou,	-	*A buffalo.*
Djara,	- -	*A horse.*
Vavee,	-	*A hog.*
Doomba,	-	*A sheep.*
Kefavoo,	-	*A goat.*
Guaca,	-	*A dog.*
Maio,	- -	*A cat.*
Mannu,	-	*A fowl.*
Carow,	- -	*The tail.*
Pangoutoo,	-	*The beak.*
Ica,	- -	*A fish.*
Unjoo,	- -	*A turtle.*
Nieu,	- -	*A cocoa-nut.*
Boaceree,	-	*Fan palm.*
Calella,	- -	*Areca.*
Canana,	-	*Beetle.*
Aou,	-	*Lime.*
Maanadoo,	-	*A fish-hook.*
Tata,	- -	*Tatou, or marks on the skin.*
Lodo,	- -	*The sun.*
Wurroo,	-	*The moon.*
Aidaffee,	-	*The sea.*

No. 8.   K k   Alica,

Ailea,	- -	*Water.*
Aoe,	• -	*Fire.*
Maate,	- -	*To die.*
Tabudge,	-	*To sleep.*
Tatee too,	- -	*To rise.*
Uffe,	- -	*One.*
Lhua,	- -	*Two.*
Tullu,	- -	*Three.*
Uppah,	• -	*Four.*
Lumme,	- -	*Five.*
Unna,	• -	*Six.*
Pedu,	- -	*Seven.*
Arru,	• -	*Eight.*
Saou,	- -	*Nine.*
Singooroo,	-	*Ten.*
Singurunguffe,	-	*Eleven.*
Lhuangooroo,	-	20.
Singaflu,	-	100.
Setuppah,	-	1000.
Selacuffa,	•	10,000.
Serata,	- -	100,000.
Sereboo,	. -	1,000,000.

It is here neceffary to obferve, that this ifland has not been laid down in any of the charts hitherto publifhed, and as to our account of it, let it be remembered, that except the facts in which we were parties, and the account of the objects which we had an opportunity to examine, the whole is founded merely upon the report of Mr. Lange, upon whofe authority it muft therefore reft.

Of the iflands in the neighbourhood of Savu, the principal is Timor, which is annually vifited by the Dutch refidents on the other iflands, in order to make up their accounts. Some of the towns on the north fide of Timor are in the hands of the Portuguefe; but the Dutch poffefs a far greater proportion of the ifland, on which they have built a fort, and erected feveral ftore-houfes. There are three fmall iflands, called the Solars, which produce great abundance of the various neceffaries of life, that are carried in fmall veffels to

the

the Dutch fettlements on the ifland of Timor. Thefe iflands are low and flat, and one of them has a commodious harbour. To the weftward of the Solars lies the little ifland of Ende, in the poffeffion of the Portuguefe, who have built a confiderable town on the N. E. point of it ; and clofe to the town is an harbour where fhips may ride in fafety. The ifland of Rotte has a Dutch refident, whofe bufinefs is fimilar to that of Mr. Lange on the ifland of Savu. Rotte produces, befides fuch things as are common to other iflands, a confiderable quantity of fugar, which is made to a great degree of perfection. There is likewife a fmall ifland lying to the weft of Savu, the chief produce of which is the areca nut, of which the Dutch receive in exchange for European commodities, as large a quantity every year as load two veffels.

About two years before the Endeavour was in thefe feas, a French fhip was wrecked on the coaft of Timor : fhe had been lodged on the rocks feveral days, when the wind tore her to pieces in an inftant, and the Captain, with the greater part of the feamen were drowned ; but the lieutenant and about eighty men, having reached the fhore, travelled acrofs the country of Concordia, where their immediate wants were relieved, and they afterwards returned to the wreck, in company with fome Dutchmen and Indians, who affifted them in recovering all their chefts of bullion, and other effects. This done they returned to Concordia, where they remained feveral weeks; but in this interval death made fuch havock among them, that not above half their number remained to return to their native country, which they did as foon as a veffel could be fitted out for them.

On Friday, the 21ft of September, in the morning, we got under fail, and bent our courfe weftward, along the north fide of the ifland of Savu, and of another lying to the weftward of it, which at noon bore S. S. E. diftant two leagues. At four in the afternoon, in latitude 10 deg. 38 min. S. and longitude 238 deg. 28 min. W. we difcovered a fmall low ifland. In the evening of the 23d, we got clear of the iflands, and

on the 26th, our latitude by obfervation was 10 deg.
51 min. S. and our longitude 252 deg. 11 min. W.
On the 28th, we fteered all day N. W. with a view
of making the land of Java, and on the 30th, Capt.
Cook took into his poffeffion the log-book and journals,
at leaft all he could find of the officers, petty officers.
and feamen, whom he ftrictly enjoined fecrecy with
refpect to where they had been. At feven in the evening we had thunder and lightning, and about twelve by
the light of the flafhes we faw the weft end of Java.

On Monday, October the 1ft, at fix o'clock in the
morning, Java Head bore S. E. by E. diftant five
leagues. Soon after we faw Prince's Ifland, and at
ten Cracatoa, a remarkable high peaked ifland. At
noon it bore N. 40 E. diftant feven leagues. On
the 2nd, we were clofe in with the coaft of Java, in
fifteen fathom water, along which we ftood. In the
forenoon a boat was fent afhore, in order to procure
fome fruit for Tupia, who was at this time extremely
ill. Our people returned with four cocoa-nuts, and a
fmall bunch of plantains, for which they had paid a
fhilling; but fome herbage for the cattle the Indians
gave our feamen, and affifted them to cut it. The country had a delightful appearance, being every where covered with trees, which looked like one continued
wood. About eleven o'clock we faw two Dutch Eaft
Indiamen, from whom we heard with great pleafure,
that the Swallow had reached the Englifh channel in
fafety, having been at Batavia about two years before.
We alfo learnt, that there was ftationed here a fly boat
or packet, to carry letters, as was faid, from the Dutch
fhips, that came hither from Batavia, but the Captain
thought it was appointed to examine all fhips, that
fhould have paffed the ftreight. We had now been
fome hours at anchor, but in the evening a light breeze
fpringing up, we got under fail, yet having little wind,
and a ftrong current againft us, we reached no further by
eight in the morning, of the 3d, than Bantam Point.
We now perceived the Dutch packet ftanding after us,
but the wind fhifting to the N. E. fhe bore away. We
were now obliged to anchor; which we did in twenty-
                                                twa

two fathom water, at about two miles from the fhore. At fix o'clock in the evening, the country boats came along fide of us, on board one of which was the maf-ter of the packet. They brought in them fowls, ducks, parrots, turtle, rice, birds, monkeys, and other arti-cles, with an intention to fell them, but having fixed very high prices on their commodities, and our Savu ftock being not yet expended, very few articles were purchafed. The captain indeed gave two dollars for twenty-five fowls, and a Spanifh dollar for a turtle, which weighed about fix and thirty pounds. We might alfo for a dollar have bought two monkeys, or a whole cage of rice-birds. The mafter of the packet brought with him two books, in one of which he de-fired of our officers, that one of them would write down the name of our fhip and commander; the place from whence we came; to what port bound; with fuch other particulars relating to ourfelves, as we might think proper, for the information of any of our countrymen who might come after us. In the other book the maf-ter himfelf entered the names of our fhip and its cap-tain, in order to tranfmit them to the governor and council of the Indies. We perceived, that in the firft book many fhips, particularly Portuguefe, had made enteries of the fame kind with that for which it was prefented to us. Mr. Hicks, our lieutenant, however, having written the name of the fhip, only added "from Europe." The mafter of the packet took notice of this, but faid, that he was fatisfied with any thing we thought fit to write, it being intended folely for the in-formation of our friends.

Friday the fifth, we made feveral attempts to fail with a wind that would not ftem the current, and as often came to an anchor. In the morning a proa, with a Dutch officer, came along-fide of us, and fent to Cap-tain Cook a printed paper in exceeding bad Englifh, duplicates of which he had in other languages, all re-gularly figned, in the name of the governor and council of the Indies, by their fecretary; the contents whereof were the following enquiries, contained in nine quef-tions.

1. The

1. The ſhip's name, and to what nation ſhe belonged?

2. If ſhe came from Europe, or any other place?

3. From what place ſhe had laſt departed?

4. Whereunto deſigned to go?

5. What and how many ſhips of the Dutch company by departure from the laſt ſhore there layed, and their names?

6. If one or more of theſe ſhips, in company with the Endeavour, is departed for this or any other place?

7. If during the voyage any particularities is happened, or ſeen?

8. If not any ſhips in ſea, or the ſtreights of Sunda, have ſeen, or hailed in, and which?

9. If any other news worth of attention, at the place from whence the ſhip laſtly departed, or during the voyage, is happened?

BATAVIA in the Caſtle.
By order of the Governor General, and the
Counſellors of India,
J. BRANDER BUNGL. Sec.

The officer obſerving, that the captain did not chuſe to anſwer any of the above queſtions, except the firſt and fourth, he ſaid that the reſt were not material, though it was remarked that juſt afterwards he affirmed he muſt diſpatch the paper to Batavia, at which place it would arrive by the next day. This examination was rather extraordinary, and the more ſo, as it does not ſeem to have been of any long ſtanding.

As ſoon as the Dutch officer departed, the anchor was weighed, but in four hours the ſhip was forced to come to an anchor again, till a breeze ſprang up; ſhe then held on her courſe till the next morning, when on account of the rapidity of the current, the anchor was dropped again. At laſt we weighed on the 8th, and ſtood clear of a large ledge of rocks, which we had almoſt ran upon the preceding day. But in the forenoon we were once more obliged to anchor near a little iſland that was not laid down in any chart on board.

It

It was found to be one of thofe called the Milles Ifles: Mr. Banks and Dr. Solander having landed upon it, collected a few plants, and fhot a bat which was a yard long, being meafured from the extreme points of the wings ; they alfo killed a few plovers on this ifland, the breadth of which does not exceed one hundred yards, and the length five hundred; they found a houfe and a little fpot of cultivated ground, and on it grew the Palma Chrifti, from which the Weft Indians make their caftor oil.

In a little time after the gentlemen returned to the fhip, fome Malays came along-fide in a boat, bringing with them pompions, dried fifh, and turtle, for fale ; one of the turtles, which weighed near one hundred and fifty pounds, they fold for a dollar, and feemed to expect the fame piece of money for their fruit ; but it being hinted to them that a dollar was too much, they defired that one might be cut, and a piece of it given to them, but this not being complied with, they at length fold twenty-fix pompions for a Portuguefe pe-tacka. When they departed, they intimated their wifhes, that this tranfaction might not be mentioned at Batavia.

We now made but little way till night, when the land-breeze fpringing up, we failed to the E. S. E. and on the following day, by the affiftance of the fea-breeze, came to an anchor in the road of Batavia. At this place we found a number of large Dutch veffels, the Harcourt Eaft-Indiaman from England, which had loft her paffage to China, and two fhips belonging to the private trade of our India company. The Endeavour had no fooner anchored, than a fhip was obferved, with a broad pendant flying, from which a boat was difpatched to demand the name of the veffel, with that of the commander, &c. To thefe enquiries Captain Cook gave fuch anfwers as he thought proper, and the officer who commanded the boat departed. This gentleman, and the crew that attended him, were fo worn out with the unhealthinefs of the climate, that it was apparent many deaths would follow : yet at prefent there was not one invalid on board of our fhip, except the

the Indian Tupia. The captain now difpatched an officer to the governor of the town, to apologize for the Endeavour's not faluting: for he had but three guns proper for the purpofe, except fwivels, and he was apprehenfive that they would not be heard. The fhip was fo leaky, that fhe made about nine inches water in an hour, on the average; part of the falfe keel was gone; one of her pumps was totally ufelefs, and the reft fo much decayed, that they could not laft long. The officers and feamen concurring in opinion that the fhip could not fafely put to fea again in this condition, the captain refolved to folicit permiffion to heave her down; but as he had learned that this muft be done in writing, he drew up a petition, and had it tranflated into Dutch.

On Wednefday, October the 10th, the captain and the reft of the gentlemen went on fhore, and applied to the only Englifh refident at Batavia; this gentleman, whofe name was Leith, received his countrymen in the politeft manner, and entertained them at dinner with great hofpitality. Mr. Leith informed us, that a public hotel was kept in town, by order of the Dutch governor, at which place merchants and other ftrangers were obliged to lodge, and that the landlord of the hotel was bound to find them warehoufes for their goods, on the condition of receiving ten fhillings on every hundred pounds of their value, but as the Endeavour was a king's fhip, her officers, and the other gentlemen, might refide where they thought proper, only afking leave of the governor, whofe permiffion would be inftantly obtained. Mr. Leith added, that they might live cheaper in this way than at the hotel, if they had any perfon who fpoke the Batavian tongue, whom they could rely on to purchafe their provifions, but as there was no fuch perfon among the whole fhip's crew, the gentlemen immediately befpoke beds at the hotel. In the afternoon Captain Cook attended the governor-general, who received him politely, and told him to wait on the council the next morning, when his petition fhould be laid before them, and every thing that he folicited fhould be granted. Late in the even-

ing

ing of this day, there happened a moſt terrible ſtorm of thunder and lightning, accompanied with very heavy rain. In this ſtorm the main-maſt of a Dutch Eaſt Indiaman was ſplit and carried away by the deck; and the main-top-maſt and main-top-gallant-maſt were torn to pieces; it is ſuppoſed, that the lightning was attracted by an iron ſpindle at the main-top-gallant-maſt-head. The Endeavour, which was at a ſmall diſtance from the Dutch ſhip, eſcaped without damage, owing, moſt probably, to the electrical chain which conducted the lightning over the veſſel.—A centinel on board the Endeavour, who was charging his muſ-quet at the time of the ſtorm, had it ſhaken out of his hand, and the ram-rod broken to pieces; the elec-trical chain looked like a ſtream of fire, and the ſhip ſuſtained a very violent ſhock.

On Thurſday the 11th, Capt. Cook waited on the gentlemen of the council, who informed him that all his requeſts ſhould be complied with. In the interim the other gentlemen made a contract with the maſter of the hotel, to furniſh them and their friends with as much tea, coffee, punch and tobacco, as they might have occaſion for, and to keep them a ſeparate table, for nine ſhillings a day Engliſh money: but on the condition that every perſon who ſhould viſit them, ſhould pay at the rate of four ſhillings and ſix pence for his dinner, and the ſame ſum for his ſupper and bed, if he choſe to ſleep at the hotel; they were like-wiſe to pay for every ſervant that attended them fifteen pence a day. It was ſoon diſcovered, that they had been much impoſed on; for theſe charges were twice as much as could have been demanded at a private houſe. They appeared to live elegantly, but at the ſame time were but ill ſupplied. Their dinner conſiſted of fifteen diſhes, all ſerved up at once; and their ſupper of thir-teen, but of theſe, nine or ten were of the moſt ordi-nary, becauſe the cheapeſt, (poultry) that could be pur-chaſed, and even ſome of theſe diſhes were obſerved to be ſerved up four times ſucceſſively: a duck, which was hot at dinner, was brought cold in the evening, the next day ſerved up as a fricaſſee, and was converted

No. 9.   L l   into

into forced meat at night. We, however, only fared as others had done before us : it was the conftant cuftom of the confcientious mafter of the hotel, to treat all his guefts in the fame manner : if we took no notice of it, all was well, for the landlord had the better cuftomers of us : if we remonfirated againft fuch treatment, the table was better fupplied from time to time, till, in the end, we had no reafon to complain. However, after a few days, Mr. Banks hired for himfelf and party, a fmall houfe, next door to the hotel, for which he paid forty-five fhillings per month ; but they were far from having the conveniencies and privacy they expected: for no perfon was permitted to fleep in it as an occafional gueft, under a penalty ; and Dutchmen were continually running in without the leaft ceremony, to afk what was to be fold, it being a cuftom for moft private perfons in Batavia to be furnifhed with fome articles of traffic. Every one here hires a carriage, and Mr. Banks engaged two. Thefe carriages are open chaifes ; they hold two perfons, and are driven by a man fitting on a kind of coach-box : for each of thefe Mr. Banks paid two rix-dollars a day.

Our Indian friend Tupia had hitherto continued on board on account of his diforder, which was of the bilious kind, yet he perfifted in refufing every medicine that was offered him. Mr. Banks fent for him to his houfe, in hopes that he might recover his health. While in the fhip, and even in the boat, he was exceedingly liftlefs and low fpirited, but he no fooner entered the town than he feemed as if reanimated. The houfes, the carriages, ftreets, people, and a multiplicity of other objects, wholly new to him, produced an effect like the fuppofed power of fafcination. But if Tupia was aftonifhed at the fcene, his boy Tayeto was perfectly enraptured. He expreffed his wonder and delight with lefs reftraint. He danced along the ftreet in a kind of extacy, and examined every object with a reftlefs curiofity which was each moment excited and gratified. Tupia remarked particularly the variety of dreffes worn by the paffing multitude, concerning which he made many enquiries. Being informed, that here were people of
. different

different nations, each of whom wore the habit of his respective country, he desired that he might conform to the custom, and appear in that of Otaheite; and some South-sea cloth being sent for from the ship, he dressed himself with great expedition and dexterity. The people of Batavia, who had seen an Indian brought thither in M. Bougainville's ship, named Otourou, mistook Tupia for that person, and frequently asked if he was not the same. About this time we had procured an order to the superintendant of the island of Ouruft, where the ship was to be repaired, to receive her there, and by one of the ships that sailed for Holland, an account was sent to Mr. Stephens, secretary to the admiralty, of our arrival at this place. Here the captain found an unexpected difficulty in procuring money for the expences that would be incurred by refitting the Endeavour; private persons had neither the ability nor inclination to advance the sum required; he therefore sent a written application to the governor himself, who ordered the Shebander to supply the captain with what money he might want out of the company's treasury.

Thursday the 18th, early in the morning, after a delay of some days, we ran down to Ouruft, and laid the ship along-side of the wharf, on Cooper's Island, in order to take out her stores. After little more than nine days, we began to experience the fatal effects of the climate and situation. Tupia sunk on a sudden, and grew every day worse and worse. Tayeto, his boy, was seized with an inflammation on his lungs. Mr. Banks and Dr. Solander were attacked by fevers, and the two servants of the former became very ill; in short, almost every person both on board and ashore fell sick in a few days, owing, as we imagined, to the low swampy situation of the place, and the numberless dirty canals, that intersect the town in all directions.

On the 26th, when few of the crew were able to do duty, we erected a tent for their reception. Tupia, of whose life we began to despair, desired to be removed to the ship, in hopes of breathing a freer air; however this could not be done, as she was unrigged, and preparing

paring

paring to be laid down at the careening-place; but on the 28th, Mr. Banks conveyed him to Cooper's Island, or as it is called here, Kuypor, and, as he seemed pleased with the spot near which the ship lay, a tent was pitched for him. When the sea and land breezes blew over him, he expressed great satisfaction at his situation. On the 30th Mr. Banks returned to town, having, from humanity alone, been two days with Tupia, whose fits of an intermitting fever, now became a regular tertian, and were so violent as to deprive him of his senses while they lasted, and left him so weak, that he could scarcely crawl from his bed. At the same time Dr. Solander's fever increased, and Mr. Monkhouse, our surgeon, was confined to his bed.

On Monday the 5th of November, after many unavoidable delays, the ship was laid down, and the same day Mr. Monkhouse, our surgeon, fell a sacrifice to this fatal country; whose loss was more severely felt, by his being a sensible, skilful man, and dying at a time when his abilities were most wanted. Dr. Solander was just able to attend his funeral, but Mr. Banks, in his turn, was confined to his bed. Great, inexpressibly great was our distress at this time; the prospect before us in the highest degree discouraging; our danger such as we could not surmount by any efforts of our own, for courage, diligence, and skill, were all equally ineffectual; and death was every day making advances towards us, when we could neither resist nor fly. The power of disease, from the pestiferous air of the country, daily gaining strength, several Malay servants were hired to attend the sick, but they had so little sense either of duty or humanity, that the patient was obliged frequently to get out of bed to seek them.

Friday the 9th, our Indian boy Tayeto paid the debt of nature, and poor Tupia was so affected at the loss, that it was doubted whether he would survive it till the next day. In the mean time the ship's bottom having been carefully examined, it was found to be in a worse condition than we apprehended. The false keel was considerably gone to within twenty feet of the stern post; the main keel was injured in many places; much

of

of the fheathing was torn off; and feveral planks were greatly damaged : two of them, and half of a third, particularly, for the length of fix feet, were fo worn, that they were not above an eighth part of an inch thick, and the worms had made their way quite into the timbers : yet, in this condition, the Endeavour had failed many hundred leagues, where navigation is as dangerous as in any part of the globe. How much mifery did we efcape, by being ignorant that fo confiderable a part of the bottom of the veffel was thinner than the fole of a fhoe, and that every life on board depended on fo flight a barrier between us and the unfathomable ocean !

Dr. Solander and Mr. Banks were now fo worn down by their diforders, that the phyfician declared they had no chance for recovery but by removing into the country. In confequence of this advice a houfe was hired for them, at the diftance of about two miles from the town, which belonged to the mafter of the hotel, who engaged to fupply them with provifions, and the ufe of flaves. As they had already experienced the unfeeling inattention of thefe fellows to the fick, they bought each of them a Malay woman, who, from the tendernefs of their fex made them good nurfes. While thefe gentlemen were taking meafures for the recovery of their health, we received an account of the death of our faithful Tupia, who funk at once after the lofs of his boy, Tayeto, whom he loved with the tendernefs of a parent. When Tayeto was firft feized with the fatal diforder, he feemed fenfible of his approaching end, and frequently faid to thofe that were about him Tyau mate fee, " My friends I am dying;" he was very tractable, and took any medicines that were offered him : they were both buried in the ifland of Edam.

On the 14th, the bottom of the fhip was thorougly repaired, and much to Capt. Cook's fatisfaction, who beftowed great encomiums on the officers and the workmen at the Marine-yard ; in his opinion there is not one in the world, where a fhip can be laid down with more convenient fpeed and fafety, nor repaired with

more

more diligence and fkill. At this place they heave down with two mafts, a method we do not now practife ; it is, however, unqueftionably more fafe and expeditious to heave down with two mafts than one, and the man muft want common fenfe, or be ftrangely attached to old cuftoms, who will not allow this, after feeing with what facility the Dutch heave down and refit their largeft veffels at Ouruft. At this time Capt. Cook was taken ill. Mr. Sporing alfo, and a failor who attended Mr. Banks, were feized with the deadly intermittents, and only ten of the fhip's company were capable of doing duty. As to Mr. Banks and Dr. Solander, they recovered flowly at their country-houfe, which was open to the fea-breeze, and fituated upon a running ftream ; circumftances that contributed not a little to a free circulation of air. Yet notwithftanding thefe perplex-ing obftacles, though harraffed by a contagious difeafe, and alarmed by frequent deaths, we proceeded in rig-ging the fhip, and getting water and neceffary ftores aboard: the ftores were eafily obtained and fhipped, but the water we were obliged to procure from Batavia, at the rate of fix fhillings and eight-pence a leager, or one hundred and fifty gallons.

On the 25th, in the night there fell fuch a fhower of rain, for the fpace of four hours, as even all of us had caufe ever to remember. The water poured through every part of Mr. Banks's houfe, and the lower apart-ments admitted a ftream fufficient to turn a mill. As this gentleman was now greatly reftored in health, he went to Batavia the following day, and was furprized to fee that the inhabitants had hung their bedding to dry. About the 26th of this month the wefterly monfoon fet in ; it blows in the day-time from the N. or N. W. and from the S. W. during the night; previous to this, there had been violent fhowers of rain for feveral nights. The mufquitoes and gnats, whofe company had been fufficiently difagreeable in dry weather, now began to fwarm in immenfe numbers, rifing from the puddles of water like bees from a hive; they were extremely trou-blefome during the night, but the pain arifing from the fting, though very fevere, feldom lafted more than half

an

an hour, and in the day-time they feldom made their
attack. The frogs kept a perpetual croaking in the
ditches, a certain fign that the wet feafon was commenced, and that daily rain might be expected.

· The ship being repaired, the fick people received on
board her, and the greater part of her water and ftores
taken in, fhe failed from Ouruftbn the 8th of December;
and anchored in the road of Batavia: twelve days were
employed in receiving the remainder of her pi ovifions,
water, and other neceffaries, though the bufinefs would
have been done in much lefs time, but that fome of the
crew died, and the majority of the furvivors were fo ill;
as to be unable to give their affiftance.

· On the 24th, Capt. Cook took leave of the governor,
and fome other gentlemen, who had diftinguifhed
themfelves by the civilities they fhewed him ; but at
this juncture an incident occurred, that might have
produced confequences by no means defirable A
failor belonging to one of the Dutch fhips in the road of
Batavia, deferted from the veffel, and entered himfelf on
board the Endeavour. The captain of the Dutch fhip
having made application to the governor, claiming the
delinquent as a fubject of the States General, the governor iffued his order for the reftoration of the man;
when this order was delivered to him, he faid, that the
man fhould be given up, if he appeared to be a Dutchman. As the captain was at this time on fhore, and
did not intend going on board till the following day,
he gave the Dutch officer a note to the lieutenant, who
commanded on board the Endeavour, to deliver the
deferter on the condition above-mentioned. On the
following day the Dutchman waited on Capt. Cook, in-
forming him, that the lieutenant had abfolutely refufed
to give up the feaman, faying he was an Irifhman, and
of courfe a fubject of his Britannic Majefty; Capt.
Cook applauded the conduct of his officer, and added,
that it could not be expected that he fhould deliver up
an Englifh fubject. The Dutch officer then faid, he
was authorifed, by the governor, to demand the fugitive
as a Danifh fubject, adding that his name was entered
in the fhip's books as having been born at Elfineur;

I   to

to this Capt. Cook very properly replied, that the governor muſt have been miſtaken, when he gave this order for delivering the deſerter, who had his option whether he would ſerve the Dutch or the Engliſh; but in compliment to the governor, the man ſhould be given up, as a favour, if he appeared to be a Dane, but that in this caſe, he ſhould by no means be demanded as a right, and that he would certainly keep him, if he appeared to be a ſubjeçt of the crown of Great Britain. The Dutchman now took his leave, and he had not been long gone before the captain received a letter from the commanding officer on board, containing full proof, that the man was an Engliſh ſubjeçt. This letter the captain carried to the ſhebander, deſiring him to lay it before the governor, and to inform him, that the man ſhould not be delivered up on any terms whatever. This ſpirited conduçt on the part of Capt. Cook, had the deſired effeçt; and thus the matter ended.

This day the captain, attended by Mr. Banks and the other gentlemen who had hitherto lived in the town, repaired on board the ſhip, which got under ſail the next morning. The Endeavour was ſaluted by the fort, and by the Elgin Eaſt Indiaman, which then lay in the road; but ſoon after theſe compliments were returned, the ſea-breeze ſetting in, they were obliged to come to anchor. Since the arrival of the ſhip in Batavia Road every perſon belonging to her had been ill, except the ſail-maker, who was more than ſeventy years old, yet this man got drunk every day while we remained there. The Endeavour buried ſeven of her people at Batavia, viz. Tupia and his boy, three of the ſailors, the ſervant of Mr. Green the aſtronomer and the ſurgeon; and at the time of the veſſel's ſailing, forty of the crew were ſick, and the reſt ſo enfeebled by their late illneſs, as to be ſcarcely able to do their duty.

CHAP. XII.

A defcriptive Account of the Town of Batavia, and the circumjacent Country—Its various Produ&ions particularized—The Manners, Cuftoms, and Way of Living of the Inhabitants fully defcribed—The Endeavour fails from Batavia to the Cape of Good Hope—An Account of the Inhabitants of Prince's Ifland, with a comparative View of their Language, with that of the Malay and Javanefe—The Arrival of the Endeavour at the Cape of Good Hope—Obfervations on the Run from Java Head to that Place—The Cape and St. Helena defcribed—Remarks on the Hottentots—The Endeavour returns to England, and anchors in the Downs on Wednefday, June 12, 1771.

BAtavia, fituated in 6 deg. 10 min. S. latitude, and 106 deg. 50 min. E. longitude from the meridian of Greenwich, is built on the bank of a large bay, fomething more than twenty miles from the Streight of Sunda, on the north fide of the ifland of Java, on a low boggy ground. Several fmall rivers, which rife forty miles up the country, in the mountains of Blaeuwen Berg, difcharge themfelves into the fea at this place, having firft interfected the town in different directions. There are wide canals of nearly ftagnated water in almoft every ftreet, and as the banks of the canals are planted with trees, they appear at firft very agreeable; but thefe trees and canals combine to render the air peftilential. Some of the rivers are navigable, more than thirty miles up the country; and indeed, the Dutch appear to have chofen this fpot to build the town on, for the fake of water-carriage, in which convenience Batavia exceeds every place in the world, except the towns of Holland. A writer who publifhed an account of this place near 50 years ago, makes the number of houfes at that time 4760, viz. 1242 Dutch houfes, and 1200 Chinefe houfes, within the walls; and 1066 Dutch houfes, and 1240 Chinefe houfes, without the walls, with 12 houfes for the vending of arrack. The ftreets

No. 9.   M m   of

of Batavia being wide, and the houfes large, it ftands
on more ground than any place that has only an equal
number of houfes. In dry weather a moft horrid
ftench arifes from the canals, and taints the air to a
great degree ; and when the rains have fo fwelled their
canals that they overflow their banks, the ground-floors
of the houfes, in the lower part of the town, are filled
with ftinking water, that leaves behind it dirt and flime
in amazing quantities. The running ftreams are fometimes as offenfive as the ftagnated canals, for the bodies
of dead animals are frequently lodged on the fhallow
parts, where they are left to putrify and corrupt the
air, except a flood happens to carry them away ; this
was the cafe of a dead buffalo, while the crew of the
Endeavour were there, which lay ftinking on the fhoal
of a river, in one of the chief ftreets for feveral days.
They fometimes clean the canals ; but this bufinefs is
performed in fuch a manner, as fcarcely to make them
lefs a nuifance than before, for the bottom being cleared
of its black mud, it is left on the fide of the canal till
it is hard enough to be taken away in boats, and as there
are no houfes for neceffary retirement in the whole
town, the filth is thrown into the canals regularly once a
day ; fo that this mud is a compound of every thing
that can be imagined difagreeable and offenfive.

The new church in Batavia, is a fine piece of building, and the dome of it may be feen far off at fea.
This church is illuminated by chandeliers of the moft
fuperb workmanfhip, and has a fine organ : moft of
the other public buildings are ancient, conftructed in
an ill tafte, and gave a very compleat idea of Dutch
clumfinefs. Their method of building their houfes
feems to have been taught them by the climate. On
the ground-floor there is no room but a large hall, a
corner of which is parted off for the tranfaction of
bufinefs ; the hall has two doors, which are commonly
left open, and are oppofite each other, fo that the air
paffes freely through the room, in the middle of which
there is a court, which at once increafes the draft of
air, and affords light to the hall ; the ftairs, which are
at one corner, lead to large and lofty apartments
above.

above. The female flaves are not permitted to fit in any place but the alcove formed by the court, and this is the ufual dining place of the family.

Batavia is encompaffed by a river of fhallow water, the ftream of which is very rapid ; within this river, which is of different widths in various places, is an old ftone wall, much decayed in many places, and within the wall is a canal wider in fome places than in others, fo that there is no entering the gates of the town but by croffing two draw-bridges ; there are but few on the ramparts, and no perfons are permitted to walk there. There is a kind of citadel, or caftle, in the N. E. corner of the town, the walls of which are both broader and higher than they are in other parts ; it is furnifhed with a number of large guns, which command the landing-place.

Apartments are provided in this caftle for the governor-general and all the council ; and in cafe of a fiege they have orders to retire thither. In the caftle are likewife a number of ftore-houfes, in which the effects belonging to the company are depofited. The company have in their poffeffion large quantities of gun-powder, which is kept in different places, that the lightning may not deftroy the whole ftock at once ; a great number of cannon are likewife laid up within the caftle. There are a great many forts built in different parts of the country, feveral miles diftant from Batavia, moft probably erected to keep the natives in fubmiffion ; and befides thefe there are a number of fortified houfes, each mounting eight guns, which are fo ftationed as to command the canals and the roads on the borders. There are houfes of this kind in many parts of the ifland of Java, and the other iflands in its neighbourhood, of which the Dutch have obtained poffeffion. The Chinefe having rebelled againft them in the year 1740, all their principal houfes were demolifhed by the cannon of one of thefe fortified houfes, which is in the town of Batavia, where, likewife, there are a few more of them.

The roads of this country are only banks between the ditches and canals, and the fortified houfes being

erected

erected among the moraffes near thefe roads, nothing
is eafier than to deftroy them, and confequently to
prevent an enemy from bringing any heavy artillery
near the town : if, indeed, an enemy be only hindered
a fhort time in his approach, he is effectually ruined,
for the climate will preclude the neceffity of the ufe of
weapons for his deftruction. Before the Endeavour
had been a week at Batavia, her crew began to feel the
ill effects of the climate ; half of them were rendered
incapable of doing their duty before the expiration of
a month. They were informed, that it was a very uncommon thing for 50 foldiers out of 100 brought from
Europe, to be alive at the expiration of the firft year,
and that of the fifty who might happen to be living,
not ten of thofe would be in found health, and, probably, not lefs than half of them in the hofpital.

In Batavia all the white inhabitants are foldiers, and,
at the expiration of five years fervice, they are bound
to hold themfelves in readinefs to go to war, if they
fhould be wanted, and the younger inhabitants are
frequently muftered ; but as they are neither trained
nor exercifed after the expiration of the five years before-
mentioned, the little they have learned is foon forgotten. The Indians, of whatever nation, who refide
here, and have either been made free, or were born fo,
are called Mardykers ; but neither thefe nor the Chinefe
are acquainted with fire-arms, yet as thefe people are
faid to poffefs great perfonal bravery, much might be
expected from their expert ufe of their daggers, fwords
and lances. It would be a laborious tafk to attack
Batavia by land, and it is not poffible to make any
attack at all by fea, for the fhallownefs of the water
would hinder any veffels from advancing within can-
non-fhot of the walls ; indeed there is barely depth of
water for a fhip's long-boat, except a narrow channel,
called the river, which extends half a mile into the
harbour, and is ftrongly bounded on each fide with
piers, the other end of it being directly under the fire
of the caftle, while its communication with the canals
of the town is prevented by a boom of wood, which is
every

every night~fhut precifely at fix o'clock, and never opened till the following day.

In the harbour of Batavia, any number of fhips may anchor, the ground is fo excellent that the anchor will never quit its hold. This harbour is fometimes dangerous for boats, when the fea-breezes blow frefh; but, upon the whole, it is deemed the beft and moft commodious in all India. There is a confiderable number of iflands, which are fituated round the outfide of the harbour, and all thefe are in the poffeffion of the Dutch, who deftine them to different purpofes. On one of them, which is called Purmerent, an hofpital is erected, on acconnt of the air being purer than it is at Batavia. In a fecond, the name of which is Kuyper, are erected numbers of warehoufes, wherein are lodged the rice and fome other commodities, which belong to the Dutch Eaft-India Company; at this ifland thofe fhips belonging to different nations, which are to be repaired at Ouruft, unload their cargoes: and it was here that the ftores of the Falmouth man of war were laid up, when fhe was condemned on her return from Manilla; her warrant officers, of whom mention has been made in the account of Captain Willis's voyage, were fent to Europe in Dutch fhips about half a year before the Endeavour anchored in the road of Batavia. A third of thefe iflands, the name of which is Edam, is appropriated to the reception of certain offenders, whofe crimes are not deemed worthy of death, and thither they are tranfported from Holland, and detained from five to forty years, in proportion to the heinoufnefs of the offence they have committed: making of ropes is the principal part of the employment of thefe criminals.

The environs of Batavia have a very pleafing appearance, and would in almoft any other country, be an enviable fituation. Gardens and houfes occupy the country for feveral miles, but the former are fo covered with trees, that the advantage of the land having been cleared of the wood that originally covered it, is almoft wholly loft; while thefe gardens and the fields adjacent to them are furrounded by ditches which yield a
difagreeable

disagreeable smell; and the bogs and moraffes in the adjacent fields are still more offenfive. For the fpace of more than thirty miles beyond the town, the land is totally flat, except in two places, on one of which the governor's country-feat is built, and on the other they hold a large market; but neither of thefe places is higher than ten yards from the level of the plain. At near forty miles from the town the land rifes into hills, and the air is purified in a great degree; to this diftance the invalids are fent by their phyficians when every other profpect of their recovery has failed, and the experiment fucceeds in almoft every inftance, for the fick are reftored to health; but they no fooner return to the town, than their former diforders revifit them. On thefe hills the moft opulent of the inhabitants have country feats, to which they pay an annual vifit. Thofe who refide conftantly on the hills, enjoy an almoft perpetual flow of health; and moft of the vegetables of Europe grow as freely there as in their native ground: the ftrawberry in particular flourifhes greatly, which is a fufficient proof of the coolnefs of the air.

In this country rice is very plentiful, and, in order to be brought to perfection, fhould lie under water more than half the time it is growing: but they have a fort which grows on the fides of the hills, which is unknown in the Weft-India iflands; this fort is planted when the wet feafon commences, and the crop is gathered in, foon after the rains are over. The maize, which grows near Batavia, is gathered while young, and roafted in the ear. The land likewife produces carrots, celery, parfley, afparagus, onions, radifhes, cabbages, lettuces, cucumbers, lentiles, kidney-beans, hyffop, fage, rue, Chinefe white radifhes, which when boiled, are not unlike a parfnip, common potatoes, fweet potatoes, wet and dry yams, millet, and the egg plant, the fruit of which, when broiled and eaten with falt and pepper, is moft exquifite food. Amazing crops of fugar are produced here, and, while the quantity is beyond comparifon greater, the care of cultivation is inconceivably lefs than in the Weft-India iflands. White fugar is retailed at two-pence half-penny the pound; and arrack

is

is made of the molasses, with a small addition of rice, and the wine of the cocoa-nut. The inhabitants likewise raise a little indigo for their own use, but do not export it.

The fruits of this country are near forty in number, and of some of these there are of several kinds. Pine-apples grow in such abundance, that they may be purchased at the first hand, for the value of an English farthing; and we bought some very large ones for a half-penny a piece at the fruit-shops, and their taste is very excellent. They grow so luxuriantly, that seven or eight suckers have been seen adhering to one stem. The sweet oranges of Batavia are good of their kind, but very dear at particular times. The shaddocks of the West-Indies, called here pamplemooses, have an agreeable flavour. Lemons were very scarce when the Endeavour lay in the harbour, but limes were altogether as plentiful, and sold at little more than two-pence the score. There are many kinds of oranges and lemons, but none of them excellent. Of mangoes there are plenty, but their taste is far inferior to the melting peach of England, to which they have been compared. It is said that the heat, and extreme dampness of the climate does not agree with them, yet there are many different kinds of them. Of bananas, there are an amazing variety of forts, some of which being boiled, are eaten as bread, while others are fried in batter, and are a nourishing food: but of the numerous forts of fruit, three only are fit to be eaten: one indeed is remarkable, because it is filled with seeds, which are not common to the rest. Grapes are sold from one shilling to eighteen pence a pound, though they are far from being good. The tamarinds are cheap and plentiful; but as the method of preserving them, which is in salt, renders them a mere black lump, they are equally nauseating to the sight, and to the palate. The water melons are excellent of their kind, and are produced in great abundance. The pompions are boiled as turnips, and eaten with salt and pepper. This fruit is admirably adapted to the use of voyagers, as it will keep many months without care, and makes an excellent pye,

pye, when mixed with the juice of lemons and fugar.
The papans of this country are fuperior to turnips, if
the cores are extracted, after paring them when they
are green.   The guava has a ftrong fmell, and a tafté
not lefs difagreeable : it is probable, that the guava of
the Weft-Indies, which many writers have diftinguifhed
by their praifes, has a very different flavour. The
fweet fop is a fruit that has but little flavour: it abounds
in large kernels, from which the pulp is fucked.   The
tafte of the cuftard-apple very much refembles the difh
from which its name is taken.   The cafheu apple produces a nut which is not unknown in England, but the
fruit has fuch an aftringent quality, that the Batavians
feldom eat of it : the nut grows on the top of the apple.   The cocoa-nut is plentiful in this country, and
there are feveral kinds of this fruit, the beft of which
is very red between the fhell and the fkin.   The jamboo
is a fruit that has but little tafte, but is of a cooling nature : it is confiderably lefs than a common-fized apple,
and thofe that have grown to their full fize, are always
the beft ; its fhape is oval, and its colour a deep red.
Of the Jambu-eyer, there are two kinds, the white
and the red : they are fhaped like a bell, and are fomething bigger than a cherry : they have no kind of tafte
but that of a watry acid.   The Jambu-eyer mauwar,
fmells like a rofe, and its tafte is not unlike that of
conferve of rofes.   The mangoftan is of a dark red colour, and not larger than a fmall apple : to the bottom
of this fruit adhere feveral little leaves of the bloffoms,
while on its tops are a number of triangles combined
in a circle, it contains feveral kernels ranged in
a circular form, within which is the pulp, a fruit of
moft exquifite tafte ; it is equally nutritious and agreeable, and is conftantly given to perfons who are trou-
bled with inflammatory or putrid fevers.   The fweet
orange of this country is likewife given in the fame diforders.   The pomegranate of thefe parts differs in nothing from that generally known in England. The durion takes its name from the word dure, which, in the
language of that country, means prickles, and the name
is well adapted to the fruit, the fhell of which is covered

vered with fharp points, fhaped like a fugar-loaf: its contents are nuts not much fmaller than chefnuts, which are furrounded with a kind of juice refembling cream; and of this the inhabitants eat with great avidity: the fmell of this fruit is more like that of onions, that any other European vegetable, and its tafte is like that of onions, fugar, and cream intermixed: the infide of the durion, when ripe, is parted, lengthways, into feveral divifions. The nanca is a fruit that fmells like garlick and apples mixed together: its fize in the gardens of Batavia, is not bigger than that of a middling fized pompion, and its fhape is nearly the fame: it is covered with prickles of an angular form. We were informed that, at a place called Madura, it has been known to grow to fuch an enormous fize as to require the ftrength of two men to carry it. The champada is in all refpects like the nanca, only that it is not fo large. The rambutan contains a fruit within which is a ftone, that is perhaps the fineft acid in the world: this fruit is not unlike a chefnut with its hufk on; and it is covered with fmall prickles of a dark red colour, and fo foft as to yield to the flighteft impreffion. The gambolan refembles a damafcen both in colour and fize, and is of a very aftringent nature. The boa bidarra taftes like an apple, and is likewife extremely aftringent: its fize is that of a goofeberry, its form round, and its colour yellow. The nam nam makes an excellent fritter, if fried in batter, but is not efteemed when raw: the rind of it is rough, its length is about three inches, and its fhape not unlike that of a kidney. The catappa and the canare are two fpecies of nuts, the kernels of which are like thofe of an almond, but fo hard, that it is almoft impoffible to break them. The madja contains a pulp of a fharp tafte, which is eaten with fugar: this fruit is covered with a hard fhell. The funtal is a fruit fcarcely fit to be eaten, being at once aftringent, acid, and of a moft unpleafant tafte, yet it is publicly fold in the ftreets of Batavia: it contains a number of kernels, which are inclofed in a thick fkin. The falack is nearly of the fize of a fmall golden pippin, and contains a few kernels of a yellow colour, the tafte of which is

No. 9.   N n   not

not unlike that of a strawberry; but the covering of this fruit is very remarkable, as it confists of a number of scales, resembling those of a fish. The chesrema and the blimbing, are two four fruits, exceedingly well adapted to make four sauce, and pickles. The blimbing besse is another fruit of the same kind, but considerably sweeter.

Of the fruits not in season when Captain Cook was at Batavia, are the boa atap, and the kinship, which he saw preserved in sugar: and there are several other sorts which the Batavians are fond of, but they are never eaten by strangers : among those are the moringa, the guilindina, the killer, and the soccum; this last has the appearance of the bread-fruit which is produced in the islands of the South Seas, but it is not near so good, though the tree on which it grows is almost exactly like the bread-fruit tree. At Batavia vast quantities of fruit are eaten. There are two markets held weekly, at distant places, for the better accommodation of those who reside in different parts of the country. Here the fruit-fellers meet the gardeners, and purchase the goods at low rates. We are told it is not uncommon to see fifty or sixty loads of pine-apples carelesly thrown together at those markets. Flowers are strewn by the inhabitants of Batavia and Java, about their houses, and they are constantly burning aromatic woods and gums, which is supposed to be done by way of purifying the air from the stench that arises from the canals and ditches about the town.

In this country sweet scented flowers are plentiful, many species of which being entirely unknown, are worth remarking. The combang tonquin, and combang carenassi, are particularly fragrant flowers, which bear scarcely any resemblance to any of those flowers with which we are acquainted. They are very small, and seem to be of the dog's-bane species. The camunga which is more like a bunch of leaves than a flower, is of a singular smell, but very grateful. The bon tanjong is of a pale yellow cast, and has a very agreeable smell; it is about an inch and a half in circumference, and consists of pointed leaves, which give

it

it the appearance of a ftar. The champacka fmells
fomewhat like a jonquil, but is rather of a deeper yellow. A large tree upon the ifland produces this flower.
There is alfo an extraordinary kind of flower called
fundal malam, which fignifies the intrigue of the
night. This flower has no fmell in the day-time, but
as night comes on, it has a very fragrant fcent, and is
very much like the Englifh tuberofe. Thefe flowers
being made into nofegays of different fhapes, or ftrung
upon thread, are carried through the ftreet for fale on
an evening. The gardens of the gentlemen produce
feveral other forts of flowers befides thefe which we
have mentioned, but they are not offered to fale, becaufe there is not a fufficient plenty of them. A plant,
called the pandang, is produced here, the leaves of
which being fhred fmall, and mixed with other flowers,
the natives of both fexes fill their cloaths and hair with
this mixture, which they likewife fprinkle on their beds,
and fleep under this heap of fweets, a thin piece of
chintz being their only covering.

Formerly the only fpice that grew on the ifland of
Java was pepper. A confiderable quantity is brought
from thence by the Dutch, but very little of it is made
ufe of in the country. The inhabitants perfer cayan
pepper, and are fond of cloves and nutmeg, but thefe
firft are too dear to be commonly ufed. Near the ifland
of Amboyna are fome little ifles, on which the cloves
grow, and the Dutch were not eafy till they all became
their property. Scarcely any other nutmegs are found
but on the ifland of Banda, which however furnifhes
enough for all the nations that have a demand for that
commodity. There are but few nutmeg-trees on the
coaft of New Guinea. The ifland of Java, of which
we have already fpoken, produces horfes, buffaloes,
fheep, goats, and hogs. The fort of horfes faid to
have been met with here when the country was firft
difcovered, appeared to be nimble animals though
fmall, being generally feldom above thirteen hands
high. The horned cattle of this country are different
from thofe of Europe. They are quite lean, but of a
very fine grain. The Chinefe and the natives of Java

eat

eat the buffaloes flefh, which the Dutch conftantly refufe, being impreffed with a ftrange idea that it is fever-
ifh. The fheep are hairy like goats, and have long ears:
they are moftly found to be tough and ill-tafted. There
happening to be a few from the Cape of Good Hope
at Batavia, fome of them were purchafed at the rate of
one fhilling a pound. The hogs, efpecially thofe of
the Chinefe ftock, are very fine food, but fo fat, that
the lean is feparately fold to the butchers, who are Chinefe; the fat, they melt and fell to their countrymen to
be eaten with their rice. Yet though thefe hogs are fo
fine, the Dutch prefer their own breed, and the confequence is that thefe latter are fold at extravagant rates.

As the Portuguefe fhoot the wild hogs and deer, they
are fold at a moderate price, and are good eating. As
to the goats of this country they are as indifferent as the
fheep. Dogs and cats are found here in abundance,
and there are numbers of wild horfes at a confiderable
diftance from Batavia, on the mountains. There are
a few monkeys feen near the town; but there are many
on the mountains and defart-places, where there are
alfo tygers, and a few rhinocerofes.

Of fifh an aftonifhing quantity is taken here, and all
are fine food, except a few that are fcarce; yet the inhabitants will not eat thofe that are found in abundance,
but purchafe thofe which are worfe and fcarcer, a circumftance that contributes to keep up the price of the
latter. A prejudice likewife prevails among the Dutch
which prevents them from eating any of the turtle
caught in thefe parts, which are very good food, though
not equal to thofe that are found in the Weft-Indies.
Very large lizards are common at Batavia; fome of
them are faid to be as thick as a man's thigh; and Mr.
Banks fhot one five feet long, which being dreft, proved
very agreeable to the tafte. We found fnipes of two
different forts; and thrufhes might have been purchafed
of the Portuguefe, who were the only dealers in this
fort of birds, and venders of wild fowl in the country.
In the ifland are palm-wine, and arrack. Of the former
are three forts, the firft of which is drank in a few
hours after it is drawn from the tree, and is moderately
                                                        fweet;

fweet; the fecond and third forts are made by fermentation, and by putting feveral forts of herbs and roots
into the liquor.

In Java, the religion of Mahomet is profeffed, for
which reafon the natives do not make ufe of wine publicly; but in private few of them will refufe it. They
alfo chew opium, whofe intoxicating qualities prove its
recommendation to the natives of India.

If we exclude the Chinefe, and the Indians of different nations, who inhabit Batavia and its environs,
the inhabitants only amount to a fmall number, not a
fifth part of whom are faid to be Dutchmen, even by
defcent. The Portuguefe out-number all the European
fettlers on the ifland. The troops in the fervice of the
ftates of Holland, are compofed of the natives of almoft all the nations of Europe; but the greater part
of them are Germans. When any perfon goes to refide at Batavia, he is obliged to enter firft as a foldier,
to ferve their company for five years. Afterwards he
applies for a leave of abfence to the council, which being granted as a thing of courfe, he engages in any bufinefs that he thinks proper to chufe. There is however
a fort of policy in this matter, fince the Dutch have thus
always a force ready to arm and join their troops in
this country upon any emergency; all places of power
and profit are held by the Dutch, and no foreigner has
any fhare in the management of public affairs.

Notwithftanding all the men of other countries are
bound to obferve the rules above-mentioned, yet women from all parts may remain here unmolefted. It appeared that the whole place could not furnifh fifty females who were natives of Europe; yet the town
abounded with white women, who were defcended from
Europeans, that had fettled there at different times, all
the men having paid the debt of nature; for fo it is,
that the climate of Batavia deftroys the men much
fafter than the women. Thefe women follow the delicate cuftom of chewing beetle, after the example of the
native Javanefe, whofe drefs they imitate, and whofe
manners they copy, in all refpects. Mercantile bufinefs is conducted at Batavia with the flighteft trouble
imaginable.

imaginable. When a merchant receives an order for goods of any kind, he communicates the contents of it to the Chinese, who are the universal manufacturers. The Chinese agent delivers the effects on board the ship for which they are befpoke, and taking a receipt for them from the mafter of the veffel, he delivers it to the merchant, who pays the Chinese for the goods, and referves a confiderable profit, without the leaft trouble, rifque, or anxiety. But when a merchant imports goods of any kind, he receives them himself, and lodges them in his own warehoufes. It may be wondered that the Chinese do not fhip the goods on their account, but from this they are reftricted, and compelled to fell them to the merchants only. The inhabitants of Java diftinguifh the Portuguese by the name of Oranferanc, that is, Nazarene-men; but thefe ufe the general term of Caper, or Cafir, refpecting all who do not profefs the religion of Mahomet, and in this they include the Portuguese. But the Portuguese of Batavia are fo only in name; for they have neither any connection with, or knowledge of the kingdom of Portugal, and they have changed the religion of the church of Rome, for that of Luther; with the manners of the natives, they are wholly familiarifed, and they commonly fpeak their language, though they are able to converfe in a corrupt kind of Portuguese. They drefs in the habit of the country, with a difference only in the manner of wearing their hair; their nofes are more peaked and their fkin of a deeper caft than that of the natives. Some of them are mechanics and artificers, others fubfift by wafhing of linen, and the reft procure a maintenance by hunting.

The Indians of Batavia, and the country in its neighbourhood, are not native Javanefe, but are either born on the feveral iflands from whence the Dutch bring their flaves, or the offspring of fuch as have been born on thofe iflands; and thefe having been made free either in their own perfons or in the perfons of their anceftors, enjoy all the privileges of freemen. They receive the general appellation of believers of the true faith. The various other Indian inhabitants of this country attach

themfelves

themfelves each to the original cuftoms of that in which themfelves or their anceftors were born; keeping themfelves apart from thofe of other nations, and practifing both the virtues and vices peculiar to their own countries. The cultivation of gardens, and the confequent fale of flowers and fruit afford fubfiftence to great numbers of them : thefe are the people who raife the beetle and areca, which being mixed with lime, and a fubftance that is called gambir, the produce of the Indian continent, is chewed by perfons of all ranks, women as well as men : indeed fome of the politer ladies make an addition of cardamom, and other aromatics, to take off the difagreeable fmell with which the breath would be otherwife tainted. Some of the Indians are very rich, keep a great number of flaves, and live, in all refpects, according to the cuftom of their refpective countries, while others are employed to carry goods by water : and others again fubfift by fifhing. The Oranflams, or believers of the faith, feed principally on boiled rice, mixed with a fmall quantity of dried fhrimps and other fifh, which are imported from China, and a little of the flefh of buffaloes and chickens; they are fond of fruit, of which they eat large quantities, and with the flour of the rice they make feveral forts of paftry. They fometimes make very fuperb entertainments, after the fafhion of their refpective countries ; but, in general, they are a very temperate people; of wine they drink very little, if any, as the religion of Mahomet, which they profefs, forbids the ufe of it. When a marriage is to be folemnized among them, all the gold and filver ornaments that can be procured, are borrowed to deck out the young couple, who, on thefe occafions, never fail to make the moft fplendid appearance; fumptuous entertainments are given by thofe who can afford them, which continue twelve or fourteen days, and frequently more, during all which time the women take care that the bridegroom fhall not vifit his wife privately, though the wedding takes place previous to the feftival. All thefe Indians, though they come from different countries, fpeak the Malay language if it deferves that name. On the ifland of Java there are

2

are two or three different dialects, and there is a language peculiar to every small island ; it is conjectured
that the Malay tongue is a corruption of the language
of Malacca.   The hair of thefe people, which is black
without a fingle exception, grows in great abundance ;
yet the women make ufe of oils, and other ingredients, to increafe the quantity of it : they faften it to
the crown of the head with a bodkin, having firft twifted it into a circle, round which they place an elegant
wreath of flowers, fo that the whole head-drefs has a
moft beautiful appearance.   It is the univerfal cuftom
both with the men and women, to bathe in a river once
every day, and fometimes oftener, which not only pro-
motes health, but prevents that contraction of filth,
that would be otherwife unavoidable in fo hot a climate.
The teeth of the Oranflams have fome particulars in
them well worthy of notice. With a kind of whetftone
they rub the ends of them till they are quite flat and
even ; they then make a deep groove in the teeth of the
upper jaw, in the centre between the bottom of each
tooth and the gum, and horizontally with the latter ;
this groove is equal in depth to a quarter of the thicknefs of the teeth ; yet none of thefe people have a rotten tooth, though according to the dentifts of England
and France, fuch a thing muft be unavoidable, as the
tooth is placed much deeper than what we call the
enamel.   The teeth of thefe people became very black
by the chewing of beetle, yet a flight wafhing will take
off this blacknefs, and they will then become perfectly
white ; but they are very feldom wafhed, as the depth
of the colour is very far from being thought difagreeable.   Moft of our readers muft have heard of the Mo-
hawks ; and thefe are the people who are fo denominated,
from a corruption of the word amock, which will be
explained by the following ftory and obfervations. To
run amock is to get drunk with opium, and then feizing
fome offenfive weapon, to fally forth from the houfe,
kill the perfon or perfons fuppofed to have injured the
Amock, and any other perfon that attempts to impede
his paffage, till he himfelf is taken prifoner or killed
on the fpot.   While Captain Cook was at Batavia, a
                                                    perfon,

perfon, whofe circumftances in life were independent, being jealous of his brother, intoxicated himfelf with opium, and then murdered his brother, and two other men who endeavoured to feize him. This man, contrary to the ufual cuftom, did not leave his own houfe, but made his refiftance from within it; yet he had taken fuch a quantity of the opium, that he was delirious, which appeared from his attempting to fire three mufquets, neither of which had been loaded, nor even primed. Jealoufy of the women is the ufual reafon of thefe poor creatures running amock [or a-muck] and the firft object of their vengeance is the perfons whom they fuppofe to have injured them. The officer, whofe bufinefs it is to apprehend thefe unhappy wretches, is furnifhed with a long pair of tongs, in order to take hold of them without coming within the reach of the point of their weapon. Thofe who may be taken alive, which is not often the cafe, are generally wounded; but they are always broken upon the wheel; and if the phyfician, who is appointed to examine their wounds, thinks them likely to be mortal, the punifhment is inflicted immediately, and the place of execution is generally the fpot where the firft murder was committed. A number of abfurd cuftoms prevailed among thefe people, and opinions no lefs ridiculous. They believe that the devil, whom they call Satan, is the author of ficknefs and adverfity; therefore, when fick, or in diftrefs, they offer meat, money, and other things, as propitiatory facrifices. Should one among them be reftlefs, or fhould he dream for two or three nights fucceffively, he imagines the devil has laid his commands upon him, when, upon neglect to fulfil, he concludes his punifhment will certainly be ficknefs or death, though fuch commands may not be revealed with fufficient perfpicuity. To interpret his dream therefore, he ftrains his wits to the uttermoft, and if, by taking it literally, or figuratively directly, or by contraries, he can put no explanation that fatisfies him, he applies to the Cawin or prieft, who unravels the myfterious fuggeftions of the night, by a comment, in which it generally appears, that Satan wants victuals or money. Thefe are placed

No. 9.   O o   on on a little plate of cocoa-nut leaves, and hung upon the branch of a tree near the river, fo that it feems not to be the opinion of thefe people, that in prowling the earth the devil " walketh through dry places." Mr. Banks once afked, whether they thought Satan fpent the money, or eat the victuals; they faid, that as to the money it was confidered rather as a mulet upon an offender, than a gift to him who had enjoined it; and that therefore if it was devoted by the dreamer, it did not fignify into whofe hands it came, and they fuppofed it was generally the prize of fome ftranger who wandered that way; but refpecting the meat, they were clearly of opinion, that, although the devil did not eat the grofs parts, yet by bringing his mouth near it, he fucked out all its favour without changing its pofition, fo that afterwards it was as infipid as water.

Another fuperftitious notion of this people is ftill more unaccountable. They imagine that women, when delivered of children, are at the fame time delivered of a young crocodile; and that thofe animals being received carefully by the midwifes, are immediately carried down to the river, and put into the water. The family in which fuch a birth is fuppofed to have happened, conftantly puts victuals into the river for their amphibious relation, efpecially the twin, who as long as he lives, goes down to the river at ftated times, to fulfil his fraternal duty; for an omiffion of which, according to the general opinion, he will be vifited with ficknefs or death. We are at a lofs to account for an opinion fo extravagant and abfurd, efpecially as it feems to be unconnected with any religious myftery, and how it fhould be pretended to happen by thofe who cannot be deceived into a belief of it by appearances, nor have any apparent intereft in the fraud, is a problem ftill more difficult to folve. The ftrange belief of this abfurdity, however, is certain, for which we had the concurrent teftimony of every Indian who was queftioned about it; and as to its origin, it feems to have taken its rife in the iflands of Celebes and Boutou, at which places many of the inhabitants keep crocodiles in their families; but however that be, this opinion has fpread

over

over all the eastern islands, even to Timor and Cream, and weftward as far as Java and Sumatra. The cro-codile twins are called sudaras, and we shall here re-late one of the innumerable and incredible stories, in proof of their exiftence, as was confidently affirmed, from ocular demonftrations; yet for the credibility of this relation we will not vouch.

At Bencoolen was born and bred among the Englifh a young female flave, who had learnt a little of the lan-guage. This girl told Mr. Banks that her father, when on his death bed, informed her that he had a crocodile for his fudara, and in a folemn manner charged her to give him meat when he fhould be dead, telling her in what part of the river he was to be found, and by what name he was to be called up. That in confe-quence of her father's injunctions, fhe repaired to that part of the river he had defcribed, and ftanding upon the bank, called out Radja Pouti, "white king;" where-upon the crocodile came to her out of the water, and eat from her hand the provifions fhe had brought him. Being defired to defcribe this paternal uncle, fhe faid, that he was not like other crocodiles, but much hand-fomer, that his body was fpotted and his nofe red; that he had bracelets of gold upon his feet, and ear-rings of the fame metal in his ears. This ridiculous tale was heard by Mr. Banks patiently to the end, and he then difmiffed the girl, without reminding her, that a crocodile with ears was as ftrange a monfter as a dog with a cloven foot. Not long after this a fervant whom Mr. Banks had hired at Batavia, a fon of a Dutchman by a Javanefe women, told his mafter, that he had feen a crocodile of the fame kind, and it had been feen by feveral others both Dutchmen and Malays. This crocodile the fervant faid was very young, two feet long, and its feet were ornamented with bracelets of gold. I cannot credit thefe idle ftories, faid Mr. Banks. The other day a perfon afferted that crocodiles had ear-rings, and you know that cannot be true, becaufe cro-codiles have not ears. Ah, Sir, replied the man, thefe fudara oran are unlike other crocodiles; for they have five toes upon each foot, a large tongue that fills their

mouth,

mouth, and ears likewife, though indeed they are very
fmall. Who can fet bounds to the ignorance of cre-
dulity and folly! However, in the girl's relation were
fome things in which fhe could not be deceived; and
therefore muft be guilty of wilful falfehood. Her father might command her to feed a crocodile, in confequence of his believing it to be his fudara; but its
coming out of the river at her call, and eating the food
from her hand, muft have been a fable of her own invention, and being fuch, it was impoffible that fhe could
believe it to be true. However, the girl's ftory, and
that of the man's, evinces, that they both believed the
exiftence of crocodiles that were fudaras to men; and
the fiction invented by the girl may be eafily accounted
for, if we do but confider, how earneftly every one defires to make others believe what he believes himfelf.
The Bougis, Macaffars, and Boetons, are fo firmly perfuaded that they have relations of the crocodile fpecies,
that they perform a periodical ceremony in remembrance of them. Large parties go out in a boat, furnifhed with great plenty of provifions, and all kinds of
mufic. They then row backwards and forwards, in
places of the river where crocodiles and allegators are
moft common, finging and weeping by turns, each in-
voking his kindred, till a crocodile appears, when the
mufic inftantly ftops, and provifions, beetle, and tobacco,
are thrown into the water. This civility is intended
to recommend themfelves to their relations at home;
not without hopes, perhaps, that it will be accepted
inftead of more expenfive offerings which may not be
in their power to pay.

The Chinefe ftand in the next rank to the Indians,
and are very numerous, but poffefs very little property.
Many of them live within the walls, and are fhop-
keepers. We have already mentioned the fruit-fellers
of Paffar Piffang; but others have a rich ftock of European and Chinefe goods. However, the far greater
part of thefe people live without the walls, in a quarter
by themfelves, which is called Campang China. Moft
part of them are carpenters, jo'ners, fmiths, taylors,
flipper-makers, dyers of cotton, and embroiderers. They

maintain

maintain the character of induftry, univerfally beftowed upon them; and many are fcattered about the country, where they cultivate gardens, fow rice and fugar, or keep cattle and buffaloes, whofe milk they bring every day to town. Yet notwithftanding their commendable fpirit of induftry, we muft obferve, there is nothing honeft or difhoneft, provided there is no danger of a halter, that the Chinefe will not readily do for money; and though they work with much diligence, nor are fparing of their labour, yet no fooner have they laid down their tools, than they begin to game either at cards or dice, or at other diverfions altogether unknown among Europeans. To thefe they apply with fuch eagernefs, as fcarcely to allow time for neceffary re-frefhments of food and fleep. In manners they are al-ways rather obfequious; and in drefs they are remark-ably neat and clean, in whatever rank of life they are placed. A defcription of their perfons or drefs is un-neceffary, feeing the better kind of China paper com-mon in England, exhibits an exact reprefentation of both, though perhaps with fome flight exaggerations. With refpect to their eating, they are eafily fatisfied; but the few that are rich have many favory difhes. The food of the poor is rice, with a fmall proportion of flefh or fifh; and they have the advantage of the Mahomedan Indians, on account of their religion; for the Chinefe, being under no reftraint, eat, befides pork, dogs, cats, frogs, lizards, ferpents, and a great variety of fea animals, which the other inhabitants do not con-fider as food. They alfo eat many vegetables, which an European, except he was perifhing with hunger, would not tafte. They have a fingular cuftom refpect-ing the burying their dead; for they cannot be prevailed upon to open the ground a fecond time, where the body has been depofited. On this account, in the neighbour-hood of Batavia, their burying-grounds contain many hundred acres; and the Dutch, pretending this to be a wafte of land, will not fell any for this purpofe, un-lefs at an exorbitant price. The Chinefe, however, contrive to raife the purchafe money, and afford another inftance of the folly and weaknefs of human nature, in

transferring

4

transferring a regard for the living to the dead, and making that an object of folicitude and expence, which cannot receive the leaft benefit from either. Under the influence of this univerfal prejudice, they take an uncommon method to preferve the body entire, and to prevent the remains of it from mixing with the earth that furrounds it. To this end they enclofe it in a large thick wooden coffin, hollowed out of folid timber like a canoe. This when covered and let down into the grave, is furrounded with a coat of mortar, called chinam, about eight or ten inches thick, which in a fhort time cements, and becomes as hard as ftone. The relatives of the deceafed attend the funeral ceremony, with a confiderable number of female mourners, hired to weep. In Batavia, the law requires, that every man fhould be interred according to his rank, which is in no cafe to be difpenfed with; fo that if the deceafed has not left fufficient to pay his debts, an officer takes an inventory of what was in his poffeffion when he died, and out of the produce buries him in the manner prefcribed, leaving only the overplus to his creditors.

The loweft clafs of people in this country are the flaves, by whom the Dutch, Portuguefe, and Indians, whatever their rank or fituation, are conftantly attended. They are bought in Sumatra, Malacca, and almoft all the Eaftern Iflands: but the natives of Java, very few of whom live in Batavia, are exempted from flavery, under the fanction of very fevere penal laws, feldom we believe violated. Thefe flaves are fold from ten to twenty pounds fterling each; but girls, if handfome, will fetch fome times a hundred. Being of an indolent difpofition, they will not do much work, and are therefore content with a little victuals, fubfifting altogether upon boiled rice, and a fmall quantity of the cheapeft fifh. They are natives of different countries, on which account they differ from each other extremely both in perfon and temper. The Papua, as they are here called, or the African negroes are the worft, moft of them thieves and all incorrigible; confequently they may be purchafed for the leaft money. The next clafs to thefe are the Bougis and Macaffars, both from the ifland of Celebes;

Celebes; who, in the higheft degree are lazy, though not fo much addicted to theft as the negroes; yet they are of a cruel and vindictive fpirit, whereby they are rendered exceeding dangerous, efpecially as to gratify their refentment, they make no fcruple of any means, nor of facrificing life itfelf. Befides thefe there are Malays and flaves of other denominations: but the beft, and of courfe the deareft, are thofe brought from the ifland of Bali; and the moft beautiful women from Nias, a fmall ifland on the coaft of Sumatra; but being of a tender and delicate conftitution, they quickly fall a facrifice to the unwholefome air of Batavia. All thefe flaves are wholly in the power of their mafters, who may inflict upon them any punifhment that does not take away life; and fhould one die in confequence of punifhment, though his death may be proved not to have been intended, yet the mafter is called to a fevere account, and generally fentenced to fuffer capitally. For this reafon a mafter feldom corrects a flave with his own hands, but by an officer called a marineu, one of whom is ftationed is every diftrict. The duty of this officer is to quell riots, and take offenders into cuftody; but more particularly to apprehend runaway flaves, and punifh them for fuch crimes as the mafter has fupported by proper evidence; the punifhment, however, is not inflicted by the marineu in perfon, but by flaves who are appointed to the bufinefs. The punifhment is ftripes, the number being proportioned to the nature of the offence; and the inftruments are rods made of rattans, which are fplit into tender twigs for the purpofe, and every ftroke draws blood. A common punifhment cofts the mafter a rixdollar, and a fevere one a ducatoon, about fix fhillings and eight-pence. The mafter is alfo obliged to allow a flave, as an encouragement, three dubbelcheys, equal to about feven-pence half-penny a week; this is alfo done to prevent his indulging his ftrong temptations to fteal.

Refpecting the government of this place we can fay but little. We obferved a remarkable fubordination among the people. Every houfe-keeper has a certain fpecific rank, according to the length of time he has

ferved

ferved the company. The different ranks thus acquired
are diftinguifhed by the ornaments of the coaches, and
the dreffes of the coachmen: fome ride in plain coaches,
fome are allowed to paint them with different devices,
and fome to gild them. The coachmen alfo are obliged
to appear in clothes quite plain, or ornamented in various manners and degrees.

The chief officer in this place has the title of governor-general of the Indies, to whom the Dutch governors of all other fettlements are fubordinate; and
they are obliged to repair to Batavia in order to have
their accounts paffed by him. Should they appear to
have been criminal, or even negligent, he detains them
during pleafure; fometimes three years; for they cannot without his permiffion quit the place. The members of the council, called by the natives Edele Heeren,
and by the Englifh, Idoleers, are next in rank to the
governor-general. Thefe affume fo much ftate, that
whoever meets them in a carriage, are expected to rife
up and bow, and after this compliment, they drive to
one fide of the road and ftop, till the members of the
council are paft : their wives and children expect alfo
the fame homage, and it is commonly paid them by the
inhabitants. Some Englifh Captains have thought
this a flavifh mark of refpect, derogatory to their dignity as fervants of his Britannic majefty, and for this
reafon have refufed to pay it; neverthelefs, when in a
hired coach, nothing but a menace of immediate death
could prevent the coachman from honouring the Dutch
grandee, at the expence of their mortification.

With refpect to the diftribution of juftice, it is adminiftered in Batavia by the lawyers, who have peculiar
ranks of diftinction among themfelves. Their deci-
fions in criminal cafes feem to be fevere with refpect to
the natives, but lenient in a partial degree to their own
people. A chriftian is always indulged with an opportunity of efcaping before he is brought to trial,
whatever may be his offence, and when convicted, he
is feldom punifhed with death. On the contrary, the
poor Indians are hanged, broken upon the wheel, and
even impaled alive. As to the Malays and Chinefe,
they

they have judicial officers of their own, named captains and lieutenants, who determine in civil cafes, fubject to an appeal to the Dutch tribunal. The taxes laid upon thefe people by the company are very confiderable, among which, that exacted for liberty to wear their hair is not the leaft. The time of payment is monthly, and to fave the charge and trouble of collecting them, notice is given of this by hoifting a flag upon the top of a houfe in the middle of the town, and the Chinefe find that it is their intereft to repair thither when a payment is due without delay.

At Batavia the current money confifts of ducates, valued at one hundred and thirty-two ftivers; ducatoons, eighty ftivers: imperial rix-dollars, fixty; rupees, thirty; fchellings, fix; double cheys, two ftivers and a half; and doits one fourth of a ftiver. During our ftay here Spanifh dollars were at five and five-pence; and we were told they were never lower than five fhillings and four-pence, even at the company's warehoufe. For Englifh guineas the exchange upon an average was nineteen fhillings; for though the Chinefe would give twenty fhillings for fome of the brighteft, thofe that were much worn were valued at only feventeen fhillings. There are two forts of coin current here of the fame denomination; thefe are milled and unmilled; the former of which is of moft value. A milled ducatoon is valued at eighty ftivers; and an unmilled one at no more than feventy-two. A rix-dollar is equal to forty-eight ftivers, about four fhillings and fix-pence Englifh currency. All accounts are kept in rix-dollars and ftivers, which here, at leaft, are nominal, like our pound fterling.

On Thurfday, the 27th of December, early in the morning, we weighed, left the harbour of Batavia, and ftood out to fea. On the 29th, after much delay by contrary winds, we weathered Pulo Pare, and ftood for the main. On the fame day paffed a fmall ifland between Batavia and Bantam, called Maneater's ifland. On Sunday the 30th, we weathered Wapping and Pulo Babi iflands, and the next day, being the 31ft, we ftood over to the Sumatra fhore.

On the morning of this new year's day, being Tuefday, January the 1ſt, we ſteered for the
Java ſhore, and continued our courſe, as
the wind permitted us, till three o'clock in the afternoon of the 5th, when we caſt anchor on the ſouth-
eaſt ſide of Prince's Iſland, in eighteen fathom water, in order to recruit our ſtores, and procure refreſhments for the ſick, many of whom were much worſe
than they were at our departure from Batavia. Mr.
Banks and Dr. Solandar, accompanied by the captain
and other gentlemen, went aſhore. We met upon the
beach ſome Indians, by whom we were conducted to
one, who, they ſaid, was their king. Having exchanged a few compliments with this perſon, we entered
upon buſineſs, but in ſettling the price of turtle could
not agree. Upon this we took leave, the Indians diſperſed; and we proceeded along ſhore in ſearch of a
watering-place. We happily ſucceeded in finding a
very convenient one, and had no reaſon to believe, with
care in filling, it would prove agreeable to our wiſhes.
On our return, ſome Indians, who remained with a
canoe upon the beach, ſold us three turtle, but we were
obliged to promiſe, that we would not tell the king.
On Sunday the 6th, we renewed with better ſucceſs our
traffic for turtle. About noon the Indians lowered
their demands ſlowly, inſomuch, that before the evening they accepted our ſtipulated price, and we had turtle in plenty. In the mean time, the three we had pur-
chaſed were ſerved to the ſhip's company, who, till
yeſterday, had not fed on ſalt proviſions from the time
of our arrival at Savu, which was now near three
months. Mr. Banks, in the evening, paid a viſit to the
king, by whom he was received very graciouſly at his
palace, in the middle of a rice field, notwithſtanding
his majeſty was buſily employed in dreſſing his own
ſupper. The day following, Monday the 7th, the Indians reſorted to the trading place with fowls, fiſh,
monkeys, ſmall deer, and ſome vegetables; but no turtle appeared till next day, Tueſday the 8th, after which
ſome were brought to market every day, while we ſtaid,

but

but the whole quantity together was not equal to that
we bought the day after our arrival.

Friday the 11th, Mr. Banks having received intelligence from a fervant he had hired at Batavia, that the
Indians of this ifland had a town fituated near the fhore,
to the weftward, he determined to go in fearch of the
fame. With this view he fet out in the morning, accompanied by the fecond lieutenant; and apprehending his vifit might not be agreeable to the natives, he
told fuch of them as he met, that he was in fearch of
plants, which was indeed alfo true. Having come to
a place where there were three or four houfes, they met
with an old man, of whom they ventured to make a
few enquiries concerning the town. He would have
perfuaded them, that it was at a great diftance; but
perceiving they proceeded forward, he joined company,
and went on with them. The old man attemped feveral times to lead them out of the way, though without fuccefs; but when at length they came within fight
of the houfes, he entered cordially into their party, and
conducted them into the town, the name of which is
Samadang. It confifts of about four hundred houfes,
and is divided by a brackifh river into two parts, one
called the old, and the other the new town. When
they had entered the former, they were accofted by feveral Indians whom they had feen at the trading place,
and one of them undertook to carry them over to the
new town, at two-pence per head. The bargain being made, they embarked in two fmall canoes, placed
along-fide of each other, and lafhed together, to prevent their over-fetting. They landed fafely, though
not without fome difficulty; and when they came to
the new town, the people fhewed them every mark of
a cordial friendfhip, fhewing them the houfes of their
king and principal people. Few of the houfes were
open at this time, the inhabitants having taken up
their refidence in the rice-grounds, to defend their
crops againft the birds and monkeys, who without this
neceffary precaution would deftroy them. When their
curiofity was fatisfied, they hired a large failing boat

for

for two rupees, value four fhillings, which conveyed
them to the bark time enough to dine upon one of the
fmall deer, weighing only forty pounds, which proved
to be exceeding good and favory food.   In the evening
we again went on fhore, to fee how our people went on,
who were employed in wooding and watering, when we
were told, that an axe had been ftolen.   Application
was immediately made to the king, who, after fome
altercation, promifed, that the axe fhould be reftored
in the morning; and it was accordingly brought to us
by a man, who pretended, that the thief, afraid of a
difcovery, had left it at his houfe in the night.

   On Sunday, the 13th, having nearly compleated our
wood and water, Mr. Banks took leave of his majefty,
to whom he had made feveral trifling prefents, and at
parting gave him two quires of paper, which he gra-
cioufly accepted.   During their converfation, the king
enquired, why the Englifh did not touch at the ifland
as they had ufed to do.   Mr. Banks replied, that the
reafon was, he fuppofed, becaufe they found a deficiency
of turtle, of which there not being enough to fupply
one fhip, many could not be expected; and to fupply
this defect, Mr. Banks advifed his majefty to breed cattle, buffaloes, and fheep; but he did not feem difpofed
to adopt this prudent meafure.

   On Monday, the 14th, we had got on board a good
ftock of frefh provifions, confifting of turtle, fowl,
fifh, two fpecies of deer, one about the fize of a fheep,
the other not bigger than a rabbit; alfo cocoa-nuts,
plantains, limes, and other vegetables.   The deer,
however, ferved only for prefent ufe, for we could feldom keep one of them alive more than twenty-four
hours.

   The trade on our parts, was carried on chiefly with
Spanifh dollars, the natives feeming not to fet value
upon any thing elfe; fo that our people who had a general permiffion to trade, parted with old fhirts and
other articles, which they were obliged to fubftitute for
money to great difadvantage.   On Tuefday, the 15th,
in the morning, we weighed, with a light breeze at
N. E.

N. E. and stood out to sea. We took our departure from Java Head, which is in latitude 6 deg. 49 min. S. and in longitude 253 deg. 12 min. West.

Prince's Island, where we were stationed about ten days, in the Malay language, called Pulo Selan, and in that of the inhabitants, Pulo Pancitan, is a small island, situated in the western mouth of the streight of Sunda. It is woody, a very small part of it having been cleared. We could perceive no remarkable hill upon it; but a small eminence, just over the landing place, has been named, by the English, the Pike. Formerly this place was much frequented by India ships belonging to various nations, especially from England; but of late they have forsaken it, because the water is bad, and touch either at North Island, or at New Bay, a few leagues distant from Prince's Island, at neither of which places any considerable quantity of other provisions can be procured; and, upon the whole, we must give it as our opinion, that Prince's Island is more eligible than either of them; for though, as we have already observed, the water is brackish, if filled at the lower part of the brook, yet higher up we found it excellent.

The first, second, and perhaps the third ship, that arrives here in the season, may be well supplied with turtle; but such as come afterwards must be content with small ones. What we purchased were of the green kind, and cost us, at an average, about three farthings a pound. They were neither fat nor well flavoured, which circumstance we imputed to their being long kept in pens of brackish water, without food. The fowls are large, and we bought a dozen of them for a Spanish dollar, which is about five pence a piece. The small deer cost us two-pence a piece, and the larger, two only of which were brought to market, a rupee. The natives sell many kinds of fish by hand, and we found them tolerably cheap. Cocoa-nuts, if they were picked, we bought at the rate of a hundred for a dollar; and if taken promiscuously, one hundred and thirty. Plantains we found in abundance; also

pine-

pine-apples, water-melons, jaccas, and pompions, befides rice, yams, and feveral other vegetables, all which
we purchafed at reafonable rates.

In this ifland the inhabitants are Javanefe, and their
Raja is fubject to the Sultan of Bantam. In their manners and cuftoms they refemble the Indians about Batavia; but they are more jealous of their women, for all
the time we were there, we faw not any of them, except
one by chance in the woods, as fhe was running away
to hide herfelf. They profefs the Mahomedan religion;
but not a mofque did we difcover in the whole ifland.
While we were among them, they kept the faft called
by the Turks Ramadan, with extreme rigour, not one
of them touching a morfel of victuals, nor would they
chew their beetle till fun-fet. Their food is likewife the
fame with that of the Batavian Indians, except the addition of the nuts of the palm, by eating of which,
upon the coaft of New Holland, fome of our people
were made fick, and fome of our hogs poifoned. We
enquired by what means thefe nuts were deprived of
their noxious deleterious quality, and were informed,
that they firft cut them into thin flices, and dried them
in the fun, then fteeped them in frefh water for three
months, and afterwards, preffing out the water, dried
them a fecond time in the fun; but after all, we found
they are eaten only in times of fcarcity, when they mix
them with their rice to make it go farther.

The houfes of thefe people are built upon piles, or
pillars, and elevated about four or five feet above the
ground. Upon thefe is laid a floor of bamboo canes, at
fuch a diftance from each other, as to leave a free paffage, for the air from below. The walls alfo are of bamboo, interwoven hurdlewife, with fmall fticks, and faftened perpendicularly to the beams which form the
frame of the building; it has a floping roof, fo well
thatched with palm-leaves, that neither the fun, nor
rain can find entrance. The ground plot, upon which
the building is erected, is an oblong fquare. On the
fide is the door, and in the fpace between that and the
other end of the houfe, in the center, towards the left
hand,

hand, is a window. A partition runs out from each
end of the houfe, which continues fo far as to leave an
opening oppofite the door. Each end of the houfe,
therefore, to the right and left of the door, is divided
into two apartments, all open towards the paflage from
the door to the wall on the oppofite fide. In that on the
left hand, next to the door, the children fleep; that
oppofite to it is for the ufe of ftrangers; in the inner
room, on the left hand, the mafter and his wife fleep;
and that oppofite to it is the kitchen. The only difference between the poor and the rich, with refpect to
thefe houfes, confifts in their fize : but we muft except
the royal palace, and the houfe of one Guadang, the
next man in riches and influence to the king ; for thofe
inftead of being wattled with fticks and bamboos, are
enclofed with boards. Thefe people have occafional
houfes in the rice fields, at the feafon when they are infefted with the birds and monkeys. They differ only
from their town houfes, by being raifed ten feet inftead
of four from the ground.

The inhabitants of this ifland are of a good difpofition ; and dealt with us very honeftly ; only like other
Indians, and the retailers of fifh in London, they would
afk twice, and fometimes thrice as much for their commodities as they would take. As what they brought
to market belonged, in different proportions, to a confiderable number of the natives, they put all that was
bought of one kind, as cocoas or plantains together,
and when we had purchafed a lot, they divided the money that was paid for it among the proprietors, in a
proportion correfponding with their contributions.
Sometimes, indeed, they would change our money,
giving us 240 doits, amounting to five fhillings, for a
Spanifh dollar, and ninety-fix, amounting to two fhillings, for a Bengal rupee.

The natives of Prince's Ifland have a language of
their own, yet they all fpeak the Malay language.
Their own tongue they call Catta Gunung, the language
of the mountains. They fay, that their tribe originally
migrated from the mountains of Java to New Bay, and
then

then to their prefent ftation, being driven from their firft fettlement by tygers, which they found too nume-rous to fubdue. Several languages are fpoken by the native Javanefe, in different parts of their ifland; but the language of thefe people is different from that fpoken at Samarang, though diftant only one day's journey from the refidence of the Emperor of Java. The following lift contains feveral correfponding words in the languages of Prince's Ifland, Java, and Ma-lacca.

PRINCE'S ISLAND.	ENGLISH.	JAVANESE.	MALAY.
Jalma, -	*A man.*	Oong Lanang,	Oran Lacki Laki.
Becang, -	*A woman.*	Oong Wadong,	Parampuan.
Oroculatacke,	*A child.*	Lari, -	Anack.
Holo, -	*The head.*	Undafs, -	Capalla.
Erung, -	*The nofe.*	Erung, -	Edung.
Mata, -	*The eyes.*	Moto, -	Mata.
Chole, -	*The ears.*	Cuping, -	Cuping.
Cutock, -	*The teeth.*	Untu, -	Ghigi.
Beatung, -	*The belly.*	Wuttong, -	Prot.
Serit, -	*The backfide.*	Celit, -	Pantat.
Pimping, -	*The thigh.*	Poopoo, -	Paha.
Hulloctoor,	*The knee.*	Duncul, -	Lontour.
Metis, -	*The legs.*	Sickil, -	Kauki.
Cucu, -	*A nail.*	Cucu, -	Cucu.
Langan, -	*A hand.*	Tangan, -	Tangan.
Ramo Langan,	*A finger.*	Jari, - -	Jaring.

In this fpecimen the different parts of the body are chofen, becaufe they are eafily obtained from thofe whofe language is unknown; and it is worthy of obfervation, that the Malay, the Javanefe, and the language in Prince's Ifland, have words, which if not exactly fimilar to thofe ufed in the South-Sea Iflands, are manifeftly derived from the fame fource, as will appear from the following lift.

SOUTH-

South-Sea.	Malay.	Javanese.	Prince's Island.	English.
Mata,	Mata,	Moto,	Mata,	*An eye.*
Maa,	Macan	Mangan,	——	*The ear.*
Einu,	Menum,	Gnumbe,	——	*To drink.*
Matte,	Matte,	Matte,	——	*To kill.*
Outou,	Coutou,	——-	——	*A loufe.*
Euwa,	Udian,	Udan,	——	*Rain.*
Owhe,	——	——	Awe,	*Bamboo-cane.*
Eu,	Soufou,	Soufou,	——	*A beaft.*
Mannu,	——	Manny,	Mannuck,	*A bird.*
Eyea,	Ican,	Iwa,	———	*A fifh.*
Tapao,	——	Tapaan,	———	*The foot.*
Tooura,	Udang,	Urang,	———	*A lobfter.*
Eufwhe,	Ubi,	Urve,	———	*Yams.*
Etannou,	Tannam,	Tandour,	———	*To bury.*
Enammou,	Gnammuck,	———	———	*A mufchito.*
Hearu,	Garru,	Garu,	———	*To fcratch.*
Taro,	Tallas,	Talus,	———	*Cocoa-roots.*
Uta,	Utan,	——	———	*In-land.*

But the fimilitude in thefe languages is more remarkable in words expreffing number, which feems to
prove that they have one common root. Mr. Banks,
with the affiftance of a negro flave, born at Madagafcar,
and who was on board an Englifh fhip at Batavia, drew
up the following comparative table, from whence it
will appear, that the names of numbers, in particular,
are in a manner common to all thefe countries: but we
muft obferve, that in the ifland of Madagafcar, the
names of numbers, in fome inftances, are fimilar to all
thefe, which is a difficulty not eafy to be folved; yet
the fact will appear unqueftionable from the following
lift of words, drawn up, as we have obferved, by Mr.
Banks.

SOUTH-SEA ISLANDS.	MALAY.	JAVANESE.	PRINCE'S ISLE.	MADA-GASCAR.	ENG-LISH.
Tahie,	Satou,	Sigi,	Hegic,	Iffe,	One.
Rua,	Dua,	Lorou,	Dua,	Rua,	Two.
Torou,	Tiga,	Tullu,	Tollu,	Tellou,	Three.
Haa,	Ampat,	Pappat,	Opat,	Effats,	Four.
Reina,	Lima,	Limo,	Limah,	Limi,	Five.
Wheney,	Annam,	Nunnam,	Gunnap,	Ene,	Six.
Hetu,	Tudju,	Petu,	Tudju,	Titou,	Seven.
Waru,	Delapau,	Wolo,	Delapan,	Walon,	Eight.
Iva,	Sembilan,	Songo,	Salapan,	Sivi,	Nine.
Ahoura,	Sapoulou,	Sapoulou,	Sapoulou,	Tourou,	Ten.

From the fimilitude between the Eaftern Tongue and that of the South-Sea, many conjectures may be formed concerning the peopling of thofe countries, which cannot eafily be referred to Madagafcar. The people of Java and Madagafcar appear to be a different race: the Javanefe has long hair, and his complexion is of an olive caft; whereas a native of Madagafcar is black, and his hair woolly; yet this will not conclude againft the opinion of their having had common anceftors: and, poffibly, the learning of ancient Egypt might run in two courfes, one through Africa, and the other through Afia, diffeminating the fame words in each, efpecially terms of number, which might thus become part of the language of people who never had any communications with each other.

In the month of February we held on our courfe, and made the beft of our way for the Cape of Good Hope; but now the fatal feeds of difeafe, our people had imbibed at Batavia, began to appear, with the moft alarming fymptoms, in dyfenteries and flow fevers. Our fituation in a fhort time was truly deplorable, and the fhip was little better than an hofpital, in which thofe who did duty, were too few to attend thofe who were confined to their hammocks. Many of thefe were in the laft ftage of the deftructive diforder; and almoft

every

every night we committed a body to the fea. Mr.
Banks was among the number of the fick, and for fome
time we defpaired of his life. In the courfe of fix weeks
we buried Mr. Sporing, a gentleman of Mr. Banks's
retinue, Mr. Parkinfon, his natural hiftory painter, Mr.
Green the aftronomer, the boatfwain, the carpenter, and
his mate. Mr. Monkhoufe the midfhipman, our jolly
fail-maker, and his affiftant, the cook, the corporal of
the marines, two of the carpenter's crew, a midfhipman,
and nine failors; in all three and twenty perfons, befides
the feven that we had buried at Batavia. Such was the
havock difeafe made among our fhip's company,
though we omitted no means, which we conceived
might be a remedy; and to prevent the infection from
fpreading, we purified the water taken in at Prince's
Ifland with lime, and wafhed all parts of the bark between decks with vinegar.

Friday the 15th of March, about ten o'clock P, M.
we brought the fhip to an anchor off the Cape of
Good Hope. Capt. Cook repaired immediately to the
governor, who chearfully promifed him every refrefhment the country afforded; on which a houfe was
hired for the fick, and it was agreed they fhould be
lodged and boarded for two fhillings each man per day.
Our run from Java Head to the Cape afforded few
obfervations that can be of ufe to future navigators,
but fome occurrences we muft not pafs over in filence.
We had left Java Head eleven days before we got the
general S.E. trade-wind, during which time, we did not
advance above 5 deg. to the fouthward, and 3 deg. to
the W. having an unwholefome air, occafioned probably
by the load of vapours, which the eaftern wind, and
wefterly monfoons, bring into thefe latitudes, both of
which blew in thefe feas, at the time we happened to be
there. Our difeafes were certainly aggravated by thofe
poifonous vapours, and unwholefome air, particularly
the flux, which was not in the leaft degree checked by
any medicine; fo that whoever was feized with it, confidered himfelf as a dead man; but we no fooner got
into the trade wind, than we felt its falutary effects.

It

It is true, we buried several of our crew afterwards, but they were such as had been taken on board in a state so low and feeble, that there were scarcely a possibility of their recovery. We suspected at first, that this dreadful disorder might have been generated by the water that we took on board at Prince's Island, or by the turtle we purchased there; but this suspicion we found to be groundless; because all the ships that came from Batavia at the same season, suffered in like manner, and some even more severely, though none of them touched at Prince's Island in their way.

Not many days after our departure from Java we were attended by the boobies for several nights successively, and as these birds are known to roost every night on shore, we concluded land was not far distant; perhaps it might be the island of Selam, which in different charts is very differently laid down both in name and situation. After these birds had left us, we were visited by no more, till we got nearly a-breast of Madagascar, where in latitude 27 deg. three quarters S. we saw an albatrofs, the number of which increased every day, with others of different kinds, particularly one about the size of a duck, of a very dark brown colour, with a yellowish bill; and they became more numerous as we approached the shore. When we got into soundings, we were visited by gannets, which we continued to see as long as we were upon the bank that stretches off Anguillas to the distance of forty leagues, and extends along shore to the eastward, from Cape False, according to some charts, one hundred and sixty leagues. The real extent of this bank is not exactly known; it is however useful as a direction to shipping when to haul in, in order to make the land.

At the time the Endeavour lay at the Cape of Good Hope, the Houghton Indiaman sailed for England. She had buried near forty of her crew, and when she left the Cape, had many of her hands in a helpless condition, occasioned by the scurvy. Other ships likewise experienced a proportionable loss by sickness; so that

our

our fufferings were comparatively light, confidering that we had been abfent near three times as long. We continued at the cape till the 13th of April, in order to recover the fick, procure ftores, and to do fome neceffary work upon the fhip and rigging. When this was finifhed we got all the fick on board, feveral of whom were ftill in a dangerous ftate; and on Sunday the 14th, having taken leave of the governor, we unmoored, and got ready to fail.

The hiftory of Caffraria is well known in Europe, and a defcription of the Cape of Good Hope has been given by moft of our circumnavigators; yet we think a particular account of this country will be acceptable to our numerous fubfcribers; and they will meet with fome particulars which fell under our obfervation, that have either been wholly omitted or mifreprefented in other narratives.

Caffraria, or Caffreria is well fituated for navigation and commerce, both which advantages are almoft wholly neglected. The interior part of the country is fertile, but wants the benefit of cultivation. The inhabitants are naturally fagacious, but their faculties are abforbed in indolence; thus both the lands and minds of the people require improvement; but left cultivation in the firft fhould introduce luxury, and information in the laft produce difobedience, neither of thefe are encouraged by the politic Dutch, who poffefs a great part of the fea coaft. This country extends about feven hundred and eighty miles from N. to S. that is, from Cape Negro to the Cape of Good Hope, from hence turning N. E. to the mouth of the river Spiritu Santo, it runs about fix hundred and fixty miles; and proceeding up the country almoft to the equinoxial line, it is about one thoufand feven hundred and forty miles farther. In fome places it is nine hundred, and in others not above fix hundred broad. Caffraria is fo named from the Caffres, its inhabitants; though fome authors affirm, that this name is a term of reproach given by the Arabs to all who have but confufed notions

of

of the deity, and which the Portuguese have by mistake applied to these people.

The Cape of Good Hope, which is the most southern part of Africa, was first discovered, A. D. 1493, by Bartholomew Diaz, admiral of a Portuguese fleet, who on account of the boisterous weather he met with when near it, distinguished it by the name of Cabodos totos Tormentos, or the Cape of all Plagues; since which, no place in the universe has been more spoken of, though little of the country, except the coast, has been penetrated or known. The reason why it has so much attracted the attention of mariners of all nations, is, their being under a necessity of frequently calling there for water or other refreshments, and also of doubling it, in their voyages to the East-Indies. But John king of Portugal, not liking the name which his admiral had bestowed upon this large promontory, changed it to that of Cabode Bona Esperanca, the "Cape of Good Hope," which appellation it has ever since retained.

Neither Diaz, nor his successor Vasco de Gama, though they saw the Cape, thought proper to land: but in 1498 the Portuguese admiral, Rio del Infanta, was the first who ventured ashore; and from his report, Emanuel, king of Portugal, on account of the eligibility of the situation, determined to establish a colony there; but the Portuguese, who are naturally pusillanimous, having taken it into their heads, that the inhabitants of the Cape were cannibals, were too much afraid of being devoured, to obey their sovereign in making the settlement he intended: however, some time after, another body of those timid adventurers made good their landing, under the conduct of Francis d'Almeyda, a viceroy of Brasil, when the Portuguese were shamefully defeated by the scarce armed, and unwarlike natives. The viceroy and fifty of his men being killed in the engagement, the remainder retired with precipitation to their ships. The Portuguese were much disappointed and chagrined at the idea of such martial superiority in a people by them deemed at once savage and despicable.

ble. They determined to be revenged; but not having magnanimity enough to shew a becoming resentment, they contrived a moft inhuman and cowardly expedient. About two years after, touching at the cape, they landed with all the appearance of amity, accompanied with ftrong profeffions of friendfhip, and under this mafk brought with them a large cannon loaded with grape fhot. The unfufpecting natives, overjoyed by the gift of fo great a treafure, began to drag it away by the means of two long ropes, which had been previoufly faftened to the muzzle. Great numbers laid hold of the ropes, and many others went before by way of triumph, when the treacherous Portuguefe firing off the cannon, a prodigious flaughter enfued, as moft of the people ftood within the range of the fhot. Many were killed, feveral wounded; and the few who efcaped, abandoned with the utmoft precipitation the fatal prefent.

About the year 1600, the Dutch began to touch at the cape, in their way to and from the Eaft-Indies; and becoming annually more fenfible of the importance of the place, they effected a fettlement in 1650, which fince that time hath rifen to great power and opulence, and been of effential fervice to that nation. M. Van Ricbeeck, a furgeon, in his return from India, obferving the conveniency of the place for a fettlement, and laying before the Dutch Eaft-India Company a plan of its advantages, the fcheme was approved, and the projector appointed governor. This adventurer failing with four fhips to the cape, entered into a negotiation with the people, who, in confideration of fifty thoufand guilders, or four thoufand three hundred and feventy-five pounds fterling, agreed to yield up to the Dutch a confiderable tract of country round the cape. Van Ricbeeck, in order to fecure his new purchafe, immediately erected a ftrong fquare fort; laid out a large garden, and planted it with a great variety of the productions from Europe, that he might render the place as commodious and agreeable as poffible. Having thus fuccefsfully founded a fettlement, the Dutch Company

3

propofed,

propofed, in order the more effectually to eftablifh it, that every man, who would fettle three years at the cape, fhould have an inheritance of fixty acres of land, provided that during that fpace he would fo improve his eftate, as to render it fufficient to maintain himfelf, and contribute fomewhat towards the maintenance of the garrifon; and at the expiration of the time, he might either keep poffeffion of it, or fell it, and return home. Induced by thefe propofals, many went to feek their fortunes at the cape, and were furnifhed on credit with cattle, grain, plants, utenfils, &c. The planters, however, at length grew weary of their habitations for want of conjugal fociety: therefore the governors of the company, to prevent their leaving the place, provided them with wives from the Orphanhoufes, and other charitable foundations. In procefs of time they greatly increafed, and fpread themfelves farther up the country, and along the coaft, till they occupied all the lands from Saldanna Bay, round the fouthern point of Africa, to Noffel Bay, on the E. and afterwards purchafed Terra de Natal, in order to extend their limits ftill farther.

It appears, however, that on the firft fettlement of the Dutch at the cape, all the Hottentot tribes did not acquiefce in the fale of the country to foreigners; for the Gunyemains diffented from the agreement of the others, and, in 1659, difputed the poffeffion of the purchafed territories with the Dutch. They always made their attack in boifterous weather, as thinking the fire-arms then of lefs ufe and efficacy; and upon thefe occafions they would murder indifcriminately all the Europeans they could meet, burn down their houfes, and drive away their cattle. At length a Hottentot, called by the Dutch Doman, who had refided fome time at Batavia, and afterwards lived at Cape Town, retired to his countrymen, and perfuaded them, that it was the intent of the Europeans to enflave them, and ftirred them up to war. Accordingly they took up arms, and, being headed by Doman, attended by another chief named Garabinga, they committed great depredations.

But

But the Hottentots themfelves at length growing tired of the war, one hundred of them, belonging to one nation, came unarmed to the Dutch fort, with a prefent of thirteen head of fine excellent cattle, in order to fue for peace. This, it may be imagined, was readily granted by the Dutch, who were heartily fick of a con-teft, in which themfelves were fuch great lofers, without reaping any advantages from it.

Notwithftanding all that has been faid to the con-trary, no country we faw during the voyage, makes a more forlorn appearance, or is in reality a more fterile defart. The land over the cape, which conftitutes the peninfula formed by Table Bay on the N. and Falfe Bay on the S. confifts of high mountains, altogether naked and defolate: the land behind thefe to the E. which may be confidered as the ifthmus, is a plain of vaft extent, confifting almoft wholly of a light kind of fea fand, which produces nothing but heath, and is utterly incapable of cultivation. All the fpots that will admit of improvement, which together bear about the fame proportion to the whole as one to one thoufand, are laid out in vineyards, orchards, and kitchen grounds; and moft of thefe little fpots lie at a confiderable diftance from each other. There is alfo the greateft reafon to believe, that in the interior parts of the country, that which is capable of cultivation, ef-pecially what is fituated at no great diftance from the coaft, does not bear a greater proportion to that which is barren ; for the Dutch told us, that they had fettle-ments eight and twenty days up the country, a diftance equal at leaft to nine hundred miles, from which they bring provifions to the cape by land ; fo that it feems reafonable to conclude, that provifions are not to be had within a lefs compafs. While we were at the cape, a farmer came thither from the country, at the dif-tance of fifteen days journey, and brought his children with him. We were furprifed at this, and afked him, if it would not have been better to have left them with his next neighbour. Neighbour! faid the man, I have no neighbour within lefs than five days journey of me.

No. 10.   R r   Surely

Surely the country muſt be deplorably barren in which thoſe who ſettle only to raiſe proviſions for a market, are diſperſed at ſuch diſtances from each other. That the country is every where deſtitute of wood is a certain fact ; for timber and planks are imported from Batavia, and fuel is almoſt as dear as food. We ſaw not a tree, except in plantations near the town, that was ſix foot high ; and the ſtems, that were not thicker than a man's thumb, had roots as thick as an arm or leg, ſuch is the influence of the winds here to the diſadvantage of vegetation, without conſidering the ſterility of the ſoil.

Cape Town is the only one the Dutch have built here, and it conſiſts of about a thouſand houſes neatly built of brick, whited in general on the outſide. They are covered only with thatch, for the violence of the S. E. winds would render any other roof inconvenient and dangerous. The ſtreets are broad and commodious, croſſing each other at right angles. In the main one is a canal, on each ſide of which is planted a row of oaks, that have grown tolerably well, and yield an agreeable ſhade. In another part of the town is alſo a canal, but the ſlope of the ground in the courſe of both is ſo great, that they are furniſhed with locks at intervals of little more than fifty yards. The houſes in general have pleaſant gardens behind, and neat court yards before them. Building, as well as tillage, is greatly encouraged here, and land given for either purpoſe to thoſe who chuſe to accept of it; but then the government claims an annual tenth of the value of the former, and produce of the latter, and a tithe of all purchaſe money when eſtates are ſold. The town extends from the ſea ſhore to the Company's garden, ſpreading along Table Bay. The fort is in a valley at a ſmall diſtance, its form pentagonal, it commands the landing-place, and is garriſoned by two hundred ſoldiers. The governor's ſtorehouſes are within it, other officers beſides himſelf have apartments here, as well as ſix hundred ſervants : the ſame number of ſlaves are lodged in a commodious building in the town, which is divided into two wards, the one for the men, the other for the women ;

women ; and there is a houfe of correction for the reception of diffolute perfons of either fex. The hofpital for fick feamen is of effential ufe to the Dutch
fleets in going to or returning from India. The church
is a large edifice, elegantly plain ; but the roof and
fteeple are thatched, for the reafon already mentioned.
Thatching indeed, from the nature of the hurricanes,
feems abfolutely neceffary ; but from the method in
which it was formerly done, it appears that it was frequently attended with danger, and we were informed,
there ufed to be fhelving pent houfes erected on both
fides the ftreets, to fhelter paffengers in rainy weather ;
but thefe brought. the inhabitants under fuch dangers
and inconveniences, that they were all pulled down by
order of government. Sailors and Hottentots were
continually affembling, and fmoaking their pipes under
them, and fometimes, through careleffnefs fet them on
fire. The government laid hold of that occafion to rid
the ftreets of thofe fellows that were continually pefter-
ing them, by publifhing an order, which is ftill in
force, and from time to time republifhed, that no Hottentot, or common failor, fhall fmoke in the ftreet,
and that upon prefuming fo to do they fhould be tied
to the whipping poft and be feverely lafhed. This has
kept the ftreets clear of all who have no bufinefs there ;
for it. is with great difficulty that either the feamen or
Hottentots can forbear fmoaking while they are awake,
if they have tobacco, which they are feldom without.
What is moft to be admired at the cape is the company's garden, where they have introduced almoft all
the fruits and flowers that are found in the other three
quarters of the globe; moft of which are improved, and
flourifh more than they did in their refpective climates
and countries from whence they were brought ; and the
garden is watered with fprings that fall down from Table mountain juft above them. Apples and pears are
planted here, with the grapes of Afia, as well as thofe
of Europe, all of a delicious flavour. Here are alfo
excellent lemons, oranges, citrons, figs, Japan apples,
and a great variety of other fruits. In this place a much

greater proportion of the inhabitants are Dutch than in
Batavia; and as the town is fupported principally by
entertaining ftrangers, and fupplying them with neceffaries, every man to a certain degree, imitates the manners and cuftoms of the nations with which he is chiefly
concerned.   The ladies, however, are fo faithful to the
mode of their country, that not one of them will ftir
without a chaudpied, or chauffet, which is carried by
a fervant, that it may be ready to place under her feet,
whenever fhe fits down : though few of thefe chauffets
have fire in them, which indeed the climate renders
unneceffary.

Notwithftanding the natural fterility of the climate,
induftry has fupplied this place with all the neceffaries, and even luxuries of life in the greateft profufion.
The beef and mutton are excellent, though the oxen
and fheep are natives of the country: the cattle are
lighter than ours, more neatly made, and have horns
that fpread to a much wider extent.   The fheep are
clothed with a fubftance between wool and hair, and
have tails of an enormous fize: we faw fome that
weighed twelve pounds, and we heard there were many
much larger.   Good butter is made from the milk of
cows, but the cheefe is very much inferior to our own.
Here are hogs and a variety of poultry; alfo goats, but
thefe laft are never eaten.   Hares are to be found exactly like thofe in Europe; likewife many kinds of an-
telopes; quails of two forts, and buftards, all well flavoured, but not juicy.   The fields produce European
wheat and barley; the gardens European vegetables;
fruit of all kinds; befides plantains, guavas, jambu,
and other Indian fruits, but thefe are not in perfection;
the plantains, in particular, are very bad, and the
guavas no larger than goofeberries.   The vineyards
alfo produce wines of various forts, but not equal to
thofe of Europe, except the Conftantia, which is made
genuine only at one vineyard, about ten miles diftant
from the town.   There is another vineyard near it,
where wine is made, and called by the fame name, but
it is greatly inferior.

With

With refpect to the animals of this country, the wild differ in nothing from thofe found in other parts. There are great numbers of domeftic animals in the various colonies and fettlements at the cape, and the woods and mountains abound with wild beafts. The horfes, which were brought originally from Perfia, are of a bay or chefnut colour, and rather fmall. The dogs have a very unfightly appearance, and are of little ufe. Among the wild beafts, the elephant claims the firft place. The rhinoceros is of a dark afh colour, and has a fnout like a hog. A horn projects about two feet from the nofe, refembling in fhape a plough fhare, and of a grey dingy colour. With this he tears up the ground, pulls up trees by their roots, throws large ftones over his head, and rips up the elephant, to whom he is a mortal enemy. Another horn of about fix inches long, turns up from his forehead. His legs are fhort, his ears fmall, and his fenfe of fmelling furprizingly acute. When he fcents any thing he purfues in a right line, and tears up every thing in his way ; but his eyes being exceeding fmall and fixed, he can only fee ftrait forward, fo that it is eafy to avoid him by ftepping afide, as he is a long time in turning himfelf about, and longer ftill in getting fight again of the object. He will not attack a man without being provoked, or unlefs he is dreffed in fcarlet. When he has killed any creature, he licks the flefh from its bones with his rough tongue, which is like a rafp. He feeds much on herbs, thiftles, and a plant refembling juniper, and which, from its fondnefs of it, is called rhinoceros-bufh. The blood, fkin, and horn of this animal, are medicinally ufed, and faid to be very efficacious in many diforders. Wine, poured into cups made of the horn, bubbles up in a ftrange kind of fermentation, appearing as if boiling. Should a fmall portion of poifon be put into the wine, the cup fplits; but if poifon only is poured into the cup, it flies into a thoufand pieces ; hence cups made of this horn are deemed excellent fafeguards, and, on that account, independent of their falubrious qualities, are highly valued. At the cape, wolves are of

two

two kinds; the one refembles a fheep-dog, and is
fpotted like a tyger; the other is like an European
wolf: they both prowl about, and do great mifchief in
the night-time, but lie concealed in the day. Lions,
tygers, leopards, &c. alfo abound here, and are fo
troublefome, that the perfon who kills one of either
fort, is rewarded with twenty-five florins, or fifty fhillings. The flefh of the lion is efteemed equal to venifon, and the fat is much valued. Here are much larger
buffaloes than in Europe. They are of a brown colour: the horns are fhort, and curve towards the neck,
where they incline to each other. Between them is a
tuft of hair upon the forehead, which adds to the fiercenefs of the look. The fkin is exceeding hard, and the
flefh rather tough. He is a ftrong fierce creature, and
is enraged at any thing red, like many other animals.
We faw here elks five feet high, with horns a foot long.
This is a very handfome creature, having a beautiful
head and neck, flender legs, and foft fmooth hair of an
afh colour. Their upper jaw is larger than the under,
the tail about a foot in length, and the flefh by the cape
epicures is faid to exceed the beft beef. They run
fwift, and climb the rocks with great agility, though
they ufually weigh about four hundred pounds each.
Another fingular animal is that called ftink-box, from
its offenfive fmell both living and dead; it is about the
fize of a common houfe dog, and made much like a
ferret. The goats are of various fpecies. One, called
the blue goat, is of a fine azure colour. The fpotted
goat is larger, and beautifully marked with brown,
white, and red fpots. The horns are a foot long. The
flefh fine eating. The rock-goat is no larger than a
kid, but very mifchievous in the plantations. The di-
ving-goat is much like the tame one, and receives its
name from its method of fquatting down in the grafs
to hide itfelf. We faw another animal called a goat,
without any additional appellation, it is of the fize of a
hart, and extremely beautiful. The hair of the fides
and back is grey, ftreaked with red, and that on the
belly white. A white ftreak paffes from his forehead to

3   the

the ridge of his tail, and three others furround his body in circles. The female hath no horns; but thofe of the male are three feet in length, and the flefh is exceedingly delicate. The horns of the hart do not branch like thofe of Europe; but the roebuck is in every refpect like ours. Wild cats are of feveral forts. The firft the Dutch call the civit cat, not that it is really the animal of that name, but becaufe of the fine fcent of the fkin. The next is called the tygercat, from its being very large, and fpotted like a tyger. The third fort is the mountain cat, which, as well as the tame cat, refembles thofe of Europe. The fourth fpecies is denominated the blue cat, from its colour, having a fine blue tinge, with a beautiful red lift down its back. There is a fpecies of mice peculiar to this country, called the rattle-moufe, which is about the fize of a fquirrel, and makes a rattling noife with its tail. It is very nimble, lives upon nuts and acorns, and purs like a cat. Among the hogs with which this country abounds, is the wild hog, or rather wild boar, which is very fierce, and harbours in woods; and the earth hog, which is of a red colour, and without teeth: this lodges like a badger in holes, and feeds upon ants; thefe he procures by forcing his long rough tongue into their hills, from whence he draws it with a great number glued thereto. Many jackalls, fome ermines, baboons, monkeys, &c. are found about the cape; and frequently do great mifchief in the gardens, orchards, and vineyards. The porcupine is very common, and its flefh efteemed delicious. There are two forts of wild affes in this country, one of which is a beautiful creature, called the zebra, and bears a greater affinity in make and fhape to the horfe than the afs. Indeed the ears are fomewhat like thofe of the latter animal, but in all other refpects it has a much more noble appearance. It is admirably well made, exceeding lively, and fo extremely fwift, that it throws almoft every purfuer at a diftance. Its legs are fine; it has a twifted tail, round flefhy haunches, and a fmooth fkin. The females are white and black, and the males white

white and brown. Thefe colours are placed alternately in the moft beautiful ftripes, and are parallel, diftinct, and narrow. The whole animal is ftreaked in this admirable manner, fo as to appear to a diftant beholder as if covered with ribbons. Moft naturalifts affirm, that the zebra never can be tamed. That which was prefented to her prefent majefty queen Charlotte, and kept feveral years at the ftables near Buckingham-gate, continued vicious till its death, though it was brought over young, and every poffible means ufed to render it tractable: it fed upon hay, and the noife it made rather refembled the barking of a maftiff dog, than the braying of an afs. The camelopardalis, we were informed, has been found in the countries round the cape. Captain Carteret, having, by order of his prefent majefty, performed a voyage round the world in the Swallow floop of war, mentions this animal in a letter to the late Dr. Matty, fecretary to the Royal Society. "From the fcarcity of this creature (fays he) as I believe none have been found in Europe, fince Julius Cæfar's time (when I think there were two of them at Rome) I imagine a more certain knowledge of its reality will not be difagreeable to you, as the exiftence of this fine animal has been doubted by many. The prefent governor of the Cape of Good Hope has fent out parties of men on inland difcoveries, fome of which have been abfent from eighteen months to two years, in which traverfe they have difcovered many curiofities. One of thefe parties croffed many mountains and plains, in one of which they found two of thefe creatures, but they only caught the young one. This they endeavoured to bring alive to Cape Town, but unfortunately it died. They took off his fkin, and it has, as a confirmation of this truth, been fent to Holland." The fkin here alluded to is now in the cabinet of natural hiftory at Leyden. Linnæus ranks this animal among the deer kind. Its head is like that of a ftag; the horns are blunt, about fix inches long, covered with hair, but not branched. The neck refembles a camel's, only longer, being neat feven feet. It has a mane like that of a horfe; feet, ears,

ears, and a tongue like thofe of a cow; flender legs,
the fore ones being confiderably longer than the hinder;
the body is but fmall, covered with white hair, and
fpotted with red; the tail is long, and bufhy at the
end; the upper jaw contains no fore teeth; he moves
both the fore feet together when he runs, and not one
after the other like other animals; he is eighteen feet
long from the tail to the top of the head, and is fixteen
feet from the ground when he holds up his head.

A great variety of birds and fowls are found at the
cape, both wild and tame. Here are three forts of
eagles, namely, 1. The bone breaker, who feeds on
tortoifes; to obtain the flefh of which it ufes this fingular method. Having carried the tortoife aloft in the
air, it drops it upon fome hard rock, by which means
the fhell is broken, and the eagle can eafily come at its
prey. 2. The dung-eagle, which tears out the entrails
of animals to fubfift on, and, though no bigger than a
common goofe, is exceeding ftrong and voracious.
3. The duck-eagle, fo called becaufe it feeds principally on ducks. Here are alfo wild geefe of three forts.
1. The water goofe, which refembles ours. 2. The
mountain goofe, which is the largeft of all, having a
green head, and green wings. 3. The crop goofe, fo
named from its remarkable large craw, of which bags,
pockets, and tobacco-pouches are made. All thefe
kinds of geefe are fuch good eating, fo plentiful, and
fo eafily taken, that the people of the cape do not
think the tame goofe worth the trouble of breeding.
But of all the numerous birds that are to be found here,
the flamingo is one of the moft fingular. It has a long
neck, and is larger than a fwan: the legs are remarkably long, and of an orange tawny, and the feet are
like thofe of a goofe: the bill contains blue teeth with
black points; the head and neck are intirely white;
the upper part of the wings are of a bright flame colour, and the lower black.

Reptiles are very numerous at the cape, particularly
the following ferpents, 1. The tree ferpents, fo called
from refembling the branch of a tree, and from being

No. 10.   S s   fond

fond of winding itfelf about trees. 2. The afh coloured afp, fpcckled with white and red, which is feveral yards long. 3. The fhoot ferpent, fo named from
the amazing velocity with which it darts itfelf at an
enemy. Some call it the eye ferpent, on account of the
numerous white fpots refembling eyes, with which its
fkin is marked. 4. The blind flow-worm, a black
fcaly ferpent, fpotted with brown, white, and red.
5. The thirft ferpent, or inflamer, a moft venomous
and dangerous ferpent, about three quarters of a yard
long; it has a broad neck, black back, and is very
active. 6. The hair ferpent, which is about three feet
in length, as thick as a man's thumb, and received its
name from its yellow hair. Its poifon is fo malignant,
that nothing but the ferpent ftone can prevent its being
mortal. This ftone is faid to be an artificial compo-
fition, prepared by the Bramins in India, who keep the
fecret to themfelves. It is fhaped like a bean, in the
middle whitifh, the reft of a fky-blue. Whenever
this is applied, it fticks clofe without bandage or fupport, and imbibes the poifon till it can receive no more,
and then drops off. Being laid in milk, it purges itfelf
of the venom, turning the milk yellow, and fo is applied again, till by its not fticking, it proves that the
poifon is exhaufted.

The neighbouring fea affords a plentiful fupply of
fifh to the inhabitants of the cape. The meat of the
fea cows is much admired. The flying fifh, which has
wings like a bat, is reckoned a great delicacy. The
brown fifh is as big as an ox, and is deemed good food
either frefh or falted. The bennet is near three feet
long, and weighs about feven pounds: the eyes and
tails are red; the fins yellow, and the fcales purple,
with gold ftreaks. The meat is of a crimfon colour,
and fo remains after it is dreffed; neverthelefs it is delicious eating. The gold fifh has a ftreak from head to
tail, circles round his eyes of a gold colour, it is eighteen inches long, weighs about a pound, and its flefh of
an exquifite tafte. The braffem is found only about the
cape. Of this fifh there are two forts; the one has a
black

black back, and purple head; the other is of a dark blue colour, and the former is rounder than the latter. They are both cheap and wholefome food. The ftone braffem is good either frefh or falted, refembles a carp in make, but is more delicious in tafte. One fpecies of this fifh is called flat-nofe, from the fhape of the head, and is much more valued than the other fort. The red ftone fifh is exceeding beautiful to the eye, and exqui-fite to the tafte : the back is fcarlet fpotted with blue, and befpangled with gold; the eyes are of a bright red, and furrounded with a filver circle, and the belly is of a pale pink colour, has a fhining filver tail, refembles a carp both in fhape and tafte, and weighs about a pound. Of fhell-fifh, which are innumerable, there is a fingular fpecies called klin-koufen, which has an up-per and under fhell, thick, rough, twifted, and incrufted. In vinegar the cruft will drop off, and the fhell exhi-bits an admirable pearl colour. Sea-funs and fea-ftars, are fmall round fhell-fifh, and receive their denomina-tions from the great variety of prickles, which fhoot from them like rays of light. The fifh called pagger has a prickly fhell, and is much dreaded by the people of the cape, as a wound from one of its protuberances turns to a mortification, unlefs great care is taken to prevent it. The fea-fpout refembles a piece of mofs fticking faft to the rocks. It is of a green colour, emits water, and within is like a tough piece of flefh. The torpedo, or cramp-ray is a very curious fifh. The body is circular, the fkin foft, fmooth and yellow, marked with large annular fpots; the eyes fmall, and the tail tapering. It is of different fizes, and weighs from five to fifteen pounds. The narcotic or benumbing quality of this fifh was known to the ancients, and hath furnifhed matter of fpeculation to the philofophers of all ages. If a perfon touches it when alive, it inftantly deprives him of the ufe of his arm, and has the fame effect if he touches it with a ftick. Even if one treads upon it with a fhoe on, it affects not only the leg, but the thigh upwards. They who touch it with the feet are feized with a ftronger palpitation than even thofe

who

who touch it with the hand: this numbnefs bears no refemblance to that which we feel when a nerve is a long time prefled, and the foot is faid to be afleep: it rather appears to be like a fudden vapour, which pafling through the pores in an inftant, penetrates to the very fprings of life, from whence it diffufes itfelf all over the body, and gives real pain. The nerves are fo affected, that the perfon ftruck imagines all the bones of his body, and particularly thofe of the limb that received the blow, are driven out of joint. All this is accompanied with a univerfal tremor, a ficknefs of the ftomach, a general convulfion, and a total fufpenfion of the faculties of the mind. In fhort, fuch is the pain, that all the force of our promifes and authority could not prevail upon a feaman to undergo the fhock a fecond time. It has been obferved, that the powers of this fifh decline with its ftrength, and intirely ceafes when it expires. This benumbing faculty is of double ufe to the torpedo: firft it enables it to get its prey with great facility; and fecondly it is an admirable defence againft its enemies, as by numbing a fifh of fuperior force with its touch, it can eafily efcape. The narcotic power of the torpedo is greater in the female than the male. According to Appian, it will benumb the fifherman through the whole extent of hook, line and rod. The flefh of this remarkable fifh having, however, no pernicious quality, is eaten by the people of the cape in common with others.

The air at the Cape of Good Hope is falutary in a high degree; fo that thofe who bring difeafes from Europe generally recover health in a fhort time; but the difeafes that are brought hither from India are not fo certainly cured. The weather at the cape may be divided into two feafons, namely, the wet monfoon, and the dry monfoon; the former begins in March, and the latter in September; fo that fummer commences at the cape about the time that it concludes with us. The inconveniences of the climate are exceflive heat in the dry feafon, and heavy rains, thick fogs, and N. W. winds in the wet feafon. Thunder and lightning are

never

never known here but in March and September. Water feldom freezes, and when it does, the ice is but thin, and diffolves upon the leaft appearance of the fun. In the hot weather, the people are happy when the wind blows from the S. E. becaufe it keeps off the fea-weeds which otherwife would float to the fhore, and corrupt there. The appearance of two remarkable clouds, which frequently hang over the fummits of the two mountains of Table-hill and Devil-hill, commonly enable the inhabitants of this country to prognofticate what weather will happen. The clouds are at firft fmall, but gradually increafing, they at length unite into one cloud, which invelops both mountains, when a terrible hurricane foon enfues. A gentleman, who refided many years at the cape, fays, " The fkirts of this cloud are white, but feem much compacter than the matter of common clouds. The upper parts are of a lead colour, owing to the refracted rays of light. No rain falls from it, but at times it difcovers great humidity, when it is of a darker hue; and the wind iffuing from it is broken, raging by gufts of fhort continuance. In its ufual ftate, the wind keeps up its firft fury, unabated, for one, two, three, or eight days, and fometimes a whole month. The cloud feems all the time undiminifhed, though little fleeces are feen torn from the fkirts from time to time, and hurried down the fides of the hills, vanifhing when they reach the bottom; fo that during the ftorm the cloud feems to be fupplied with new water. When the cloud begins to brighten up, thofe fupplies fail, and the wind proportionably abates. At length the cloud growing tranfparent, the wind ceafes." During the continuance of the S. E. winds, the Table-valley is torn by furious whirlwinds. If they blow warm, they are generally of fhort duration, and in this cafe the cloud foon difappears; but when the wind blows cold, it is a fure fign it will laft long, except an hour or two at noon, or midnight when it feems to recover new ftrength, and afterwards renews its boifterous rage.

Near the cape the water of the ocean is of a green colour,

colour, owing principally to the coral fhrubs, and the weed called tromba. The firft, while in the water, are green and foft; but when expofed to the air, they grow hard, and change their colour to white, black, or red. The latter are ten or twelve feet in length, hollow within, and when dry, become firm and ftrong. They are often framed into trumpets, and the found they produce is very agreeable to the ear.

The fources of the rivers in this country are in the mountains: they glide over a gravelly bottom, are clear, pleafant, and falubrious; but other ftreams are dark, muddy, and unwholefome. Here are a few brackifh fprings, whofe waters medicinally ufed, greatly purify the blood; and feveral hot baths are very efficacious in various diforders. Upon the whole, the reputation of the cape waters is fo great, that every Danifh fhip returning from India, is obliged to fill a large cafk with the clear fweet water that abounds here for the ufe of his Danifh majefty.

The foil in general about the cape confifts of a clayey earth, and is fo fat, that it requires but little manuring. White and red chalk are found in abundance; the former is ufed by the Dutch, to whitewafh their houfes, and the latter by the Hottentot women to paint their faces. Various bituminous fubftances of feveral colours are found in Drakenftoin colony, particularly a kind of oil which trickles from the rocks, and has a very rank fmell. With refpect to minerals, filver ore has been found in fome of the mountains, and alfo feveral iron mines. The Namaqua Hottentots, who are fituated above three hundred miles from the cape, bring copper to trade with the Dutch.

When we fpeak of agriculture, it is to be obferved, that the Europeans of the cape, and their lands, are implied; for the Hottentots in general deteft the very idea of cultivation, and would fooner ftarve than till the ground, fo greatly are they addicted to floth and indolence. The working of the plough here is fo laborious from the ftiffnefs of the foil, that it frequently requires near twenty oxen to one plough. The fowing

feafon

feafon is in July, and the harveft about Chriftmas. The corn is not thrafhed with a flail, but trod out by horfes or oxen, on an artificial floor made of cow-dung, ftraw, and water, which when mixed together cements, and foon becomes perfectly hard. It is laid in an oval form. The cattle are confined by halters which run from one to the other, and the driver ftands in the middle, where he exercifes a long ftick to keep them continually to a quick pace. By this method half a dozen horfes will do more in one day, than a dozen men can in a week. A tythe of the corn belongs to the Dutch Company, and the reft they purchafe at a price ftipulated between them and the hufbandmen.

We have already obferved of the inhabitants of the cape, that their numbers bear a greater proportion to the natives and ftrangers, than thofe in Batavia ; and have only to add, that the women in general are very handfome : they have fine clear fkins, and a bloom of colour that indicates a purity of conftitution, and high health. They make the beft wives in the world, both as miftreffes of a family and mothers, and there is fcarcely a houfe that does not fwarm with children. The common method in which ftrangers live here, is to lodge and board with fome of the inhabitants, many of whofe houfes are always open for their reception ; the rates are from five fhillings to two a day, for which all neceffaries are found. Coaches may be hired at twenty-four fhillings a day, and horfes at fix ; but the country affords very little temptation to ufe them. There are no public entertainments, and to thofe that are private, all ftrangers of the rank of gentlemen are always admitted.

We come now to fpeak of the Caffres or natives of this country, none of whofe habitations, where they retain their original cuftoms, are within lefs than four days journey from Cape Town ; thofe that we faw at the cape were all fervants to Dutch farmers, whofe cattle they take care of, and are employed in other drudgery of the meaneft kind. There are fixteen Hottentot

nations,

nations, which inhabit this fouthern promontory; at leaft, there are fo many that hold a correfpendence with the Dutch, though it is prefumed, there are many more to the northward.

The ftature of the Hottentot men is from five to fix feet in height.   Their bodies are proportionable, and well made: they are feldom either too fat or lean, and fcarce ever any crooked or deformed perfons amongft them, any farther than they disfigure their children themfelves by flatting and breaking the griftles of their nofes, looking on a flat nofe as a beauty.   Their heads as well as their eyes, are rather of the largeft: their lips are naturally thick; their hair black and fhort like the negroes, and they have exceeding white teeth : and after they have taken a great deal of pains with greafe and foot to darken their natural tawny complexions, re-femble the negroes pretty much in colour.   The women are much lefs than the men; and what is moft remark-able in them, is a callous flap or fkin that falls over the pudenda, and in a manner conceals it.   The report of which ufually excites the curiofity of the European failors, to vifit the Hottentot villages near the cape, where a great many of thofe ladies, on feeing a ftranger, will offer to fatisfy his curiofity for a half-penny, before a crowd of people, which perfectly fpoils the character that Mr. Kolben has given of their modefty.

The head of the men are covered with greafe and foot mixed together; and going without any thing elfe on their heads in the fummer-time, the duft fticks to it, and makes them a very filthy cap, which they fay cools them, and preferves their heads from the fcorching heat of the fun; and in the winter, they wear flat caps of cat-fkin or lamb-fkin, half dried, which they tie with a thong of the fame leather under their chins.   The men alfo wear a kroffe or mantle, made of fheep-fkins or other fkins, over their fhoulders, which reaches to the middle; and, being faftened with a thong about their neck, is open before.   In winter they turn the woolly or hairy fides next their backs, and in fummer the other : this ferves the man for his bed at night; and

this

this is all the winding-fheet or coffin he has when he dies. If he be a captain of a village, or chief of his nation, inftead of a fheep-fkin, his mantle is made of tyger-fkins, wild cat-fkins, or fome other fkins they fet a value upon : but though thefe mantles reach no lower, generally, than their waifts, yet there are fome nations who wear them as low as their legs, and others that have them touch the ground.

A Hottentot alfo hangs about his neck a greafy pouch, in which he keeps his knife, his pipe and tobacco, and fome dahka (which intoxicates like tobacco) and a little piece of wood, burnt at both ends, as a charm againft witchcraft. He wears alfo three large ivory rings on his left arm, to which he faftens a bag of pro-vifions when he travels. He carries in his right hand two fticks, the firft called his kirri, which is about three feet long, and an inch thick, but blunt at both ends ; the other, called his rackum-ftick, about a foot long, and of the fame thicknefs, but has a fharp point, and is ufed as a dart, to throw at an enemy or wild beaft ; which he feldom miffes, if he be within diftance. In his left hand he has another ftick, about a foot long, to which is faftened a tail of a fox or wild cat ; and this ferves him as a handkerchief to wipe off the fweat. They wear a kind of fandals, alfo made of the raw hide of an ox or elephant, when they are obliged to travel through ftoney countries ; and fometimes have bufkins, to preferve their legs from bufhes and briars ; but ordinarily their legs and thighs have no covering.

The women wear caps, the crowns whereof are a little raifed ; and thefe are made of half dried fkins, and tied under their chins. They fcarce ever put them off night or day, winter or fummer. They ufually wear two kroffes or mantles, one upon another, and, as thefe are only faften-ed with a thong, about their necks, they appear naked down to the middle : but they have an apron, larger than that of the men to cover them before, and another of ftill larger dimenfions that cover their hind parts. About their legs they wrap thongs of half dried fkins, to the thicknefs of a jack-boot, which are fuch a load to them,

No. 11.   T t   that

that they lift up their legs with difficulty, and walk very much like a trooper in jack-boots: this ferves both for a diftinction of their fex, and for ornament. But this is not all their finery: if they are people of any figure, inftead of a fheep fkin, they wear a tyger fkin, or a mantle of wild cat fkin. They have alfo a pouch hanging about their necks, in which they carry fome-thing to eat, whether they are at home or abroad, with their dahka, tobacco, and pipe. But the principal ornaments both of men and women are brafs or glafs beads, with little thin plates of glittering brafs and mother of pearl, which they wear in their hair, or about their ears. Of thefe glafs or brafs beads ftrung, they alfo make necklaces, bracelets for the arms, and girdles, wearing feveral ftrings of them about their necks, waift, and arms, chufing the fmalleft beads for their necks: thofe are fineft that have moft ftrings of them, and their arms are fometimes covered with bracelets from the wrift to the elbow. The largeft beads are on the ftrings about the middle: in thefe they affect a variety of colours, all of which the Dutch furnifh them with, and take their cattle in return. There is another kind of ornament peculiar to the men, and that is, the blad-der of any wild beaft they have killed, which is blown up, and faftened to the hair as a trophy of their valour. Both fexes powder themfelves with a duft they call bachu; and the women fpot their faces with a red earth or ftone (as ours do with black patches) which is thought to add to their beauty, by the natives; but, in the eyes of Europeans, renders them more frightful and fhocking than they are naturally. But as part of their drefs, we ought to have mentioned, in the firft place, the cuftom of daubing their bodies, and the infide of their caps and mantles, with greafe and foot. Soon after their children are born, they lay them in the fun, or by the fire, and rub them over with fat or butter, mixed with foot, to render them of a deeper black, it is faid; for they are naturally tawny: and this they continue to do almoft every day of their lives, after they are grown up, not only to increafe their beauty, but to render their limbs
fupple

fupple and pliable. As fome nations pour oil upon their heads and bodies, fo thefe people make ufe of melted fat : you cannot make them a more acceptable prefent than the fat or fcum of the pot that meat is boiled in to anoint themfelves.

Nor are the Hottentots more cleanly in their diet than in their drefs; for they choofe the guts and entrails of cattle and of fome wild beafts (with very little cleanfing), rather than the reft of the flefh, and eat their meat half boiled or broiled; but their principal food confifts of roots, herbs, fruits or milk : they feldom kill any of thofe cattle, unlefs at a feftival ; they only feed on fuch as die of themfelves, either of difeafes or old age, or on what they take in hunting ; and, when they are hard put to it, they will eat the raw leather that is wound about the womens legs, and even foles of fhoes ; and, as their mantles are always well ftocked with lice of an unufual fize, they are not afhamed to fit down in the public ftreets at the cape, pull off the lice, and eat them. And we ought to have remembered, that they boil their meat in the blood of beafts when they have any of it. They rather devour their meat than eat it, pulling it to pieces with their teeth and hands, difcovering a canine appetite and fiercenefs : they abftain, however, from fwines-flefh, and fome other kinds of meat, and from fifh that have no fcales, as religioufly as ever the Jews did. And here it may not be improper to fay fomething of the management of their milk and butter: they never ftrain their milk, but drink it with all the hairs and naftinefs with which it is mixed in the milking by the Hottentot women. When they make butter of it, they put it into fome fkin made in the form of a foldier's knapfack, the hairy fide inwards ; and then two of them taking hold of it, one at each end, they whirl and turn it round till it is converted into butter, which they put up for anointing themfelves, their caps and mantles with, for they eat no butter ; and the reft they fell to the Dutch, without clearing it from the hairs and dirt it contracts in the knapfack. The Hollanders, when they have it indeed, endeavour to feparate the

naftinefs

naftinefs from it, and fell to the fhipping, that arrives
there, frequently for butter of their own making; and
fome they eat themfelves (but furely none but a Dutchman could eat Hottentot butter) and the dregs and
dirt that is left they give to their flaves; which having
been found to create difeafes, the governor of the cape
fometimes prohibits their giving their flaves this ftuff by
public ediᵭ; which is not, however, much regarded.
The butter-milk, without any manner of cleaning or
ftraining, the Hottentots drink themfelves; giving
what they have to fpare to their lambs and calves.
Their ufual drink is cow's milk or water, and the women fometimes drink ewe's milk; but this the men
never touch: and it is obferved, that the women are
never fuffered to eat with the men, or come near them,
during the time of their menfes.

Since the arrival of the Dutch among them, it appears that the Hottentots are very fond of wine, brandy,
and other fpirituous liquors: thefe, and the baubles
already mentioned, the Hollanders truck for their cattle; and though a Hottentot will turn fpit for a Dutchman half a day for a draught or two of four wine, yet
do they never attempt to plant vineyards (as they fee
the Dutch often do) or think of making wine themfelves.

We fhall proceed, in the next place, to give an account
of their towns and houfes, or rather, their camps and tents.

Like the Tartars and Arabs, they remove their dwellings frequently for the conveniency of water and frefh
pafture: they encamp in a circle formed by twenty or
thirty tents, and fometimes twice the number, contiguous to each other; within the area whereof they keep
their leffer cattle in the night, and the larger on the
outfide of their camp: their tents, or, as fome call
them, houfes, are made with flender poles, bent like
an arch, and covered with mats or fkins, and fometimes both: they are of an oval figure, the middle of
the tent being about the height of a man, and decreafing gradually (the poles being fhorter) towards
each end, the loweft arch, which is the door or entrance, being about three feet high, as is the oppofite
                                                      arch

arch at the other end; the longeft diameter of the tent
being about twelve or fourteen feet, and the fhorteft
ten; and in the middle of the tent is a fhallow hole
about a yard diameter, in which they make their fire,
and round which the whole family, confifting of nine
or ten people of all ages and fexes, fit or lie night and
day in fuch a fmoak (when it is cold, or they are dreffing of victuals) that it is impoffible for an European
to bear it, there being ufually no vent for the fmoak
but the door, though fome have feen a hole in the top
of fome of their huts, to let out the fmoak, and give
them light. Such a circle of tents or huts as has been
defcribed, is called by the Hottentots a kraal, and fometimes by the Europeans a town or village; but feems
to be more properly a camp: for a town confifts of
more fubftantial buildings, and is feldom capable of
being removed from one place to another: whereas
thefe dwellings confift of nothing more than fmall
tent-poles, covered with fkins or mats, which are moveable, and carried away upon their baggage oxen whenever they remove with their herds to a diftant pafture.
As to the furniture of their tents; they confift of little
more than their mantles which they lie on, fome other
fkins of wild beafts they have killed or purchafed, an
earthen pot they boil their meat in, their arms, and
perhaps fome other trivial utenfils. The only domeftick
animals they keep are dogs, as ugly in their kind as
their mafters, but exceeding ufeful to them in driving
and defending their cattle.

The Hottentots are agreed by all to be the lazieft ge-
neration under the fun: they will rather ftarve, or eat
dried fkins, or fhoe foles at home, than hunt for their
food; and yet, when they apply themfelves to the
chace, or any other exercife, no people are more active
and dexterous than the Hottentots; and they ferve the
Europeans often with the greateft fidelity and application, when they contract to ferve them for wages:
they are alfo exceeding generous and hofpitable; they
will fcarce eat a piece of venifon, or a dift of fifh they
have catched, or drink their beloved drams alone, but

call

call in their neighbours to partake with them as far as it will go.

Concerning their government, people agree, that every nation has its king or chief, called konquer, whofe authority devolves upon him by hereditary fucceffion ; and that they do not pretend to elect their refpective fovereigns. That this chief has the power of making peace and war, and prefides in all their councils and courts of juftice : but then his authority is faid to be limited ; and that he can determine nothing without the confent of the captains of the feveral kraals, who feem to be the Hottentot fenate. The captain of every kraal, whofe office is hereditary alfo, is their leader in time of war, and chief magiftrate of his kraal in time of peace ; and, with the head of every family, deter-mines all civil and criminal caufes within the kraal ; only fuch differences as happen between one kraal and another, and matters of ftate, are determined by the king and fenate. The Dutch, fince their arrival at the cape, have prefented the king, or chief of every nation of the Hottentots in alliance with them, with a brafs crown; and the captains of each kraal with a brafs-headed cane, which are now the badges of their refpective offices; formerly they were diftinguifhed only by finer fkins, and a greater variety of beads and glit-tering trifles. In their councils their king fits on his heels in the center, and the captains of the kraals fit in like manner round about him. At his acceffion, it is faid, he promifes to obferve their national cuftoms ; and gives them an entertainment, killing an ox, and two or three fheep, upon the occafion ; on which he feafts his captains, but their wives are only entertained with the broth: but then the next day, we are told, her Hottentot majefty treats the ladies, and their hufbands are put off in like manner with the foup.

The captain of each kraal alfo, at his acceffion, en-gages to obferve the cuftoms of his kraal, and makes an entertainment for the men, as his lady does the next day for the women ; and, though thefe people fhew their chiefs great refpect, they allow neither their king

I or

or inferior magiftrates any revenue; they fubfift, as other families do, upon their ftock of cattle, and what they take in hunting.

Having no notion of writing or letters, they can have no written laws: but there are fome antient cuftoms, from which they fcarce ever deviate. Murder, adultery, and robbery, they conftantly punifh with death; and, if a perfon is fufpected of any of thefe crimes, the whole kraal join in feizing and fecuring him; but the guilty perfon fometimes makes his efcape to the mountains, where robbers and criminals like himfelf, fecure themfelves from juftice, and frequently plunder the neighbouring country; for no other kraal or nation of Hottentots will entertain a ftranger, unlefs he is known to them, and can give a good reafon for leaving his own kraal. If the offender is apprehended, the captain affembles the people of his kraal in a day or two; who, making a ring, and fitting down upon their heels, the criminal is placed in the center of them: the witneffes on both fides are heard, and the party fuffered to make his defence: after which, the cafe being confidered, the captain collects the fuffrages of the judges; and, if a majority condemn him, the prifoner is executed on the fpot. The captain firft ftrikes him with a truncheon he carries in his hand, and then the reft of the judges fall upon him and drub him to death: then wrapping up the corpfe in his kroffe or mantle, it is carried to fome place diftant from the kraal, where they bury it. In civil cafes alfo, the caufe is determined by a majority of voices, and fatisfaction immediately ordered to the injured perfon, out of the goods of the perfon that appears to be in the wrong. There is no appeal to any other court: the king and his council, confifting of the captains of the kraals, never interpofe unlefs in matters that concern the public, or where the kraals are at variance. To which we may add, that the Hottentots cattle and perfonal eftate defcend to his eldeft fon: he cannot difinherit him, or give his effects to his other children; but, as for property in lands, or any certain real eftate, no man has any; the

whole

whole country is but one common, where they feed
their cattle promifcuoufly, moving from place to place,
to find water or frefh pafture as neceffity requires. Even
the feveral nations have no ftated bounds ; but ufe fuch
tracts of land as their anceftors did before them : it is
true, their refpective limits fometimes create great differences between the feveral nations, and occafion
bloody wars ; which brings us now to treat of their
arms, and the arts and ftratagems they ufe in war.

The arms of a Hottentot are, 1. His lance, which
refembles a half-pike, fometimes thrown, and ufed as a
miffive weapon ; and at others, ferves to pufh with in
clofe fight, the head or fpear whereof is poifoned.
2. His bow and arrows, the arrows bearded and poifoned likewife, when they engage an enemy or wild
beaft they do not intend for food. Their bows are made
of iron, or olive-wood ; the ftring, of the finews or
guts of fome animal : the quiver is a long narrow cafe,
made of the fkin of an elephant, elk, or ox, and flung
at their backs, as foldiers fling their knapfacks. 3. A
dart of a foot long, which they throw exceeding true,
fcarce ever miffing the mark they aim at, though it is
not above the breadth of half a crown ; thefe alfo are
poifoned, when they engage an enemy or a wild beaft
that is not to be eaten : and laftly, when they have
fpent the reft of their miffive weapons, they have recourfe to ftones, feldom making a difcharge in vain ;
and, what is moft remarkable in their fhooting or
throwing arrows, darts, or ftones, they never ftand ftill,
but are all the while fkipping and jumping from one
fide to the other, poffibly to avoid the ftones and darts
of the enemy. They are all foot, and never engage on
horfeback ; but have difciplined bulls or oxen taught to
run upon the enemy, and to tofs and diforder them ;
which thefe creatures will do with the utmoft fury on
the word of command, not regarding the weapons that
are thrown at them : for though the Hottentots have
number of large elephants in their country, they have
not yet learned the art of taming them, or training
them up to war, as the military men in the Eaft Indies
do.

do. Every able bodied man is a foldier, and poſſeſſed of a ſet of ſuch arms as has been deſcribed; and on the ſummons of his prince, appears at the rendezvous with all imaginable alacrity and contempt of danger, and every man maintains himſelf while the expedition laſts. As their officers, civil and military, have no pay, ſo neither do the private men expect any; a ſenſe of honour, and the public good, are the ſole motives for hazarding their lives in their country's ſervice.

The Hottentots, in war, have very little conception of diſcipline, nor indeed is it poſſible they ſhould; for the only method of raiſing an army, is, for the kraal captains to order the people to follow them; the only method of maintaining one, is by hunting as they march: and the only way of deciding a diſpute between two nations, is, by fighting one battle; the ſucceſs of which determines the whole affair. In an engagement, they attack with an hideous yell, fight in great confuſion, and put more confidence in their war oxen than their own ſkill: for, as we have hinted above, theſe animals, when trained to the buſineſs, are better diſciplined and much more formidable, than the Hottentots themſelves. The principal inducements to their entering into a war at any time, is the preſervation of their territories. As they have no land marks or written treaties to adjuſt the exact bounds of every nation, they frequently diſagree about the limits of their reſpective countries; and, when any neighbouring nation grazes their cattle upon a ſpot of ground another claims, ſatisfaction is immediately demanded; and, if it be not given, they make repriſals, and have recourſe to arms. But this is not the only occaſion of wars amongſt the Hottentots: they are not always that chaſte and virtuous people Mr. Kolben has repreſented them; ſome tempting Helen (for Hottentots poſſibly may appear amiable in one another's eyes, with all the greaſe and carrion they are cloathed with) has ſmitten a neighbouring chief, perhaps, who prevails on his people to aſſiſt him in the rape of the deſired female; and this frequently ſets their tribes together by the ears. The

ftealing each others cattle is another caufe of deadly
ftrife; for though each kraal punifhes theft among
themfelves with death, yet it is looked upon as an he-
roic act to rob thofe of another nation; at leaft the
body of the people are fo backward in giving up the
offender, that they frequently come to blows upon it.
When they march into the field, every man follows
his particular captain, the chief of his kraal: they
obferve little order; neither do they take the precaution of throwing up trenches to defend themfelves:
and what is ftill more furprifing, have no fhields to
defend themfelves againft miffive weapons, though
fome fay they will ward off a lance or dart, and even a
ftone, with a little truncheon about a foot long, which
they carry in their hand. The feveral companies advance to the charge, at the command of their chief;
and, when thofe in the front have fhot one flight
of arrows, they retreat and make room for thofe in the
rear; and, when they have difcharged, the former advance again, and thus alternately they continue till they
have fpent all their miffive weapons, and then they
have recourfe to ftones, unlefs they are firft broken and
difperfed by a troop of bulls: for the wife chiefs and ge-
nerals of each fide, according to the European practice,
remaining on an eminence in the rear, to obferve the
fortune of the day, when they obferve their people are
hard preffed, give the word of command to their corps
de referve of bulls, who break into the body of the
enemy, and generally bring all into confufion; and
that fide that preferves their order beft, on this furious
attack of thefe bulls of Bafan, are fure to be victo-
rious. The fkill of the general feems to be chiefly in
managing his bulls; who never charge each other, but
fpend their whole rage upon the men, who have, it
feems, no dogs of Englifh breed to play againft them,
or this ftratagem would be of little fervice: but we
fhould have obferved, that as the battle always begins
with horrid cries and noife, which perhaps fupplies the
place of drums and trumpets; fo the victors infult with
no lefs noife over the conquered enemy, killing all that
.fall

fall into their hands : but they feldom fight more than
one battle, fomeneighbouring power ufually interpofing
to make up the quarrel ; and of late the Dutch perform this good office, between fuch nations as lie near,
their fettlements.. From their wars with each other, we
naturally proceed to their wars with wild beafts, with
which their country abounds more than any other ; thefe
people, it feems, efteem it a much greater honour to.
have killed one of thefe foes to mankind, than an
enemy of their own fpecies.

Inftances are not wanting of a Hottentot's engaging
fingly with the fierceft wild beafts, and killing them ;
but ufually the whole kraal or village affemble, when a
wild beaft is difcovered in their neighbourhood, and,
dividing themfelves in fmall parties, endeavour to furround him.   Having found their enemy, they ufually
fet up a great cry, at which the frighted animal endeavours to break through and efcape them : if it prove
to be a rhinoceros, an elk, or elephant, they throw their
lances at him, darts and arrows being too weak to pierce
through their thick hides : if the beaft be not killed at
the firft difcharge, they repeat the attack, and load him
with their fpears ; and, as he runs with all his rage at
the perfons who wound him, thofe in his rear follow
him clofe, and ply him with their fpears, on whom he
turns again, but is overpowered by his enemies, who
conftantly return to the charge, when his back is towards them, and fcarce ever fail of bringing the creature down, before he has taken his revenge on any of
them.   How hazardous foever fuch an engagement
may appear to an European, thefe people make it their
fport ; and have this advantage, that they are exceeding fwift of foot, and fcarce ever mifs the mark they
aim at with their fpears : if one of them is hard preffed
by the brute, he is fure to be relieved by his companions, who never quit the field till the beaft is killed,
or makes his efcape : though they fometimes dexte-
roufly avoid the adverfary, they immediately return to
the charge, fubduing the fierceft either by ftratagem or
force.   When attacking a lion, a leopard, or a tyger,

U u 2   their

their darts and arrows are of fervice to them; and therefore they begin the engagement at a greater diftance, than when they charge an elephant or rhinoceros; and the creature has a wood of darts and arrows upon his back, before he can approach his enemies, which make him fret and rage and fly at them with the greateft fury; but thofe he attacks, nimbly avoid his paws, while others purfue him, and fininfh the conqueft with their fpears. Sometimes a lion takes to his heels, with abundance of poifoned darts and arrows in his flefh: but, the poifon beginning to operate, he foon falls, and becomes a prey to thofe he would have preyed upon. The elephant, the rhinoceros, and the elk, are frequently taken in traps and pitfalls, without any manner of hazard. The elephants are obferved to go in great companies to water, following in a file one after another, and ufually take the fame road till they are difturbed: the Hottentots therefore dig pits in their paths, about eight feet deep, and four and five over; in which they fix fharp ftakes pointed with iron, and then cover the pit with fmall fticks and turf, fo as it is not difcernable: and as thefe animals ufually keep in one track, frequently one or other of them falls in with his fore feet into the pit, and the ftake pierces his body; the more he ftruggles, the deeper the weight of his monftrous body fixes him on the ftake. When the reft of the herd obferve the misfortune of their companion, and find he cannot difengage himfelf, they immediately abandon him: whereupon the Hottentots, who lie concealed, in expectation of the fuccefs of their ftratagem, approach the wounded beaft, ftab him with their fpears, and cut his largeft veins, fo that he foon expires; whereupon they cut him to pieces, and, carrying the flefh home, feaft upon it as long as it lafts. His teeth they make into rings for their arms, and, when they have any ivory to fpare, difpofe of it to the Europeans. The rhinoceros and elk are frequently taken in pitfalls, as the elephants are. The Hottentot, who kills any of thefe, or a lion, leopard, or tyger, fingly, has the higheft honour conferred

upon

upon him, and several privileges, which belong only to
such intrepid heroes. At his return from his hazardous and important service, the men of the kraal depute
one of the seniors to congratulate him on his victory,
and defire that he will honour them with his prefence;
whereupon he follows the old deputy to the aſſembly,
whom he finds, according to cuſtom, fitting upon their
heels in a circle; and, a mat of diſtinction being laid
for him in the center, he fets himfelf down upon it:
after which the old deputy urines plentifully upon him,
which the hero rubs in with great eagernefs, having firſt
fcratched the greafe off his fkin with his nails; the deputy all this while pronouncing fome words unintelli-
gible to any but themfelves. After this, they light a
pipe of tobacco, which they fmoke and hand one to
another till there remain nothing but aſhes in the pipe,
and thefe the old deputy ſtrews over the gallant man,
who rubs them in as they fall upon him, not fuffering
the leaſt duſt to be loſt. After which the neighbours
having feverally congratulated him on his advancement
to the high honour, they difperfe, and go to their refpective tents. The conqueror, afterwards, faſtens
the bladder of the furious beaſt he has killed to his
hair, which he ever after wears as a badge of his knight-
hood; and is from that time eſteemed by every one a
brave man, and a benefactor to his country. When
retired to his tent, his neighbours feem to vie which of
them ſhall oblige him moſt, and are, for the next three
days, continually fending him one delicious morfel or
other; nor do they call upon him to perform duty during that time; but fuffer him to indulge his eafe: but,
what is ſtill more unaccountable, his wife, or wives, (for
he may have more than one) are not allowed to come
near him for three days after this honour is conferred
on him; but they are forced to ramble about the fields,
and to keep to a fpare diet, left they ſhould, as Mr.
Kolben furmifes, tempt the hufbands to their embraces:
but on the third day in the evening, we are told the women return to the tent, are received with the utmoſt
joy and tendernefs; mutual congratulations pafs between

tween them; a fat sheep is killed, and their neighbours invited to the feast, where the prowefs of the hero, and the honour he has obtained, are the chief subject of their converfation.

There is fcarce any wild beaft, but the flesh is good eating, if it be not killed with poifonous weapons; but the tyger is the moft delicious morfel; and as the whole kraal partake of the feaft, the perfon who kills him meets with a double fhare of praife, as he both rids the country of an enemy, and pleafes their palates. But to return to the field fports of the Hottentots: when they hunt a deer, a wild goat, or a hare, they go fingly, or but two or three in company, armed only with a dart or two, and feldom mifs the game they throw at: yet, as has been obferved already; fo long as they have any manner of food left, if it be but the raw hides of cattle, or fhoe foles, they will hardly be perfuaded to ftir to get more; though it is true, when they apprehend their cattle in danger from wild beafts, no people are more active, or purfue the chafe of them with greater alacrity and bravery. From hunting, we proceed to treat of their fifhing; at which they are very expert; taking fifh with angles, nets, and fpears; and they get a certain fifh, called rock-fifh, particularly by groping the holes of the rocks near the fhore, when the tide is out: thefe are mightily admired by the Europeans; but having no fcales, the Hottentots will not eat them.

The manner of the Hottentots fwimming, is as particular as of his fifhing; for he ftands upright in the fea, and rather walks and treads the water, than fwims upon it, his head, neck, and fhoulders being quite above the waves, as well as his arms, and yet they move fafter in the water than any European can; even in a ftorm, when the waves run high they will venture into the fea, rifing and falling with the waves like a cork.

The next thing we fhall notice, is the marriages of the Hottentots: and it feems every young fellow has fuch regard to the advice of his father, (or rather the laws and cuftoms of the country require it) that he always

1 Tiger.............2 Lion.............3 Lioneſs...........

ways confults the old man before he enters into a treaty with his miftrefs, and if he approves the match, the father and fon, in the firft place, pay a vifit to the father of the damfel, with whom having fmoked, and talked of indifferent things for fome time, the father of the lover opens the matter to the virgin's father, who having confulted his wife, returns an anfwer immediately to the propofal : if it be rejected, the lover and his father retire without more words ; but if the offer be approved by the old folks, the damfel is called, and acquainted, that they have provided a hufband for her ; as fhe muft fubmit to their determination, unlefs fhe can hold her lover at arms end, after a night's ftruggling; for we are told, that when the parents are agreed, the two young people are put together, and if the virgin lofes her maidenhead, fhe muft have the young fellow, though fhe be never fo averfe to the match : but then fhe is permitted to pinch and fcratch, and defend herfelf as well as fhe can ; and if fhe holds out till morning, the lover returns without his miftrefs, and makes no further attempts ; but if he fubdues her, fhe is his wife to all intents and purpofes, without further ceremony ; and the next day the man kills a fat ox, or more, according to his circumftances, for the wedding dinner, and the entertainment of their friends, who refort to them upon the occafion, bringing abundance of good wifhes for the happinefs of the married couple, as is ufual among politer people. The ox is no fooner killed, but the company get each fome of the fat, and greafe themfelves with it from head to foot, powdering themfelves afterwards with buchu, and the women, to add to their charms, make red fpots with oker, or red chalk, on their black faces. The entertainment being ready, the men form a circle in the area of the kraal (for a large company cannot fit within doors) and the women form another ; the bridegroom fitting in the middle of the men's circle, and the bride in the center of her own fex. Then the prieft enters the men's circle, and urines upon the bridegroom, which the young man rubs in very joyfully. He then goes to the ladies circle,

circle, where he does the bride the same favour. Then the old man goes from the bride to the bridegroom, till he has exhausted all his store. The priest then pronounces his benediction in these words: " That they may live long and happily together ; that they may have a son before the end of the year ; and that he may prove a brave man, and an expert huntsman, and the like." After which, the meat is served up in earthen pots glazed with grease : and some of them having knives since the Europeans came amongst them, they divide their meat pretty decently ; but more of them make use of their teeth and claws, pulling it to pieces, and eating it as voraciously as so many dogs, having no other plates or napkins than the stinking corners of the napkins they wear ; and sea shells without handles usually serve them for spoons. When they have dined, a pipe is filled with tobacco, which they smoke all round, every one taking two or three whiffs, and then handing it to the next. It is singular, that though the Hottentots are immoderately fond of spirituous liquors, music and dancing, yet they do not drink the first, nor practise the latter at weddings.

The Hottentots allow of polygamy ; but seldom have more than three wives at a time ; and it seems it is death to marry or lie with a first or second cousin, or any near relation. A father seldom gives his son more than two or three cows, and as many sheep, upon his marriage, and with these he must make his way in the world ; and we do not find they give more with their daughters than a cow, or a couple of sheep ; but the latter are to be returned to the father, if the bride dies without having had any children : on the contrary, if she ever bore any children to her husband, the portion becomes his, even though the children are defunct. They do not leave their daughters, or younger sons, any thing when they die ; but all the children depend upon the eldest brother, and are his servants, or rather slaves, when the father is dead, unless the eldest brother infranchise them ; nor has the mother any thing to subsist on, but what the eldest son allows her. Their being no.

great

3

great fortunes among them, they match purely for
love ; an agreeable companion is all their greateſt men.
aim at : their chiefs intermarry frequently with the
pooreſt man's daughter ; and a brave fellow, who has
no fortune, does not deſpair of matching with the
daughter of a prince. A widow, who marries a ſecond
time, is obliged to cut off a joint of one of her fingers ;
and ſo for every huſband ſhe marries after the firſt. Either man or woman may be divorced, on ſhewing ſufficient cauſe before the captain and the reſt of the kraal ;
the woman, however, muſt not marry again, though
the man is allowed to marry, and have as many wives
as he pleaſes at the ſame time. A young Hottentot
never is maſter of a hut or tent till he maries, unleſs
his father dies and leaves him one: therefore the firſt
buſineſs the bride and bridegroom apply themſelves to,
after their marriage feaſt, is to erect a tent or hut of all
new materials, in which work the woman has as great a
ſhare as the man ; and this taking them up about a
week's time, the new married couple are entertained in
the mean time in the tents of ſome of their relations.
When they reſort to their new apartment, and come to
keep houſe together, the wife ſeems to have much the
greateſt ſhare of the trouble of it : ſhe fodders the cattle, milks them, cuts out the firing, ſearches every
morning for roots· for their food, brings them home,
and boils or broils them, while the drone of a huſband
lies indolently at home, and will ſcarce give himſelf the
trouble of getting up to eat when the food is provided
for him by the drudge his wife. The more wives he
has, ſtill the more indolent life he leads, the care of
making proviſion for the family being thrown upon
them. It is ſaid he will, in his turn, attend his cattle
in the field ; but expects every one of his wives ſhould
do, at leaſt, as much towards taking care of them as
he does. He will alſo, ſometimes, but very rarely, go
a hunting with the men of his kraal, and bring home a
piece of venifon, or a diſh of fiſh ; but this is not often ; and if he is of any handicraft trade, he may work at
it two or three hours in a week, and inſtruct his chil-

No. 11. X x   dren

dren in the art. He alfo takes upon him to fell his
cattle, and purchafe tobacco, and ftrong liquors of the
Dutch, with neceffary tools, beads and other ornaments, for which the Hottentots barter away their cattle: their wives are not permitted to intermeddle in the
bufinefs of buying and felling, this being the fole pre-
rogative of the man. When a woman brings a living
fon into the world, there is great rejoicing; but the
firft thing they do with the child, is to daub it all over
with cow-dung; then they lay it before the fire, or in
the fun, till the dung is dried: after which they rub it
off, and wafh the child with the juice of certain herbs,
laying it in the fun, or before the fire again, till the liquor is dried in, after which they anoint the child from
head to foot with butter, or fheeps fat melted, which
is dried in as the juice was: and this cuftom of anointing their bodies with fat, they retain afterwards as long
as they live. After the child has been thus fmeared
and greafed, the mother gives it what name fhe thinks
proper, which is ufually the name of fome wild beaft,
or domeftic animal. When the women is well again,
and able to leave her hut, fhe rubs herfelf all over with
cow-dung; and this filthy daubing is by thefe delicate
people termed a purification. Being thus delightfully
perfumed, and elegantly decorated with fheep's guts,
fhe is permitted to go abroad, or to fee company at
home.

If the woman has twins, and they are girls, the man
propofes it to the kraal, that he may expofe one of
them, either upon pretence of poverty, or that his wife
has not milk for them both; and this they ufually indulge one another in; they do the fame when they have
a boy or a girl; but always preferve the boys, though
they happen to have two at a birth. The expofed
child is carried to a diftance from the kraal; and if
they can find a cave or hole in the earth, that fome
wild beaft has made, they put the child alive into it;
and then having ftopped up the mouth of the den with
ftones or earth, leave it there to ftarve: if they cannot
meet fuch a cavity, they tie the infant to the lower
                                                     bough

bough of a tree, or leave it in fome thicket of bufhes, where it is frequently deftroyed by wild beafts. They do not deal thus, however, as has been obferved, by their male children : on the birth of a boy, they kill a bullock ; and if they have twins, two bullocks ; and make an entertainment for all the neighbourhood, who congratulate the parents on their good fortune ; and, as with us, the greateft rejoicings are on the birth of the firft fon.

The males, at about ten years of age, are always deprived of their left tefticle : the operation is performed with a dexterity that would furprize an European furgeon, and bad confequences are feldom or never known to enfue. A fheep is killed, and great rejoicings are made upon the occafion ; but it is to be obferved, that the men devour all the meat, and allow the women nothing but the broth. The reafon of this abfurd cuftom of mutilating their male youth is unknown : fome of the Hottentots fay, it is to make them run fwift ; but the greateft part of thefe people give their general reafon, which they ufe upon all occafions, when they are unable to account for any of their abfurd practices ; namely, That it is the Hottentot cuftom ; and has been practifed by their anceftors time immemorial. At the age of eighteen, the male Hottentots, being deemed men, are admitted into male fociety : the men of the village (if it may be fo called) fquat down, and form a circle, as is ufual upon moft public occafions, the youth fquats down without the circle, at fome diftance. The oldeft man of the kraal then rifes from the circle, and, having obtained the general confent for the admiffion of a new member, he goes to the youth, acquaints him with the determination of the men of the kraal, and concludes his harangue with fome verfes, which admonifh him to behave like a man for the future. The youth being then daubed with foot and fat, and well fprinkled with urine, is congratulated by the company in general in a kind of chorus, which contains the following wifhes : that good fortune may attend him, that he may live long, and thrive daily ; that he

X x 2   may

may foon have a beard, and many children; till it is univerfally allowed he is a ufeful man to the nation. A feaft concludes the ceremony; but the youth himfelf is not permitted to participate of any part thereof till all the reft are ferved. Having been thus admitted into male fociety, it is expected that he fhould behave ill to women in general, and to his mother in particular, in order to evince his contempt of every thing feminine. Indeed it is ufual for a youth as foon as admitted, to go to his mother's hut, and cudgel her heartily, for which he is highly applauded by the whole kraal; and even the fuffering parent herfelf admires him for his fpirit, and protefts that the blows do not give her fo much pain, as the thoughts of having brought fuch a mettle-fome fon into the world afford her pleafure. The more ill treatment he gives his mother, the more efteem he obtains; and every time he ftrikes her fhe is in the higheft raptures, and thanks providence for having bleffed her with fuch a fpirited child. So egregioufly will cuftom counteract the very dictates of nature, and impofe upon the underftanding of the ignorant.

It may be proper now to fay fomething of thofe officers amongft them, which the Europeans generally deno-minate their priefts. Thefe perfons are called furri or mafter, and are elected by every kraal: they are the men who perform the ceremony of making water at their weddings, and other feftivals; the furri alfo is the perfon who extracts the left tefticle from the young males at eight years of age; for all which he has no ftated revenue, but a prefent now and then of a calf or a lamb, and makes one at all their entertainments. Every kraal alfo has its phyfician, as well as its prieft, who are perfons that have fome fkill in phyfic and fur-gery, and particularly in the virtues of falutary herbs; thefe alfo are chofen by a majority of voices, and make it their bufinefs to look after the people's health: but have no other reward neither for their pains, than voluntary prefents. And fuch is the opinion of the Hottentots of thefe phyficians, that, if they cannot effect a cure, they conclude they are certainly bewitched; as the

the doctor himself also never fails to give out : whereupon application is made to some pretended conjurer for relief; and if the patient happens to recover, it gives the cunning man, as we call him, a mighty reputation. The physician and surgeon, as has been hinted, is the same person; and though these gentlemen scarce ever saw a body dissected, it is said, they have pretty good notions of anatomy: they cup, bleed, make amputations, and restore dislocated limbs, with great dexterity : cholicks and pains in the stomach they relieve by cupping. Their cup is an horn of an ox, the edges cut very smooth : the doctor, having sucked the part where the pain lies, claps on the cup; and, after it has remained some time, till he thinks the part is infensible, he pulls off the horn-cup, and makes two or three incisions, half an inch in length, with a common knife, having no other instrument: after which, he applies the cup again, which falls off when it is full of blood, but the patient, it is said, suffers great pain in the operation. If the pain removes to another part, they rub it with hot fat; and, if that does not ease the pain, they use the cup again on the part last affected; and, if the second cupping does not relieve the patient, they give him inward medicines, being infusions or powders of certain dried roots and herbs. They let blood in plethories and indispositions of that kind, having no other instrument than a common knife; and, if bleeding will not effect the cure, they give the patient physic. For headachs, which they are pretty much subject to in calm weather, they shave their heads in furrows, as they do when they are in mourning; but a brisk gale of wind usually carries off the head-ach, without any other application; and this they do not often want at the cape. They seldom make any other amputations, than of the fingers of such women as marry a second time, or oftner : and, in this case, they bind the joint below that which is to be cut off very tight, with a dried sinew, and then cut off the joint at once with a knife, stopping the blood with the juice of myrrh-leaves; after which, they wrap up the finger in some healing herbs,

4   and

and never any part of the finger receives any hurt beyond the amputation. They have little or no skill in setting fractured limbs ; but are pretty dexterous at restoring of dislocations.

The Hottentot physician, in case he meets with a foul stomach, gives the juice of aloe leaves ; and, if one dose will not do, repeats it two or three days ; and, for any inward ail, they give chiefly the powders, or infusions of wild sage, wild figs and fig leaves, buchu, garlic or fennel : but, whatever the disease be, it seems the patient never fails to sacrifice a bullock, or a sheep, upon his recovery.

The Hottentots are exceedingly superstitious, and fond of divination. In order to know the fate of a sick person, they flay a sheep alive ; after having its skin intirely taken off, if the poor animal is able to get up and run away, it is deemed a propitious omen ; but, on the contrary, if the excruciating pain kills it, they imagine that the patient will certainly die, and accordingly give him up intirely to nature, without taking any further care of him.

Whatever they believe of departed souls, they have no notion either of heaven or hell, or of a state of rewards or punishments ; this is evident from the behaviour of a dying Hottentot, and those about him ; neither he or his friends offer up any prayers to their gods for the salvation of his soul ; or even mention the state of departed souls, or their apprehensions of his being happy or miserable after death : however, they set up terrible howlings and shriekings, when the sick man is in his last agonies ; and yet these very people are frequently guilty of murdering their antient parents, as well as their innocent children ; for when the father of a family is become perfectly useless and superannuated, he is obliged to assign over his stock of cattle, and every thing elfe he has in the world, to his eldest son ; and in default of sons, to his next heir male : after which, the heir erects a tent or hut in some unfrequented place, a good distance from the kraal or camp he belongs to ; and, having assembled the men of the kraal, acquaints

them

them with the condition of his fuperannuated relation, and defires their confent to expofe him in the diftant hut ; to which the kraal fcarce ever refufe their confent. Whereupon a day being appointed to carry the old man to the folitary tent, the heir kills an ox, and two or three fheep, and invites the whole village to feaft and be merry with him ; and at the end of the entertainment, all the neighbourhood come and take a formal leave of the old wretch, thus condemned to be ftarved or devoured by wild beafts : then the unfortunate creature is laid upon one of their carriage oxen, and carried to his laft home, attended to the place, where he is to be buried alive, by moft of his neighbours. The old man being taken down, and fet in the middle of the hut provided for him, the company return to their kraal, and he never fees the face of a human creature afterwards; they never fo much as enquire whether he was ftarved to death, or devoured by wild beafts : he is no more thought of, than if he had never been. In the fame manner they deal with a fuperannuated mother ; only as fhe has nothing fhe can call her own, fhe has not the trouble of affigning her effects to her fon. Whenever the Hottentots are upbraided with this unparallelled piece of barbarity, they reply, it would be a much greater cruelty to fuffer an old creature to languifh out a miferable life, and to be many years a dying, than to make this quick difpatch with them ; and that it is out of their extreme tendernefs they put an end to the lives of thefe old wretches ; all the arguments in the world againft the inhumanity of the cuftom, can make no impreffion on them : and, indeed, as long as the Dutch have refided at the cape, they have not been able to break them of one fingle cuftom, or prevail with them to alter any part of their conduct, how barbarous or abfurd foever : and, it feems, the captain of a kraal is not exempted from feeing his funeral folemnized in this manner, while he is alive, if he happens to become ufelefs. And this leads us to treat of fuch funerals as are folemnized after the perfon is really dead.

The fick man, having refigned his breath, is immediately

mediately bundled up, neck and heels together, in his
sheep-skin mantle, exceeding close, so that no part of
the corpse appears : then the captain of the kraal with
some of the seniors, search the neighbouring country
for some cavity in a rock, or the den of a wild beast,
to bury it in, never digging a grave, if they can find
one of these within a moderate distance. After which,
the whole kraal, men and women, prepare to attend the
corpse, seldom permitting it to remain above ground
more than six hours. When all things are ready, all
the neighbourhood assemble before the door of the deceased, the men sitting down on their heels in one
circle, and resting their elbows on their knees (their
usual posture) as the women do in another : here they
clap their hands, and howl, crying, Bo, bo, bo ; (i. e.
father) lamenting their loss. The corpse being then
brought out on that side the tent, where the person
died, and not at the door, the bearers carry him in
their arms to the grave, the men and women follow it
in different parties, but without any manner of order,
crying all the way, Bo, bo, bo! and wringing their
hands, and performing a thousand ridiculous gestures
and grimaces, which is frequently the subject of the
Dutchmen's mirth; it being impossible, it is said, to
forbear laughing at the antic tricks they shew on such
an occasion. Having put the corpse into the cavity
prepared for it, they stop up the mouth of it with ant
hills, stones, and pieces of wood, believing the ants will
feed on the corpse, and soon consume it. The grave
being stopped up, the men and women rendezvous
again before the tent of the deceased, where they repeat
their howling, and frequently call upon the name of
their departed friend : after which two of the oldest
men get up ; and one of them going into the circle
of the men, and the other into the circle of the
women, urine upon every one of the company; and,
where the kraals are so very large, that two cannot find
water enough for this ceremony, they double or treble
the number. Then the old men go into the tent of
the deceased ; and, having taken up some ashes from
the

the fire-place, they fprinkle them upon the bodies of the people, bleffing them as they go : and, if the deceafed was a perfon of diftinction, this is acted over again feveral days. But we fhould have remembered, that the ceremony always concludes with an entertainment. If the deceafed had any cattle, a fheep is killed on the occafion; and the caul being powdered with buchu, is tied about the heir's neck, who is forced to wear it while it rots off, which is no great penance, all ftinks being perfumes to a Hottentot. All the relations alfo wear the cauls of fheep about their necks; which it feems is their mourning, unlefs the children of the deceafed are fo poor, that they cannot kill a fheep; and then they fhave their heads in furrows of about an inch broad, leaving the hair on of the fame breadth between every furrow.

It is not an eafy matter to come at a Hottentot's religious notions; he is fparing of his words, and laconic in his anfwers upon all occafions; but when religious topics are introduced, he generally conceals his fentiments in filence. Some on this account have doubted whether the Hottentots have any religion at all : but the moft intelligent among the Dutch at the cape pofitively affirm, that they believe in a Supreme Being, whom they ftile Gounya Taquoa, or God of gods, and fancy that his place of refidence is beyond the moon. They allow that Gounya Taquoa is a humane benevolent being, yet they have no mode of worfhipping him ; for which they give this reafon, " That he curfed their firft parents for having greatly offended him, on which account their pofterity have never from that time paid him adoration." They believe that the moon is an inferior vifible god, and the reprefentative of the high and invifible: that fhe has the direction of the weather ; and therefore they pray to her when it is unfeafonable. They never fail to affemble and worfhip this planet at the new and full moon, let the weather be never fo bad ; and though they diftort their bodies, grin and put on very frightful looks, crying and howling in a terrible manner, yet they

No. 11.   Y y   have

have fome expreffions that fhew their veneration and
dependance on this inferior deity ; as, 'Mutfchi Atze,
I falute you ; you are welcome : Cheraqua kaka chori
Ounqua, grant us pafture for our cattle and plenty of
milk.' Thefe and other prayers to the moon they repeat, frequently dancing and clapping their hands all
the while; and, at the end of every dance, crying, Ho,
ho, ho, ho! raifing and falling their voices, and ufing
abundance of odd geftures, that appear ridiculous to
European fpectators ; and which no doubt, made them
at firft, before they knew any thing of their language,
conclude, that this could not be the effect of devotion,
efpecially when the people themfelves told them, it was
not an act of religion, but only intended for their diverfion. They continue thus fhouting, finging and dancing, with proftrations on the earth, the whole night,
and even part of the next day, with fome fhort intervals, never refting, unlefs they are quite fpent with the
violence of the action; and then they fquat down upon
their heels, holding their heads between their hands,
and refting their elbows on their knees ; and, after a
little time, they ftart up again, and falling to finging
and dancing in a circle as before, with all their
might.

The Hottentots alfo adore a fly about the bignefs of a
hornet, called by fome the gold beetle : whenever they
fee this infect approach their kraal, they all affemble
about it, and fing and dance round it while it remains
there, ftrewing over it the powder of buchu, by bota-
nifts called fpiræam ; which when it is dried and pul-
verized, they always powder themfelves with it at feftivals. They ftrew the fame powder alfo over the tops
of their tents, and over the whole area of the kraal, as
a teftimony of their veneration for the adored fly.
They facrifice alfo two fheep as a thankfgiving for the
favour fhewn their kraal, believing they fhall certainly
profper after fuch a vifit : and, if this infect happens
to light upon a tent, they look upon the owner of it
for the future as a faint, and pay him more than ufual
refpect.

refpect. The beft ox of the kraal alfo is immediately facrificed, to teftify their gratitude to the little winged deity, and to honour the faint he has been pleafed thus to diftinguifh: to whom the entrails of the beaft, the choiceft morfel in their opinion, with the fat and the caul is prefented; and the caul being twifted like a rope, the faint ever after wears it like a collar about his neck day and night, till it putrifies and rots off; and the faint only feafts upon the entrails of the beaft, while the reft of the kraal feed upon the joints, that are not in fo high efteem among them: with the fat of the facrifice alfo the faint anoints his body from time to time, till it is all fpent; and, if the fly lights upon a woman fhe is no lefs reverenced by the neighbourhood, and entitled to the like privileges. It is fcarce poffible to exprefs the agonies the Hottentots are in, if any European attempts to take or kill one of thefe infects, as the Dutch will fometimes feem to attempt, to put them in a fright: they will beg and pray, and fall proftrate on the ground, to procure the liberty of this little creature, if it falls into a Dutchman's hands; they are on fuch an occafion, in no lefs confternation than the Indians near Fort St. George, when the kite, with a white head, which they worfhip, is in danger. If a foldier takes one of thefe alive, and threatens to wring the neck of it off, the Indians will gather in crowds about him, and immediately collect the value of a fhilling or two, to purchafe the liberty of the captive bird they adore. But to return to the Hottentots: they imagine if this little deity fhould be killed, all the cattle would die of difeafes, or be deftroyed by wild beafts; and they themfelves fhould be the moft miferable of men, and look upon that kraal to be doomed to fome imminent misfortue, where this animal feldom appears.

The Hollanders have fent feveral reverend divines to the cape as miffionaries, who have fpared no pains to bring the Hottentots off from their idolatry, and induce them to embrace Chriftianity; even their covetoufnefs and ambition have been applied to, and temporal re

wards

wards offered them, on condition of their being inftruded in the principles of Chriftianity. But no motives whatever, whether thofe relating to this or another
ftate, have yet been able to make the leaft impreffion on
any one of them: they hold faft and hug their ancient
fuperftitions, and will hear of no other religion. The
reafon that they neither imitate the Europeans in their
building, planting or cloathing, is becaufe they imagine themfelves to be religioufly obliged to follow the
cuftoms of their anceftors ; and that, if they fhould
deviate from them in the leaft of thefe matters, it might
make way for a total change of their religion and manners, which they cannot think of without abhorrence.
One of the Dutch governors at the cape bred up an
Hottentot from his infancy, obliging him to follow the
fafhions and cuftoms of the Europeans, to be taught
feveral languages, and to be fully inftruded in the principles of the Chriftian religion, cloathing him hand-
fomely, and treating him, in all refpeds, as a perfon
for whom he had a high efteem ; and let him know,
that he defigned him for fome beneficial and honourable
employment. The governor afterwards fent him a
voyage to Batavia, where he was employed, under the
commiffary his friend, for fome time, till that gentleman died ; and then he returned to the Cape of Good
Hope: but, having paid a vifit to the Hottentots of
his relations and acquaintance, he threw off all his fine
cloaths, bundled them up, and laid them at the governor's feet; and defired he would give him leave to re-
nounce his Chriftianity, and live and die in the religion
and cuftoms of his anceftors ; only begged the governor
would give him leave to keep the hanger and collar he
wore for his fake; which while the governor was deli-
berating with himfelf upon, fcarce believing the fellow
to be in earneft, the young Hottentot took the opportunity of running away, and never came near the cape
afterwards, thinking himfelf extremely happy that he
had exchanged his European cloaths for a fheep fkin,
and the reft of the Hottentots drefs and ornaments:
the

the Englifh Eaft India company, we are informed, made the like experiment, bringing over two of that nation hither, whom they cloathed decently after the European manner, and ufed them, in all refpects, with the greateft goodnefs and gentlenefs, hoping, by that means, to be better informed of the condition of their country, and whether it might be worth the while to make a fettlement there : but the two Hottentots only learnt Englifh enough to bewail their misfortune in being brought from their country and their friends; and, after two years trial of them, being again fet on fhore at the cape, they immediately ftripped off their European cloaths, and, having taken up the fheep fkin mantle again, rejoiced beyond meafure for their happy efcape from the Englifh.

The poor Hottentots fometimes employ themfelves in making arms, viz. bows and arrows, lances and darts, bartering them with the rich for cattle, to begin the world with: others get elephants teeth, and what they do not ufe in making rings and ornaments for themfeves, are generally difpofed of, it is thought, to the Portuguefe and other Europeans, who touch at Terra de Natal, and other parts of the eaftern or weftern coaft. The Hottentots fell very few teeth to the Dutch; though it is manifeft they kill abundance of elephants : they fupply the Hollanders however with cattle, and take wine, brandy or tobacco, in return; and an ox may be purchafed of them for a pound of tobacco, and a large fheep for half a pound. As to coin, the reader will conclude they have none; nor do they ever fee any, unlefs fome fmall pieces of money the Dutch fometimes give them for their wages at the cape; and it muft not be forgot, that the Hottentots find abundance of oftrich's eggs in the fand, which they barter with the fea-faring men, that touch at the cape, for brandy and tobacco; every failor almoft being proud of bringing home one of thefe egg fhells to his friends, after he has fried and eaten the yolk, which

makes

makes a large pancake, and is pretty good food, but rather of the strongest.

Their butchers are said to be great artists in their way, and to handle a knife as dexterously as an anatomist : having tied the hind and fore legs of a sheep, they throw the creature on his back, and with cords, two of them extend it to its full stretch, while a third rips it up ; so that all the entrails appear : then, with one hand, he tears the guts from the carcase, and, with the other, stirs the blood, avoiding as much as he can the breaking any of the blood-vessels about the heart ; so that the sheep is a long time a dying : in the mean time he gives the guts to another, who just rids them of the filth, and rinces them in water, and part of them are broiled and eaten amongst them, before the sheep is well dead : having scooped the blood out of the body of the animal with their hands or sea shells, they cut the rest of the guts in small pieces, and stew them in the blood, which is the Hottentots favourite dish. An ox also is killed in the same barbarous manner; being thrown upon his back, and his legs extended with cords, he is ripped up, and his guts taken out first ; in which cruel operation the beast is half an hour a dying : they separate the parts with great exactness, dividing the flesh, the bones, the membranes, muscles, veins, and arteries, and laying them in several parcels every thing entire. The bones also are taken out of the flesh, and laid together in such order, that they might be easily formed into an exact skeleton : these they boil by themselves, and get the marrow out of them, with which they anoint their bodies. Of the sheep skin, as has been observed already, they make a mantle, if it be large ; but, if it is small, they cut it into thongs, to adorn their women's legs : and the hide of an ox serves either to cover their tents, or to make girts and straps of, with which they bind their baggage on their carriage oxen when they decamp ; and, if they have no other use for their ox-hides, they lay them by, and eat them when they want other food.

They

They have another artificer, who is both felmonger and taylor : that is, he dreſſes ſkins after their way, and then makes them into mantles: he takes a ſheep ſkin juſt flayed off, and, rubbing it well with fat, the ſkin becomes tough and ſmooth ; and, if it be for one of his countrymen, he rubs it over alſo with freſh cow-dung, and lays it in the ſun till it is dry : then he rubs it with fat and cow dung again ; which he repeats ſe-veral times, till it becomes perfectly black, and ſtinks ſo, that no European can bear it ; and then, with a lit-tle ſhaping and ſewing, it is a compleat mantle for a Hottentot : but, if it be dreſſed for a Duchman, he only rubs the ſkin well with fat, which ſecures the wool from coming off. If he be to dreſs an ox's hide, he rubs the hairy ſide with wood aſhes ; then ſprinkling it with water, rolls it up, and lays it a day or two in the ſun ; which expedients effectually brings off the hair ; this ſkin is then well greaſed, ſtretched out, and dried again, when it is deemed good leather.

Their ſmiths do not only faſhion their iron, but melt it from the ore : they find plenty of iron ſtones in ſeve-ral parts of their country ; and having got a heap of theſe, they put them into a hole in the ground, heated and prepared for their purpoſe : then they make a fire over the ſtones, which they ſupply with fuel, and keep up till the iron melts; and then it runs into another hole, which they make for a receiver, a little lower than the firſt : as ſoon as the iron in the receiver is cold they break it to pieces with ſtones; and, heating the pieces again in other fires, beat them with ſtones, till they ſhape them into the heads of lances, darts, arrows, and bows, and ſuch weapons as they uſe ; for they ſcarce ever form any other utenſils, but arms of this metal : they get the hardeſt flat ſtone, according to monſieur Vogel, and, laying the iron upon it, as upon an anvil, beat it with another round ſtone, which ſerves them for a hammer; then they grind it upon the flat ſtone, and poliſh it as nicely as any European artificer could do with all his tools : they have ſome copper ore too, which

which they melt in like manner; but they make only toys and ornaments for their drefs of this metal: nor, indeed, do they ever work in iron, but when they want weapons. They would never labour, if their neceffities did not fometimes compel them to it: but, when they do, no people work harder, or more indefatigably; for they never leave a piece of work, till they have finifhed it.

The ivory-turner makes the ivory rings that are worn ornamentally about the arms; and confidering that his only tool is a common clafp knife, which he procures from the Dutch, the wormanfhip has great merit.

The potter or maker of earthen veffels is another art; but this, it feems, they are all dexterous at, every family making the pots and pans they want. For thefe they ufe only the earth of ant-hills, clearing them of all fand and gravel; after which, they work it together with the bruifed ant eggs, that are faid to conftitute an extraordinary cement. When they have moulded thefe materials into a kind of pafte, they take as much of them as will make one of their pots, and fafhion it by hand upon a flat ftone, making it of the form of a Roman urn; then they fmooth it within and without very carefully, not leaving the leaft roughnefs upon the furface; and, having dried it in the fun two or three days, they put the pot into a hole in the ground, and burn it, by making a fire over it; and, when they take it out, it appears perfectly black: every family alfo make their own mats, with which they cover their tents or huts; but this is chiefly the bufinefs of the women: they gather the flags and rufhes by the river fide, or weave or plat them into mats fo clofely, it is faid, that neither the weather or light can penetrate them.

The laft artificer we fhall mention is the rope-maker, who has no better materials, than fuch flags and rufhes as the mats are made of; and yet they appear almoft as ftrong as thofe made of hemp: the Dutch, at the cape, buy

buy and ufe them in ploughing, and in draught-carriages.

As to the way of travelling here, the natives all travel on foot, except the aged and infirm; and thefe are carried on their baggage oxen. As there are no inns or places for refrefhment, the travelling Hottentot calls at the kraals in his way, where he meets with a hearty welcome from his countrymen, who endeavour to fhew their hofpitality to ftrangers, whether of their own country or of Europe. Such indeed is the general urbanity of thefe people, and their ftrict integrity when any confidence is placed in them, that when the Hollanders travel either on foot or horfeback, if they cannot reach an European fettlement, they alfo call at the kraals of the Hottentots, where they are complimented with a hut, and fuch provifion as they have, or they may lie in the area of the kraal, in the open air, if they pleafe, and the weather be good; and here they are fecure, both from robbers and wild beafts; for the bufhis banditti on the mountains are dangerous, as they give no quarter; but the Hottentot nations in general hold them in abhorrence, and unanimoufly concur in feizing and punifhing them upon all occafions.

Their language is very inarticulate and defective; one word fignifies feveral things, the definitive meaning being determined by the manner of pronouncing; and the pronunciation is fo harfh and confufed, that they feem to ftammer in all they fpeak. Hence, though they are eafily taught to underftand other languages, they can feldom be brought to fpeak them with any degree of intelligibility.

We fhall here fubjoin a fmall Hottentot vocabulary, for the fatisfaction of the curious; khauna, fignifies a lamb; kgou, a goofe; bunqvaa, trees; knomm, to hear; quaqua, a pheafant; tkaka, a whale; horri, beafts in general; knabou, a fowling piece; qua-araho, a wild ox; ounequa, the arms; quienkha, to fall; likhanee, a dog; konkequa, a captain; quas, the neck; quan, the heart; kgoyes, a buck or doe; tikquoa, a god ; komma, a houfe; khoaa, a cat, kowkuri, iron; konkerey, a hen ; thoukou, a dark night; tkoume, rice ; ghoudie, a fheep; toya, the wind ; ttkaa, a valley; tkaonoklau, gunpowder ; kamkamma, the earth; quaouw, thunder ; duckatere, a duck; kamma, water ; quayha, an afs; naew, the ears; kirri, a ftick; nombha, the beard ; ka-a, to drink ; duriefa, an ox; hek-kaa, an ox of burden ; ounvie, butter; houteo, a fea-dog; bikgua, the head ; kamma, a ftag ; kouquik, a pigeon ; anthuri, to-morrow ; kou, a tooth ; khamouna, the devil; hakqua, a horfe ; koo, a fon ; kammo, a ftream ; tika, grafs; toqua, a wolf; koanqua, the mouth; khou, a peacock ; gona, a boy ; gois, a girl; khoakamma, a baboon ; kerhanehou, a ftar; mu, an eye ; tquaffouw, a tyger.

The Hottentots have only ten numerical terms, which they repeat twice to exprefs the multiplication of the firft term, and three times to exprefs the re-mulplication of the latter. Their terms are : q'kui, one ; k'kam, two ; kouna, three ; kakka, four ; koo, five ; nanni, fix ; hounko, feven ; khiffi, eight ; khaffi, nine ; ghiffi, ten.

Thus have we given a circumftantial and full account of the cape, its inhabitants, productions, and adjacent country; from whence the French, at Mauritius, are fupplied by the Dutch with falted beef, bifcuit, flour, and wine : the provifions for which the French contracted this year were five hundred thoufand lb. weight of falt beef, four hundred thoufand lb. of flour ; four hundred thoufand lb. of bifcuit, and one thoufand two hundred leagers of wine. We have only to add to this account a few obfervations on the bay, and garrifon. The former is large, fafe, and exceeding convenient. It is indeed open to the N. W. winds, but they feldom blow hard ; yet as they fometimes occafion a great fea, the fhips moor N. E. and S. W. The S. E. winds blow frequently with great fury, but their direction being right out of the bay prevents them from being dangerous. For the conveniency of landing and
                                                                    fhipping

shipping goods, a wharf of wood is run out near the town, to a proper diſtance. Water is conveyed in pipes to this wharf, and many large boats and hoys are kept by the Company to carry ſtores and proviſions to and from the ſhipping in the harbour. This bay is co-vered by a ſmall fort on the E. ſide of the town, and cloſe to the beach; and is alſo defended by ſeveral out-works and batteries extending along the ſhore, as well on this ſide of the town as the other; nevertheleſs they are by their ſituation expoſed to the ſhipping, and in a manner defenceleſs againſt an enemy of any force by land. As to the garriſon, this conſiſts of eight hun-dred regular troops, beſides militia of the country, in which laſt is comprehended every man able to bear arms. By ſignals they can alarm the country in a very ſhort time, and when theſe are made, the militia is to repair immediately to their place of rendezvous in the town.

On Sunday, the 14th of April in the morning, we weighed, ſtood out of the bay, and anchored at five in the evening under Penguin, or Robin Iſland. Here we lay all night, and being prevented from ſailing by the wind, the captain diſpatched a boat to the iſland for a few trifling articles, which we had omitted to take in at the cape; when our people drew near the ſhore, they were warned by the Dutch not to land at their peril. At the ſame time ſix men, armed with muſ-quets, paraded upon the beach. The commanding officer in the boat did not think it prudent to riſk the lives of his men, on account of a few cabbages, and therefore returned without them to the ſhip. To this iſland the Dutch at the Cape baniſh ſuch criminals as are not thought worthy of death, for a certain number of years, according to the nature of their crimes. They are employed as ſlaves in digging lime-ſtone, which though ſcarce upon the continent is here in great abun-dance. A Daniſh ſhip touched at this iſland, having been refuſed aſſiſtance at the cape, and ſending her boat on ſhore, overpowered the guard, and then took as many of the criminals as were neceffary to navigate her home; for fhe had loft great part of her crew by ficknefs. To this incident we attributed our repulfe; concluding, that the Dutch, to prevent a fimilar refcue of their prifoners, had ordered their garrifon at this place, not to fuffer any boat of foreign nations to land the crew, and come afhore.

On Thurfday the 25th, we put to fea, and about four o'clock in the afternoon died our mafter, Mr. Robert Mollineux, a youth of good parts, but unhappily for his own felf prefervation too much addicted to intemperance, a habit we would caution all thofe who undertake long voyages to avoid, if they have any regard to their perfonal fafety. We now continued our voyage without any other remarkable incident; and on Monday the 29th, we croffed our firft meridian, having circumnavigated the globe from E. to W. and confequently loft a day, for which upon correcting our reckoning at Batavia, we made an allowance. On Monday the 1ft of May, we came to anchor at break of day, before James's fort in the ifland of St. Helena; and as we propofed to refrefh here, Mr. Banks employed his time in vifiting the moft remarkable places, and in furveying every object worthy of notice.

St. Helena is fituated in the Atlantic ocean, in fix degrees W. longitude, and fixteen S. latitude, almoft in the midway between Africa and America, being twelve hundred miles diftant from the former, and eighteen hundred from the latter. It was fo named by the Portuguefe, who difcovered it on St. Helen's-day. This ifland is 36 miles long, 18 broad, and about 61 in circumference. It is the fummit of an immenfe mountain rifing out of the fea, and of a depth unfathomable at a fmall diftance round it. It may be difcerned at fea, at above twenty leagues diftance, and looks like a caftle in the middle of the ocean, whofe natural walls are of that height, that there is no fcaling them. The fmall valley called Chapel-valley, in a bay on the eaft fide of it, is defended by a battery of forty or fifty great
                                                              guns,

guns, planted even with the water; and the waves dafh-
ing perpetually on the fhore, make it difficult landing
even here. There is alfo one little creek befides, where
two or three men may land at a time; but this is now
defended by a battery of five or fix guns, and rendered
inacceffible. No anchorage is to be found any where
about the ifland, but at Chapel-valley bay, and as the
wind always fets from the S. E. if a fhip overfhoots
the ifland ever fo little, fhe cannot recover it again.
The feat of volcanoes has been found to be the higheft
part of the countries in which they are found. Hecla
is the higheft hill in Iceland; and the Peak of Teneriffe
is known to be the covering of fubterraneous fire.
Thefe are ftill burning: but there are other mountains
which bear evident marks of fire that is now extinct:
among thefe is St. Helena, where the inequalities of
the ground, and its external furface, are evidently the
effects of the finking of the earth; and that this was
caufed by futerraneous fire, is equally manifeft from
the ftones, for fome of them, efpecially thofe in the
bottom of the valleys, are burnt almoft to cinders. This
ifland, as the Endeavour approached it on the windward
fide, appeared like a rude heap of rocks, bounded by precipices of an amazing height, and confifting of a kind of
ftone, which fhews not the leaft fign of vegetation: nor is it
more promifing upon a nearer view. Sailing along fhore,
we came near the huge cliffs, that feemed to overhang
the fhip. At length we opened Chapel-valley, which
refembles a trench, and in this valley we difcovered the
town. The fides of it are as naked as the cliffs next
the fea; but the bottom is flightly cloathed with herbage. In its prefent cultivated ftate, fuch appeared
the ifland to us; and the firft hills muft be paffed,
before the country difplays its verdure, or any other
marks of fertility.

In Chapel-valley, a little beyond the landing place,
is a fort where the governor refides with the garrifon;
and the town ftands juft by the fea-fide. The greater
part of the houfes are ill built. The church, which
was

was originally a mean ſtructure, is in ruins; and the market-place nearly in the ſame condition. The town conſiſts of about forty or fifty buildings, conſtructed after the Engliſh faſhion, whither the people of the iſland reſort when any ſhipping appears, as well to aſſiſt in the defence of the iſland, as to entertain the ſeamen if they are friends: for the governor has always ſentinels, on the higheſt part of the iſland, to the windward, who give notice of the approach of all ſhipping, and guns are thereupon fired, that every man may reſort to his poſt. It is impoſſible for an enemy to approach by ſea in the night time, and if diſcovered the day before, preparations are ſpeedily made for his reception.

Notwithſtanding the iſland appears a barren rock on every ſide, yet on the top it is covered with a fine layer of earth, producing grain, fruits, and herbs of various kinds; and the country after we aſcended the rock, is diverſified with riſing hills and plains, plantations of fruit trees and kitchen gardens, among which the houſes of the natives are interſperſed, and in the open fields are herds of cattle grazing, ſome of which are fatted to ſupply the ſhipping, and the reſt furniſh the dairies with milk, butter, and cheeſe. Hogs, goats, turkeys, and all manner of poultry alſo abound, and the ſeas are well ſtored with fiſh. But amidſt all this affluence, the people have neither bread nor wine of their own growth; for though the ſoil is proper for wheat, yet the rats that harbour in the rocks, and cannot be deſtroyed, eat up all the ſeed, before the grain is well out of the ground; and though their vines flouriſh and produce them grapes enough, yet the latitude is too hot for making wine. This they have therefore from the Canaries, the Madeiras, or the Cape, as well as their flour and malt. Their very houſes are ſome of them brought from Europe ready framed, there being no timber on the iſland, trees not taking deep root here on account of the rock that lies ſo near the ſurface: however, they have underwood enough for neceſſary uſes.

ufes. Befides grapes, they have plantains, bananas, figs, lemons, and fuch other fruits as hot countries ufually produce. They alfo raife kidney beans, and fome other kinds of pulfe in their gardens ; and the want of bread they fupply with potatoes and yams.

In the year 1701, there were upon the ifland about two hundred families, moft of them Englifh, or defcended from Englifh parents. Every family has a houfe and plantation on the higher part of the ifland, where they look after their cattle, fruits, and kitchen garden. They fcarce ever come down to the town, unlefs it be to church, or when the fhipping arrives, when moft of the houfes in the valley are converted into punch-houfes, or lodgings for their guefts, to whom they fell their poultry, and other commodities; but they are not fuffered to purchafe any merchandize of the fhips that touch here. Whatever they want of foreign growth or manufacture, they are obliged to buy at the company's warehoufe, where twice every month, they may furnifh themfelves with brandy, European or Cape wines, Batavia arrack, malt, beer, fugar, tea, coffee, china, and japan-ware, linen, calicoes, chintz, muflins, ribbands, woollen-cloth and ftuffs, and all manner of cloathing, for which they are allowed fix months credit. Among the very few native productions of this ifland muft be reckoned ebony, though the trees are now nearly extinct. Pieces of this wood are frequently found in the valleys of a fine black colour, and a hardnefs almoft equal to iron ; thefe pieces, however, are fo fhort and crooked, that no ufe can be made of them. There are few infects here, but upon the tops of the higheft ridges a fpecies of fnail is found, which has probably been there fince the original creation of their kind. It is indeed very difficult to conceive how any thing not formed here, or brought hither by the diligence of man, could find its way to a place fo fevered from the reft of the world, by feas of immenfe extent,

The Portuguefe, who difcovered this ifland in 1502,

ftored

2

ftored it with hogs, goats, and poultry, and ufed to touch at it for water and frefh provifions in their return from India; but we do not find they ever planted a colony here; or, if they did, having deferted it afterwards, the Englifh Eaft-India Company took poffeffion of the ifland A. D. 1600, and held it till 1673, without interruption, when the Dutch took it by furprize. However, the Englifh, commanded by Capt. Munden, recovered it again within the fpace of a year, and took three Dutch Eaft India fhips that lay in the road at the fame time. The Hollanders had fortified the landing place, and planted batteries of great guns to prevent a defcent; but the Englifh being acquainted with a fmall creek where only two men could go abreaft, climbed up to the top of the rocks in the night time, and appearing next morning at the backs of the Dutch, they threw down their arms, and furrendered the ifland without ftriking a ftroke: but, as we have before obferved, this creek has been fince fortified: fo that there is now no place where an enemy can make a defcent with any probability of fuccefs.

The affairs of the Eaft-India Company are managed here by a governor, deputy-governor, and ftorehoufe-keeper, who have certain fettled falaries allowed, befides a public table, well furnifhed, to which all commanders, mafters of fhips, and eminent paffengers are welcome. The natives fometimes call the refult of their deliberations fevere impofitions; and though relief might perhaps be had from the company in England, yet the unavoidable delays in returning anfwers to addreffes at that diftance puts the aggrieved under great hardfhips; and on the other hand, was not the fituation of this ifland very ferviceable to our homeward-bound Eaft-India fhips, the conftant trouble and expence would induce the company to abandon the ifland; for though it is furnifhed with the conveniencies of life, the merchants find no other profitable commodities there. The mafters of the plantations keep a great many blacks, who, upon fevere treatment, hide themfelves

themfelves for two or three months together, keeping among the rocks by day, and roving at night for provilions: but they are generally difcovered and taken.

The children and defcendants of white people have not the leaft red in their cheeks, in all other places near the tropics; but the natives of St. Helena are remarkable for their ruddy complexions and robuft conftitutions. Their healthfulnefs may, in general, be afcribed to the following caufes. They live on the top of a mountain always open to the fea breezes that conftantly blow here: they are ufually employed in the moft healthful exercifes of gardening and hufbandry; the ifland is frequently refrefhed with moderate cooling fhowers; and no noxious fens, nor falt marfhes annoy them. They are ufed alfo to climb the fteep hill between the town in Chapel-valley and their plantation; which hill is fo fteep, that, having a ladder in the middle of it, they call it Ladder-hill; and this cannot be avoided without going three or four miles about; fo that they feldom want air or exercife, the great prefervers of health. As to the genius and temper of thefe people, they feemed to us the moft honeft, the moft inoffenfive, and the moft hofpitable people we ever met with of Englifh extraction, having fcarce any tincture of avarice or ambition. We afked fome of them, if they had no curiofity to fee the reft of the world, and how they could confine themfelves to fo fmall a fpot of earth, feparated at fuch a diftance from the reft of mankind? They replied, that they enjoyed the neceffaries of life in great plenty: they were neither parched with exceffive heat, or pinched with cold; they lived in perfect fecurity; in no danger of enemies, of robbers, wild beafts, or rigorous feafons; and were happy in the enjoyment of a continued ftate of health: that as there were no rich men among them (fcarce any planter being worth more than a thoufand dollars) fo there were no poor in the ifland, no man being worth lefs

No. 12.   3 A

lefs than four hundred dollars, and confequently not obliged to undergo moie labour than was neceffary to keep him in health.

Our thoughts were now employed on returning to our native fhore ; and having fufficiently recruited our ftores, on Saturday the 4th of May, we weighed, and failed out of the road in company with the Portland man of war, and his convoy, confifting of twelve fail of Eaft Indiamen. With this fleet we continued our courfe for England until Friday the 10th, when perceiving they out-failed us, and confequently might make their port before us, Capt. Cook, for this reafon, made the fignal to fpeak with the Portland, upon which Capt. Elliot came on board the Endeavour ; to whom a letter for the admiralty was delivered, with a box, containing the common log books of the fhip, and the journals of fome of the officers. We did not lofe fight of the fleet till Thurfday the 23d, when they parted from us ; and about one o'clock in the afternoon, we loft our firft lieutenant, Mr. Hicks, an active, fkilful, judicious, and ufeful officer. He died of a confumption, of which lingering diforder he difcovered fome fymptoms when he left England ; fo that it may be truly faid, that he was dying the whole voyage ; and his decline was very gradual till we arrived at Batavia, from whence to the time of his diffolution, the flow confuming difeafe gained ftrength daily. The whole fhip's company attended the funeral rites, and in the evening we committed his body to the fea with the ufual ceremonies. The next day the captain appointed Mr. Charles Clerk, a young man, to act in the room of Mr. Hicks.

We now every day drew nearer our defired haven ; but what muft be the condition of our once good fhip, the Endeavour, may eafily be imagined, from a flight recollection of the hardfhips fhe had furmounted, and the dangers fhe had providentially efcaped. At this time our rigging and fails were fo weather-beaten,

that

that every day fomething was giving way. However, we held on our courfe, without any material occurrence that might endanger our fafety, till Monday the 10th of June, when, to our great joy, Nicholas Young, the boy who firft difcovered New Zealand, called out land from the maft head, which proved to be the Lizard. The next day, being Tuefday, the eleventh, we proceeded up the channel. On Wednefday the 12th, with the pleafing hopes of feeing our relatives and friends, exciting fenfations not to be defcribed by the pen of the moft able writer, we paffed Beachy Head. At noon, to our inexpreffible joy we were a-breaft of Dover; and about three o'clock, P. M. we came to an anchor in the Downs. When we landed at Deal, our fhip's company indulged freely that mirth, and fociable jollity, common to all Englifh failors upon their return from a long voyage, who as readily forget hardfhips and dangers, as with alacrity and bravery they encounter them.

We cannot clofe this book without joining in that general cenfure, which has been juftly beftowed on Dr. Hawkefworth, the late compiler of a former account of this voyage of the Endeavour. An infidel may imbibe what deiftical chimeras may be beft adapted to the gloomy temper of his mind ; but we cannot but think him highly culpable in forcing them into a work of this kind ; for though it may be faid, that, with refpect to efficient and final caufes, the opinion of a general and particular Providence will form one and the fame conclufion, yet we think it is of great comfort to all men, particularly to thofe who can trace the wonders of an almighty hand in the deep, to be fenfible of a merciful interpofition, concerned, and ever attentive to their fupport, prefervation, and deliverance in times of danger. Befides, this fentiment of a divine agent fuperintending, and correcting the diforders introduced by natural and moral evil, is, undoubtedly a fcripture-doctrine ; and from the deductions of the mere light

of

of nature, it muſt appear unreaſonable to ſuppoſe, that the firſt Great Cauſe who planned the whole grand ſcheme of creation, ſhould not be allowed to interfere with reſpect to particular parts, or individuals? as occaſion, circumſtances, or times may require. And whoever has duly conſidered the wonderful protection of the Endeavour in caſes of danger the moſt imminent, particularly when encircled, in the wide ocean, with rocks of coral, her ſheathing beaten off, and her falſe-keel floating by her ſide, a hole in her bottom, and the men by turns fainting at the pumps, cannot but acknowledge the exiſtence of a Particular Providence. The hiſtory of Joſeph can only afford a more ſtriking inſtance of the interpoſition of a divine inviſible hand. This our countrymen experienced ; and we have good authority to aſſert, that our company in the Endeavour do acknowledge, notwithſtanding the private opinion of the above mentioned compiler, that the hand of ſuperior power was particularly concerned in their protection and deliverance. This omniſcient and omnipotent power it is the incumbent duty of every chriſtian to believe, confide in, and adore.

A New